# WANT YOU GONE

# WANT YOU GONE

## CHRIS BROOKMYRE

Little, Brown

LITTLE, BROWN

First published in Great Britain in 2017 by Little, Brown

1 3 5 7 9 10 8 6 4 2

Copyright © Christopher Brookmyre 2017

The right of Christopher Brookmyre to be identified as the author of this work has been asserted by him in accordance with the Copyright, Designs and Patents Act 1988.

A CIP catalogue record for this book is available from the British Library.

Hardback ISBN 978-1-4087-0717-3
Trade paperback ISBN 978-1-4087-0718-0

Typeset in Caslon by Palimpsest Book Production Limited, Falkirk, Stirlingshire
Printed and bound in Great Britain by Clays Ltd, St Ives plc

Papers used by Little, Brown are from well-managed forests
and other responsible sources.

Little, Brown
An imprint of
Little, Brown Book Group
Carmelite House
50 Victoria Embankment
London EC4Y 0DZ

An Hachette UK Company
www.hachette.co.uk

www.littlebrown.co.uk

For Nick Witcher, Steve Finn and Kerry Fraser-Robinson.

# THE BITTER END

He's never known such cold, such merciless, pervasive cold. It is enveloping him completely, like the embrace of a wraith, and he is being crushed in its grip.

His limbs are useless, still twitching in spasms, tiny echoes of the convulsions that rendered him helpless, and he can see his stilted, strangled breaths escaping from his mouth as tiny wisps. Pain is still pulsing through him, a pain he can feel from his internal organs to his every extremity. There is a buzzing in his ears, tiny explosions dancing in his eyes like a miniature firework display.

The temperature is so low that it feels as though the air itself is biting him, but worst of all is what lies beneath. The floor is like a giant radiator in reverse, draining warmth from every point of contact, and given he is lying flat on his back, that means close to half the surface of his body.

His assailant is standing over him, staring down from the blank smiling face of a Guy Fawkes mask.

He thinks he sees a fleeting gleam in a black-gloved hand, there for a twinkling, then it's gone. It's hard to tell among the flashes he's seeing, the after-effects of the electroshock device.

'I want you to know why this is happening to you, and I want you to understand why it's happening now.'

There is such anger in the voice, an anger that speaks of years of hatred; years of waiting.

Why didn't he see this betrayal coming? How could he have walked so blind into the jaws of a trap?

'You thought you had reinvented yourself, didn't you: turned your reputation around. I wanted you to touch that better future. I wanted you to believe you could once again be what you used to . . . before I took it all away.'

1

High on the wall he sees the dark glass of a CCTV camera lens, and with it comes a realisation colder even than the floor. Too late, he understands the significance of the mask, and that it is practical rather than symbolic.

It is the mask that confirms what he thought he glimpsed is indeed a blade.

It is the mask that tells him he is about to die.

# PART ONE

# CELL BINDING (I)

I was always afraid that this story would end with me in prison. Turns out I was right.

Not exactly a major spoiler though, is it? I mean, we both already know that part, so it's how I got here that really matters.

I'm going to tell you everything, and I'm not going to hold back to spare anyone's feelings. I have to be totally honest if I'm looking for honesty in return. I'll warn you up front, though. Much of what I'm about to say is going to be difficult for you to hear, but there are things about me that I need you to understand. You're not going to like me for some of what I did and said, and the way you personally come across isn't always going to be flattering either, but it's important that you get a handle on how everything looked from my point of view.

It doesn't mean I feel that way now, or that I was right to think what I did back then. It's just how it was, you know?

There are a lot of places I could start, but I have to be careful about that. Certain choices might imply I'm pointing the finger, and I'm not. I know who's to blame for everything that happened. No need for any more deceptions on that score. So I'm not going right back to childhood, or to when my dad died, or even to when the police raided the flat and found a shitload of drugs and a gun. Because this isn't about any of that stuff, not really. To me, this all starts a few weeks ago, with me sitting in a waiting room, looking at a human time-bomb.

# THE READER

I know the man is going to explode several minutes before the incident takes place. It is only a matter of time.

He is sitting opposite me in the waiting area, shifting restlessly on the plastic bench, his limbs in a state of constant motion: sudden jerks and twitches beating out a code I can read only too clearly. His head is an unkempt ball of hair, his matted locks merging with enough beard to kit out a whole bus full of hipsters. He looks across at me every few seconds, which makes me scared and uncomfortable, though I know he's not picking me out specifically. His eyes are darting about the room the whole time, not alighting on a single sight for more than a second, like a fly that won't land long enough to be swatted.

I am afraid of catching his eye, so I keep my gaze above him, where a row of posters glare back at me from the wall. They all seem intended to threaten, apart from the ones encouraging people to grass on their neighbours. 'We're closing in,' says one. 'Benefit thieves: our technology is tracking you,' warns another. 'Do you know who's following you?' asks a third. They feature images of people photographed from above at a steep angle, making them look tiny and cornered as they stand on concentric circles. To drive the point home, another poster shows an arrow thwocking into a bull-seye: 'Targeting benefit fraudsters'.

I have done nothing wrong but I feel guilty and intimidated. I feel like a criminal simply for being here. I have rehearsed what I am going to say, gone over it and over it in front of the bedroom mirror. I know my arguments, and have tried to anticipate how the officials might respond. I was feeling ready when I left the house, coaching myself all the way here, but now I think I've got no chance. I'm wasting my time. I want to leave, want to run, but I can't. I need the money. I desperately need the money.

I glance towards the counter. Above the woman on reception there is a poster stating 'In the UK illegally? Go home or face arrest.' Bold text proudly announces there were '86 arrests last week in this area'. There are no people on this poster, but if there were, I know what they would look like. They would look like me.

One nation, I think. The Big Society.

I know the poster they'd really like to print. It would say: 'Are you white enough to live here? If not, fuck off back to Bongo Bongo Land.'

A woman emerges from the interview rooms and shuffles towards the exit without looking up. I can tell things didn't go well for her. She is followed shortly by one of the staff: a grey-haired white bloke.

There is also a Chinese woman doing interviews. It's already half an hour after my appointment, and both she and Grey Hair have each come out a couple of times since I arrived. I've been watching them very carefully.

I hope I get the Chinese lady. She seems relaxed, if a little tired. The grey-haired guy is like a coiled spring.

He calls out a name and the twitchy bloke opposite stands up. He walks towards the interview rooms, following Grey Hair, who has barely looked at him. Part of me is pleased that Grey Hair is now occupied, as I must surely be due in next, but the part of me that reads people knows something bad is about to happen.

The Chinese lady comes out again and I sit up straighter in my chair, willing my name to be called. It isn't.

More people drift in and take up the empty spaces on the benches. There has to be a dozen people in here, and the only one talking is a woman in the corner trying to stop her toddler from kicking off. But, to me, there is a growing cacophony in the room, ratcheting up my anxiety. They ain't saying anything, but I can sense all of their tension, anger, fear and hurt.

I have always been able to gauge people's true states of mind, regardless of what their faces or their words are trying to say. I can read their expressions, their micro-gestures, their body language, the tone of their voices. It comes so naturally that it took me a long time to realise other people didn't see all these things too.

Sometimes it's a blessing, but right now they might as well be shouting at me. I am in a room full of desperation, all of it telling me that my efforts here are doomed.

I hear a growing sound of male voices dampened only slightly by thin walls. One is getting increasingly angry, the other low but insistent, authoritative. One rising up, the other not backing down. Unstoppable force, immovable object. I hear a clattering, what sounds like a chair skidding across the floor. An alarm sounds and suddenly members of staff I have never seen appear from side offices and rush towards the interview room. One of them is a security guard. I hear several thumps, the sound of feet on furniture, voices raised in rage, in command, in panic. Someone shouts, demanding that the twitchy man calm down. This is like trying to put out a fire with lighter fluid.

I am terrified. I feel the tears running down my cheeks. I want to leave but I know that if my name gets called and I'm not there, I've blown it.

The shouting grows louder, the twitchy man's angry words degenerating into nothing but roaring, which itself gives way to a low moan as his rage exhausts itself. He is led out shortly afterwards. He looks numb and dazed, like he barely knows where he is. He is crying.

Grey Hair stands watching him retreat for a few moments, letting out a long sigh and supporting himself with a firm hand against a doorframe. Someone asks him if he wants a break. He shakes his head. He definitely does need a break, but I can tell that what he *wants* is to unload his frustrations, to exercise his power. He disappears into the interview room then comes out again a few seconds later.

'Samantha Morpeth,' he barks out.

# VILLAINS

It takes only a few minutes; less time than they spent subduing the twitchy man.

I sit down, separated from Grey Hair by a desk that now has several rubber scuff marks down one side. I am close enough to read his badge. Close enough to smell his sweat.

His name is Maurice Clark. His face is like a recently slammed door. There are papers strewn around the floor of his office, the place still reeling from the twitchy man's rage. I'm guessing the same could be said for the inside of Maurice Clark's head. If I asked him to repeat my name, which he called out moments ago, he would probably have forgotten it.

'The change to your mother's circumstances means that she is no longer eligible for the Carer's Allowance. That is why the payments have stopped. It's very simple.'

He puts it delicately, but I feel a hint of contempt. The delicateness was actually a way of rubbing it in.

'Yes, but it's me who should be receiving the allowance now, and it hasn't been transferred.'

All my planning and rehearsing is for nothing. When I speak, my voice feels like it is coming from down a well: timid and faint, lacking any conviction. I always get this way when I am dealing with people like him: people in authority, angry people, aggressive people. I can't deal with confrontation. It makes me shrink and fade.

Maurice Clark, by contrast, seems to get louder and bigger and firmer.

'It hasn't been transferred because you are not eligible to receive it either.'

'But I'm the one who—'

9

'Miss Morpeth, the rules are very clear. You cannot claim this allowance if you are in full-time work or in full-time education.'

'Full— But I'm only at a sixth-form college.'

As the words come out, tiny and hoarse, I know they are worthless.

Clark stares back at me with this look that says I just underlined his point. He doesn't care. He's hurting. He's frustrated. The only thing this guy wants right now is to say no. If there was a way for him to help me, he wouldn't.

All the things I was supposed to say become like illegible scribbles in my mind, the paper they're written on burning. I feel the tears roll again. I am hopeless. I am pathetic. A fucking victim.

I leave the benefits office with the same defeated walk as the woman I watched earlier, like I'm carrying Maurice Clark on my bloody shoulders. However, when I get out on to the high street, a glance at my phone tells me that, little as I feel like it, I'll need to pick up the pace. I ended up waiting about three quarters of an hour for a two-minute interview, and now I'm running late. It's a good half an hour to the Loxford School, and it's already twenty-five to four.

Instinctively I wonder when the next bus is due, then remember that it's a luxury I can't afford.

The implications are starting to sink in. I feel weighted down but I don't have the option to slow my pace. Grey Hair spelled it out. If I want the Carer's Allowance, I have to drop out of school. I won't be able to sit my exams, but then that won't matter, as uni isn't going to be a possibility now anyway.

I might have read it wrong, but I got the sense there was something else the guy could have told me. On a different day he might have done. Or maybe he is always a prick.

I get the head down, earphones in. I am blotting out the world as I hurry along the pavement, slaloming shoppers and push-chairs and gaggles of office staff on smoke-breaks. I barely glance up before I hit the junction. That is where I see them: Keisha, Gabrielle and all that lot. But worse than that, they've seen me. I can't cross the road to avoid them. I know they'll cross too, and it will be worse if they know I tried to get away. It's like if you run, they have to chase. It's the rules.

I wish I was with Lilly. They wouldn't bother me then. God, that sounds so pathetic, hiding behind her. Wouldn't be the first time, though.

I can see the malicious delight on Keisha's face, even from twenty yards. I can't take this today, not on top of everything else, and I can't be held up. I can't be late.

But then the gods smile. A bus slows to a crawl as it approaches a red light at the junction, and I step on without hesitation. As it pulls away again, I see Keisha and Gabrielle staring at me through the window, a nasty look of satisfaction on both their faces. They all know what just happened.

The bus gets me to Lilly's school with time to spare, but as I peer through the railings I can't help calculating what it has cost me: what I could have bought for the fare that has been taken from my Oyster card. It's all going to be the finest of margins from now on. But what really stings is that it isn't the bus journey that has truly cost me: it was not facing down Keisha and her harpies. That was an avoidable expense. A coward tax.

I watch the first of the kids appear, their wheelchairs coming out of the big double doors on to a gently sloping ramp. The rest will start streaming out of a different entrance separated from the car park by a fence. I am always amazed at everyone's patience as several of the pupils are loaded on to minibuses, the hydraulic platforms slowly lifting one wheelchair at a time. I couldn't handle that: being powerless, waiting ages every day while your time bleeds from you.

One of the buses is heading to an after-school facility at the Nisha Leyton Centre, a day-care complex that provides services for adults with learning disabilities.

I realise that's another item on the big list of things I urgently need to look into. I'm going to have to find a job, and there aren't many of those that will let me knock off around half past three every day so I can be standing here dutifully at the Loxford School's gates to collect my younger sister.

*Being There For Lilly* could be the title of my brief and boring autobiography. It certainly feels like the story of my life.

We moved around so much growing up, and it was difficult enough to fit in and make friends at each new place without Lilly always following me around. The other kids never saw me as an individual: they saw the little Down syndrome girl first and her big sister was merely part of the package.

'She's my half-sister,' I sometimes told them, out of a need to distance myself. I always felt ashamed later, and it hurts now to remember saying it. Bloody stupid anyway. Half the kids I went to school with had brothers and sisters from different mums and dads.

Lilly emerges carrying an art folder – it catches the wind and she needs a second's attention to get a better grip. I see Lilly before Lilly sees me. I always love that, because it means I can savour the moment when Lilly reacts. Her face lights up like she hasn't seen me in days, and it makes me feel, just for an instant, like I'm the most special person in someone's life.

These days that moment lasts only until I remember that it's true. Right now I'm all Lilly's got.

'I've painted Batgirl. She's fighting Harley Quinn.'

Lilly loves comics, especially girl superheroes.

She makes to open the folder but I head her off, leading her towards the pelican crossing.

'Show me when we get home. It's a bit breezy right now.'

'It's not finished. I'm going to finish it at home. I need some new colouring pens. Can we buy some new colouring pens?'

I wish the answer could be yes.

'Was Cassie back in school today after her tummy bug?'

A change of subject often does the trick. Lilly will forget about the pens until she gets home, where she can make do with what she's already got or more likely start drawing something new.

'Yes. She's feeling better.'

Lilly is quiet for about a hundred yards, seemingly lost in her thoughts. It's long enough for me to think the question is not coming. But then it does.

'Is Mum home yet?'

I stifle a sigh, trying not to vent my frustration. Every night we go through this. Is she pretending she doesn't understand? Is it a kind of protest? Then I remember how long it took Lilly to understand about her dad.

'No, she's not home yet. She won't be home for a long time. She told you that, remember? When we went to see her.'

'But why is she there? Why won't she come home?'

'Because they won't let her out.'

'Why won't they let her out?'

I give vent to a sigh. It's that or a scream.

'Because she's in jail, Lilly.'

# TELEPHONE BANKING

'Good morning, HR, Don Corrigan speaking.'

His tone is breezy, someone whose day hasn't gone wrong yet.

'Oh, hi, Don,' comes the reply, matching his friendliness. 'This is Morgan Bell over at Corporate Security in Holborn.'

'Oh. How can I help?'

Don sounds suddenly guarded but trying to disguise it. Like talking to a cop: he's sure he's got nothing to answer for, but slightly edgy all the same.

'It's nothing heavy, don't worry. How are things over in Canary Wharf? I haven't been in the building for a while. They ever fix that big digital thermometer above the lobby?'

'No, it's still twenty-eight degrees every day, including January.'

He's relaxed again, friendly. He sounds like he wants to help. Maybe not help get the ball rolling on a massively high-profile hack of his employer, the RSGN Bank, but cooperative even so.

'Look, apologies if this isn't your remit, but I'm chasing up a list Human Resources was supposed to have sent us more than a week ago. I'm organising a security awareness seminar for new employees. They were meant to send me the names of anyone who has started in the last three months.'

'At Holborn as well, or just Canary Wharf?'

'Just Canary Wharf. I already got the list from our end, but only because I was able to go down to HR in person. I'm not having a lot of luck and I'm right up against a deadline now.'

'Do you know who was compiling it for you?'

'I've been back and forth between so many people that I've forgotten the name. Can you do a quick search? For all I know it might turn out there's nobody eligible and that's why I never got a list.'

'Okay, give me a second to get into the right system.'

There is a *clack-clack* of keys, a pause, an impatient sigh.

'Sorry,' Don says, but it's a good sorry. 'Computer's a little slow this morning.'

He's under control. He's going to deliver.

'Ah, here we go. There's actually quite a few. Fourteen results.'

'I'd better get busy, then. Can you email me their names and contact details? You'd really be digging me out of a hole.'

'Sure thing. I can send you this list right away. What's your email?'

'It's morgan.bell@RSGN_blue.com,' I reply. 'Major thanks, I really appreciate this.'

'RSGN Blue? I've never seen that address before.'

'It's a new thing. Part of the rebranding: certain departments are getting a colour.'

'You should have it now. Has the email come across okay?'

'It's just appeared. That's brilliant. Thanks.'

'You're welcome. Sorry about the delay. Will my email address be changing, then?'

'You'd have heard by now if it was. Don't worry, it's completely meaningless anyway. They'll probably ditch it again as soon as they've printed the new stationery.'

Don laughs in agreement and the call comes to a polite end.

'Good morning, Customer Communications.'

'Yeah, good morning. I'm looking for Sonya Donovan?'

'Yeah, that's me. How can I help?'

'This is Morgan Bell at Corporate Security over in Holborn. Don't panic, we're not about to have you escorted from the building or anything.'

'God, well that's a relief.'

Sonya sounds on the back foot but cheery, eager to please. She's not been in the job long, which is, after all, why she's been chosen from the list Don helpfully supplied.

'It was November you joined us, right? How are you liking it at RSGN? Settling in okay?'

'Yes, great.'

'Glad to hear it. I'm calling because it's coming up on our files that you haven't had a computer security audit yet. Is that right?'

'Er, no, I mean yes, that's right, I haven't. I was at a briefing when I started, but . . .'

'Yes, that's the standard briefing. The audit is something different. Don't worry, it's only a check-up to make sure you're okay with all the protocols. It's pretty painless and very rarely results in you being escorted from the building.'

Sonya chuckles, nervous but keen. Don's list said she was forty-one. She sounds mumsy: cheerful, responsible, cooperative.

'We're doing this now?' she asks.

'It should only take a couple of minutes, but if you're about to go for lunch I can schedule you for an after-hours audit. I've got a window at six forty-five tonight, or my colleague Mazood could fit you in at eight tomorrow morning.'

'No, no, if it's only going to take a little while . . .'

'It really is. Firstly, were you happy with the IT security briefing you received when you first arrived at RSGN? Was it clear enough? Did you understand it all?'

'Yes, totally. It was pretty similar to other places I've worked.'

'And so you're confident about your own security practices? You're never thinking: I *hope* this is okay?'

'No, never. I'm not dealing with anything sensitive here anyway. Despite the name, Customer Communications doesn't deal with any customer accounts. We're part of Marketing.'

'Okay, but as an aside I would warn you never to assume any information isn't sensitive.'

'Of course. Absolutely.'

'Have you had any communication that you were worried might be suspect?'

'Do you mean emails? I know not to open any attachments: that was all covered in the briefing.'

'Good. And have you ever been given any media – a disk or a flash drive – that originated outside of RSGN?'

'No, never. Again, that was covered in the—'

'Yes, I appreciate that. But not everybody remembers the briefing so well when it comes to the day-to-day, which is why we have to audit.'

'Of course.'

'Now, to confirm, your email is sonyadonovan@RSGN.co.uk and your login name is "sonyadonovan", all one word?'

'No, it's "sdonovan".'

'Oh dear. And you were doing so well.'

'What's wrong?'

'You just told me your username, and I could be anybody.'

'Oh, jeez, I'm sorry.'

'It's okay. This is why we have audits. I'd say seventy per cent of people get tripped by that one the first time. Now, more importantly, your password. Is it easily guessable?'

'No. Well, I don't know. I'm not sure now.'

'I'd better test it for you, then. We've got software that calculates how long it would take an automated program to crack it. If your password comes in at less than a certain figure, we have to insist you change it. So, what's yours?'

Sonya takes a breath, then sighs, letting out a chuckle.

'No. You're testing me again, aren't you?'

'Hey, you're catching on. Rule number one, and rules number two through fifty, are never tell anyone else your password. And we recommend you change it every three months as a further precaution. Would you like me to take you through that right now, so you know how to do it?'

'Sure, yes, that would be great.'

'It's very straightforward. Then that's us done and we can both get off to lunch. I'm starving, actually.'

'God, me too.'

Sonya listens carefully, following the instructions until she has reached the Change Password screen.

'Okay, just this once, because it's your first time doing this, in case anything goes wrong, I want you to change the password to "testpass", all lowercase, then press Save.'

'Testpass, got it. Okay, it's gone through.'

'Now I need you to log out of the system, then when you log in again, go to the Change Password screen and put in a proper password. And make sure nobody is in sight of your monitor when you do.'

'Understood. I'm logging back in now. No, hang about. It's saying "User already logged on". It's not letting me in.'

'It's okay, don't panic. Sometimes it takes the system a while to update itself. When do you get back from lunch?'

'Two o'clock.'

'Oh, no bother. It will be sorted long before that. And if it's not, my extension is . . . well, actually I'll be out of the office this afternoon, so I'll give you my mobile.'

'Thanks. And is that it now? The audit?'

'Yes. All done. Thank you, Sonya. You've given me everything I needed.'

And she sure has. Because at this point, the hacker known as Buzzkill is already inside the system, having logged on to the RSGN Bank – username 'sdonovan', password 'testpass' – the very second Sonya logged out. And Buzzkill has a whole hour to go exploring before she comes back.

# THE TOMORROW PEOPLE

'There are few more impressive sights than a Scotsman on the make,' according to J.M. Barrie, who might not qualify as an entirely object-ive source. His fellow countryman Jack Parlabane would like to believe Barrie's words are true, but right now he is more certain of the fact that 'wanting it too much' looks the same on a Scotsman as it does on every other nationality, and 'impressive' definitely does not seem the appropriate adjective. That's why nobody ever thought to use Desperation as a brand name for shower gel.

He is in a café in Shoreditch, sitting opposite Candace Montracon and Lee Williams, respectively the founder and the London bureau chief of *Broadwave*. The place is a former greasy spoon that has been given the full gentrification make-over, though with the hipster 'ironic' twist that it is serving pretty much the same menu as in its previous incarnation. The principal differences are that the walls have been stripped back to their bare bricks, the crockery is now uniformly black and square, and the brown sauce comes in a pewter ramekin. Oh, and that it's a tenner for a roll and sausage.

There are not many things in this world that would entice Parlabane to tolerate such an establishment, but the prospect of a job with *Broadwave* is one of them.

'You've been in the game a long time,' Candace states. 'Going all the way back to the early nineties.'

Parlabane can't quite read her tone, but from the fact that she makes the early nineties sound like it could be the Victorian era, he's not so sure she thinks his longevity is an entirely positive attribute. The phrase 'veteran reporter' has already been used, which he is not delighted about, but he is sufficiently familiar with the terms 'disgraced reporter' and 'former reporter' as to make his peace with it.

'I started unusually young,' he tells them, hoping this shaves a few years off their perceptions of his age. 'It helped when I was first investigating scams in Glasgow. I looked too innocent to be a cop or a reporter.'

'And from there you were headhunted to join a major investigative team here in London, before moving out to LA.'

'Yeah,' Lee chimes in, her gushy excitement pouring forth in contrast to Candace's detached cool. 'You went undercover investigating corruption in the LAPD. Seriously hardcore.'

'How do you know about that?' Parlabane asks, partly to hide his delight at how pleased she looks.

'Travin Coates, one of your colleagues from back then heads up our west coast features desk,' Candace says. 'We were talking about the Black Widow story and he said he'd worked for you. Gave you a good reference, said we should hit you up.'

Parlabane nods, wondering where his stock is right now. He thought he was being, if not headhunted, then at least asked to audition, and reckoned that was on the strength of his career overall. If the Diana Jager scoop is the principal reason they are looking at him, then the ground feels a lot shakier beneath his feet. That story put him back on the radar after a difficult few years, but the attention it brought was always likely to be transitory. There is a very good chance that it merely made *Broadwave* curious, and now that they have the chance to run the rule over him, they will see that he is not what they were hoping for.

This would be a massive kick in the plums, because *Broadwave* is very much what Parlabane is hoping for. There are precious few opportunities left in traditional print journalism, even for individuals who haven't burned quite so many bridges, so he is running out of time to find a future. *Broadwave* is a burgeoning cross-media entity that has evolved from a completely new perspective upon news and technology. While other outlets are struggling to manage the change from their old analogue platforms, often drowning under the weight of their own legacies, *Broadwave* is a product of the digital age.

It was started in San Francisco by Candace Montracon, whose background was in tech start-ups rather than journalism or television, so its models and paradigms derived from Silicon Valley rather than Fleet Street. It wasn't trying to be anything that had gone before, which was perhaps why it quickly developed such a strong brand in a crowded and hyper-competitive market. What had impressed Parlabane was that in a web full of clickbait and content dilution, *Broadwave* was all about substance. When a big story broke, it went deep: its features were lengthy and detailed, its interviews wide and prolific.

Critics called it 'Broadfunnel', because it was one of the first places would-be reporters and ordinary punters sent their blogs, vlogs and phone-cam footage in the hope of a payment or simply a credit. Candace called this 'crowdsourcing the news', and hired a new breed of editors whose job was about filtering and compiling content from the deluge of material that came to them over the wires. It wasn't a scattershot strategy: this new breed needed strong news sense, and worked closely with a staff of experienced reporters who helped shape the coverage across multiple media. The results weren't merely garnering page hits: *Broadwave*'s features were regularly being picked up by newspapers, and its logo was becoming a familiar sight in the corner of video footage shown on network news.

He hadn't sent them a CV and no vacancy had been advertised. They called him, and he was on a flight the next morning. He met them at their London offices, in a basement off Kingsland Road.

In his excited haste Parlabane had scribbled down the words 'perseverance works' next to the postcode dictated by the intern he spoke to. As he walked from Old Street Tube station, he couldn't remember whether this had been a warning that the place was difficult to find or a sentiment to himself regarding his own tenacity. It turned out to be the name of the building.

He was met in the reception area by a heavily tattooed young woman sporting close-cropped, pink-dyed hair and a pair of pink eighteen-hole Doc Marten boots. She had an iPhone in her left hand and was clutching a copy of *Diva* in her right. She looked twenty-five at most and Parlabane assumed she must be the intern he had spoken to until she greeted him by name in a strong southern Welsh accent. That was what turned enough cogs in his head for him to be able to respond by saying: 'You must be Lee.'

He didn't know if he got points for that, but she did seem genuinely pleased to see him.

He only got a brief look at the place through the reception windows before Lee ushered him back out again, saying they would be meeting Candace around the corner for brunch.

Hence his current location in this po-mo greasy spoon, where Parlabane is coming to suspect that his glimpse through the windows is as close to *Broadwave* as he's going to get.

'I'm not gonna ask you to blow smoke. That doesn't tell me nothing I don't know. What I really want to ask is what you think is *wrong* with *Broadwave*.'

It is Candace who speaks. Parlabane wonders whether his insight is genuinely being sought or whether this is some kind of truth-to-power test. Candace Montracon is a tall and striking black Hispanic transsexual whose path to a nine-figure net worth before the age of thirty was not greased by favour, privilege or Ivy League connections. There was no 'small loan of a million dollars'. Hers is an intimidating power to speak truth to, but Parlabane also reckons her bullshit detection and tolerance levels are calibrated so that truth is the only path. He is also working on the premise that Candace didn't get where she is without a fine appreciation for hustle.

This is his chance to pitch.

'That's not a question you would be asking if you didn't already know the answer. *Broadwave*'s Achilles heel right now is that in news terms, while you've got great reach and fast reflexes, you're reactive rather than dynamic. Something happens and you're all over it, big with the analysis and the follow-up. Not so much with the scoops. You're great at covering stories, but you aren't breaking them.'

Candace shows barely any response, but Parlabane is looking carefully enough to detect just the slightest affirmation. It's barely a nod, the merest movement of her head, but it's enough to say: Tell me more.

'You guys thought the whole "democratisation of information" thing combined with your crowdsourcing model would mean the stories would come to you. You'd be the ideal safe haven for whistle-blowers, for leaks and confidential sources: people who wouldn't go

22

to the mainstream media because they didn't trust them for what-ever reason. It didn't happen though, because it doesn't work like that.

'New media, old media, certain principles endure, and one of them is that it's all about contacts. If you've got a nervous source wanting to reach out, they're going to reach out to someone they know, or at least someone they feel they can quantify. People trust individuals, not brands; no matter how hot and sexy that brand is. And that goes tenfold in the political sphere.'

Candace fixes him with a penetrating stare.

'And I gather the political sphere is one in which you are well-travelled.'

Lee wades in before Parlabane can answer, speaking with what he is surprised to discern as alacrity.

'He broke some seriously major stories.'

Lee turns to look at him, eyes wide. She is actually fangirling.

'I mean, Jesus, the Midlothian NHS Trust scandal, the murder of Roland Voss, a massive blackmail conspiracy at the Scottish Parliament. That was swashbuckling shit. You were a lightning rod back then.'

As they departed the *Broadwave* offices, Lee had informed him that the premises had once housed a typesetting business, asking if he remembered what it was like to use paste-up boards and bromides. He replied in the affirmative, which seemed to delight Lee but made Parlabane feel like a relic.

It is proving something of a leitmotif as the interview progresses.

'And how's your contact book looking these days?' Candace asks.

It is what in Glasgow they call a double dunt. She is not only pointing out the stark absence of such lightning-rod political scoops in Parlabane's more recent career, but deftly introducing the sensitive subject of the reason why.

Parlabane finishes chewing a small mouthful of his roll and sausage; probably about a quid's worth.

'I guess you're asking whether I'm as good as my greatest triumphs or as bad as my worst mistakes.'

'It would be fair if the answer was "somewhere in between", but we both know it ain't about fair. Especially now. It's all about the brand. Hitler Diaries: that was embarrassing because it told everyone the news company wanted it to be true more than they worried about it being right. When you're the goddamn *Sunday Times*, you can recover from that. We don't got the institutional cachet of having a century or two of operational history behind us. In the new media, you're only credible while you're cool and you're only cool while you're credible. What I'm asking is if you can still get people to pick up the phone.'

Parlabane feels punctured, skewered with pinpoint accuracy through his own Achilles heel. The Leveson Inquiry had laid bare his more morally questionable (and at times downright illegal) methodology, and in his desperation to restore his reputation he had taken the bait in a honey trap set by the intelligence services. What he thought was a major scoop about military collusion in overseas false flag operations turned out to be a deliberate hoax planted to flush out a leak. He had wanted it to be true more than he had worried about it being right.

'I can still find a story where nobody knew there was one,' he replies. 'My Black Widow exclusive proves that much.'

He winces inside. He's actually bringing up the Black Widow story himself now. Not waving but drowning.

Candace looks impassive, though Parlabane is grateful her look is not one of pity.

'It was a big story, a great scoop,' she concedes. 'But not so much about your contact book as about being in the right place at the right time.'

Parlabane takes a sip of tea. He's sure this last was supposed to rile him, maybe to see how he reacted or maybe evidence that Candace has seen enough and wants to wrap this up.

He figures he's got one last opening here, and then it's over.

'You ever watch football, Candace?'

'Do you mean soccer? Sometimes.'

'I took her to West Ham against Swansea,' Lee says, her grin and her accent suggesting the points went west.

'I once heard an interview with a striker who had scored the only goal of the game, a tap-in from six yards,' Parlabane says. 'Someone had come up to him afterwards and said: "You got your money easy today." He laughed because the guy had no idea what it took to be in the right place at the right time for that six-yard tap-in. It's the most valuable skill in the game, and a striker who's got that is worth a fortune.'

'That's true,' Lee agrees, but then she wrinkles her nose. That's when he knows for sure that he's lost it.

'It wasn't really a *Broadwave* kind of story, though,' Lee goes on. 'I mean, it was a great scoop, obviously, but affairs, cheating, marriage breakdown: it's a bit tabloidy. Not quite our speed.'

She's still smiling, but he can see the regret in it. He has disappointed her. She wanted him to prove he was still relevant, that he was still the guy she had read about. Essentially she wanted the reporter he was when he was her age.

Parlabane picks up the remains of his roll, an overpriced breakfast looking like the only thing he's going to get out of this interview.

He looks across at the women on the other side of the table and thinks about some of the editors and colleagues he used to work with. So many *men* he used to work with. He can imagine the way they would respond to the idea of Lee as their news editor.

*I don't care what job title she's been given, I'm not listening to some little girl. What can she tell me about this game when she's only twenty-five?*

Parlabane's response would be to listen to her very carefully, because she's got that job title and she's only twenty-five.

He used to think he wanted the media to be the way it once was, but these were the comfort fantasies of an ageing man. Instead he can glimpse what the industry might become were it run by young tyros such as Candace and Lee, rather than by old filth like Kelvin MacKenzie and Paul Dacre.

Candace signals for the bill with the slightest glance to the waitress. It is subtle and minute yet effective, unequivocal, and in that tiny gesture Parlabane can see the future leaving without him.

# THE USUAL REASONS

<Buzzkill> So would some noble gentleman care to oblige a
    fellow and do the needful with these password hashes?
<Cicatrix> Who invited Little Lord Fauntleroy?
<Buzzkill> Sorry, forgot myself. Spent all day at the riding
    school teaching dressage.

*Buzzkill changes language mode to Internet Relay Chat.

<Buzzkill> Can anybody hook a brother up?
<Stonefish> NYPA.
<Cicatrix> Yeah NYPA. What the hell are you going after a
    bank for?
<Buzzkill> Striking back at the patriarchy. And for the lulz.
<Stonefish> Strike back on your own then. Sounds like
    you're turning SJW.
<Buzzkill> Get rekt, fuckhead.
<Juice> Hey. Show a bit of respect up in here.
<Cicatrix> What's up your butthole?
<Juice> My boy Blayze died today.
<Cicatrix> Shit. Sorry man.
<Stonefish> Yeah. Sucks, dude. He close? Family?
<Juice> Family. Found him dead on the couch this morning.
    Must have lay there all night.
<Buzzkill> That's awful. You okay?
<Juice> Hurting. Bad.
<Stonefish> You were close?
<Juice> Yeah. I fuckin loved that budgie.
<Stonefish> lol
<Cicatrix> Fuck you, skrub.

<Juice> Rekt.
<Stonefish> Rest in kill poor Blayze.

*Buzzkill lights candle.
*Buzzkill mourns the budgie.

K-zag joined channel #Uninvited_specops

<K-zag> Sup. What I miss?
<Stonefish> Juice's budgie died and Buzzkill wants to take
   down a bank.
<K-zag> For revenge?
<Buzzkill> No. For the usual reasons.

The usual reasons. Buzzkill smiles typing that.

Once you're in the guts of it, it's hard to remember what first sparked the motivation for a hack. In this case it was a TV news report about the Royal Scottish Great Northern Bank doling out super-fat bonuses to its top dogs, like these skrubs needed a hot meal. This was coming on the heels of the revelations that the RSGN had been illegally rigging the Libor rates as well as helping its richest clients dodge what meagre taxes were still due after they had parked the rest of their money in Panama or the Virgin islands.

Stonefish was on the wind-up, using SJW. It stands for social justice warrior, which admittedly Buzzkill can be, sometimes. Nothing is sacred with the Uninvited crowd, and it is unwise to let them know what you really care about. Nothing is to be taken seriously, and anything you say can and will be used against you. That said, you don't have to be selling the *Socialist Worker* outside Euston to think these RSGN chancers are taking the piss.

The TV reporter laid it all out, what they'd been up to, then their shameless spokeswombat spewed out quotes giving it the L'Oréal defence: Because we're worth it. Buzzkill's response was: Fuck these ass-clowns.

But Buzzkill has thought 'fuck these ass-clowns' about plenty of people before, and not decided to deploy any hack-fu against them.

Seeing the report merely prompted the response: 'Hmmm. I wonder I wonder I wonder.'

So truth is it's not about social justice, any more than the rest of the Uninvited crew – regardless what they might claim – will be doing it for the lulz. They do it for the usual reasons: because they can; or simply to find out *if* they can.

A bank would ordinarily be a non-starter (come on, it's a *bank*), but at the tail-end of that news story, the reporter mentioned that the RSGN was in the middle of a rebranding exercise. It was the usual suit-think: they were trying to clean up their image by re-designing their logo and launching a new slogan. It was hardly going to make everybody forget that they were doling out seven-figure bonuses to their execs while everybody else was still paying for their ten-figure bail-out, but it did present a skilled hacker with a possibility.

A trip down Canary Wharf was called for, to that glass-and-chrome supervillain HQ from where you see the TV guys reporting every time the RSGN gets caught on the fiddle. Buzzkill had a wander around, scoped the place, took some notes: such as the fact that it had this gigantic digital thermometer hanging in the middle of the vestibule, permanently showing the wrong temperature. It was about forty feet up and obviously a bitch of a thing to get to, so apparently it had been like that a while, as it hadn't been twenty-eight outside for months.

Around midday, an upmarket deli joint full of suits having lunch seemed an inviting destination. Buzzkill sat there a long time, sipping from a bottle of water and being comfortably ignored, blending into the background. To a shower of corporate zones the hacker was practically invisible.

Buzzkill huddled there tapping at a laptop which had a modified webcam attached to the side by a clip. It was designed to look like it was pointing at the user, but all the time the tiny high-definition camera was focused on the screen of whichever device happened to be open on an adjacent table. That way the resourceful hacker-about-town was able to see the address of the site they were logging into in order to keep working for the Man during their lunch hours: committed, professional, dedicated.

Slaves. Drones. Losers.

After that, of course, a username and password would be required.

Sonya's login proved sufficient to facilitate a thorough poke around, allowing the download of a ton of emails and a fact-finding tour of the Customer Communications department's local network. Sonya's lowly credentials weren't going to provide access to anything truly tasty, but it was a foot in the door: enough to get names, job titles, contact details, and from that to develop a picture of the department's structure, the terminology they used and crucially the codename they had given the rebranding project: White Frost.

Hacking works by increments: once you're inside, even at the ground floor, you can usually score something that will help you access the next level; and sometimes you really luck out. In this case it was the discovery that Customer Communications had a policy of hot-desking, so staff were logging in from different computers. This meant that each machine stored a list of passwords for all of the user accounts that had logged into it. They were encrypted, but still, it represented an express elevator to the penthouse. Buzzkill only needed the right executive credentials to make it move.

That's what the internet relay chatroom request for hashes was all about, and why the guys were joyfully giving out grief about it. It takes a varied pool of talents to make something like this happen, and though everybody loves to showcase their skillz, they also love the power it gives them when they can dangle their refusal over a friend in need.

You don't only have to ask politely, you have to ask canny. Don't sound like you want it too much. Don't sound like you're on a crusade.

That's why Stonefish said NYPA. Not Your Personal Army. He was joking, though. He knew Buzzkill wasn't on a crusade, same as they both knew nobody was going to miss out on being part of this big a win. This would see Uninvited getting headlines right around the globe. Jesus, even LulzSec and Anonymous never hit a bank.

# A GOOD WALK SPOILED

'Hello, can I speak to Jonathan Rockwood please?'

'Who is this?'

'My name is Les Dillon. I'm from—'

'Les, it's not a good time to talk. I'm on the golf course, so . . .'

'I appreciate that, and I'm very sorry to interrupt your game on a Sunday morning, sir, but I'm with IT and I need to inform you of some server outages in case they affect you.'

'Wait, server outages?'

'Yes, sir. There's been a suspected breach and we've been investigating a possible malware intrusion. The damage looks limited at this stage but the worry is that we don't know how far it might have spread.'

'What are you telling me?'

'Well, ordinarily we wouldn't be going so belt and braces, but because of White Frost we've been ordered to take everything up a notch, security-wise. We're having to wipe the potentially affected servers and restore from back-up.'

'I've got a deadline for a major project fast-approaching. I can't afford any delays.'

'I know, sir. I'm aware you're in charge of customer-side website content for the rebrand, which is why I've been instructed to let you know about this immediately, and to ask which servers you've been using for the White Frost project.'

'We're using Sierra Nine and Sierra Eleven.'

'I was kind of hoping that wasn't going to be your answer.'

'Shit. How long is this going to take?'

'We'll be getting them back up one by one, but some are likely to be down for several days.'

'Several days? That's just not on. Absolutely not. There has to be a quicker solution.'

'With respect, sir, it's not like re-installing Windows. We're going to have to rebuild entire databases, and the compiling process—'

'I don't care about the technicalities. This work is crucial to White Frost, do you understand? For fuck's sake, there has to be something you can do.'

'This is not my doing, sir. I appreciate you're upset, but you're not the first person I've had this conversation with. Everybody wants to be head of the queue to get their work up and running again.'

'I apologise. I'm shooting the messenger here. But you have to see the situation I'm in. White Frost is supposed to be going live in less than a fortnight, and . . .'

'I understand, sir. I suppose there is— No.'

'What?'

That little note of desperate, eager hope in his voice is music to any hacker's ears.

'Well, the only thing I can think to do might get me into a boatload of trouble if it goes south.'

'I'll vouch for you. What is it?'

'It would involve me creating a new partition on the server and copy-pasting your project files to that while everything else gets wiped. Problem is, if it later turns out the malware has infected your stuff, then we're back to where we started and we'll have to repeat the whole exercise further down the line. Except, when I say we, I mean whoever is doing my job after I get fired.'

'I'll take full responsibility. You can have that in writing if you like.'

'That won't be necessary, Mr Rockwood. I'll take you at your word. What I am going to need from you is a list of the directories where you're storing the materials you want protected.'

'Absolutely. Absolutely. I can email that from right here.'

'I'm also going to need your username and password.'

Rockwood takes a breath, about to answer. Then he stops, and there is a moment's pause.

'Wait. Who did you say you were?'

There is no panic. Buzzkill is ready for this. It's not an exact science. It never goes smooth, exactly the way you planned it. It's not about whether you get the specific information you were phishing for: it's about how you can improvise with the information you do get.

The very reason for this call to Rockwood is that Plan A got derailed. It's okay, though. Without this brief exchange, Buzzkill wouldn't have scored the additional information regarding which servers Rockwood is keeping the goodies on; and better yet, which specific directories contain the White Frost assets.

Plan A involved Stonefish decoding Rockwood's password hash and then Buzzkill was simply going to log in and see how far his clearance level took things. Password hashes are long gobbledegook strings of numbers and letters that represent the encrypted versions of login details. It's so that a computer or website doesn't store your actual password for some curious and enterprising individual to get hold of. Hashes can be decrypted, though. Guys like Stonefish live for it. It's like a religious meditation the way he describes it: descending into this trance-like flow state in which hours pass without him noticing. He said one time he actually wet himself a bit because by the time he realised that he needed to pee, it was so urgent that he didn't make it to the bathroom fast enough.

Stonefish had delivered. That wasn't the problem.

<Buzzkill> Were you trolling me with that password for
   Rockwood?
<Stonefish> You're saying it was wrong?
<Buzzkill> I'm saying it didn't work.
<Stonefish> Did you key it in right? It was jacknicklaus78,
   all lowercase.
<Buzzkill> I copy-pasted it.
<Stonefish> Shit. I swear jacknicklaus78 was definitely what
   I got from the hash.
<Buzzkill> Not doubting you. Just checking, because I can't
   afford too many wrong attempts in case he gets an alert.
<Stonefish> Definitely not messing with you man.

It may have been an older document. Maybe Rockwood last logged on from that particular machine a while ago and had changed his password since, or perhaps he changed it regularly. Buzzkill really hates people who do that.

But there are ways to use someone's old password in order to get his new one.

'Les Dillon,' Buzzkill tells him. 'I'm with IT.'

'Where are you based?'

'I'm mostly at Radogan House over in Holborn.'

Buzzkill uses the specific name of the premises rather than merely the geographic.

'Who's your boss over there?'

It's a safe bet he knows naff-all about RSGN's IT personnel, and if Buzzkill made up a name it would call his bluff, but you don't leave shit like that to chance. Les Dillon is the name of the person who is genuinely on-duty today for the IT department. Buzzkill knows this for a fact, having called first thing and checked.

'Tallat Kumar. Do you want to talk to him instead? Because if you do, please don't tell him what I just offered to do for you.'

'No, it's okay. But I'm not comfortable giving my login details over the phone. You could be anybody.'

'I understand. And to be honest I'm not comfortable risking my job over bypassing your files in the server rebuild, so maybe it's best if we leave it.'

Buzzkill lets Rockwood think about this, reminding him that Les is his only chance of getting a fast result.

'No, no. What if I came in right now and logged in for you?'

'I'm on a bit of a clock here. It's really now or never.'

Limited time offer!

'I could be there in forty-five minutes.'

'I really can't wait that long. Tell you what, though. I can call up your details and read you back the password you used when we first set up your user account.'

'How do you have access to that?'

'Through something else that could get me fired. We keep a record of people's initial password in case they screw up the primary registration. It's why we recommend regularly changing your pass-word. Please don't tell anyone I told you about it.'

33

'No, I won't.'

'Anyway, I'm looking at your file now and it appears your initial password was "jacknicklaus78". Would that be right?'

'Yes. Well, I don't think that was my original password, but I did use it.'

'It's what we've got on file. Are you happy to give me your new one now?'

'Sure. It's "tomwatson77". Username "jrockwood".'

'Got it. Thank you.'

'And can you guarantee my work will be safe from the server meltdown?'

'As soon as you tell me the directories you want protected.'

'You're a life-saver. I owe you big time.'

'No, you don't. Because this didn't happen, remember?'

'Understood.'

'Now, I don't need to say that when you get into work tomorrow, you should change your password . . .'

# LIFE IN CAPTIVITY

I take off my jacket, my boots, my watch, my bangles and my earrings, placing them in a grey plastic tray which is lifted by a grey-faced woman and shunted on to a grey conveyor belt beneath the most harsh and nasty strip lighting. There is a bloke in front of me, waiting for the nod to go through the metal detector. He smells like he has spent the morning rolling around in a giant ashtray. I hate the smell of cigarettes on clothes worse than I hate the smell of the smoke itself. It smells of mornings after: of not knowing who I am going to find in the house, crashed out on the couch or in my mum's bed.

I stand there in my socks, waiting my turn, like I've done so many times in so many airports. Today, though, I know that once I have passed through security, the only journey waiting for me will be a guilt trip.

Ash-Man shuffles through the arch then I am beckoned forward. I always feel nervous that these things might beep, but vastly more so here. If you forget to remove your phone or whatever at Heathrow, they're only going to make you go through again. Here, they might think you're trying to smuggle contraband. I resent the fact that they are looking at me and actually thinking I might be a criminal.

But the worst part is I can't hold it against them: after all, I am the daughter of one.

I take a seat in the waiting room where they hold you until it's officially visiting time, and not a fraction of a second before. I am surrounded by people who look hatchet-faced and aggressive, people I am careful not to make eye contact with, but who I feel driven by instinctive caution to scrutinise.

A rational voice tells me these are only visitors, the same as me, but they aren't the same as me. They all seem tougher than me. They don't look scared like I feel scared.

They are bristling with attitude, some of them openly and often pointlessly disrespectful towards the staff. It is as though they are laying down boundaries, standing on the same side of the line as their friend or relative who is inside.

I am suddenly self-conscious about being so cooperative and polite, smiling at the staff like some stupid girl. That is me, though: always afraid of getting into trouble. Always trying to please the teacher.

I can hear Keisha and Gabrielle's voices, mocking how I spoke in class, mocking how I behaved, mocking how I dressed. Considering they were all in the same school uniform, it showed you how little those bitches needed to work with.

'You fucking fink you're better'n us, don't ya?'

'No, I don't.'

'Yes, you fucking do. Just cause you always get your sums right and you talk all proper. It's paffetic. You fink you're a fucking genius. You're fucking nuffing, that's what you are. Nobody fucking knows you exist except the fucking teachers.'

*No, I don't.*

That really told them. Put them in their place good and proper.

I don't get what's wrong with how I talk. I moved around a lot growing up, rarely long in one place, so although I understand their slang, I feel self-conscious using it, because it's not mine. There's a few Geordie words that feel more natural, but I tend to shy off using them too, because they only remind me of how I don't belong.

Keisha's right, though. I am pathetic. Always a target. Always a victim.

It still burns inside when I remember what they did to me in fourth form. They must have got bored of the endless verbal abuse and tripping me up in corridors. Or maybe it finally dawned on them that *they* were the ones who thought I was better than them, and this light-bulb moment inspired a rare bout of creativity.

They cornered me on the way home one afternoon, lying in ambush behind the high flats: Keisha, Gabrielle, Martine and Paula. I always took the long way home because I knew the others tended to cut through the park. They must have doubled back, or maybe they had bunked off the last class and were on their way to hang around the shops.

'Martine says you've got maffs homework,' Keisha stated.

Martine was in the top set for maths alongside me, but she never got shit for it because she was one of their mates, and had been for ever. I had only been at the school a year at this point.

'You're gonna fail it,' Gabrielle said.

I thought she was simply trying to goad me, before it hit me that this wasn't a prediction, but an order.

'You're gonna fail it or we're gonna fuck you up.'

Martine stood there arms folded, giving me evils. She was going to let them know if I complied. Martine was a hanger-on, someone who wouldn't be pushing anybody around if she wasn't in with that lot, so she was enjoying wielding some power. I wondered if it had been her idea, a way of scoring points with Keisha and Gabrielle.

In case I thought this might be an empty threat, Keisha punched me in the stomach so hard I thought I was going to be sick. Then they all walked away, but they weren't laughing like they usually did once they'd had their fun. That was how I knew for sure they were planning to follow up.

I was in hell after that, wrestling with what to do. I wrote out a version of my homework that I had calculated to be a narrow fail: something that would score less than 50 per cent, but where the marks were lost in ways believable enough to the teacher that it wouldn't be obvious I was taking a dive.

I couldn't sleep that night, and sometime around two in the morning I ripped up the failed homework and started again. I had tried to convince myself otherwise, but deep down I knew that if I did this for them once, they would repeat the drill. They were doing this because they had run out of ways to hurt me, so I couldn't give them a new one.

It was my only means of defiance. I couldn't stand up to them face to face, even one on one, but I could still give them all a big fuck you in the only way possible. I stayed up the rest of the night, taking extra care over the homework, making sure I missed nothing.

I scored 98 per cent, my highest mark ever.

It felt good for about a second, seeing the look on Martine's face, but as soon as maths was finished, my legs were like jelly and my stomach was imploding. I was useless in my other classes, tired from being up all night and distracted by thoughts of how I might get home.

I stayed in sight of the staffroom window during breaks and even held off having a pee so as to avoid the toilets. My bladder was bursting by the last class, a constant, growing, piercing pain.

In my desperation to get home, I opted to race through the park, running all the way, reckoning they would be waiting for me on my normal route. I was wrong. I ran right into them, and as Keisha fronted up to me, fists balled, I pissed myself in front of everyone. Not only them, but half the school. They all laughed and took photos. It was on Facebook before I got home.

The door to the visit room opens from the inside, preceded by a jangle of keys and a distinctive clunk. It is the constant rhythm of this place, like hi-hat and bass drum.

I am last inside, letting everyone else file through before me, not wanting to get in anyone's way. I don't like the feeling of being in a crowd, even the sense of bustle when too many people are trying to get through one doorway.

Same as last time, I look past my mother at first before recognising her. She is in a faded blue prison-badged polo shirt, identical to all the other women, one that looks as though it has been through the machine a couple of thousand times. Before she went inside, I had never seen her in anything so basic and indistinct, and I know that being forced to wear the same thing as anyone else is an insult. For someone who worked as a nurse for years, Mum has always had an aversion to uniforms. The skin on her arms looks ashy. I've never seen that on her before. She must have run out of moisturiser.

She isn't smiling. Instead she has a searching, quizzical look on her face.

'Where's Lilly?'

Not 'How are you?' or 'Thanks for coming'.

'Why didn't you bring her?'

'It's Wednesday. She's at school.'

Where I should be, I don't add.

'Oh, Jesus, like it matters if she misses a morning. Not like she's studying for her GCSEs.'

'She doesn't like it if her routine is disrupted. Neither does the school.'

'Yeah, but I haven't seen her in over a week. She gets upset if she doesn't see me.'

I sit down on a hard plastic chair. Mum didn't stand up, so there weren't going to be any hugs. If I'd brought Lilly, sure, but I haven't.

I take a moment, readying myself to say this. I feel exposed. The light in here is too bright, too harsh.

'Not getting to see you upsets Lilly, but not as much as seeing you in here and then leaving again. She doesn't understand why you can't just come home. We've been twice and she's cried for hours after each time.'

'You think I don't cry afterwards too?'

Maybe not after this time, I reckon, but I say nothing.

'You think I like it here?' Mum demands.

I still stay silent. I've made my point.

'How is Lilly? Is she eating okay? Are you making sure you're there on time at school, because she gets real scared if she comes out that door and she can't see someone she knows.'

I feel my hackles rise. I gaze across, meeting my mum's insistent eyes. The horrible threads and dry skin aside, I think Mum is looking better than she has done in a long time. It must be harder to get drugs in here than the stories make out, though coffee is an exception, I guess, because she looks kind of wired. She is more alert, more awake, and now that she is straightened out, she has to occupy her ever-restless mind with other things, and that means micromanaging my care of Lilly from a distance.

'Lilly is fine. Me not so much.'

Mum tuts, like this is merely whining she could do without. I press on, though. Talking this stuff out was the reason I made myself come here.

'I got a letter this morning telling us the housing benefit's being cut because we now have a spare room.'

Mum's face is a mixture of outrage and confusion.

'We don't have a spare room.'

'We do now. So we either have to move somewhere smaller or make up the difference, which just got harder because they already said they won't transfer the Carer's Allowance to me because I'm not eligible.'

'Why not?'

'Because I'm still at the college. They don't give it to people in full-time education, same as they don't give it to you if you're earning more than a hundred quid a week. Or at least more than a hundred quid that they know about,' I add.

Mum sighs at this dig, nostrils flaring. She folds her arms and sits back in her chair. I brace myself. I know the signs: another helping of tough love coming up. I can barely remember the last time I enjoyed any other kind.

'Well, you're gonna have to get a job, Sam.'

She says it with a dry, humourless laugh, like I'm being thick or in denial and need the hard truth pointing out.

'What about my exams? What about going to uni?'

Mum holds out her palms in a display of frustration, indicating her situation.

'I don't know if you noticed, but circumstances have changed.'

This is Mum all over. She acts like this is something that simply happened, and happened *to* her rather than something she brought upon herself.

'If you want it so badly, you'll make it work. Change your application to somewhere in London, find a part-time job. Plenty of other students manage.'

'And I could too, but not if I have to be there for Lilly. Dropping her off every morning, picking her up every afternoon, staying around the house all the time she's home.'

'Welcome to my life, before *this* happened. You don't think I could have spread my wings if I didn't have Lilly to think about?'

*Well, no,* I don't say. *You definitely didn't spread them very far all the times you had me looking after her, running to get to school on time after I dropped Lilly at hers, sprinting again to be there for her at the end of the day. Those wings never seemed to take you past your dealer's house, and half the time they never lifted you from the sofa.*

The hardest part is that I remember my mum being someone different, someone who was always in control. She was never passive, feeling sorry for herself and acting like a victim. She was full of energy and ideas, looking for every angle she could play.

That was before Dad died, though. Everything turned to shit after that.

'You're her mother.'

'And you're her sister.'

'It's not the same. I'm nineteen.'

'What, and I've had my time, is that what you're saying? I can't believe you sometimes, Samantha. You're so selfish. What would Lilly think if she heard you talk about looking after her like this, as though you want rid of her.'

'That's not what I said.'

'It's what I'm hearing.'

I look down at the manky, fag-burned table. I can feel Mum's glare burning into me. I am cowed, defeated.

How did it come to this, that I could sit here and be guilt-tripped by the person who fucked everything up?

'I'm just saying, this is all falling on me, Mum, and it's a lot to handle. They're sending someone to do an assessment.'

Mum stiffens.

'Who is?'

'Social services. They need to check out the situation, make sure Lilly's being looked after properly.'

'And why wouldn't she be?'

'If we can't make the rent and I've no Carer's Allowance and her mum's in jail and I'm struggling to put food on the table, they might not view that as an ideal situation.'

'And that would suit you, wouldn't it? That's what you want. If they took her away.'

'No, I'm only—'

41

'You've always acted as if she was a burden, as if you wanted rid of her, and now you've got your chance. Is that what you came in here to tell me? Is that why you didn't bring her, so she didn't have to hear you say it?'

I can feel myself start to cry: the swelling in my throat, the trembling of my lip. The idea of Lilly ending up in care is horrifying, the furthest thing from what I want. But it is the thought of Lilly hearing that I don't want her around that is really slaying me.

It isn't true, but it isn't entirely untrue either. How do you make someone like Lilly understand that you want to have a grown-up life?

'That's not—'

'I didn't want this for you. I wanted you to have every chance, Sam. But I can't help the fact I'm stuck in here.'

*No, Mum,* I don't say. *You can't help it now, but you could have helped it when you made the choices that saw you end up in this place. Instead you're framing it, like you frame everything, as part of the ongoing martyrdom of Saint Ruth.*

'You got to promise you won't let them take her, Sam. I couldn't handle that, after everything that's happened to me. It would be the end. I grew up in those places. I know what they're like. Promise me, Sam. You have to promise me.'

I wipe my nose and my eyes with the sleeve of my jumper.

'I promise.'

# THE LAST TO KNOW

Parlabane rings the doorbell a second time, hearing music from inside but as yet no sound of footsteps, no cry of 'Be right with you'. He has been blowing around London like an empty crisp poke, and now he's stranded on a stranger's doorstep, quite probably until the song ends and a third ring stands a better chance of being heard.

He is staying – or intending to stay – at his friend Mairi's place in Hoxton. She is out of the country but she told him he was free to crash there when they spoke on Skype yesterday. She said he could pick up the keys from her next-door neighbour, though he wouldn't be home until the evening.

After his brunch in Shoreditch, Parlabane really wanted to head all the way home to Edinburgh but he didn't have any return travel booked. He had told himself this was to keep his options open: maybe look up a few people, refresh some old contacts socially and professionally. But the embarrassing truth – one that fortunately he doesn't have to admit to anyone else – is that he had actually been hoping *Broadwave* would offer him a job on the spot, so that if they asked when he could start, he would be able to answer: 'Right away.'

Jesus, whit a riddie.

He recalls the polite smiles, the sterile 'We'll be in touch', an assurance as valuable as 'We'll keep your details on file'.

Concerned that the music might be a DJ mix with no gaps, he gives the door a few firm thumps: not quite polis strength, as he doesn't want to be rude, but voluble enough. It works.

All Mairi told Parlabane about her neighbour is his name and that he works as a make-up artist. The door is opened by a tall, attractive and flamboyantly camp man with Latin features and a Hispanic accent. He initially regards his visitor with surprise and suspicion, but before Parlabane can say anything, his face flashes with realisation and he smiles.

'Are you Jack?'

'That's right.'

'Is you been standing there long? I'm so sorry. I been cooking, and with the extractor fan and the music . . . Come on in. You want some chicken?'

'Oh, no, no. I don't want to impose. I just need the keys . . .'

'Come on in, it's nothing. I made too much anyways. It's the marinade: I can't get the quantities right if I do like a reduced batch, so I end up making a ton and I'm eating it for days. Come on, if I got company I got an excuse to make caipirinhas.'

Parlabane is feeling about as sociable as a jihadi in a synagogue. He wants to go next door and pull a quilt over his head, but this guy is doing him a favour as well as extending his courtesy, so he ought to be polite. Besides, a drink sounds pretty good right now.

'That would be most welcome. You're very kind. Han, isn't it?'

Han leads him into the flat, its layout a mirror image of Mairi's, though it doesn't seem as cramped and tiny due to being less chaotically cluttered. Parlabane would confess he was expecting décor tending towards the fabulous, but instead he finds himself in something of a geek cave; though undeniably a tastefully curated geek cave. There are models and figurines on glass shelves, several autographed movie stills framed on the walls. Upon closer inspection he sees that they are not commercial prints but on-set photographs.

Parlabane thought Han worked in a salon. Mairi neglected to specify that he was a visual effects make-up artist.

'Alejandro,' he explains. 'Han for short. Who doesn't wanna be Han?' he adds, nodding towards a classic *Star Wars* poster.

Parlabane follows him to the minute kitchen, but waits in the doorway as there is barely enough room for two people to stand in there. The chicken smells great. Han mixes him a drink.

'How long you known Mairi? You guys worked together? You in the music biz too?'

'I've known her about thirty years, though with a gap of about

44

fifteen without seeing her. She was my friend's little sister once upon a time.'

Han pauses as he is about to take a mouthful from his caipirinha.

'Oh, wait. I know who you are. You're the *guy*, you're the journalist.'

Han's eyes bulge with enthusiasm, simultaneously delighted and impressed. Unfortunately it only reminds Parlabane of Lee Williams' fangirling this morning. He doesn't feel like he's 'the journalist' today. He certainly doesn't feel like 'the *guy*'.

'She told me all about you. Well, she told me what she was allowed to, because I know there was some NDA shit went down that nobody's supposed to know. But whatever you did, you were her hero, man. Oh, yeah, she *likes* you.'

Parlabane can't help a bashful smile. There is something irresistibly warm and endearing about Han; perhaps it's that he is so unselfconscious, albeit bordering on indiscreet. He makes Parlabane feel a little bit gay; or at least makes him flirt briefly with wishing that he was. Would it all have worked out better for him that way, he wonders.

When he spoke to Mairi yesterday, he couldn't help but feel there was a weird vibe between them; not awkwardness, but not as comfortable as it was before. She was friendly enough – she had offered him the use of her flat, for God's sake – but there was a strange sense of her keeping her distance. It was almost like he had recently made a move and she'd said no, and this was their first time talking since.

Maybe this is how it goes, he told himself. He had his chance back in Berlin, but chose not to take it, partly because he felt responsible for her at the time, but mainly because he was still in denial over the terminal state of his marriage. He had suggested they see if they still felt the same after she returned from accompanying Savage Earth Heart, the band she managed, on tour. It was a mature and rational decision, and had reaped the rewards it deserved. Whoever said love worked out for them because they had been rational and mature?

'She told me she really thought something was gonna happen there,' Han goes on. 'But then you friend-zoned her.'

He gives Parlabane a curious look: part scrutiny, part admonishment.

'We had been through some scary stuff. People sometimes get confused about their feelings at times like that. Plus I knew she was going to be jetting off all over the globe for months at a time. All in all, it seemed the . . . sensible thing.'

Han nods like he understands, though he may not agree with Parlabane's choices.

'She's off travelling again,' continues Parlabane. 'She'll be gone for weeks. Australia and New Zealand, then twenty more dates in the US. Apart from Skype calls, I haven't seen her in months.'

'Oh, I hear you. I ain't hardly seen her much either, though they was back for a couple days last week.'

'They?'

Parlabane feels something tighten inside him. If he was previously unsure whether he really did have feelings for Mairi, then the verdict just came in.

'Yeah. Her and, you know, ah, what's his name, yeah, like in that movie about the devil kid.'

Parlabane takes a gulp of the caipirinha. He needs to swallow so that he can deal with the lump in his throat. He also needs the alcohol.

'Damien?'

'Yeah, yeah. He's the guitarist, right? Got that whole broody dark thing going on? Handsome, sure. I like that little bass player, though. He cute.'

Parlabane needs another gulp.

'She was with Damien? Like *with* with Damien?'

'What, she didn't say nothing?'

'No, but it's, you know, her business.'

'Shit, though, maybe she keeping it quiet because he's in the band. Guess I shouldn't be telling you, then, if you're a journalist. You're a friend though, so you ain't gonna blab. Plus if she wanted to keep it quiet, she should have kept it quiet, if you know what I'm saying. Walls in this place are paper-thin. Or come to think, maybe she never said nothing because it's a new thing; they was certainly going *at it* like when it's a new thing.'

Parlabane is still standing in the kitchen doorway, a few feet from Han, but he suddenly feels like he is a thousand miles distant. They are in the same place but not in the same moment. The one mercy is that Han doesn't appear to notice.

'Gonna be an issue if they're on tour, you'd think. I mean, if he's in the band and she's the manager, there could be problems ahead. I guess he's not so sensible, though.'

Ouch.

'Anyway, Mairi said you were in town for an interview. How'd that go?'

# HIGH JINKS AND EXPLOITS

<Buzzkill> This is mission control for #bankjob. Everybody good to go?

<K-zag> I am already hard.

<Juice> Package is prepped.

<Stonefish> So we're really doing this?

<Buzzkill> No, we're running Bank Hack Simulator. It's on Steam Greenlight if you want to grab yourself a copy. WTF. Yes we're really doing this. You pussing out?

<Stonefish> I'm good to go. Just thought this might be a good time for everybody to take a moment to consider what we're about to get into here. We're talking about a bank.

<K-zag> These RSGN skrubs are a bank? I thought they were a farming collective. Buzzkill, why didn't you tell us this?

<Stonefish> I'm just making sure everybody understands that this is a new line we're crossing. We should savour it, but we should also be under no illusions about how deep the shit is here. This will be big. They'll be bitching about stock prices dropping tomorrow, the knock-on effect in the markets, all that shit. And they will come after us for this, like we never saw before.

<Juice> I sure hope so. I'm shorting RSGN shares.

<Buzzkill> Internets is serious business.

<Stonefish> Jeez, Buzzkill, that meme is almost as old as you'll be by the time you get out of prison.

<Buzzkill> So you are pussing out.

<Juice> It's an inevitability that one day someone is gonna go Sabu on us and sell us out to the Feds. My money has always been on Stone.

<Stonefish> Damn right. I'm compiling logs on all you
   motherfuckers. But it would blow my cover if I pussed
   out of a big op like this, so fuck it, I'm in.

Buzzkill feels relief reading this, but is kind of annoyed at Stonefish. Why is he making such a big deal over that fact that it's a bank? It's just another hack. They're breaking the same bullshit laws and they're not hurting anybody. All they're doing is what they always do: messing with some smug ass-clowns who have seriously got it coming.

It's no mystery why he's antsy, though. Nobody could blame him for that. They're all nervous. That's part of the buzz. This is when it gets crazy.

The weird thing is that technically the hacking is already done. Buzzkill has been up in those servers for days – they all have – since that nice Mr Rockwood whose golf game got interrupted was kind enough to tell Les from IT his password. (Rockwood changed it first thing Monday morning, sensible chap, but by then Buzzkill had already created a ghost account in the system, cloning his access privileges, then shared the login details with the Uninvited crew.)

There is a crucial difference between penetrating a system and announcing to the world that you've done it. It's kind of a 'no harm, no foul' deal, as the whole point is that nobody knows any crime has been committed. In fact, it's a whole other thrill to go snooping around servers and networks undetected. Buzzkill once read an online interview with Ferox, a legendary hacker from the early days of the internet, in which he admitted that the companies he was known to have penetrated back then were only the tip of the iceberg.

Buzzkill has had secret logins to certain places for years, and some nights goes back simply for the sake of nostalgia. LulzSec and Anonymous sat on some of their hacks for months, even years. In certain cases it was a question of waiting for the right time to go public; in others it was about patiently watching to see what else an exploit might open up if they waited for developments; and in still other instances they simply decided, for whatever reason, not to act.

LulzSec got inside the NHS's computer system, for example. They quietly sent an email to the network administrators telling them about the vulnerability they had discovered. They said: 'We mean you no harm and only want to help you fix your tech issues.'

When you do go public and hit a site, you know you're probably cashing in your access privileges, but it's always worth it for the rush.

&lt;Juice&gt; So if everybody is lubed up, let's crime.

&lt;Buzzkill&gt; Steady. Tote board is light. Cicatrix, you in or you out?

&lt;Buzzkill&gt; Cicatrix? Hello? Paging Cicatrix, come in, over?

&lt;K-zag&gt; Maybe had to go pee-pee.

*Buzzkill taps microphone.

&lt;Buzzkill&gt; Is this thing on? Cicatrix? You there? Got a major hacking operation about to kick off here. That ring any bells?

&lt;Cicatrix&gt; Shit. Sorry. Having issues with my VPN.

&lt;Juice&gt; Having issues with a VPL? If you're worried about a visible panty line, go commando girl.

&lt;K-zag&gt; Just watch out for those upskirt paparazzi shots.

&lt;Cicatrix&gt; Shit. Shit. Shit. No joke. I'm gonna have to bail on this one.

&lt;Stonefish&gt; That blows. You sure you can't get it fixed?

&lt;Cicatrix&gt; What do you think I've been doing the past three hours? I can't risk it.

&lt;Stonefish&gt; Not when we're hitting a bank.

&lt;Buzzkill&gt; What about your files? We need that shit.

&lt;Cicatrix&gt; I'll fire them over to Juice. He knows how to run the install.

&lt;Buzzkill&gt; Okay.

&lt;Cicatrix&gt; Sorry Buzzkill.

&lt;Buzzkill&gt; Shit happens.

Buzzkill feels for Cicatrix, and is pissed off that they will have to do this without his talents. He has put a lot of effort into this, but he is right not to suit up if he has issues with his VPN. A virtual private network is to a hacker what a mask is to a bank robber. It's how they hide their locations and prevent their activities from being traced.

Anonymity is the most valuable currency in the game, and is not to be given up cheaply. They try very hard not to give away personal details, and troll each other if there is ever a hint that they have slipped up. Some hackers even try to cloud their geographic locations, avoiding coming online around the same regular schedule, or deliberately showing up during hours that might be assumed to indicate another time zone. To Buzzkill, online time is too precious to be going dark for the sake of concealing a longitude shared by like fifty million people. That said, talking openly about living in London deliberately dangles the possibility of a double bluff.

It seems likely Cicatrix lives in the UK too, something Stonefish is quick to deduce when he takes a look at the files Cic has fired across to him.

<Stonefish> So I'm guessing it's all fish and chips and tea and crumpets chez Cicatrix?
<Cicatrix> WTF you talking about??
<Stonefish> Your politics betray you, Skywalker. You know a shitload about this bank. No wonder you're pussing out. Don't shit where you eat and all that.
<Cicatrix> Well apples and pears, lor love a duck. Whatever. Just don't mess up my handiwork.

Buzzkill knows from Jonathan Rockwood's emails and from sifting through his network precisely when the RSGN is launching its shiny rebrand. The developers are uploading a reskin of the website tonight, so that it is live when RSGN starts running its new ad campaign on UK TV tomorrow evening.

Uninvited are all over White Frost. They know what all the files are called, they know where they are stored and they know when the RSGN's Customer Communications department are scheduled to replace the website's existing content with the new stuff. The true

51

beauty of it is that the RSGN will be uploading the hacked version of its own website, doing Uninvited's work for them.

It's a matter of swapping out the legitimate files and overwriting them with Uninvited's improved versions, by giving the new files the same names. Cicatrix created some very polished graphics for this, and Stonefish is carefully placing them in just the right locations.

It's possible to do a smaller-scale version of this if some dick at work is pissing you off (and you have, ahem, managed to finesse his login details). You wait until he's got a big PowerPoint presentation coming up and then 'improve' his pptx document by sticking some quality porn stills four or five slides in, so that he's well into his stride by the time the bomb goes off. Extra points if you can also hack his phone or cloud storage and put his own selfie-porn in there.

Uninvited are not hacking anything financial, by the way. None of them is that good, or that bad. They're not blackhats. They don't steal from people. Juice probably wasn't joking about shorting shares, but that's not the same as theft or fraud. He's well into that stuff, and showed the others how to set up an account on a site he uses, but Buzzkill didn't feel right about risking the cash, not to mention the potential digital trail.

On the RSGN site, the links taking people to their bank account information are still live: that stuff runs on a completely different frame and connects to infinitely more secure servers. If it was in the real world, the account login portals would be the tellers at their windows, and the Customer Communications content would be the posters on the wall.

Essentially you could say that Uninvited are just defacing those posters, but you'd be selling them extremely short, and not in the way Juice likes.

Stonefish reports that the installs are complete and the overwrites verified.

K-zag confirms that he has absolute control over the Sierra Nine and Sierra Eleven servers.

Juice is running a program that lists who is logged on to the Customer Communications intranet. He is copy-pasting the updates into the Uninvited chatroom so that they can watch RSGN fuck themselves over in real time.

These guys are legends.

Buzzkill's right index finger is repeatedly hitting F5 to refresh the bank's homepage as it sits open on the screen. The page stays as it is for a stubbornly long time. Then there is the tell-tale delay as updated content begins to load, before rsgn.co.uk reveals the redesign from hell.

Buzzkill is almost literally living the meme: rolling on the floor laughing. Uninvited deliver again.

But this is just the start. The real fun will begin about thirty seconds after the good folks at RSGN notice the damage. That's when they'll find that they can't change the content back because Uninvited have locked them out of their own system.

# THE MAKEOVER

A couple of hours later Parlabane is feeling less pain. The chicken was very good, and the caipirinhas are playing their part, but what helped the most was simply opening up and talking to someone else about his day. It doesn't look quite so bleak once it's been refracted through the detached lens of someone else's perspective.

It never does. No longer having that is the hardest thing about not being married any more.

Han gets up and lifts both their glasses.

'You want another?'

'I probably shouldn't, but what the hell.'

As Han strides off to the kitchen, his height making him seem all the more mismatched beneath the flat's low ceiling, Parlabane reflexively snatches a quick look at his phone, concerned not to seem rude, especially as Han is still talking.

'You ask me, these *Broadwave* people wouldn't get you to come down here, waste your time – waste *their* time – if they didn't think you had something they might want.'

He briefly scans his emails for anything from *Broadwave*, uncertain whether no news is good news, then has a glance at Twitter, which causes him to gape when he sees what is trending both UK and worldwide.

'Everything you talked about today, they knew all that without you getting on a plane. It's not about what happened already, it's about what you do next.'

In less than two seconds he is looking at rsgn.co.uk. It seems the site has had visitors, though at first he can't detect what is wrong.

The centrepiece of the page is an image Parlabane recognises from fresh new posters he has been seeing all day on the Tube and at bus stops, the flagship image of RSGN's latest design revamp.

They each show a smiling and photogenic – but conspicuously not too sexy – member of staff standing in a welcoming posture: one hand beckoning the viewer as a valued customer, the other holding an iPad with the bank's logo on the screen. The new slogan, which no doubt some bunch of spunk-weasels in Camden got paid seven figures for, reads: 'How can we help you?'

On the posters he saw examples male and female from across the ethnic spectrum, but the face chosen for the website is predictably female, blonde and about as Caucasian as it is possible to get without actually being a member of the royal family.

Parlabane observes that the RSGN logo on the iPad is rotating, his eyes drawn to a smaller line of inset text stating: 'Click on the tablet to discover what we're all about.'

He clicks, and an image expands from the iPad to fill the frame around the grinning branch manager from Whitebread-upon-Twee. This is where the fun begins. It is an animated graphic comprising two rotating digital counters, one above the other, with captions beneath explaining what the figures show. The top one displays, in real time, how much money the RSGN has made since the user surfed to the site; the other how much the bank's senior executives have made in the same period, if last year's earnings and bonuses are a reliable guide. A third counter, not moving, shows how much the taxpayer gave to the RSGN in the 2008 bail-out.

Parlabane spots a hand-swipe icon at the bottom of the graphic, captioned: 'See what else we've been up to.'

With each swipe the image is replaced by another graph or bar chart. One shows the amount of tax estimated to have been avoided by the 'high net worth' clients of the RSGN's Swiss-based private banking arm. Another displays the estimated number of people murdered by the Central American drug cartels the bank was revealed to have been knowingly laundering money for. As a kicker, a third graphic plots on the Y-axis the number of RSGN executives pros-ecuted each year by the British authorities for their roles in the bank's various crimes and scandals, against an X-axis timeline running from 2008 to the present. The graph is blank, permanently flatlining at zero.

Parlabane quickly checks the customer login portals. They still work. It is only the image content that has been affected, but nobody is going to want to move money on a page bearing hacked graphics.

The RSGN's whole ad campaign and rebrand is going to have to be scrapped. Every poster he saw today will be taken down, the image corrupted by being rendered instantly synonymous with the bank's past misdemeanours and its present security embarrassment.

But that's going to be the least of their worries. Several of the tweets he saw made mention of the fact that though the UK markets are closed for the day, New York is still trading. He can picture another real-time counter displaying how much money this is wiping off share prices.

This is going to be messy.

Parlabane scrolls down to see what other damage has been done. He sees a photograph of the RSGN's chief executive officer and other board members at a black-tie dinner, sipping champagne with the then Chancellor of the Exchequer. They are moist-eyed with laughter, some doubled over, almost spilling their drinks at something Osborne has said.

A caption reads: 'And then I told them we're all in this together!'

Finally, at the bottom of the page, there is a brief message:

Dear RSGN,

You have had visitors. The reality fairy has dropped by and given your corporate image a vigorous make-over with her magic truth wand.

You really should have expected us.

There is no name, only an icon:

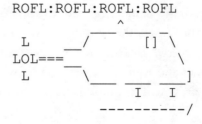

It is signature enough: an instantly recognisable hallmark. This was Uninvited.

One name immediately leaps to mind:

Buzzkill.

Han walks back in from the kitchen, carrying two more caipirinhas.

'Seems simple enough to me,' he says. 'These *Broadwave* folks, they want someone who can find them a story they couldn't find themselves. A story nobody else got.'

# SECRET SELVES

I remember Dad talking about getting the beer scooter home, his Geordie accent still playing in my head as I recall the words. I didn't understand it, never having been drunk, but I do now: it is about being so distracted that you aren't aware of having travelled. The bus has almost reached Barking, and so I must have been on it forty minutes, yet I have no memory of the journey.

I have been thinking about my situation, about my conversation with Mum and the options it has left me. I don't know how I thought or even hoped Mum would react: it wasn't like I expected her to reveal the location of a secret stash of money to tide things over. Or to say: 'Well, maybe it's past time I told you who your birth father was, in case he wants to step in and help out.'

I only wanted to talk about what I was dealing with, and for Mum to give me some sympathy. Some fucking credit, at least.

As the bus slows approaching my stop, it hits me that I have allowed myself to be defined by two things. One is Lilly; and the other is my inability to stand up for myself, most problematically against my mother.

That meeting at the prison was our whole relationship in micro-cosm. Me being told I am selfish for wanting anything other than whatever suits Mum. Being told I don't love Lilly if I ever express my frustrations at being landed with responsibility for her yet again.

*What, and I've had my time, is that what you're saying?*

Well, yes. You got to make your own decisions, Mum. Some bad shit happened that wasn't your fault, but that doesn't excuse all the other bad shit that definitely was. And the bad shit didn't only happen to you. In fact, some of it didn't happen to you at all. It only *affected* you, sometimes far less than it affected other people.

*I can't believe you sometimes, Samantha. You're so selfish. What would*

*Lilly think if she heard you talk like this about looking after her, as though you just want rid of her.*

Was it selfish to want more than the first zero-hours minimum wage job that would allow me to get by as long as it fitted around the Loxford School timetable? I love Lilly, but my whole life can't be *about* Lilly. I am her sister, not her mother.

The doors hiss closed and I step down on to the pavement, still so immersed in my thoughts that I fail to notice I am walking straight towards Keisha. With her headphones in and her head down, Keisha hadn't noticed either, until I hopped off the bus and directly into her path.

She is wearing a Burger King uniform, which is perhaps why I didn't notice her and sense the danger.

As our eyes meet, Keisha looks briefly upset, an unfamiliar vulnerability in her normally aggressive expression. I can tell she hates being seen like this, and hates me all the more for having done so.

I bow my head and resume my progress, saying nothing. After the initial surprise, there seems a brief moment when it is understood that we can both walk away pretending it hasn't happened.

Only in my mind, it turns out.

'Hey. *Hey.* You fuckin' lookin' at me? Yeah, you was. I saw you fuckin' lookin' at me.'

Keisha is following me, speeding up to keep pace. Keisha never walks fast, as it ruins the air of supreme indifference she loves to give off. Her blood is up. This briefest of encounters has really narked her.

'I'm fuckin' talkin' to you. You fuckin' stop and look at me when I'm fuckin' talkin' to you.'

We are on the main drag and there are plenty of people around. I understand that Keisha is unlikely to do anything physical to me in front of so many witnesses – not now that there could be adult-scale consequences – but it was never the violence I most feared from Keisha and her mates. The physical assaults were almost a release when they came, as that meant the other part was over: the confrontation, the ranting, the loud voices, the rising anger.

'I saw you checking out my uniform, you snide bitch. You think I'm shit, don't ya.'

Something inside tells me that if I stop and face Keisha, that will get it over with, that her fury will burn itself out. But everything else inside tells me to get away from the angry, shouting person who is burning up with rage and hate.

'You think I'm shit, but at least my mum ain't in fuckin' prison. And at least I ain't got no fuckin' mong for a sister.'

That stops me, like a switch over which I have no control.

'Don't say that about Lilly.'

'I'll say it if I like, because it's true. I looked it up. She's got Down syndrome. That's where the word *mong* comes from, 'cause they used to be called mongoloids.'

*Oh, wow, you looked something up*, I don't say. *That's a breakthrough moment for you. And did your lips move while you were reading it, like they used to in class?*

'Yeah, you're fuckin' clamped, ain't ya? Always thought you was so smart. Least I never pissed myself. That's all anybody will ever know about you.'

*No, at* most *you never pissed yourself,* I don't retort. *And that's all anybody will ever know about you.*

But that is when the worst of it hits me. I am not better than Keisha, and I'm not going to be either. I am going to be applying to Burger King and anywhere else that might have me, first thing tomorrow. Then someday soon Keisha is going to walk into wherever that might be and see me standing there. It is going to be the best day of Keisha's life.

I get back to the flat, the anger and impotence churning away, burning me up from the inside. I want to lock myself away, maybe go to sleep right now and hope I feel better the next day, but neither of these is an option. I have Lilly to pick up in a couple of hours.

The kettle has just boiled when I hear a knock at the door. It is loud and insistent, and my first thought is Old Bill. Then I remember about the inspection from the social. I thought that was next month but maybe they say that so they can come early and catch you unawares, get a more accurate snapshot.

I look around the place, reckoning it seems tidy enough, but wonder what someone else might see, what evidence they would be looking for that would seem invisible to me. There isn't time to do anything about it.

I open the door and find three men standing there. I recognise them straight away. They are bad news: low-lives my mum had dealings with. Drug dealings mostly. The two in front are Ango and Griff. I know that Ango's surname is Angola, which is the only exotic thing about either of this pair. They both look like they were born in a hoody and jogging bottoms.

They work for the guy standing behind them, known as Lush. His real name is Lucius Cresswell. When I first heard it, I pictured some public school type in a cravat who might burst into tears if you dissed his favourite opera singer. I was wrong on multiple counts.

'My mum's not home,' I say, but even as I speak they are pushing past me and into the flat.

'Yeah, I know,' says Lush. 'She's inside. I heard. But that don't mean she gets a holiday from owing me money.'

'I don't have any,' I say weakly, my voice fading to a dry nothing.

'It'll have to be payment in kind, then, won't it.'

Behind him I can see Ango unplugging the TV and the DVD player, carelessly spilling Lilly's discs on the carpet. Griff heads down the hall, rooting through the bedrooms. He comes out of mine a few seconds later carrying the laptop that had been sitting on my desk.

Neither of them speaks. They are quick and efficient, business-like, as though I had hired them for a removal.

I just stand and watch, thinking Lilly would have put up more of a fight.

# SUMMONING THE DEVIL

Parlabane's finger hovers over the Send button, instinctive caution forcing him to take a moment to consider if he really wants to do this. He's had some strong coffee but he drank rather a lot of Han's caipirinhas. He's three sheets to the wind and he knows his judgement ought to be clearer before making such a decision, but equally, he knows that chemically induced disinhibition might be a necessary prerequisite for going through with it.

Fuck it, he thinks. When did he ever get anywhere interesting by playing it safe?

He tells himself he has perhaps overestimated the risk here. Maybe the fact that the danger is unquantifiable is what makes it disproportionately worrying. With other people, you're scared because of what you know they might do to you. With someone like Buzzkill, the scariest thing is what you *don't* know (and can't imagine) they might do to you. In fact, the whole issue with Buzzkill is that Parlabane has no idea who or what he's dealing with.

Buzzkill is a cypher. A ghost. His identity is so fiercely protected that Parlabane has never even heard his voice. Most contact between them is carried out by text or instant messaging, and on the occasions vocal communication has proven necessary, Buzzkill has used a modified sat-nav voice system to ventriloquise himself. It's not even a voice-disguiser, but a text-to-speech program, indicating that Buzzkill doesn't even want to give away the patterns and cadences of his delivery.

He has predictably been described as a cyber-terrorist by the tears-and-snotters tendency among the right-wing commentariat, and once as 'the cyber-Banksy' in a typically over-intellectualising piece in the *Guardian*. Parlabane used to think that 'cyber-vandal' was a more accurate description of someone who got their rocks off by imaginatively defacing websites: not a threat, only a nuisance. But that was before Buzzkill paralysed Parlabane's own computer, ransacked what he thought were his most carefully protected files and essentially blackmailed him into helping with a hack into the editorial and archive systems of the *Clarion* newspaper, where he was working at the time.

If it had merely been blackmail, however, he could have made his peace with it. Instead, Buzzkill offered to reciprocate. That was where the trouble really began. Buzzkill helped him hack into an MoD laptop – a *stolen* MoD laptop – in what turned out to be the biggest disaster of his career.

But while Parlabane thought he was cashing in his quid pro quo, Buzzkill refused to see it like that.

'Friends don't keep score,' was how the hacker put it.

On the surface it sounded generous, but Parlabane couldn't help feeling menaced by the implications for it being a two-way street.

He quickly decided that he never wanted to find himself owing Buzzkill favours, given that the guy had already coerced him into hacking his erstwhile employer and risking jail as a consequence. However, having such a skillset to draw upon had proven way too tempting an option when other avenues were closed, and his credit line at the Bank of Buzzkill kept growing longer and longer.

He presses Send, effectively lighting up the Buzzkill bat signal. He knows he is going to the well one more time, but in his twisted half-drunk logic he tells himself he might actually be able to sell this as doing Buzzkill a favour.

There is no response for ten, then twenty minutes. Gradually sobering, Parlabane sees it as a blessing. He'd be far wiser to take stock and see how this looks in the morning. But right when he is thinking of folding the laptop shut and heading for the unaccustomed comfort of Mairi's bed (his previous stays always involving the sofa), there is a chime.

An icon appears: a goofy-looking fish superimposed over a biohazard symbol. It is Buzzkill's secret token: an icon that guarantees it's him on the other end.

'You rang,' states the sat-nav voice.

It is frustratingly devoid of emotion; no nuance to be read, no clue as to the speaker's state of mind. There are only words.

Parlabane enjoys no such protection. He long ago taped over his laptop's webcam due to his awareness of how Buzzkill might be remotely controlling it, but as he speaks into the inbuilt microphone he hopes he doesn't sound tipsy. Nothing he can do about it, though: the only thing more conspicuous than slurred speech is over-precision.

'I was wondering if you might know anything about the reality fairy and her wand of truth.'

'How do you know it's *her* wand? You know the rules: there are no women on the internet.'

'Don't change the subject. I think your prints are all over that wand. Are you in Uninvited?'

'The first rule of Uninvited is we do not talk about Uninvited.'

That's a yes.

'Well, that would put you in a minority tonight. There are *a lot* of people talking about Uninvited right now.'

Parlabane waits for a response, considering his next gambit if nothing is forthcoming.

Buzzkill proves that he is already a move or two ahead, able as always to read where Parlabane is going.

'You looking for a scoop, Jack?'

Parlabane takes a breath.

'It's more about what I can offer *you* for a change. If you give me some quotes, I can help people understand your motivations. Show your side of the story before the authorities and their media mouthpieces start filling in the blanks with whatever shit suits their own agendas: saying you're working for the Chinese, the Russians, Islamic State or whoever.

There is a pause, a very long pause. Parlabane is reassured by the sight of the icon that Buzzkill is still there, but he is on tenterhooks expecting the goofy fish to vanish at any second.

'One condition.'

Get in.

'Sure.'

'Direct quotes. Absolutely no paraphrasing.'

64

'You got it.'

'Cool. We on the record now?'

Parlabane is frantically fidgeting with an app, trying to get the laptop to record the audio. He's pretty sure he's made an arse of it, so he sits his phone next to the computer instead and uses that. He now feels 100 per cent sober: heart thumping, brain alert. He already knows he's not sleeping for about four more hours.

'As of now, yes.'

'We're hackers on steroids. Our motivation is twofold. We do it because we can. We do it for the lulz. That is a corruption of lol.'

'I know what it is.'

'Direct quotes, Jack.'

He's being trolled here, he knows. Hackers love their memes and they love their pranks. Buzzkill wants to get certain phrases into his media statement purely for the juvenile amusement of himself and his comrades-in-code, but Parlabane is happy to play along on this occasion. It's the price of doing business, and it's cheaper than usual today.

'How many of you are there in Uninvited?'

'I literally can't answer that. The figure is growing all the time. It's over nine thousand.'

'Lulz aside, you had to have your reasons for what you did today. There were some strong points being made. You've caused the RSGN massive embarrassment.'

'If the RSGN are embarrassed, then it will be a first. Nothing else appears to have shamed them.'

'The financial implications are bound to be enormous, the fall-out considerable. Do you have any thoughts for the money this is going to cost?'

'Yes. They should tote it up and take it out of next year's executive bonuses. That way nobody loses a penny except the people who deserve to.'

'They're going to come after you with everything they've got.'

'The harder they try, the harder they'll fail.'

'The CEO is calling for sentences commensurate with an act of terrorism. This is chiming well with the government's new cybercrime czar who is already ramping up the rhetoric for using this as the perfect excuse to drive through more digital-surveillance legislation.'

'Just proves the more you hate it, the stronger it gets.'

'Are you talking about them or you?'

'Both. But they should dial down on the anger. They're not the only ones who can escalate things. We don't forgive, we don't forget.'

'You're not going to catch them with their pants down a second time.'

'That's what they think. Even if they tighten up their security tonight, it's already too late. We plan ahead. We didn't hack RSGN tonight. We did it ages ago: we simply chose tonight as our moment to reveal it. We've hacked into a lot of things but we don't always go on the offensive. We don't come after you unless you give us a reason.'

Parlabane silently clenches his fist and allows a smile to play across his face. He has an inside angle on the hottest story in the country right now, maybe the world.

Even in that sterile sat-nav voice, these words are incendiary. Buzzkill delivers again. Buzzkill always delivers.

Nobody at *Broadwave* is going to say *this* isn't their speed.

# ONE MAN'S TRASH

I check my phone and see that there's time enough for a trip to the recycling centre before I have to be at the Loxford. It's not so far out of my way and I'm a fast walker, always. Nobody bothers you if you're walking at pace. Even chuggers know to go after the low-hanging fruit, unless the street is really quiet.

When I get there, old Jaffer greets me. 'Hey, Sam. Not seen you in a little while. You keeping busy?'

I have come today because he's usually in the cabin on a Wednesday. He's got a son, Ahmed, at Loxford in the year below Lilly. Ahmed's got some severe form of autism that means the part of his brain that's supposed to process relationships and emotional interaction isn't wired right. I always feel sorry for Jaffer and his wife when I watch them collecting him from school, because whereas Lilly lights up at seeing me, Ahmed's whole thing is that he's completely indifferent.

Jaffer once said that if he dropped dead on the kitchen floor, Ahmed would walk over him to get to the fridge. Doesn't stop him loving Ahmed, though. Him and Karima dote on the kid, but it must be tough when there's no signal coming back the other way.

'You got anything for me?' I say.

'Yes. Been saving these. You can take your pick. Or take the lot.'

I smile when I see the haul he's unearthed for me, two laptops in equal states of disrepair. Treasure. People simply chuck them away these days, sometimes when they're not even knackered. They want the newest, fastest, slimmest, shiniest, and often they can't even be bothered with the hassle of selling the old one. They reckon if they can't use it anymore, who the hell is going to pay money for it?

Even the supposedly broken ones don't always take much to restore to a bootable condition, and if they can't be saved, they can always be raided for their RAM or other components.

The ones that are in the best nick I give a bit of a digital MoT, and then Jaffer's cousin sells them on from his shop up in Barnet. I get a bung for those, but that's quite rare. Mostly I'm taking home machines that are just about salvageable, and I don't always need them to run. They're useful as decoys, you see. Laptops have a habit of disappearing from the Morpeth household. If it's not my mum's drug-dealer leeches lifting them to cover unpaid debts, it's her waster drug buddies stealing them when I'm not home.

See, I've told you about how pathetic I am. A victim. A doormat. But I need you to understand that there's another side to me, a person nobody gets to walk all over. Samantha Morpeth is merely my crappy avatar for playing in the world's biggest and shittest role-playing game: Real Life™.

Who I really am is the person that exists online. To me, that's the world that matters. And in that world, I'm not pathetic, I'm not a victim and I'm not a doormat. I'm a fucking supervillain.

# ONLINE PREDATOR

The smaller machine has a cracked screen and a broken hinge, but it will serve its function fine. After I get home with Lilly I take it to my room and sit on my bed, giving the exterior a brush-up. The spare cable I have doesn't fit it, but that doesn't matter: it only has to trail from a nearby socket. Once I'm happy that it looks the part, I place it on the desk, closed, waiting for the next thieving cockroach to fuck off with it, while leaving my real laptop undisturbed.

The older and larger of Jaffer's finds has got a DVD drive. Result. The operating system is corrupted and the wireless is fried, but the machine itself is still functional, so once I've cooked dinner and filled in a bunch of forms the Social have sent me, I gently coax the thing back into life. It's not going to run the latest *Sacred Reign* RPG, but it will do for Lilly to watch her shows on, since there's no TV and no DVD player any more.

I reflect that it's a good job they didn't realise her comics might be worth something, but these moronic gangsta-bots are too ignorant to read anything other than what appears on their social media feeds.

I tell Lilly the TV had to go for repair. She is delighted by the idea of having her own private and portable DVD setup, which she can take to her room if she wants.

We watch a couple of episodes of *Teen Titans* together. I let her stay up later than usual because she's excited over the novelty, then I tuck her up and make sure she's not going to be upset again about Mum not being here. She seems settled tonight, though. Her new personal TV has proven a good distraction. I make a mental note to find a decoy for that too.

I go back to the kitchen and do the washing up that's been left from dinner, postponed because fixing the DVD laptop was a priority. Once it's dried and put away, I hang up the laundry that's been sitting in the drum since the cycle ended an hour ago, before ironing Lilly's clothes for the next day: uniform *and* sports kit, as it's a Thursday.

I go back down the hall and turn the light off so that it doesn't spill inside when I stick my head around the door to Lilly's room. I can't see her face because she is lying with her back to me, but I can hear the steady and comforting rhythm of her breathing.

She's asleep.

It's time for me to suit up.

I slide my bed away from the wall, then I lean over it and roll back the carpet from the edge. It reveals an access hatch for getting into the space beneath the floorboards. I discovered this when we once had a problem with the lights and I watched the electrician remove this pre-cut section of floorboards before crawling out of sight.

I reach down and haul out the neoprene bag containing my real laptop, booting it up from a tiny memory card I keep in the lining of my bra. Then I check which of my neighbours' Wi-Fi signals is strongest tonight and quietly connect.

None of the Uninvited crew is in our chat channel yet, so I check out a few of the message boards I like to use. Hacktivism started on sites like these. It's like the opposite of social media. You don't have an avatar or a screen name: all posters are listed as Anonymous, which is where the name came from.

I must have been nine or ten years old when Anonymous first really saddled up, going after the Church of Scientology, but it has never troubled me to be turning up late to the party. I'm familiar with the Rules of the Internet, but I've got a few of my own, and one is that: 'Whenever you show up somewhere online, you always just missed the golden age.'

Besides, I'm only here for the lulz.

I scroll a few threads, a familiar mix of silly images and even sillier arguments. Then I see that somebody has posted a Facebook head-shot of a girl and is asking for help hacking into her online photo storage. That spurs me into action.

I screenshot the page and fire up Photoshop.

I log on to Facebook as Jools: she is one of sixteen fake profiles I've currently got running, all but three of them girls. I usually get the headshots from Eastern European accounts, girls in Slovenia being unlikely to happen across their own photo on an English-language profile. I friend all my own accounts to get the ball running, and my fellow hackers can be relied upon to provide a boost, because we all friend each other's fake profiles. Then I populate the feeds with photos and status updates copy-pasted from real accounts for added authenticity. Facebook is more active these days about closing down dormant or suspected false accounts, so I have to put a lot of time and imagination into keeping my fake profiles convincing.

It's amazing how deep you can get sucked into spectating upon other people's lives. I spend hours cherry-picking images and postings from individuals I've never met, weaving them into a made-up background for girls who don't exist.

I search Keisha Deacon and find four results. In descending order I see two white girls and a *Hunger Games* logo, the girls both pictured in classic selfie pose: arm out holding the phone so that it shoots from a flattering downward angle. Beneath these three is the Keisha I'm looking for. She's gone for the mirror shot, head tilted and lips pouty. I'm not sure whether she's trying to look sultry or bad-ass, but mainly the effect is that she looks pissed off and unwelcoming, so in that respect it's a good likeness.

I copy-paste her picture into Photoshop and get to work.

Keisha is going to need to see a face she can believe in. I change my Jools profile's manga avatar to a studious-looking white girl with a hint of emo about her. She looks friendly but not too pretty, smart but not trendy, a geek but not a nerd. Her timeline is full of gaming references and superhero memes. She's someone Keisha would never friend, for the same reasons that Keisha is going to trust her implicitly a few minutes from now.

I send Keisha a private message.

&lt;Jools&gt; You don't know me, but I was on a message board and saw this. I thought you should be warned what they're trying to do to you.

Attached to the private message is the screenshot I took from the hacker forum, amended so that it is Keisha's Facebook avatar that appears in the post asking for help in hacking her photo accounts.

I wait, and less than a minute later there is a reply.

<Keisha> omg were did u c this?
<Jools> The worst place on the internet. A board where hackers hang out. These are the people who got J-Law's nudes. If they can hack her, they can hack you. They live for this shit.
<Keisha> omg pls help me. can u help me?

I nod to myself. Keisha wouldn't be worried if all she had in her photo account was a few selfies and two dozen pictures of her dinner. She's got n00dz.

<Jools> That's why I got in touch. This shit pisses me off. I'm a hacker too. I lurk on there and help stop these raids. It all depends on whether I can track the girl down before they do. Looks like we got lucky this time.

Keisha doesn't ask any tricky questions, like how Jools could track her down from a single photo. It always helps when you've got a mark who's not so bright.

Ever wonder why there's so much bad grammar and spelling mistakes in phishing emails? You've probably thought to yourself: stupid fraudsters, you're not going to fool anyone if you can't even take the time to get that stuff right. That's because you don't understand. It's deliberate. If you're smart enough to spot the mistakes, you're not their target. But if you're thick enough not to notice that they can't even spell, there's a better chance that you'll be thick enough to fall for their scam.

Which isn't to say you're too smart to fall for a different scam. You might think otherwise, but has anyone ever got you to share your "pornstar name", where you combine your first pet's name and

72

your mother's maiden name? You know, the answers to the two default security questions on every account you ever registered?

> \<Keisha\> omg thank u so much
> \<Jools\> Don't thank me yet. We need to lock down your
>     account. Where do you keep your photos?
> \<Keisha\> cloudvault
> \<Jools\> Any other photo accounts? iCloud? OneDrive?
> \<Keisha\> No just cloudvault
> \<Jools\> Good. Gives us a better chance if we're only
>     securing one thing. If I get in first, I can lock your
>     account down and secure it against attacks. I need your
>     email address and password, and you need to be quick,
>     because we're against the clock. If they get there before
>     me, there's nothing I can do.

She sends me the login details as fast as she can type them. She doesn't pause to think, doesn't skip a beat.

Her password is 'specialK'. Seriously.

I download everything. It's a few gigabytes' worth, so I give her a running commentary on my bullshit progress while it's all coming through. She doesn't ask what 'locking out' these hackers involves. The correct answer is, of course, 'Not being stupid enough to send an anonymous stranger your password.'

> \<Jools\> I think I've secured it, but you can never be sure.
>     These guys always have more tricks up their sleeves. You
>     should change your password, right now, and after that
>     change it monthly. Add the month, like specialK02 for
>     February, specialK03 for March.

Fifty quid says she does this verbatim, thinking it's genius, without changing the specialK part. Not even after what's about to happen to her.

> \<Keisha\> omg thx so much u r a legend u saved my ass

73

Quite literally, I'm betting: to my hard drive.

I scroll through my haul, past hundreds of shots of Keisha, her idiot mates and her poser boyfriend, until I strike gold. Nude selfies: a selection of arm's length downward angle and mirror shots. A pic of her on a bed giving her boyfriend a hand-job. Oh yeah, here we go: two frames later it's in her mouth.

It's a good look for her, I reckon.

I upload a selection of the pics to a file-sharing site, then I send the link to everybody she's Facebook friends with, and to everybody I can think of from our school who she's definitely not *any* kind of friends with.

For good measure I post the images on a couple of message boards as well, and by that time the guys are starting to show up on our chat channel.

I begin typing:

<Buzzkill> Helluva result last night chaps. So now that we've successfully hit a bank, any fun suggestions for what's next?

# THE WALK OF SHAME

Parlabane stirs from a vivid dream about drinking coffee to find a mug of the stuff sitting on the bedside table. He gazes up through blurry vision and sees Lee Williams staring down at him, looking amused. She is wearing an Afghan Whigs T-shirt – *his* Afghan Whigs T-shirt – and nothing else.

His eyes are open but he would hesitate to describe his status as awake. Nothing is quite making sense yet. He recognises his surroundings, though they aren't his home, and he recognises the woman standing by the bed, but the fact of her being here doesn't fit. The fact that she is, as of a few days ago, technically his boss is not helping.

She catches him taking in her bare legs and the look of confusion mixed with mild alarm etched on his face.

'Don't freak out, we didn't do anything.'

This merely makes him more confused, given the fragments from last night that are starting to emerge, if not quite assemble.

She giggles and clambers over him to the other side of the bed, beside which there is another cup of coffee perched on the opposite nightstand.

'Only messing with you, sleepyhead. We did everything.'

Lee laughs again at his semi-conscious bafflement, starkly contrasted by her lively energy. He begins to recall the Broadwave party, how much they drank, how late they were up and how, indeed, they did everything. Several times.

She has no right to be in this condition, he thinks. Then he remembers her age, which explains much but makes him feel so much worse in so many ways.

'I partially sussed your espresso machine. Couldn't work out how the frother thing works so I made us Americanos.'

'Thank you. You've sussed more than me. It's not my espresso machine. It's not my flat. My friend Mairi is letting me stay here while she's away on tour.'

'Ah. That tracks. I was wondering about all the cushions and the White Company bed linen.'

Parlabane takes a gulp of coffee and feels the memories of the previous evening wash back into his mind like the liquid is washing down his throat.

He had been on a night out with his new colleagues, celebrating his Uninvited scoop and the job it bagged him. The session started at Perseverance Works before progressing to Soho and then back to Hoxton. Adding to the dream-like haze is his difficulty in comprehending how these people were labouring under the collective misapprehension that he was cool; none more so, it appeared, than Lee.

She had said she lived nearby, her way of explaining why she was jumping into a cab with him as he was leaving the final bar. Now that the fog is clearing, he doesn't recall ever telling her where he was staying.

'You don't live nearby, do you?' he states.

She smiles coyly.

'Not exactly. Camberwell.'

He gulps down more coffee, wondering about this weird sensation that is gripping him from the gut. He realises it's fear.

'So what do we do next?' she asks, apropos nothing specific. Her expression is beckoning and sincere.

Parlabane really doesn't know whether she means here in this bed, the rest of Saturday or with general regard to the future. At this point it's like years are falling off her by the second and he keeps getting correspondingly older.

What the fuck has he done?

He plays back the time they spent together, in the few days since he started work, and socially the night before. She had dialled down the fangirling, but she seemed to look up to him with a mentor-to-pupil vibe that he found all the more flattering given what a prodigy he considered her to be. He was more than comfortable with that. He didn't need to come over like he was down with the kids, so acting his age lent emphasis to his experience.

They got very friendly during the pub crawl, but the age gap provided an assurance of distance. Plus, the fact she was gay meant he wasn't tempted to listen to the little voice in every male head that was constantly suggesting behaviour that might make him seem more of a prospect.

If there was one moment that seemed to sum this up, it was when she offered him some coke and he said no.

Parlabane never touches the stuff, and it is often a source of tension. All those years married to Sarah gave him a profound respect for the properties of pharmaceuticals and a wariness of consuming them in any way that wasn't reliably measured. His private position on recreational drugs is that they should all be legal, but *talking* about doing them – and the amazing times you had on them – ought to be punishable by death. He has never said this to anyone though, so any time he gets offered, there is an awkward moment after he declines. The person offering clearly wonders whether he or she is being judged, and Parlabane reciprocally wonders whether he is too.

With Lee, there was no such awkwardness. It felt like something was mutually understood, a demarcation either side of which they could both comfortably get on with their separate roles.

So how did this happen? What did he say? What persona did he drunkenly adopt that has irretrievably fled in the cold light of day?

Lee watches his paralysed distress and her sincere look cracks into a bashful smile.

'You looked petrified, Jack. I can see the wheels turning. You're desperately trying to be a good guy and do the right thing. Problem is you don't have a roadmap for this. Don't worry about it. It was a bit of fun, that's all. It's only weird if you make it weird.'

'It's weird that I must be twenty years older than you. I don't even like it in movies when they flatter the male lead by casting him opposite a woman half his age.'

'It probably wouldn't make you feel better if I told you that was part of the attraction.'

'No, let's not go there. But I have to say, you're a lot less gay than I assumed.'

'Well, don't make any assumptions on the basis of last night either. You might be just as wrong.'

He nods, gives her a grateful smile.

'Thanks for the coffee,' he says, thanking her for a lot more besides. He is feeling some relief but his head is still in a spin.

'I've been out of the game a long time. I was married fifteen years, and since then . . .'

He lets it hang.

'Yeah,' Lee replies. 'That's why I knew you were a sure thing.'

There's nothing like getting exactly what you want to make you realise that what you thought you were missing isn't the problem.

Parlabane is walking along the banks of the Thames, past the Blade of Light, squally rain and a chill wind forcing the tourists to scurry for cover. He isn't feeling it. He isn't feeling much, that's the problem. He's been walking almost two hours. Ideally he'd be climbing, but there aren't a lot of mountains around the Home Counties, so this has had to suffice.

He got the job he wanted, in the vanguard of a media technology that hadn't even been conceived of when he first started work in this city. He can draw a line under the Leveson fall-out, declare himself professionally back on track.

Last night he had sex with a gorgeous bisexual woman almost two decades younger than him, in case he needed affirmation of his virility. Casual, no-strings sex at that, with a friend and mutually respecting colleague who was utterly cool about the situation. Wasn't that like the Holy Grail for guys?

Yet he's seldom felt so old as in realising that casual, no-strings sex was what it had been, and that it was something he couldn't handle.

He spent the past few years wishing he could go back to being who he was when he was Lee's age. Well, he's just had a taste of it and it's made him realise that he can't be twenty-five again, any more than he can redraw the past and erase his mistakes.

After Lee asked him 'So what do we do next?', in that panicked moment when options and possibilities frantically ran through his mind, he tried to picture a future with her in case that was what she wanted. He came up blank, like some plausibility buffer was preventing anything getting through.

He's over Sarah. Lee's the first new partner he's had sex with in fifteen years, and neither Sarah's name nor face crossed his mind until now. But being over Sarah is not the same as being over the end of a marriage. He had always thought he would be someone different by this point in his life: not merely a husband, but a father.

He looks across the river and sees that he is parallel with Temple Gardens. He thinks back to the strange meetings he had there, and the offer he was ultimately made by a nameless woman trying to recruit him as a spook. He had been tempted then, he had to admit: drifting aimless, needing to be needed, vulnerable to the idea of someone moulding his talents to a greater purpose.

'I don't have to sell it, Mr Parlabane. You made up your mind thirty seconds ago.'

She was right, but she blew it with that. She stepped right on his 'fuck you' reflex, though maybe that was her intention. He wasn't going to be much use as an agent of the state if he couldn't suppress it. So if it was a test, he failed with flying colours.

In that moment he defiantly told himself he could still carve out a future on his own terms. That's why he turned her down. He told himself that there was still time, that he could get *everything* back on track once he had turned his career around.

He's done that, yet here he is, still moping.

He thinks back to a couple of hours ago. As he drank the coffee Lee brought him, she noticed him start to withdraw again, and she wasn't having it.

'I've worked out your problem.'

'I only have the one?'

'I doubt that. But I've nailed the thing that's eating you this morning, for sure. You've been through a lot of shit, Jack, and you're so used to it all going wrong, you're having trouble accepting it when things go right.'

She spoke the truth, he couldn't deny it.

Things are going right, yet instead of allowing himself to feel happy about it, he is frantically searching for a catch, or even a booby trap. Perhaps this is because in his experience, the feeling that everything might be working out is a reliable precursor to a meteor coming out of the blue and putting a big hole in his life.

# WHEN WORLDS COLLIDE

I get off the District Line at Paddington and make my way up to the main concourse. I've got a tingling in my chest, a sensation that travels out to the ends of my fingers as though I'm a human tuning fork. It's like I'm in love or something. I could say it's a blind date, but it's more complicated than that. For one thing, neither I nor the person I'm going to meet even knows the sex of the other. We know quite a bit more about each other than that, though. Or at least we both think we do.

Nothing is certain. Nothing is verifiable.

*There are no girls on the internet. All girls are men and all kids are undercover FBI agents.*

I'm aware this might be a dumb move, and I can already hear my own voice telling me I told you so.

I need this, though. I can't explain why, but I need this. Actually, I can explain why. I just don't like admitting it to myself.

I am lonely. I live with another person, with Lilly, but I am lonely. There's a harsh limit on what I can talk to her about, so I feel more like a single parent than an older sister. It's not only since Mum went away either. I've felt this way for a lot longer than that. I don't have any real friends, close friends. We moved around so much when I was younger, but even now that we're settled I have never managed to fit in. I have always been shy. I'm not anti-social, but I have a hard time opening up to strangers. I like to listen more than I like to talk, which means I tend to blend into the background whether I intend to or not.

It hasn't helped that I have always been needed to look after Lilly whenever my classmates were doing extra-curricular activities, but to be honest, I've reached the stage where I don't think it's worth the effort anyway. I'll be gone from there soon, with or without my A levels.

There are a few people I speak to at school, but I can't talk to them about what's really going on in my life. I can't talk to them about the things that matter.

A while ago I carried out a few hacks on my own, including improvements I made to UKIP's website, which was how the name Buzzkill came to the attention of certain like-minded individuals. When they asked me to come on board, I had my reservations, but I never looked back. There was something far preferable to being part of a hacking collective: something more impressive, more menacing. There is a reason Anonymous's slogan is 'We Are Legion'.

Being anonymous is not about being nobody. It's about all the people you *might* be. The moment you are named, it takes that power away. That's why being part of Uninvited feels more exciting than just being Buzzkill. This is the one place in my life where I feel part of something.

That is why I am here to meet Stonefish IRL: in the real world. In the flesh.

I walk past a newsstand and see the latest *Evening Standard*. 'BANK HACKERS WILL BE HUNTED DOWN VOWS CYBERCZAR', a billboard declares confidently. The story was on the front pages of half the newspapers I saw on the Tube journey here, illustrated by a photo of the new sheriff of Interweb Creek, some gawky-looking posh-boy named Jeremy Aldergrave. He looks like he was probably attending polo matches when he was my age, while legends like Mendax and Ferox were hacking satellites and nuclear installations. I'm quaking in my boots.

I ride a short escalator down into the glass-enclosed concourse known as The Lawn. There are shops on three sides around a busy courtyard cluttered with chairs and tables. Dozens of people are hunched over coffees and snacks, crammed in next to strangers and luggage. It is difficult to tell if anyone here is with anyone else in particular, and that is why I have chosen it.

I check the time. It is about a minute to eleven. I walk a circuit around the shopfronts, wondering about every face I pass, every person seated in the courtyard. Right now any of them could be Stonefish; and to Stonefish, right now any of them could be me.

We are legion, but only while we are anonymous.

82

It is dead on eleven now. I scan the tables carefully, and that's when I spot it. It's surprisingly easy to pick out even in this crowd, but a Rubik cube is fairly distinct when everybody else is holding paper cups or sandwiches.

He is at a table close to the foot of the escalator. I must have walked past him twice. He's Chinese, around mid-twenties, peroxide blond and, to be honest, a lot better looking than I was expecting. He's wearing a *Team Fortress* T-shirt but that's the only obvious geekwear. He's slim but muscly: looks like he works out.

I reach into my rucksack and produce a cube of my own. He hasn't noticed me: he isn't anxiously scoping for his visitor, just sitting there and waiting to see what happens. I like that.

Two gap-yah types with aluminium-framed rucksacks get up from the seats alongside, so I make my move. I place my own cube down on the table and take a seat next to him.

His eyes light up. I try not to flatter myself: this isn't about what I look like, but the fact that I showed up at all. (Though I am allowed to tell myself that a smidgen of it is about what I look like.)

'There are no girls on the internet,' he says.

'I'm really a forty-eight-year-old FBI agent.'

Neither of us speaks for a while after that. We're both kind of freaked out that this is happening, but also we're super conscious that we are on precarious ground. All of the small talk we might normally make when meeting someone is potentially toxic. Where have you come from? What do you do? At this moment, we are each the most dangerous person in the other's life. And yet we both wanted this. Needed this.

It was me who asked Stonefish if he'd like to meet, but I'm pretty sure he was trailing the idea. We were the only two people in the IRC channel at the time, and he told me he was going to be in London soon. At first I thought it was another dig, playing on the fact that I've admitted where I live, but then I realised where he might be going with it.

'Weird, isn't it?' I say. 'We've so much in common, I feel like I know you, yet there's almost nothing I can think to ask you that I reckon you would answer.'

'Oh, I would answer. But you'll never know if I'm telling the truth.'

There is a Chinese flavour to his accent but I'm hearing Manchester in there too.

'There are some things we can deduce though,' I say. 'You're a Brit. That's why you homed in on Cic bringing politics into the RSGN hack. And I'm guessing you're not passing through London. You've no bag. You live here.'

'It's a fair cop, guv.'

'Why did you want to meet?'

'You asked me.'

'And you said yes. We're both taking a big risk here. What makes it worth it for you?'

'It's not that big a risk. We've seen each other's faces, but you're black and I'm Chinese, and in both cases they all look the same.'

He grins as he says this, like he got worried halfway through that I wouldn't realise he was joking. He speaks fast too, nervous and over-eager. He's coming over altogether less cool than while he was sitting there in patient silence, but I'm liking him for it.

'You didn't answer my question.'

He lifts his head, looks around briefly like he's checking the entire crowd isn't earwigging, or maybe for reassurance that we're still lost in the midst of them. Then he glances at the Rubik cube, and finally back to me.

'It's the disconnect, I guess, between what we did and seeing everyone's reactions to it here, IRL. I mean, we did this amazing thing. It's all over the TV, every newspaper, they're discussing it in Whitehall, for God's sake, and there's nobody I can physically talk to about it. You know?'

I'm already nodding.

'Do I ever.'

'And I don't mean I want to celebrate or to crow. It's just that I feel like there's an air gap between me keying code into a laptop and seeing headlines about millions being wiped off a share price. This must be what it's like to be a drone operator. You push a button and somebody dies, but you can't connect to it so you don't feel anything.'

'Totally. What's weird is I don't get a buzz from seeing the response, like I do when I am actually hacking. It seems so, I dunno, disproportionate. There are all these angry people talking about what they are going to do to us, and to me it's like they want to give me a speeding ticket for my driving in *Grand Theft Auto*, or send the cops around because I stabbed somebody in *Sacred Reign*. And what makes it all the more ridiculous is these ass-clowns think they can cross over into my realm to catch me. I'm like: it's the internet, you stupid skrubs. Chill.'

'It isn't only that, though,' Stonefish says. 'There's two sides to the air gap. All the good things I've got online are out of reach in the real world. You and the rest of Uninvited, we're like comrades in arms. We've been through so much together, and I feel this connection, but . . .'

He winces with frustration, like he can't find the words. He doesn't need them, though.

'They're only names on a screen,' I say. 'And you want them to be more than that.'

He nods. He's smiling, but it's as much in relief that someone understands. I know because I'm feeling exactly the same.

'Have you met anyone else?' he asks.

'No.'

This is the truth, but what I don't tell him is that I *almost* met up with Cicatrix several weeks ago. Cic was the one who asked, and I agreed to it for the same reasons as I'm here today.

It was his idea to meet in a railway station because it was 'literally transitory: we could be coming from anywhere'. On that occasion it was Euston, I think because he wanted to imply he would be heading north, maybe even as far as Scotland, and thus blurring the possibilities regarding where he lived. He came up with the Rubik cube thing too, and told me it was how Edward Snowden revealed himself to the *Guardian* journalists he had agreed to meet in Hong Kong when he first came forward.

My choice of The Lawn is an improvement on that day, because the place Cic suggested was more enclosed, a coffee shop with one door in and out. I sat there feeling exposed and conspicuous, so I experienced relief rather than disappointment when Cic sent me a message saying that he had chickened out. He was politely apologetic, but I got the impression that having pulled back from the brink once, he wouldn't be doing it again.

'This was a very dangerous idea,' he messaged me. 'And it took coming this far for me to realise how catastrophic it could be. We should both learn our lesson.'

I couldn't, though. I tried, but when Stonefish put out feelers, I bit down hard.

'I do live in London,' Stonefish says. It isn't the biggest concession but it is symbolic enough. 'Clapham.'

'Barking.'

'Are you a student?'

I wince, hope he doesn't pay it too much heed. There's a story there I don't want to tell. A loser's story.

'Kind of. Sixth form college.'

He covers his mouth and gives an amused gasp. It's slightly camp in a way I find irresistible.

'Oh my God. So you're still at school. If the bank and the government knew that.'

'What about you?'

'I work in IT. Big shock, right? But it's more controversial than you'd assume, if you knew my parents. Chinese family. I was supposed to go into medicine, but I've only ever been interested in computers. Big disgrace. It's like I ran away to join the circus.'

He smiles but it's not a joke. He looks sad.

'They never got me, and now they don't care.'

I have to stop myself from saying 'My mum is in prison.' The words form in my head and get ascloseasthis to my lips. I want to let him know that I understand where he's coming from, that we both came here today for the same reasons. I can't, though. It's too big a chunk of data, too easy to extrapolate from and to connect to my real name.

'I'm cripplingly shy,' I tell him. 'I feel like the real me is who I am online and this version is a flimsy 2D simulation. Online I feel like I'm capable of anything, whereas out in the world I'm permanently disappointed in myself. Part of me wishes the people who know me could see who I really am, but that's our curse, isn't it? We can't let anyone know.'

'Like superheroes,' he suggests with a self-conscious giggle.

'Supervillains,' I correct.

I expect him to share my evil grin at this, but instead he seems uncomfortable.

'I guess that's the other reason I wanted to meet,' he says. 'Ever since we hit the bank, I've been worried, and the pressure keeps building because I can't talk to anyone about it. It's so much bigger than anything we've done before. You said they're not able to cross over into our realm, but that's just it: they don't need to, because we have to live in theirs.'

I feel like I'm comforting Lilly after she's woken up in the night. He's got the same uncertain expression, the need for reassurance over something not worth the worry. There are no monsters behind the roller blinds, only shadows from passing headlights.

'Don't sweat it. The police don't know how to internet. We all wore condoms, right? Right?'

I emphasise this last, in case he's about to tell me otherwise. For a second I think of Cic bailing out because he was having issues with his virtual private network, and wonder if Stonefish had a problem too but decided to risk it because he didn't want to miss out on the op.

'Of course. I'm not reckless. *When one sees a lion, one must get into the car.* But this is so huge, the feds are going to come after us loaded for bear. LulzSec were all using condoms too, and they got caught.'

The thought of this gets me in the gut. LulzSec's virtual private network providers caved in to the authorities and suddenly the feds had logs of everything they had been up to. I flash news images of Jake Davis and Ryan Ackroyd being bundled into police cars, walking into court buildings. But then I realise Stonefish has it backwards, and the fear fades.

'That's not how they got caught, though. The feds needed to know who LulzSec were *before* they could go to their VPNs. LulzSec got caught because one of their own guys betrayed them. Sabu rolled to the FBI. That's not going to happen with us.'

Once I've walked away from Stonefish, it's like I can't escape the RSGN hack. As I make my way back down to the District Line, I keep seeing it on *Evening Standard* front pages clutched by my fellow passengers, and once I have boarded a train, it stares up at me from articles on iPads being scrolled on nearby laps.

I felt really sad about leaving him, and I had this aching regret that we couldn't share more information about each other, that we had to be mutually firewalled.

We sat there in that courtyard a long time. It was simultaneously like a first meeting of minds and a reuniting of old friends, or perhaps comrades. It felt good to reminisce about past adventures – or maybe I should say exploits – as I had never been able to share these experiences aloud before. Now that I have seen his face, it artificially revises my memories, like Lucas CGI-ing young Anakin into *Jedi*, so that I reimagine past hacks like we were there together. It is an illusion, though. I was with nobody, and what felt like actions were just words on a screen.

That's all any of it is.

It can't jump the air gap. I am insulated from reality, and for the first time that is making me feel isolated rather than secure.

A girl I vaguely recognise gets on at Upton Park. I see her on the platform as the train slows to a stop. I think she was in the year above me at school. I doubt she would ever have noticed me, but to my surprise her head lifts in pleased recognition and she heads down the carriage towards where I am sitting.

Then I realise her eyes are focused past me, on the girl sitting two along. She thumps down into the empty seat between us like it's her sofa at home, trailing perfume and hairspray.

The two of them trade greetings and trivial catch-up stuff. I pick up that the new arrival is named Mia while her mate is Julie, and that Mia is an apprentice in a hair salon while Julie is at college doing electrical engineering. The conversation is not exactly riveting, but it still bothers me to think that I've got nobody I talk to like that.

Then Mia takes it up a notch, waving her hand to show that she has remembered big news she can barely contain.

'Oh my God, did you hear about Keisha?'

'What, about the nude selfies? Who didn't? Evan sent me the link, and he's in Miami.'

Julie has dropped her voice to a half-whisper, but it is more a token than a real attempt to avoid being overheard. Her tone indicates simultaneously that this is something she shouldn't be laughing about and yet something nobody could help but find hilarious. I try to keep my smile on the inside.

'No, no, man," Mia replies. "She's in the hospital. She took a bloody overdose.'

'For real?'

'Yeah, yeah. It was everyone seeing those pictures. She couldn't handle it. Tried to off herself.'

'Oh my god, is she gonna be okay?'

'I dunno. She's in intensive care. Her mum's in a right state. All I know is Keisha ain't woke up and they don't know if she's gonna.'

# THE CALL

As always, the clouds of Parlabane's existential angst are blown away when a fresh wind carries in the scent of a new story.

He is thinking of heading for bed, feeling the need of an early one after the previous night's revelries, when his mobile buzzes, accompanied by that most seductive of sights: an unrecognised number.

He answers tentatively, opting not to confirm who he is until he has established what the call is about.

'Hello?'

There is a woman's voice on the other end.

'Is that Jack Parlabane?'

'Who wants to know?'

'I have information concerning a major data breach. I need to talk to someone about this and I saw your piece on the RSGN thing. Can we meet?'

She speaks slowly and carefully, as though she is reading a script. He pictures someone nervous about the implications of what she is doing, so it is likely she has written down what she needs to say. His caller display shows that the number wasn't withheld and that it is a landline, which makes it less likely this is a time-waster.

'A breach from where? What kind of data are we talking about? When did this happen? Has it been covered up?'

'I'm not willing to disclose any of this over the phone. If you are interested, I'm prepared to meet with you alone, somewhere public.'

Even as she speaks, he is quietly keying the phone number into his laptop as he sits on the sofa. His eyes bulge. It is an internal line from inside 6 Pancras Square: Google's London HQ.

'I'm interested. Where and when?'

She tells him nine-thirty at a café close to King's Cross. A quick check reveals that it is around the corner from where she is calling.

'How did you get this number?' he asks.

'I will be able to make that clear when we talk in person.'

And like that, suddenly nothing else matters.

# DANGEROUS CIRCLES

I collect Lilly from school, unable to lose myself in the moment when she sees me and smiles because all I can think about is Keisha lying in hospital, and Keisha's mum and the rest of her family worried sick. Lilly must pick up a vibe from me, because she starts to look worried.

She asks me when Mum's coming back. She hasn't done that in a while.

We pop into the supermarket on the way home. Lilly says she wants pizza but my purse says that's off the menu. I pick up some potatoes for baking and a tin of beans, trying not to dwell on the irony that I am eating like a student.

Over dinner I realise Lilly is talking to me and I haven't been listening. I can't get Keisha out of my head.

I don't get why she would do this over some stupid photos on the internet. I thought she was tough as leather. I thought she had no weakness. No feelings.

Lilly pulls a letter from her schoolbag, which is under the kitchen table. I am vaguely aware of having wondered why she left it there. It was to remind herself, apparently.

'It's about the trip to Chessington World of Adventures,' she says, beaming from ear to ear. She says it like the letter is telling us she's won the lottery. I had forgotten about this. Mum signed the form and sent in a deposit months ago.

Lilly was uncontainable about it. She could talk about nothing else for a fortnight, but as the trip was ages away, it gradually got relegated down her list of thoughts. Now it is right back to the top, and the countdown has only four weeks to run.

I look at the letter. The outstanding balance is due, and it's eighty quid.

Something inside me withers and goes cold. I feel anger towards Mum for putting me in this position, but that's pointless. I think carefully about how I'm going to phrase it, then brace myself to tell her.

'Lilly, about this trip,' I begin. She looks at me expectantly, like I'm about to ask what she's most looking forward to.

I can't. I just can't.

'It's going to be awesome,' I tell her.

Once the dishes are done and Lilly has gone off to read a comic, I check what I've got in cash. Forty and some shrapnel. I take out my phone and log on to my bank to check how much is left in the account. All the money Mum transferred before she went inside is in there. On the basis of my seriously pared-back outgoings, I work out how soon I need to find a job and see a wage packet before the situation becomes critical.

This is going to bring it forward, but that hardly matters. Nothing is going to change the bigger picture, which is that it's my responsibility to provide for Lilly now. She's been hurt enough lately without this treat being taken away from her.

I say to Lilly that I'm nipping out for half an hour. I should be ten minutes tops, but she hates being left in alone, so I always like to be back sooner than I've told her. I could take her with me, but she walks so slow that it really would be half an hour. It's freezing too.

The nearest ATM is out of order, so I have to go to the one on the pedestrianised stretch between Timpson and Greggs. It's all right during the day, but I always feel conspicuous walking through there at night. I don't like my intentions being readable, and it strikes me the cash machines are the only place you could be going at that time.

The ATMs are in sight when suddenly I'm aware of footsteps behind me. They're moving quickly, catching up. I'm a fast walker, so this sounds like two people at a light jog. I turn around, hoping to see some runners with their headphones in, minding their own business, but instead I'm confronted by Ango and Griff.

'Samanfa,' Ango says. 'Wot you doin' out and about on your own at this time of night?'

I say nothing, but they are either side of me now. I put a hand to the pocket where the card is, concerned about it being picked. This is a mistake. Griff is on the movement like a falcon, and in a flash he's got the card and is handing it to his mate. Ango holds it up with a flourish.

'Hold up. Looks like you is about to make a unauforised wifdrawal.'

I take a breath and find my voice. It sounds feeble and pathetic as usual. Why can I sound confident and even husky when I'm social-engineering some mark on the other end of a phone, but come over like a hummingbird on helium when I'm in the flesh?

'That's my card. Give it back.'

'Yeah, it might be your card, but it ain't your money. That's why it's unauforised. Your mum still owes Lush.'

'She's in jail,' I protest. 'It's her debt, not mine.'

'What, you're saying she never give you any? Yeah, sure. So you're gonna lift the daily max and hand it over.'

'I've forgot the PIN,' I say. 'I only just got this card.'

It's pitiful. I don't even sound like I believe myself.

Griff flashes a blade inside his jacket.

'Have a stab at it,' he says.

They escort me to the bank, one of them either side.

I look around, hoping in vain for the cops to be passing, though I know it would only piss these guys off if I stalled them that way. They know where I live.

I key in the PIN, at which point Griff nudges me aside. They lift three hundred, which is the daily limit. I check the time. It's around half eight. Three and a half hours until they can lift three hundred more, except they can't, because there's only two-forty left.

Griff hands me back the card, though. They're not going to keep it, in case I cancel it maybe. They probably think there are benefits going into the account. They want to keep this channel open for future withdrawals.

Ango fans the money like he's riffling cards.

'Leave me something,' I plead. 'My sister and me need that to live on.'

Ango puts a hand on my bottom and squeezes, running his fingers close to the seam of my jeans that runs between my legs.

'Tasty young fing like you can always find uvva ways of workin' off the debt.'

I don't tell Lilly anything when I return. I will go back to the cash machine in the morning and lift everything that's left, so that I can't get mugged like that again. Then I will go to the school office and formally drop out. I've been putting it off, kidding myself that something might change, but this has made me face the reality of it.

I'm going to take the first McJob I can find, though depending on the shifts, I'll need to speak to someone at the Loxford about after-school options.

I roll back the carpet and pull out the pouch from beneath the hatch in the floorboards. A few minutes later I'm online, scrolling message boards and scoping to see who is around in the IRC channels. I'm not feeling it, though. This is my refuge, the place I can become my true self and put distance between me and whatever shit is happening in my life, but it's not the same tonight. The air gap has been bridged in both directions. Keisha was hurt in the real world by what I did here, and now I can't escape from real world hurt by losing myself online.

I hear a chime and a message pops up stating:

Zodiac is inviting you to join new IRC channel
#careeropportunities.

I don't know anyone called Zodiac, so I click to ignore it.

On an internet relay chat server, you can create a new channel just like that, and if you've created a channel, then you have ops: operational privileges. This results in total randoms spamming invites to their new channels so they can play at king of the castle, and I often get messaged specifically because it gives them a bit of kudos if a well-known hacker joins their chat.

I tut. I can block invites from anyone not on my whitelist, but sometimes I turn the blocking off because I'm feeling sociable or mischievous. I am neither of these things tonight. I go to my settings. Oddly, the block list is active.

A few minutes later another message appears.

Zodiac is inviting you to join new IRC channel #blackmail

People post bullshit threats and prank stuff all the time. However, there's something about this I instinctively don't like. I can't rationally say why, but I know I've never felt this way about a message before.

I don't get why it's clearing the block filter, then it hits me that it must be someone on my approved list who has changed their display name.

I click Ignore again and launch *Sacred Reign*. A bit of questing through Calastria might be what I need to help take my mind off other things.

I blow some of my virtual coin on new armour and levelling up my fire sword. It's my idea of retail therapy.

I am riding towards a fortress on the back of a battlehog when I hear the message chime again. I toggle to the IRC window, intending to tell whoever it is to piss off and quit spamming me, but that is before I read the message.

Zodiac invites you to join new IRC channel
   #samanthamorpeth

Everything changes in that moment. Everything burns. I've been through some nasty shit lately, but I know that this is when my world truly falls apart.

I feel hyper-aware of my surroundings, as though somebody jacked up the settings on my senses. I see cracks in the paintwork that I never saw before, like a close-up, insect-eye view of the wall behind my laptop. I hear the TV next door, a couple arguing out on the street. It's like time has stopped.

My fingers approach the keyboard again like I'm afraid it will give me a static shock.

<Buzzkill> Delete that fucking channel name now.

Anyone on the server can see the list of channels, one of which is currently my real-world name. It is on a list of dozens, hundreds, but that's no comfort.

The channel name disappears.

Zodiac invites you to join new IRC channel #letsbefriends
Password is 24pitmanrise

That's my home address.

I join the channel, where Zodiac is the only other user listed. In other windows I am running searches and queries on his display name, the associated account and his IP. He's well shielded. I'm getting nothing.

Postings begin to appear, too fast and too large for him to be typing them. He is copy-pasting the text into the chat window, stuff he already has prepared. I see my name and address again, then the name and address of my sixth form college followed by my subjects and exam results from last term. I wince at the sight, bringing back memories of Mum's arrest just as I was about to sit my A levels. It's why I never got the grades I needed.

I see my mum's name, her present whereabouts, the charges brought against her, the sentence she was handed down. Dad's name, his date of birth, his date of death. Then Lilly's name, her date of birth, her diagnosis, the name and address of her school.

I can still hear the couple arguing, the studio laughter from next door's TV. Only a few seconds have passed since I was riding on that battlehog, but since leaving my fantasy realm, the real world I returned to has changed completely.

Zodiac posts some images: chat logs from the #Uninvited IRC channel taken during the RSGN hack; screenshots of early versions of the graphics and banners we uploaded.

Then he posts my mobile phone number. I use an app that disguises who is calling, or spoofs the source to make it appear that a call is coming from a different number, but that's not going to save me. If somebody knows the original source, the authorities will be able to trace the moves I made at every stage of the hack, from that first phone call to Don Corrigan in HR at Canary Wharf.

I think of all those angry headlines, the rants by bank execs, the vows by politicians. On my laptop screen right now is everything they would need to put me away.

I tap the keys briefly. The sound seems louder than I'm used to, echoing off the walls.

&lt;Buzzkill&gt; What do you want?
&lt;Zodiac&gt; We want you to help us.

I think of Sabu – real name Hector Monsegur – who the FBI turned, offering him a deal if he helped them catch the rest of LulzSec.

&lt;Buzzkill&gt; Are you the Feds? You want me to roll on my
    friends? I don't know anything about them other than
    their screen names.

That's when I think of Stonefish, and how I spent my day. The implications hit me like a falling anvil flattening Wile E. Coyote. How could I have been so multi-facepalmingly fucking stupid?

He got me out in the open. This was what Cicatrix feared, why he pulled back from the brink. Once I produced that Rubik cube and identified myself, I was tagged. Stonefish followed me home: him or someone working with him, watching from close by. In fact, the guy I spoke to might not even have *been* Stonefish, if Stonefish was even a single individual. Stonefish could be an account operated by a group of people.

I think back to the Chinese bloke and my first impressions, before he started telling me about himself. He struck me as not geeky enough: that was my initial instinct. That Team Fortress T-shirt was thrown in there for effect, a token to establish certain credentials. He was playing a part, and that was his job because he was good looking, charming.

<Zodiac> We're not the feds and we're not interested in
   your friends. We're only interested in you.

As soon as I read this I understand that it would be better if they
*were* the feds, because at least I would know what I was dealing
with. Whatever they want, they're using the threat of grassing me
up as leverage, which means the feds are part of the equation anyway.

Stonefish. Jesus Christ. The name itself is giving away that it's a
trap. Hackers love doing shit like that: putting something right in
front of your nose that you still can't see. You don't know a stonefish
is there – you don't see the danger – until you step on it. But once
you do, it's said the pain is horrific beyond description.

My hands reach to the keyboard again.

<Buzzkill> What do you want?

There is a long wait. I see the typing icon . . .

<Zodiac> We want you to understand that your choice is
   between going to jail and delivering exactly what we are
   about to ask of you.

# UNNAMED SOURCE

Parlabane takes a gulp of tea and checks the time on his phone. His contact is late, which is contributing to a tripartite anxiety he could do without at this time of the morning. The first aspect is that he has no idea what this person looks like, his late-night caller having refused to give him any identifying information whatsoever. The second is that with every passing moment he is becoming more concerned as to whether this skittish and anonymous whistleblower will actually show up; and the third is that he has a train to catch in a little over an hour.

The value of this last consideration is growing in direct proportion to his belief that he is about to be stood up, as his intended journey is taking him to a guaranteed story he is actually being paid to cover. Lee Williams has tasked him with going undercover as a delegate at an arms trade fair. It is a major assignment, the first time they've really taken the training wheels off him, so he can't afford to be late due to chasing a flyer, especially if the flyer never materialises.

It's 9.44. Parlabane's train leaves from Euston at 10.33.

The uncertainty takes him back to when he first worked in London, though he remembers it extracting less of a toll on his nerves when he was younger. He had to deal with some jumpy whistleblowers back then, all manner of elusive and unreliable contacts, going by aliases and codenames. There were time-wasters and attention-seekers, employees with a grudge, executives with an agenda, crooks and conmen. Sometimes there was a story at the end of it, sometimes at least a lead, and often nothing at all, but what got the adrenaline flowing was that he never knew.

For a fleeting moment of both nostalgia and regret he recalls a beguiling figure going by the single name Aurore. She made out she was a potential whistleblower, but he was never sure whether she was sounding out his reliability as a confidant or getting ready to play him somehow. He never got to find out, as he had to leave the country in a hurry when someone he was investigating set him up. It was an early instance of a meteor strike right when things seemed to be going well.

He looks around the café in case the contact is already here, nervously and surreptitiously checking him out. He can't see any viable candidates. At the table directly ahead there is a tubby bloke in frayed jeans with a hard hat at his feet, undulating ridges of builder's arse hoving into view as he reaches for the ketchup. Nearest the window is a woman in her fifties or sixties. He'd put the voice he heard much younger than that, and though he would ordinarily allow for a large margin of error in such things, he's never yet seen a Deep Throat bring two grandchildren along to the meet.

To his left there is a young black girl working intently at a laptop. She looks more like she's skipping school than she's about to start her shift at Google, but in tech you can never be sure. She closes the machine and stands up. Parlabane glances across, anticipating eye contact, thinking this could be it, but she walks past him and goes to the counter to settle her bill.

He finishes his tea, estimating how long he can plausibly wait until he needs to make a move. He is factoring both taxi and walking options, while also calculating for each how little time he would have left to speak to the woman if she did show up.

Then his phone chimes with a text. It's from an unrecognised number.

Change of venue. Waiting for you here instead.

There is no name or address, only a link. He clicks it and his browser opens but the screen remains blank. He checks the signal and confirms there is strong 4G. He replies.

Link didn't work.

A few seconds later his phone chimes again. This time the link takes him to a Google map location. It's two minutes away, if that: a Starbucks. That sounds far more Google-employee than the greasy spoon he's in right now, though the prospect of a story is the only thing that would force him to darken the door of the place.

As he pays for his breakfast he wonders irritably why she didn't simply text him the address, but what the hell. It's on his way towards Euston anyway.

He walks briskly to the specified Starbucks and stands inside the door, looking past the gaggle at the counter towards the customers already seated. All but one of them is oblivious to his scrutiny. The exception is already looking at him. It is the girl from the adjacent table at the greasy spoon, the one he assumed was too young to be working at Google. The moment she catches his eye, she beckons him with a subtle gesture.

'What was wrong with the other place?' he asks, taking the seat opposite, which happens to be a beanbag. He wonders if she chose the spot with that indignity in mind, or if it was the only one free.

'I had to verify that you were alone.'

Her voice does sound older than her appearance would indicate. It's another sign of his own advancing years that he's becoming worse at gauging these things. For all he knows she could be twenty-five.

'You asked for alone, I came alone.'

'Thank you.'

'I have a train to catch, so I'm afraid my time is limited. What is it you wanted to tell me?'

'I take it I can count on complete confidentiality here?'

'Absolutely. I have in the past gone to extreme lengths to protect my sources.'

'Good. Because this is as sensitive as it gets. I have inside information about a data breach at a major tech company.'

'And to establish the scale of what we're talking about, would this company be Google?'

She lifts her head.

'What makes you think that?'

'Call it a hunch.'

'Well, your hunch is wrong.'

'You don't work at Pancras Square?'

'No.'

He asks himself what game she's playing here. He knows she called from Google. She used a landline and didn't take any steps to withhold the number. Why wouldn't she assume he could trace her location from that?

He's making assumptions again, trying to get one step ahead of his own potential source. It happens when he isn't convinced someone is on the level: he feels an impulse to work out what is really going on. He needs to suppress it, let her talk.

'I said a data breach. It's more than that, though. Much more. I'm talking full-scale industrial espionage here. High-clearance data theft as well as old-school B&E.'

She looks anxious, impatient to be unburdened and yet she still hasn't really told him anything. His alarms are going off, but it's not his bullshit detector that's tripping them. Something's wrong here. His skin is prickling.

'Like I said, I've got a train to catch, so you'll need to cut to the specifics. I need a where, a when, a who, a what, something I can hang this on.'

'I'll get to all of those. Are you a man of your word?'

'Have you ever met a dishonest man who would answer no to that question?'

She stares back, her expression neutral.

'An honest man wouldn't avoid answering it.'

He doesn't like this. Her tone doesn't make this sound like sass or banter. With every passing moment she is coming across less like a contact and more like an adversary.

'I always protect my source,' he reiterates, though it's himself he's more worried about protecting. What is going on here?

'I need more than that. I need you to promise you will act on what I am about to tell you.'

'I can't do that until I know what you're actually talking about.'

'I'm talking about something that hasn't happened yet. That's why I need your word that you'll act.'

His danger senses are tingling, warning him that he's being set up.

'But how can I promise I'll be able to prevent it unless you tell me what it is?'

She stares back impassively.

'That's not what I'm asking. Nothing is going to prevent it from happening.'

He glances around the coffee shop, wondering which unseen eyes might be watching him.

'So if my acting on this information isn't going to stop it, why are we both here?'

He glances at his watch. He doesn't make a show of it but he doesn't completely disguise it either. He needs to check how long he's still got, and he needs to remind her of that too.

'Have you heard of Synergis?'

She asks this with a tone of doubt that indicates maybe *she* hadn't until recently. That would make sense. Synergis hasn't exactly been making waves in recent memory, but once upon a time it had been a household name.

'Aldous Syne was to British electronics in the nineties what Clive Sinclair was in the eighties,' Parlabane replies, so she knows she can skip a few pages.

She gives him a blank look, the name Clive Sinclair clearly not registering anything.

'Whatever. The point is they are the target. Synergis's research and development labs are working on some new product that they reckon is gonna revive their fortunes. The whole thing is shrouded in secrecy, highest levels of security, but it's not gonna be enough. The prototype is about to go bye-bye, along with copies of the plans, schematics, programming, the lot. Everything that would be needed to reverse-engineer the thing: that's what's going to be stolen.'

No wonder she's playing it cagey. This is big, but only if she can stand it up. Parlabane is already thinking about when he can arrange another meet if they run out of time here. He'll make sure he controls the venue next time, though.

'How do you know this?'

'That's not important right now. You ought to be more interested in who is going to be pulling this thing off.'

'Why? What's his name?'

She sits up straight, folds her arms.

'Jack Parlabane.'

# THE RECKONING

'This is a wind-up, right?' he says. 'Is this *Broadwave*'s version of a hazing ritual?'

He shifts in the beanbag, wondering if finding himself perched on this ridiculous thing was part of the prank's stage management. The young woman across the table doesn't look like she's in on the joke. Her disciplined neutral expression is finally failing her and her eyes are moistening.

'Listen, I've a train to catch and I'm done playing games. It's cards on the table time, or I'm walking. Who are you and what do you want?'

She wipes her eyes and reaches into a compact rucksack at her feet.

'Cards on the table, yeah?'

Parlabane looks down at the tiny square of paper she has placed in front of him. It shows a goofy, buck-toothed fish superimposed on a biohazard symbol.

'It's not what I want, it's what I need. I need your help, Jack.'

He looks up at her again, gaping as though someone completely different has been beamed down to replace whoever was sitting there before.

He drops his voice to a whisper.

'Jesus fuck. You're *Buzzkill*?'

The impassive expression returns, though a hint of defiance creeps in.

'What part of me weren't you expecting? Am I a little too young, a little too female or a little too black?'

Parlabane ignores this. There isn't time to go down that road. There isn't time for much, in fact, so he has to focus on what's relevant.

'Why are you coming out to me, revealing yourself after all this time?'

'Because I don't have much choice any more. I did something stupid and it gave away my identity. Somebody played me: somebody in Uninvited. Now I'm being blackmailed. They're going to go to the cops with all kinds of evidence about the RSGN hack unless I do what they want, and what they want is for me to steal this prototype from Synergis. I can't do it alone. I need your help.'

'First things first. What do I call you? What's your name?'

'The less you know about me, the better for both of us. But you can call me . . . Barb,' she decides. 'Can't exactly afford to have some random overhear you calling me by my hacker name.'

He checks the time again, discreetly this time.

How is he meant to resolve this in the few minutes he's got left before he needs to hail a cab and hope the traffic's not gridlocked? Catching a later train isn't an option. He's meeting a guy at Birmingham New Street who is holding fake credentials for him, so that he can gain entry to the arms fair. This individual is not the type to wait around in public places. If Parlabane misses the hand-off, he isn't getting in.

'I can help you, but not like this. Think it through. If you do this for these people, they don't go away. In fact, in the unlikely event that you pull it off without getting caught, you would double what they could hold over you. You'd be their toy to control for ever.'

'What other choice do I have?'

'There are cops who owe me favours. Not rank and file: senior officers. I can help bring you in.'

'What, so I can cut a deal like Sabu? Roll on my friends?'

'From where I'm sitting, it doesn't sound like they're your friends. One of them isn't, for sure, and you don't know about the rest — who else is in on this, who any of them really are.'

'That's just it, though,' she says. 'I've got nothing to offer. I don't know anything.'

'Neither did Hector Monsegur. He worked with the FBI to identify his LulzSec co-conspirators.'

'Yeah, but all it bought him was a deal to reduce his jail time. He didn't walk away free. He sold his soul and still served seven months. This way at least my fate is in my own hands, and I stay out of jail as long as I can.'

'This way is . . .' Parlabane looks around, trying to ground both of them in the reality of this coffee shop, the here and now. 'It's a non-starter. It's madness. I mean, what made you think I would even contemplate something like this?'

'Because I've nobody else to turn to and it's not exactly virgin territory for you, is it, Jack? You've been sneaking into places and snooping information your whole life. That's why I sought you out in the first place, remember?'

He knows Barb is merely another alias, but she's chosen it well. She's had a jagged little hook in him since the start.

'If by seeking me out you mean hijacking my laptop and holding my files hostage before coercing me to install malware inside the offices of my erstwhile employer, then sure.'

'Yeah, but I also helped you hack the laptop you stole when you broke into that crusty MoD guy's flat in Kensington; and I helped you analyse the data when you broke into that place in Inverness. We complement each other. You handle the physical infiltration, I handle the digital.'

'And that Kensington thing worked out so well for me, didn't it?'

'Don't pretend Inverness wasn't a result.'

'Look, I've broken into a couple of places.'

'A couple!' she splutters.

'Usually very soft targets that were defended by little more than a locked door. Yes, I can pick locks and I can climb walls. But thanks to precisely my sorts of activities – and yours – people have seriously upped their game when it comes to security. I mean, Jesus Christ, the R&D labs at Synergis? Physically and digitally that's got to be a fortress.'

She lifts her head and arches her brow, as though she has somehow turned the tables on him. He can't see how.

'Ah. So you've moved on from "won't do it" to "can't do it". That's a slippery slope. You're already thinking about how it would be a blast. That's why we're kindred spirits. We're both social engineers.

Getting people to tell you things they're supposed to be keeping secret, giving up information because they don't realise its true value. We live for this shit. We're a great team.'

Parlabane isn't buying into this one bit, and she reads it in his face.

'Or are we only a team when I'm helping you get what *you* want?'

Her expression is riven with accusation, even betrayal. Parlabane feels like shit. He knew that one day Buzzkill would come demanding the inevitable pound of flesh, and finally it is here. The thing he didn't anticipate was that he would be in a position to refuse.

'I can help you if you go to the authorities. That's it.'

'I can't go to jail,' she replies, her eyes moistening again. 'You don't understand.'

'Coming clean to the cops about being blackmailed doesn't mean you'll go to jail, especially if you're trying to prevent a crime.'

'You don't have a fucking clue. I hacked a bank, which means rich and powerful people are looking for a scalp. This Aldergrave fucker is desperate for a result on RSGN. And if I end up in jail, what happens to—'

She stops herself, shakes her head.

'I can't go to jail, Jack. I'm out of options. I wouldn't be coming to you otherwise, believe me.'

'And I'm out of time,' he replies, feeling all of a centimetre high, and knowing it will be worse as he is literally about to run away from here.

She stares balefully at him as he gets to his feet. He thought she'd look more indignant, but instead she seems simply defeated.

'You know how to find me. Soon as you're ready to accept the help I *can* offer, I'll be there for you.'

# WAR FAIR

Parlabane can't get her out of his thoughts, even as he is running flat out across the concourse of Euston Station, slaloming the somnambulant in order to reach his train on time. He always feared a reckoning from Buzzkill, but having met her under such circumstances he feels a burden of responsibility rather than debt.

He thinks of her arch tone concerning her appearance: too young, too female or too black. He'd probably have to put his hand up to two out of three. He had always pictured a white male, though her age was less of a surprise. Aside from the Hispanic Hector 'Sabu' Monsegur, who was pushing thirty, the other main players in LulzSec were white males ranging from twenty-two down to sixteen at the time of their arrests.

He can't help her the way she's asking. She looked so meekly accepting of his refusal, though: so broken. He was expecting some kind of tantrum, a protest about how he owed her.

Maybe deep down she knew she was kidding herself, and needed it spelled out to her. Maybe the best thing is for her to accept that this isn't an option, then when she comes back to him he can speak to some cops he knows: Catherine McLeod or Jenny Dalziel. It is out of both their jurisdictions but they are sufficiently senior as to be able to chaperone her through the right channels. Whoever is blackmailing her was involved in the RSGN hack, and now they are planning high-level industrial espionage.

Surely the police would be far more interested in running them down than in making a token arrest of a harmless teenager? That said, you could never be certain when political pressure was being brought to bear: she was right about that much. Press and politicians were calling for hackers' heads on sticks, as anything that undermined confidence in our banks clearly had to be dealt with (except when bankers themselves were responsible, naturally).

By late afternoon, his morning rendezvous seems a long time and a long way distant. He has made the hand-off to pick up his fake credentials, and subsequently spent the past few hours walking the halls of the trade show from hell. It's like a nightmare version of the Ideal Homes Exhibition, where all the gadgets and innovations are about ways to kill everybody in the house next door in the event that your neighbours are planning an insurgency.

He finds himself in a side hall, where a number of smaller exhibitors are offering to consult on 'security contracting'. This is the posh new name for mercenaries, though he is intrigued by the incongruous sight of a slightly built and bespectacled woman on one of the stands. Among the services listed on a pop-up banner alongside her is 'penetration testing'.

He decides to introduce himself, pausing briefly to read a text from Lee:

What's the big story?

She's checking up on him. He likes that. He texts back, telling her:

All in good time.

Parlabane approaches the woman on the stand. She puts on a professional smile, practised enough to remind him what kind of sleaze she is probably assuming him to be.

'Can you tell me a little about what you offer in terms of penetration testing?'

'Sure thing,' she replies. 'What would you like to know?'

Her accent is American, though softened by travel, he estimates. Maybe Canadian, rather: he is pretty sure he heard her finish off a conversation on her mobile in French as he approached.

'I suppose, first of all, do you guys do anything in the civilian sector? Because otherwise I'd be wasting your time. Among the interests I represent is an electronics manufacturer which is very concerned about industrial espionage.'

'Truth is we work *primarily* in the civilian sector, Mr . . .?'

He hands her one of the fake cards he's been given.

'Logan. Jack Logan.'

'We do consult on some military-level security, but it's far from our core activity.'

'So walk me through it. How does it work? When people talk about penetration testing, I mostly think of computer networks these days, which makes me picture the threat as a bunch of hackers in a basement in Donetsk; guys eating Dorritos who never even enter the same country as their target.'

She gives him an indulgent chuckle. This is good, because playing the glib and uninformed tube is what he is aiming for.

'Computer networks often control all the other security systems, so defending against cyber intrusion is still a big part of what we do. But we're also about analysing the physical vulnerability of premises. A lot of hacking requires physical intrusion in one form or another; accessing air-gapped servers, for instance. We infiltrate on all possible levels then provide an in-depth report of our methods, detailing all the weaknesses we were able to exploit.'

'And this is against live targets? Like, only the CEO or whoever knows you're coming.'

'That's right, though he usually doesn't know when. Sometimes it's the CEO who is a potential weakness, and we've been hired to demonstrate that to him.'

'Isn't it dangerous? Guards patrolling, armed police possibly getting called?'

'Most of the time we're in and out of there without anybody knowing, which is kind of the point. If a guard raises an alarm, then technically your pen test has failed.'

Parlabane is wary that he feels a tingle at the thought of pulling off an undetected infiltration inside some highly secure facility. Buzzkill wasn't completely wrong about what excites him, but he is not allowing himself to entertain the notion of what she was suggesting.

'We have on occasion penetrated installations where guards were carrying live ammunition. We are very meticulous in our safety preparation, mostly for the protection of subject personnel. There is more danger of an armed guard shooting his colleague in a panic than ever getting a bead on our guys.'

'Not so much with the shooting here in the UK, though,' he suggests hopefully.

'No, but even here, the average security guard's non-lethal load-out is getting nastier all the time: shock batons, telescopic clubs, pepper spray. Legally speaking, they're not always supposed to have these things, but there are companies on the floor right here selling them, and they're not surviving purely on exports. If you get caught somewhere you shouldn't be, you're not going to make a very credible witness when you dispute specifically what kind of hardware was used to apprehend you.'

No, Parlabane reflects, he is most definitely not going to entertain Buzzkill's crazy notion.

'So who does it take to break into these places? I mean, what kind of background and skills do your team bring to this?'

'We have a lot of different specialities. Ex-military, ex-law-enforcement, and sometimes ex-law-breaking.'

'To catch a thief . . .'

'That's right.'

'And which are you?'

She gives him a wary smile, though it's warmer than the meet-and-greet one he got earlier.

'Ex-hacker.'

'Figures.'

She gives him her card. It says: 'Lex Richardson, Solid Bett Security Partners.'

As he walks back towards the main hall, he gets another text. It's Lee again, asking:

What's the big story and why aren't we getting it?

He decides he'd better file a taster and an outline of what he has so far. He makes his way to one of the refreshment areas, where he grabs a coffee, finds a quiet corner and opens his laptop.

The first, rather large sign that something is wrong is that his desktop background has been changed. Instead of one of the generic rotation of preloaded pictures, he is confronted by a pixelated image of a blue-haired cyborg in a purple cape, a frame from the opening of Zero Wing: an early nineties video game he never played but is tediously familiar with through a meme almost as old as the internet.

'ALL YOUR FILE ARE BELONG TO ME,' states an altered version of the caption.

Parlabane's instinctive response is to check the documents he's been working on. That is when he notices that the folder names have all been changed to unreadable Japanese characters, and their icons replaced with thumbnails of photographs: personal photographs from what he had previously considered secure online storage.

He double clicks one at random and gets a message informing him that the file is locked and requires a password. Thinking fast, he remembers that the most recently accessed files can also be accessed via a list on the Start menu. When he clicks on it, the titles are in Japanese, and though the Word program does launch, what was previously a single-sheet document now displays as several hundred pages of gobbledegook. The files have been remotely encrypted.

Fucking Buzzkill.

His annoyance gives way to a more chilling thought, as he remembers about those texts from Lee.

*What's the big story?*

He lifts his phone, upon which the lock screen shows that he has an unusually high number of notifications on Twitter. He launches the app, but instead of the familiar feed, he is presented with the beginner's sign-up screen.

'No,' he says, almost involuntarily. 'Mammy, Daddy, please no.'

He is locked out of his own account, and that can only mean that Buzzkill is all up in it.

He logs in using a secondary account, from where he is able to read, with growing horror, a number of tweets ostensibly posted by himself. These are announcing an exclusive that will send shockwaves through British journalism, all accompanied by a link.

114

The link takes him to his own blog, where to his immediate but only temporary relief, there is mostly blank space. He reads a single line of text stating: 'Stand by for the most career-defining exclusive I will ever file.'

Beneath that is a digital timer, counting down.

He glances at his watch and does the arithmetic. It's an ultimatum. She's posting at midnight. But posting what?

Now he knows why she didn't simply send him a text with the address of the Starbucks she went to this morning. She knew he would click on the link to find out where to meet. The browser had gone blank. He thought the first link hadn't worked, but it had, inasmuch as it caused him to download some malicious piece of code.

This was why there were no tantrums, no emotionally over-wrought demands when he turned her down and walked away. She knew this would happen, she planned for it. In her mind it was only Phase One.

He doesn't think he's going to enjoy Phase Two.

Already on edge, he starts with a shudder as his mobile vibrates in his hand, signalling a text.

Thought you'd like a sneak preview.

His finger pauses over the accompanying link, mindful of the first one he clicked on today, which appeared to do nothing but evidently did plenty. He reckons that section of his defences has already fallen, however. It's the unseen damage that he is more concerned about. That phrase 'career-defining' has a particularly menacing resonance.

The screen fills with text and images, at the top of which is another famously mistranslated line from that same stupid early nineties game.

SOMEBODY SET UP US THE BOMB.

Parlabane feels the sweat running down inside his shirt. A bomb is what he is looking at, no mistake: counting down on his own blog page to the moment when it will put a hole in his world big enough to see from space.

It is a detailed confession of how he assisted in hacking the *Clarion*'s servers, from when Buzzkill first made contact by hijacking his laptop and ransoming his files. It catalogues times, dates, locations, methods, and what Parlabane ultimately got in return, which was Buzzkill's assistance in hacking a senior civil servant's laptop. What he thought was the scoop of his life had in fact resulted in a disaster for the newspaper that published it; a disaster for the *Clarion* of a magnitude that would only be eclipsed by the emergence of what was in front of him right now.

A confession on its own might be deniable, especially when he could demonstrate that his blog and phone had been hacked. But Buzzkill is also posting data from the hack itself, files and information that have never previously seen the light of day, and were never supposed to.

These were the stories you never run, the stories you hold over people in order to get the other stories. Top secret scandals the tabloid had been sitting on, sometimes for decades. There is art too: photos of royals, celebrities, politicians. And that isn't even the worst of it. There are also details of paid sources in the police, in government, in sport, in showbiz, complete with amounts they received for specific information.

If this came out, Parlabane wouldn't be the only one going to jail. But more damagingly, he would instantly become the most hated man in British journalism, as his actions would burn every source on that list, as well as all of the reporters dealing with them.

She is saying that if she's going down, he's coming with her: mutually assured destruction.

He dials the number the texts originated from.

She answers almost immediately. No sat-nav voice, no time delay.

She puts on a tone of false cheeriness, and he suspects she phrased her greeting in advance.

'Hi, Jack.'

'This will ruin me. It won't just send me to jail, it will finish my career: it will burn it and salt the earth. But then you knew that.'

116

'Not necessarily. Why don't you talk to your high-up friends in the police, ask them to "bring you in"?'

He has no come-back to that, and she knows it.

'This was your plan all along,' he says redundantly.

'We're in the same boat now, Jack. So you can take your chances with the authorities like you suggested I do, or you can start helping me paddle.'

He looks down at his now useless laptop, then back at the hijacked phone he is holding. He's been utterly out-manoeuvred. He doesn't have a move here. Not yet, anyway.

'Okay, you've made your point. But if I'm coming on board, even just to probe whether this madness is feasible, it's on the understanding that hitting Synergis is priority number two. Priority number one is finding out who is blackmailing you, and getting some leverage on them.'

'You're preaching to the choir on that, mate. See, we're already thinking along similar lines.'

'And you can wrap the kindred spirit shite. Have no illusions: if I get you through this, we're quits.'

'Friends don't keep score, Jack.'

'We're not fucking friends, *Barb*.'

# PART TWO

PART TWO

# MONITORS

'Take a look, Samantha.'

'Just a sec.'

'Samantha, take a look. Samantha.'

'In a minute, Lilly,' I reply, struggling not to sound testy.

I am peeling spuds for some chips while Lilly is sitting at the kitchen table, colouring in a picture. I'm getting fed up with baked potatoes and I forgot to pick up a tin of something anyway. Going with chips. Means I'll need to clean the cooker, because the fat always spits, but it'll be worth it for the change.

'Samanthaaaa,' she insists, and I lean over to see what she's working on.

It is a before and after picture of Batgirl and her secret identity.

'That's awesome,' I say, but the image has twisted me up inside, because it reminds me of the mess I'm in.

I think about Jack in that Starbucks near King's Cross. He asked for a name and I stupidly hadn't expected it. I came this close to telling him to call me Sam. I had to pluck a name out of the air and the first thing I thought of was Lilly and the comic she was reading that morning before I took her to school. Batgirl. Barbara Gordon.

I get these merciful moments when I forget all about how the world is caving in, losing myself in a task like peeling potatoes or washing the dishes. Then something brings it back to the top like an irritating pop-up window.

All it takes is for me to think of the word *Synergis* and I get this horrible churned-up sensation, suddenly wired like I necked three cans of Red Bull. What's making it worse is that the word had a nasty effect the first time I read it in one of Zodiac's messages, like the name itself tapped into something that made me uneasy, but I can't place why.

121

With that thought I dry my hands and go to my bedroom, where I open my laptop and search for Synergis on Wikipedia. It's a long entry and I'm aware I've left the chip pan on the heat with Lilly in the kitchen. I could bring my laptop into the room but for various reasons I'm still reluctant to let her know I have it, in case she says anything to anyone (mainly Mum).

I scan the page impatiently, skimming through the early stuff that's talking about 'ambulatory monitoring' and the inventor Jack mentioned, Aldous Syne. I had never heard of him and I don't know what ambulatory monitoring is either. Further down it talks about the company's decline into manufacturing low-end electronics, like generic mobile handsets, knock-off mini hi-fis and crappy clock radios. I must have seen the name on a device somewhere: maybe inside Graythorne Young Offenders Institution, where I spent the worst three days of my life. If so I don't remember, but then I've worked damn hard at blocking those seventy-two hours from my memory.

I scroll down again and read how Synergis changed hands a few times. It was most recently bought over by one of its original founders, Leo Cruz, but again the name means nothing to me.

I hear a knock at the door and I tense up, remembering the last time anyone came calling unannounced. When Lush and his gangsta-bots fronted up before, at least Lilly wasn't home. I'm not opening my door to those bastards with her in the house.

I sneak a look out of the bedroom window, which gives me a view along the outside landing. There is a smartly dressed woman standing in front of the door, holding a briefcase.

I suddenly remember. She's from the Social. She is due here for the home inspection to make sure Lilly's being looked after all right. It's not a surprise visit to catch me unawares, though it's done that anyway. I knew it was today, but I completely forgot, with everything else that's on my mind.

I open the door and she greets me with the thinnest, coldest smile I've ever seen. I never thought it was possible to turn up the corners of your mouth without giving some hint of friendliness and warmth, but she's proved otherwise.

'You must be Samantha. Mary Hardwick,' she says, holding out her ID. 'I hope I haven't caught you at a bad time. You were expecting me, yes?'

'Oh, yes. Sure.'

I smile, instinctively going into please-the-teacher mode.

'Just getting the tea organised,' I add, hoping it scores some points.

'I see.'

She starts nosing around the place while asking me questions.

'You're at sixth form college?'

'Yeah, well, I was. Had to give it up so I can earn some money. I'm starting a job at a sandwich place up in Ilford.'

'Didn't you have any plans for further education?'

This sounds like I'm being told off.

*Well, yeah, course I did, but that's gone south since you lot cancelled my Carer's Allowance,* I don't say.

She gives the living room a thorough examination, like she's thinking of buying the place.

'No TV,' she says, her tone so weirdly neutral I can't pick up anything from it.

'That's right. Lilly likes to read comics. Reading's better than TV for a child's development.'

Even as this is spilling from my mouth I am asking myself what the hell I think I'm trying to achieve. I don't know. It just came out from my nervousness.

She glances at the pile of DVDs under the table where it's so laughably obvious that the telly used to sit. She knows I saw her looking at this, and now she's got to be wondering why I barfed up that word-sick.

'Well, Lilly does have a little laptop she uses as a portable DVD player,' I add.

'And where is Lilly?'

'She's in the kitchen.'

With the open chip pan on. Jesus.

I lead her through, trying not to rush.

Lilly looks up from her colouring.

'Hello, Lilly. I'm Mary,' she says.

123

Lilly gathers her colouring and her pens and scarpers off to her bedroom. She's a sharp judge of character, that girl.

'She's shy,' I say.

Mary doesn't reply.

'What's for dinner?'

It sounds like small-talk but I've no idea how much might hinge on my answer.

'I'm making some chips.'

'With what?'

I swallow.

'Just chips, tonight. Lilly likes chips,' I add.

She says nothing and continues to look the place up and down, wrinkling her nose. She doesn't like what she's seeing, I could tell that much without any talent for reading micro-gestures.

I think of my mum asking me to promise I wouldn't let Lilly get taken into care. I made that promise, but now I'm getting this horrible vision of things being taken out of my hands. I can see how easily the process might start, how quickly it might snowball.

That's when it comes back.

I remember now why that name must have taken root in my subconscious, associated with a fear of losing everything.

A few years back, only months after Dad died, Mum found a lump on one of her breasts. She went for tests, and then she had to go into hospital to have the cancer removed.

I remember her telling us we hadn't to let anybody know we were on our own at home, fending for ourselves while she got her treatment. She said the Social might come and take us away if they found out there was nobody taking care of us, especially with Lilly having special needs.

I had looked after Lilly alone when Mum was at work, but not overnight, and not several nights on the spin. Lilly was a frightened teary mess, restless and confused, but I was the one who was truly afraid, because I was the one who truly understood. If Mum had cancer, if she was going to become ill and then die, it would all be out of our hands. We wouldn't be able to keep our situation a secret. I would lose Mum like I had lost Dad, then I would lose Lilly. We'd both end up God knows where, with God knows who.

I recall the hospital visits most vividly. We only went in a few times, but it stayed with me, and you don't remember the hanging around the house part, because that's normal. Mum was hardly ever lying in a bed when we went in. She didn't like looking helpless, so she was usually on her feet, but she always had this thing attached to her: wires leading from her chest to a little plastic box on her hip. It was called a Synapse Ambulatory Monitor. SAM, like me. She even had it on for a while after she came home. It wasn't even to do with the cancer. They made her wear it because she had developed an irregular heart rhythm and they wanted to keep an eye on it.

It didn't seem to bother her, but the sight of it always troubled me, maybe because I could never see the cancer but I could always see *it*.

I can see it now, that beige plastic box, the manufacturer's name prominent on the front.

Synergis.

# REMOTE ACCESS TROJAN

Parlabane watches his destination rise into view as he comes down Monument Street. He feels a horrible burden of inevitable fate settle upon him, like a condemned man approaching Tyburn on the back of a cart and the gallows looming before him. This will be the instrument of his destruction, and yet he is compelled to proceed towards his undoing.

He had hoped the Synergis HQ would be located in some suburban science campus of eighties-built low-rises with corresponding levels of security. Then when he clocked the address, he had nonetheless comforted himself with the possibility that it might be some carbuncle-era concrete slab, unloved and neglected as it awaited the wrecking ball that would follow a sell-off and development of the site. Instead he is looking at Tricorn House: a handsome seven-storey structure that has been sneering down on the likes of him for at least two centuries, a prestigious address where the immaculate maintenance of the stonework outside speaks forebodingly of how well-equipped it is likely to be inside.

He has on occasion thought of his more vainglorious or ill-advised ventures as tilting at windmills, but there seems nothing chivalrous and quixotic about this doomed undertaking. Don Quixote never had Sancho Panza blackmailing him to saddle up and heft the lance. Nor did he have the bastard gibbering in his earpiece the whole time.

'Are you there yet?' Barb asks. 'What does it look like?'

'Like a fucking fortress. Like our doom with a postcode.'

'Zodiac wouldn't be leaning on me if it was easy. *One does not simply walk into Synergis,*' she adds, irritatingly.

Now that she has revealed herself, she no longer seems so guarded about what lies beyond the Buzzkill persona, having previously been

126

circumspect even in her frame of reference. Instead she now seems babblingly nervous, consequently assailing Parlabane with a mix of teen argot and geek-speak that is making him feel not only old, but grateful to be so if this is youth.

He always feels like a crazy person wearing one of these Bluetooth mics, walking down a busy street talking to himself. Today, though, it represents one of the more sane and rational aspects of his behaviour. He is here to meet Synergis CEO Leo Cruz, ostensibly on an interview assignment for *Broadwave*, after pitching to Lee that his instincts indicated there was a story in the offing.

The true purpose of his visit to this intimidating redoubt is to case the joint.

'Walking in the front doors now. Going off-mic.'

'No, you're not,' she reminds him.

'Yeah, but you are, thank God.'

He pulls the earpiece away but does not disconnect the call. She will be listening in throughout, and recording everything to a hard drive for analysis later. Parlabane is wired for vision also, two miniature spy cameras hidden in his jacket and the strap of his shoulder bag.

He walks into a cavernous vestibule. His shoe leather taps a cadence on the tiled floor, but the sound barely carries to his ears. Instead it is absorbed into the greater hubbub, itself swallowed by the atrium that rises around him in stone and glass. There are dozens of people thronging the concourse, greeting visitors, hastening to meetings, couriering documents and milling around the café area at one end.

He can see glass-walled elevator shafts rising behind the reception desk, access beyond the public area protected by card-operated barriers. An aluminium column displays building information, listing the occupants floor by floor. There's an international pharmaceuticals firm, a drinks company with a portfolio of brewers and distillers spanning four continents, an internet travel firm and an electronics and communications giant.

On balance, he's probably not going to be able to sneak in a side door and grab the prototype while everybody is on their lunch.

Parlabane approaches the desk and is greeted by one of four receptionists, each kitted out with boom-mic headsets and seated before a monitor angled so that it is impossible to see the screens from his side of the counter.

'I'm Jack Parlabane. I'm here to see Tanya Collier.'

'Which company?'

'Synergis.'

The receptionist clacks away at the keyboard then relays a message over her headset. Parlabane expects to be told to take a seat and wait, but instead she asks him to look straight into a globular camera on a sliding riser, which she adjusts to his approximate eye level.

'Look at the green light and hold still for a second please, sir.'

A few moments later he is issued with a temporary pass. *Then* he is told to go take a seat and wait.

He watches people go through the barrier in both directions, their progress followed by a security guard wearing a thick-ribboned lanyard over his blazer, on hand to help in case of any technical problems or to intervene if someone is not supposed to be there. Parlabane examines the card he's been given and figures the embedded chip now contains his picture, his name, the person he's here to see and which company she works for. Whenever anyone swipes through, the system will log who came into the building, when they entered and, crucially, whether they have exited again.

A few minutes later he sees a bright and smiling young woman stride towards him, extending a hand.

'You must be Jack. Tanya Collier. We spoke on the phone. Leo's in a meeting that's overrunning, but I'm sure we can find something to keep you occupied.'

'You can give me the tour,' he suggests.

'Yeah, such as it is. Now that you've seen the lobby, you've probably seen the best of it. Just offices from here on in, really.'

'It's certainly a nice address.'

She waves him ahead of her as they reach the barrier. Parlabane makes a show of looking for a swipe dock, and the guard steps across with a helpful smile, a firm hand taking the card and pressing it to a sensor pad instead.

'Yeah, it's a legacy of when Synergis was wholly owned by Neurosphere. They've got half the building.'

'And now it's wholly owned by Leo Cruz?'

'Not wholly. There are a number of investors, but Leo holds the controlling stake. Because he was taking on a loss-making concern, part of the deal was that the rent here would be subsidised for six months in order to smooth the transition. It was widely assumed that we would be pared back and relocated, but here we still are. A lot of assumptions about Leo's buy-out have turned out to be wide of the mark.'

She says this with a note of pride and a firmness of assertion. There is a PR agenda at play here. Cruz has a reputation as an asset-stripper, and it has been speculated that the preferential terms of Neurosphere's sale of Synergis were down to the parent company effectively outsourcing its dirty work.

At the time, Neurosphere was in negotiations that would lead to it receiving major tax breaks and other subsidies in order to retain its manufacturing presence in the UK. It would not have played well were the company to close down the once iconic British brand, even though Synergis was by then a chronically loss-making subsidiary. The assumption Tanya is referring to is that Neurosphere sold cheap to Leo Cruz knowing that he would wield the axe instead.

Tanya beckons him forward into the lift, then taps her card against the control panel before pressing a button for the seventh floor. You can't even get the lift to move if you don't have the right credentials, Parlabane notes. He wonders where the stairs might be, making a note to keep an eye out for fire exits.

'Were you always with Synergis?'

'No. I already worked for Leo.'

Figures, Parlabane thinks.

'I'm aware of his reputation, so you don't need to tiptoe around it.'

'I vaguely remember a headline about Mr Cruz preparing to "eat his own young",' Parlabane admits. It was in reference to the fact that Cruz had actually been one of Synergis's founders, once upon a time. That he should return to kill off his own creation had a certain grim poetry to it, in the eyes of many commentators. Cruz had in recent years operated as a vulture feeding off the corpses of failed companies, the wide-eyed visionary who was once the great white hope of British electronics long since consumed by the monster he had become.

She responds with a knowing smile. There's something she's not saying, and she's happy to make him wait.

They emerge from the elevator into a glass-walled lobby looking down upon the teeming concourse. Dead ahead is a plush reception area, recently refurbished by the look of it. A woman behind the desk gives Tanya a smile, busy directing calls as they stride through the lobby.

Another set of security doors bars the entrance to the Synergis premises proper. Tanya taps her card in order to access the corridor beyond, then steps aside to beckon him through.

There is a glass case on a plinth against the wall a few feet inside.

'A little piece of history,' Tanya says, allowing him to have a look.

Inside is the original prototype of the device that effectively built the company.

Synergis hit its high-water mark in the early nineties, when its new chipset helped pioneer ambulatory heart monitoring and paved the way for medical miniaturisation technology in general. Christened the Synapse, the device was the brainchild of Aldous Syne, a famously flaky and reclusive electronics innovator, but its success was largely down to the determination of a hungry young entrepreneur by the name of Leo Cruz. It was Cruz who formed the company and raised the finance, hustling tirelessly until he had brought the Synapse to market.

Syne was lauded as a genius and caricatured as a typically British eccentric, emerging from nowhere to bring forth a game-changing innovation. From media impressions, admittedly cobbled together from scant resources – the guy never gave any interviews – it was easy to imagine he had knocked this thing up in his garden shed. The very quirkiness of that notion fed into the cheerleading for Syne's invention in the UK, where people were charmed by the idea that this indispensable new gizmo had not emerged from a decade's development inside a megalithic Japanese corporation, but was instead an iconic example of old-fashioned homespun invention.

However, as time went on the Synapse was quickly eclipsed by greater innovations in medical monitoring (though the NHS being what it is, the ones it had shelled out for were still in use more than a decade later), and the growing public impression of its inventor was not of a wayward genius but a one-hit wonder. While his early success had drawn comparisons with the altogether less publicity-shy Clive Sinclair, the reason Syne never had the albatross of a hubristic C5 slung around his neck was that he failed to bring anything new or radical to market again. In fact, by the time Cruz and Syne sold the firm, the name Synergis had become a byword for cheap generic knock-offs.

It was once joked on a TV panel show that the reason Aldous Syne was so reclusive was that he was actually an actor hired by Alan Sugar, and the entire Synergis venture was a long-haul ruse to make Amstrad products look good.

Its largest revenue stream in recent years had been Chinese-made, non-branded mobile handsets, and there certainly weren't any of those in display cases along the corridor. According to Parlabane's research, the perception within the industry was that its manufacturing plant in Shanghai was the only part of Synergis potentially worth anything, though only if it started making something other than Synergis products.

So far however, Cruz didn't appear to be following the script the industry had written for this. The Shanghai plant was not up for sale. There had been no redundancies, no move to smaller premises even after the six-month subsidised tenancy expired. People were unsure what he was waiting for, but then a couple of months back, it finally appeared as though the familiar process was underway.

'I gather that Synergis recently sold off its profit-making children's and educational electronics subsidiary,' Parlabane says, as Tanya leads him down a long corridor. There are windows along one wall, giving him a view of a busy open-plan office area. 'Given the company's monthly burn, many people interpreted that as an attempt to keep

131

the lights on a while longer, though nobody seems quite sure what you're keeping the lights on for.'

She gives him that same look: *I know something you don't know.*

'Do we look like we're chucking ballast out of the balloon?' she asks, indicating the activity through the windows.

'It's not a picture of resignation and despair,' he concedes. 'Though as you suggested, it does look a lot like any other office. My inner geek must have had greater expectations because you're an electronics firm. Didn't I read somewhere that you have research and development labs?'

'Yeah,' she says, her averring expression giving him hope that these might be on a different site: that eighties-built science campus rising enticingly back into view. Then she extinguishes it again.

'We have research labs upstairs. I mean, we call them labs but we're still largely talking about rooms full of computers like you're seeing here, plus a few electronics work benches.'

Parlabane's face falls, and she misinterprets the nature of his disappointment.

'There are a few toys,' she adds. 'And there's the sub-zero room for working at ultra-low temperatures. I suppose when people get suited up for that it looks pretty space-age.'

'Can I see it?

'I'll need to ask. I don't have clearance.'

'Just a look-see, peak through the glass?'

'No, that's what I mean. My card doesn't open the doors. We'd need to be escorted. I'll see what I can do, though.'

'Thanks.'

She swipes him through another set of security doors into a quieter area where the adjacent office doors are closed and there are no windows on to the corridor. His geography tells him the windows inside probably offer a view of the Thames, so this must be the executive area.

Tanya escorts him into a conference room with a large empty table, attended by sixteen unoccupied chairs.

'Leo is still in his meeting, I'm sorry. Do you mind waiting here a bit? How are you for time?'

'No rush.'

'Can I offer you a coffee?'

'No thanks, but do you have a Wi-Fi password so I can catch up on emails?'

'Oh, sure. Select Tricorn Guest and the password is 28Hill, as in the building's address.'

Parlabane looks at the list of networks that his phone has found.

'The building's guest network doesn't have the strongest signal,' he says. 'Probably a lot of users sharing the bandwidth too.'

'Neurosphere has its own guest network, but I don't know the current password for that. The 4G is usually pretty good up here, though.'

'Can you let me piggyback into something a bit more local?'

'It's not allowed.'

'You worried I'm going to hack your network? I wouldn't know where to start. Despite our recently augmented reputation, most reporters aren't that technically adept.'

'You're not most reporters, Mr Parlabane.'

With that she pops the secure delusion that she knows nothing about him.

'It's nothing personal. We've got strict data security protocols.'

'Very sensible. To be fair, I wouldn't give me access to your networks if I were you.'

She accepts his concession with good grace and leaves him to it. Parlabane waits for her to move out of sight then pops his earpiece back in.

'There's several different Wi-Fi networks showing up within Synergis,' he says quietly.

'I know.'

'How?'

'I can see what's on your mobile.'

'Jesus,' he moans. 'I'm the journalist whose phone got hacked.'

She giggles, like it's utterly trivial.

'You have a whole other version of boundary issues,' he tells her. 'Anyway, what do you make of it so far?'

'They've had proper security consultants in. She only offered you

133

the guest Wi-Fi because it will be running off a different server and won't be connected to anything else. Non-employees won't be permitted to access Synergis's own networks because at that point you're behind the firewalls.'

'What's with the four different networks?'

'It's for restricting access to different sectors of the company, so that a breach in one sector doesn't compromise anything else. And those are merely the networks your phone can detect. There will be others.'

'So we most likely need to get into a network that we not only can't access, but can't even see?'

'I am disappoint. Corporate security intensifies.'

More hacker argot, he assumes.

'Wonderful. Is there anything I've encountered so far that you would interpret as good news?'

'It's all good news. The fact that you've already got eyes and ears inside the building is an advantage I've never had before. It's about perspective: all you're seeing is locked doors, whereas I'm getting advance notice of *which* doors to unlock.'

'And do you have any thoughts on how we might achieve that? Hello? Barb?'

Yeah, that stumped you, he thinks, with scant satisfaction, which drops to precisely zero when he realises she is no longer on the line.

# NO PICNIC

'Hey. Break time is over. Come on,' says Snotworm, my charming co-worker who has appointed himself my superior by virtue of having been here a month.

I have to put my phone away, though I don't disconnect the call, as I am still recording the audio. I slip the handset into my bag, placing it where it won't get nudged. I will listen back to what I've missed later.

'Hurry up.'

He was getting chewed out by Dot, the manager, when I showed up this morning for my second day at Urban Picnic. I knew right then that he'd be on my case to make himself feel better. I've been trying hard not to give him any excuses, but I'm still learning the ropes, so mistakes are going to happen.

After my mass mail-out I got invited to two interviews on the same day: one was for a call centre, which would have suited me okay, because I wouldn't have to speak to strangers face-to-face. Give me a headset and I can become who you like: work to a script, cold-calling people who don't want to know, I don't care. They're just voices on the other end of a line.

Problem was the interview clashed with Lilly's school run. If I couldn't even make that, then there was little chance I'd be as flexible as they required in terms of actual shifts.

Which left me with the second prize: making sandwiches in the Ilford branch of a new fast-food chain. I'd have preferred a burger place, to be honest. They say the grease goes for your skin and hair, but maybe I could hide in the back out of sight and not have to work a till. It's irrational, I know, but I feel vulnerable when I have to present myself to strangers, like they could simply reach across the counter and take something from me and I'd be powerless to stop them.

135

A bloke comes in and asks for a DMP. He grunts it out, like he begrudges every syllable. I don't mind. It's easier when they ask for one of the signature specials, because then I don't have to keep asking them stage by stage what they want on their sandwich.

Snotworm sees his chance, though.

'No, no. What you doing? It's the wrong way round. The Double Meat Picnic is chicken on first, then the salad, then the ham. Jesus. All them GCSEs but you ain't that smart, is ya?'

That's the third time he's mentioned the GCSEs. Dot must have left my application lying around. Not that it's bothering him or anything.

I'm pretty sure he told me the DMP was ham first the last time he had a go at me, but I can't be sure. He makes me bin the sandwich and start again, muttering about the waste. I've got no come-back.

Snotworm wins this round.

I consider again how little I'm getting paid for putting up with this, and about how limited my prospects look in the longer term if I'm held back by my responsibility for Lilly. I hate even thinking of her as 'holding me back', because I love her, but I feel so frustrated, like I'm never going to be able to explore my true potential. With that in mind, the temptation to turn blackhat is growing by the day. It's a line I've never crossed, but I'm already a wanted criminal and I'm starting to reckon 'in for a penny'.

I can't think that way, though. What would be the point of everything that I've done to Jack – and of what Jack is doing right now – if I end up getting nicked for something else? I'm a hacker, not a thief, though that distinction is getting more blurry all the time.

I need to stay focused. Primary objective: stay out of jail. I'm not going to follow in Mum's footsteps, deluding myself that the best way to ensure Lilly's future is to go after easy money, only to end up somewhere I can't be any help to her at all. I can put up with Snotworm, same as I can deliver on what Zodiac is demanding.

I feel bad about the way I've manipulated Jack, though. I knew he wouldn't understand my situation unless I put him in the same boat, but he doesn't deserve this. I didn't have any choice, though. There was no one else I could turn to. I can't trust the Uninvited crew. Zodiac could be any one of them, not just Stonefish, and I don't want to leave any more evidence that can be used as blackmail material. The trick is to pull this off and have nobody but Jack knowing how.

I know I can trust him. I can't say why – maybe because I can't afford to think about the alternative. I believe in him, and have done for a while. That's what makes it all the worse that I'm basically making an enemy of the guy. I'm giving him all the reason in the world to hate me for ever.

# ADVERSARIES

'I think they're finishing up,' Tanya says, leaning around the door-frame.

Parlabane stands, grateful to be leaving this improvised isolation tank. It is the only space in the building where he has been at any point unsupervised, most likely because there is nothing in it of any interest or sensitivity. Not so much as a Post-it note with a name scribbled on it has been left in the place.

'Did you get your emails done?' she asks.

Parlabane takes a beat to remember the pretext for enquiring about the Wi-Fi.

'Settled for the 4G,' he tells her.

She taps her card against the sensor and leads him into a small lobby where a secretary is seated at a desk adjacent to two closed doors. There is a modernist painting dominating the wall behind her. It looks like the artist drank several tubs of paint and then puked on it.

'Are they about done, Carol?' Tanya asks.

'Any minute. Miryam is due to give them a tour of the labs on the hour.'

Even as Carol speaks, one of the doors opens and Parlabane gets his first sight of Leo Cruz in the flesh. He is glowering as he grips the door handle, switching to a neutral expression as he notices that there are witnesses outside.

Cruz looks unsettlingly young, as though he has stepped out of a magazine portrait of himself from twenty years ago. He was famously prodigious in his business success back in the day, but upon closer inspection it's apparent he's had work done. His hair is unnaturally black and shiny, the skin on his cheekbones conspicuously stretched. Parlabane sees a man clinging too tightly to the vestiges of youth, maybe trying to be the man he once was instead of settling for the one he has become. He has been through that struggle himself, and knows the only way to end it is to accept defeat. Unfortunately, to reach that understanding usually takes a sustained period of kidding yourself.

It is all handshakes and politeness as three men and two women file past him into the lobby, but Parlabane can sense tension escaping from the office like Cruz loosened the lid on a pot.

Finally a fourth male emerges, for whom Cruz cannot even muster a fake-and-shake. The other suits are already being greeted by Carol in readiness for being escorted to meet this Miryam person she mentioned, and thus their attention is elsewhere, but Parlabane has focused on where the action is.

It lasts only a couple of seconds, but there is a palpable enmity crackling in the doorway.

Something is spoken quietly. Parlabane doesn't catch it. Then the other guy strides into the lobby to join the others.

He looks like a prick, Parlabane thinks. He's not being purely pejorative: the guy has a manner about him that reminds Parlabane of a bulging erection. He holds himself super-straight, tensed up and restless, giving off an unsettling aggression. Parlabane recognises someone who needs to assert himself in any situation, perhaps as a schooldays legacy of looking like a cross between Kinski's Nosferatu and Plug from the *Beano*.

Cruz stares down at the carpet, taking a moment. Parlabane feels like he caught him naked. It's a mutually awkward start. When the CEO looks up again, however, he's got his PR face on.

'Mr Parlabane. Sorry to keep you. Come on through to my office.'

There is no third-party introduction from Tanya. Cruz knows who he is talking to. In Parlabane's experience this is seldom a good thing, but given that he's planning on robbing the place in the near future, it seems particularly unwelcome news.

Cruz shakes Parlabane's hand and leads him through an adjacent door into what is apparently the CEO's personal office. It is large and airy, tall windows affording a view across the river. Cruz gestures to him to take a seat across an expanse of desk, while Tanya asks if either of them requires anything and is dismissed when the answer is a mutual no.

Parlabane wonders how long he's got, what silent signal will summon Tanya back to get rid of him.

Cruz has barely sat down when something seems to occur to him. 'Excuse me a moment.'

He gets up and exits in a hurry, apparently in pursuit of his assistant. Perhaps he forgot to agree the signal.

Parlabane is alone in the office. Documents are scattered untidily about the desk in front of him, Cruz's PC unguarded only feet away. It seems too good an opportunity to be true, and he wonders if it is some kind of trap. A glance up towards the ceiling reveals a CCTV lens, and that's the camera he *can* see.

Nonetheless, he is close enough that several of the documents are legible, albeit upside down. Most are lists of figures or data reports that are incomprehensible without any context, but two catch his eye. One appears to be an acquisition proposal regarding a company named Optronix, and the other is a bulk purchase order for e-cigarettes.

Cruz returns, apologising for having left so abruptly. He is wearing a professional smile, but there is something unmistakably flustered about him.

'Tough meeting?' Parlabane suggests.

'Nothing I haven't been through before.'

He takes a seat, looking more relaxed to be in his office chair: home advantage.

'So, now we're both here, what do you want to talk about?'

'As I'm here from *Broadwave*, and as we have an unashamedly geeky streak running through us both personally and editorially, I'm here to ask what your plans are now that you are back where it all began at Synergis.'

Cruz sits back in his chair and says nothing, regarding his interviewer carefully as he weighs up his answer.

'No, you're not,' he states.

'I'm sorry?'

'You're not here to ask about some vague business strategy I might

140

have. That's not something I can see *Broadwave* running with, not even if I was Mark Zuckerberg. It's also not what you said on the phone to Tanya when you asked for this interview.'

Parlabane is on the back foot, trying to recall his initial pitch. Cruz jogs his memory.

'You said you had heard that we were working on a new device. You wouldn't have got in the door otherwise.'

Parlabane isn't sure where he's going with this, but these self-made business types can be somewhat unto themselves. Sometimes its affectation, sometimes it's insecurity and sometimes it's coke-fuelled psychosis.

'Sure,' he agrees. 'That is what I said. So can we talk about that?'

'No. We can talk about where you heard this. That's the only reason I agreed to speak to you.'

'Well, I fear it might be a very short interview in that case. I can't disclose my sources.'

'I appreciate you can't tell me who you heard this from. But can you tell me what exactly you heard?'

'That you have a new product in development; nothing more specific. I didn't realise this in itself was sensitive information.'

Cruz puts his knuckles to his chin, reflecting on this. He doesn't seem displeased, but it hasn't calmed his soul either.

'It's sensitive inasmuch as I think it means we have a leak. No offence, Mr Parlabane, but when someone of your reputation knows something he's not supposed to regarding my business, it makes me very jumpy.'

'None taken. But nothing I'm hearing is making it sound like you don't have something in the pipeline. Something top secret, it would appear.'

Cruz gives him an odd smile, conceding the point.

'I'm not here to break Synergis up, that much should also be apparent.'

'So I've been hearing. But the disposal of your profit-making educational electronics subsidiary was grist to that particular rumour mill. Do you have any comment on that?'

Cruz responds with a wry smile.

141

'I understand how that might be interpreted. But the truth is that I made the sale in order to streamline operations and raise capital.'

'So you're filling a war chest rather than wielding a wrecking ball? Again, the "exciting new product" hypothesis seems to be gathering momentum.'

Cruz scrutinises him again, evaluating very carefully before his next response. Parlabane can see a glint in his eye. This guy has got something big in the works, and though it remains imperative he keep his cards close to his chest, he is bursting to tell somebody *something* about it.

'I'm sorry I can't go into any detail, but yes, Synergis does have a new innovation under development. Everything is so delicate at this stage, you know? I'm treading on eggshells. I feel like an expectant father, though I'm not pacing outside the delivery suite. That's a way off yet. More like I'm waiting for a scan and hoping it says everything is still okay.'

'Was that what the meeting was about earlier? The atmosphere seemed a wee bit fraught, I couldn't help noticing.'

'Yes. There are some complex negotiations still in progress. And to be honest, I can't help feeling like karma's about to bite me on the arse.'

'How so?'

He sighs, looking torn, though it isn't clear whether he is conflicted by what is troubling him or merely by the notion of telling Parlabane about it.

'I assume you're familiar with my career. Or at least other people's accounts of my career.'

'I've done my homework,' Parlabane replies, politely neutral.

'Then we both know there aren't many articles out there in praise of my altruism or morality. I know what people think of me. Truth is, they're right. I became all of the things they said I am: a shark, a predator, an asset-stripper, a spiv, a vulture. But I wasn't always those things. I was an idealist once.'

'They say all cynics are disappointed idealists,' Parlabane suggests.

'Then I'm living proof. I won't bore you with the details of my disaffection. It was a gradual process rather than some origin-story

142

moment of transformation. But at some point, instead of being frustrated by the fact that business rewards predators rather than innovators, I stopped waiting for the world to make sense according to some notion of natural justice. You embrace the absurdity or you let it drive you mad.'

'Absurdity? Isn't it simply harsh reality?'

Cruz lets out a laugh. It's not bitter, but it sounds like it might have been, at one time.

'The London stock exchange once rallied after a slow morning when a rumour swept the trading floors that Reg Holdsworth had been appointed to the vacant chief executive's position at Tesco's. On the wires it was reported that market confidence increased because he was known to be a safe pair of hands, and there was a knock-on effect across the whole market. He was a *fictional character*. He managed the supermarket on *Coronation Street*.'

'I remember the story.'

'Then I'll raise you another. Someone got a five-year-old girl to pick hedge-fund trades for six months. She outperformed several funds whose supposed hot-shot managers were taking home seven-figure salaries for making choices that worked out worse than hers.'

'I heard about a similar experiment where the trades were picked by a dog.'

'Dogs, sure. Monkeys too. The point is it's these people's decisions that often mean your business stands or falls. There's no justice to it because there's no reason to it. So I quit whining and went to work. Won some, lost some. Mainly made a handsome living, "looting corpses" as someone described it. But even for me there was a cost to the soul. I tried to deny it to myself, but it catches up with you eventually.'

Parlabane opts not to relay the scepticism of those who believe this impossible due to Cruz not actually having a soul.

'I had an epiphany. I know, I know. Other people change their minds. Pompous, self-serving arseholes have epiphanies. But it's true. Something happened, something I didn't necessarily deserve, but it put me in the position to build something again, and to do so at Synergis. I'm not a religious or superstitious man, but you can't ignore the symbolism when it's screaming at you.'

'So how is karma threatening to bite you in the arse?'

'Because I'm vulnerable now. In order to fund this project, I've had to bring in investment, and that means diluting my stock, which in turn means loosening my grip on ownership. Now there's someone out there – one of the new investors – who is making overtures towards buying Synergis out from under me. If the other investors are tempted by his offer, there's little I can do. It's a guaranteed return for them, and a fast one too.'

Parlabane recalls the human prick and the atmosphere between the two men when Cruz first opened that conference-room door.

'How likely is it they'll sell?'

'It can be a domino effect. But individually it comes down to whether they think they'll do better if they stay for the long haul.'

'You would get a return on your own investment, though, wouldn't you?'

'If I chose to sell, sure, but my whole point is that this isn't about the money.'

'Words that I predict many people will find hard to believe actually emerged from your mouth,' Parlabane says.

Cruz looks ever so slightly wounded for a moment, but his expression is stoic.

'That's fair. That really is fair. But let me show you something.'

Cruz gets to his feet, that mercurial look on his face once again, like he's managed to keep his mouth straight but is unable to hide the smile that's in his eyes. Parlabane can't quite read the expression, but it's more than merely the satisfaction of knowing something his interviewer doesn't.

Cruz leads him through a single security door, one that opens into a stairwell. Parlabane spots a CCTV camera monitoring the space, and notes an infra-red sensor high up on the wall.

They ascend one level to a landing with two security doors. One leads to the next flight of stairs and thus into Neurosphere's premises, so Parlabane figures nobody's swipe card works on that any more. Cruz taps his ID against a panel next to the other exit, which opens into a further corridor.

Ten yards along, they turn a corner and pass through another set

144

of double-wide security doors, above which a sign states: 'Research and Development: Strictly No Unauthorised Access'. A line of slightly smaller type underneath warns: 'Tailgaters will be reported to Security. If you forgot your pass, get another.'

As they step through the doors, a security guard emerges from a tiny office, little more than a cubicle.

'I need to see your guest pass, sir,' he tells Parlabane. 'And I need you to give me your phone.'

'Oh, yeah, sorry,' Cruz says. 'Forgot to mention. We don't allow visitors to take phones inside. Or any recording devices, flash drives, USB keyfobs. You got any of that?'

Parlabane feels a shudder of paranoia about the concealed cameras. He can't fess up to this stuff now. He'll have to take his chances.

'I have a USB,' he says, handing over his keyring.

'You can pick them up again here,' the guard informs him.

Parlabane has a quick glance inside the cubicle. He sees four monitors arranged in a square on the wall, switching between views every few seconds. Beneath these upon a shallow desk is a tray full of mobile phones, USB sticks and iPads, and on a bracket clipped inside the doorframe is some kind of wand, like a metal detector. The guard hasn't opted to deploy it, for which he is truly grateful. Perhaps being in the company of the boss has conferred certain privileges. The spycams remain his secret.

They pass through into a passageway with windows on one side. Tanya was right. It looks like another open-plan office area: lots of desks and monitors, staff working intently at their screens. At the far end, Parlabane can see the execs that were at the meeting, being given their guided tour.

Cruz leads him past this and through a security door on the other side of the corridor. They emerge into another open-plan area. There are more desks and monitors, but there are also workstations equipped with bafflingly technical electronics tools, the purposes of which Parlabane can merely guess at. In here the staff are dressed in paper-like overalls, anti-static devices strapped to their wrists.

There is a grey wall extending halfway across the floor at the end of the room, a cube-like enclosure with two doors side by side.

145

'Is that the sub-zero room I heard about?'

'Yes, on the right. Everyone finds it rather impressive, but I'm actually more taken by what's next door. That's where we have our server farm. Nothing to do with me, it was put in by Neurosphere, but the clever thing is that it's all part of this amazing thermal exchange system. Server farms generate a tremendous amount of heat, which gets pumped around the building to save on fuel costs.'

The atmosphere is hushed, almost monastic in its studied calm. Cruz has stopped against a wall, making sure they are in nobody's way and offering no distraction, but everyone is working with such quiet purpose that Parlabane feels like he could be watching through a two-way mirror.

He glances at Cruz, who has that glint again, and this time Parlabane understands.

It is pride.

Whatever they are working on here, he is invested in it more than just financially.

'Can you give me a hint?' Parlabane asks.

Cruz shakes his head.

'All I can say is that the Synapse was once overtaken by new monitoring systems, and we're working on an RBA.'

'RBA?'

'Right Back Atcha.'

Cruz leaves Parlabane to consider this, having been summoned by a gesture from one of the staff who wants to show him something.

Rather than remain there like a lemon, Parlabane opts to take a wander, reckoning that as Cruz didn't tell him otherwise, he can play daft if he is challenged. He takes a closer look at the grey cube. The doors to the sub-zero room and to the server farm are both controlled by card sensors, but there appears to be an emergency override for the first, perhaps in case somebody gets stuck in there without their thermal undies and a flask of monkey.

It is as he walks around the enclosure that he sees a distinct single door on the opposite wall. It is made of steel, as is its frame. From its position in the building, Parlabane estimates that it is quite shallow, maybe only ten feet from the thick stone of the exterior wall. It is possible that he is not merely seeing a steel doorframe, but an embedded steel chamber. A small laminated sign above the handle and lock mechanism states 'Strictly No Admittance'. Not 'No Unauthorised Access'; Strictly No Admittance.

Whoever you are, you know you have no access. So fuck right off.

As he walks back towards Cruz, he stops to let a woman pass. She is carrying a tray of circuitry components that looks like someone went mad with a hammer in Dixons.

'Can you get the door for me, Charlotte?' she asks a nearby colleague.

Parlabane watches as Charlotte obliges, reaching for the handle of a nearby door marked 'Secure Disposal'. He notices that unlike all the others, this one is controlled by a keypad, into which Charlotte punches a four-digit PIN. He doesn't see the numbers clearly, but he is sure that his spy cameras will have picked them up, as well as recording the audible confirmatory touch tones.

It's on the same side as the vault, abutting the outside wall, and it's where they take their refuse. That's got to be worth something.

'Can I quote you on the RBA thing?' Parlabane asks, catching up to Cruz once more.

There is that twinkle in his eye again. Of course he can quote it.

'I never said I was off the record, did I?'

And this is where Parlabane understands the real talent Cruz brought to market once upon a time. He is a consummate salesman, for here he is selling Parlabane a mere shadow of an idea.

'Jack, I'd like you to meet someone.'

Cruz is standing beside the woman who had beckoned to him earlier. 'This is Jane Dunwoodie, our head of R&D. Jane this is Jack Parlabane, who is writing an article about us for *Broadwave*.'

Dunwoodie looks late twenties, early thirties, an intensity about her that fits with such seniority at a comparatively young age. There is a professional and determined air about her, right up until the point Cruz mentions why Parlabane is there.

She removes her latex gloves to shake his hand. Must be for anti-static protection, he reasons. He has spotted a couple of boxes of them around the workbenches.

She gives him a polite smile but she seems uncomfortable about potentially being put on the spot. It's a reaction Parlabane has seen plenty of times before. Perhaps Cruz forgets that not everybody enjoys media attention, though maybe she's just very busy right now and could do without the interruption.

'It must be exciting to be in the vanguard of a new development,' Parlabane suggests.

She seems caught in the headlights. She looks at Cruz rather than at Parlabane, which is when he understands her panicky discomfort. She isn't sure how much she's allowed to say.

'It's a tremendous opportunity,' she manages, glancing at Cruz again before she has even finished speaking, like she needs affirmation that she did okay. Parlabane recognises somebody happier tinkering in the lab than dealing with other people.

'Jane, have those new diagnostics come back, by the way?' Cruz asks.

'I've sent them through to you. Do you want to see them now?'

'While I remember.'

He guesses there is no reason Cruz can't wait until he's back at his office to see whatever she sent, and surmises that this is a wee bit of theatre for Parlabane's benefit: Cruz as the hands-on boss.

Cruz then walks him back towards the security cubicle to pick up his phone. As they turn the corner, way up ahead he can see the visiting execs at the end of their tour. They are being scanned in turn by the security guard, running that wand thing up and down them from head to toe and back again.

'What's going on there?' Parlabane asks.

'Can't be too careful. It's in the non-disclosure agreement and a condition of getting a look-see. We always scan visitors on the way out. Again, I forgot to mention it.'

'What's he scanning for? Is it in case they've pocketed a circuit board?'

'No, it's to detect any hidden recording devices. You'd be amazed how tiny a video camera can be these days.'

# DATA CACHE

Parlabane feels a wave of something cold pulse through him. He never agreed to any conditions, but there's still no way of making this look good.

'I guess you have to take the threat of industrial espionage very seriously when you're working on something new.'

'Like you wouldn't believe. When it comes to investors, truth is I need these people far more than I trust them. The only thing worse than having Synergis bought out from under me would be if someone ripped off the new project and beat me to market.'

'Yeah, that would be a sickener,' Parlabane agrees. 'Hey, do you have a loo nearby that I could use? Coffee is catching up with me.'

'Sure, just back there and around the corner. First on your right.'

'Cheers.'

He walks briskly to the toilets and locks himself inside a cubicle, contemplating his disposal options. Chucking the whole kit down the pan seems the most obvious solution, but there are wires and a miniature solid-state drive that might not flush. If someone retrieves the drive and looks at the files, it won't take long to identify who brought it here. Then he looks above the pan, at the absence of a cistern. Instead there is a fibreglass panel, behind which the plumbing is kept out of sight.

He takes a coin from his pocket and uses it to twist open the fastener on an access panel behind the u-bend. It comes away with a bit of a wrench, but that is good news, as it indicates that the hatch is not in regular use. He slips the spy cameras and the SSD down behind the kickplate and replaces the panel, trying not to think about all of the surveillance info he has just lost.

On the bright side, maybe everything he has learned today might help convince Buzzkill that this is a suicide mission after all.

Parlabane feels conspicuously furtive as he emerges from the toilets, realising how suspicious his sudden retreat may have looked. To cover this he decides to come out swinging by way of asking Cruz another question as soon as he catches up to him at the security doors.

'So who are the investors? Are they venture capitalists? Other electronics firms?'

'I'm afraid that's confidential. They're not the only ones covered by an NDA.'

'I see.'

The guard gives Parlabane back his phone and his keyring. He puts them in his pockets as Cruz holds the door open for him.

'Did you get everything you came with?' he asks.

Parlabane rides out a queasy moment of wondering whether Cruz knows what he just did in the toilets. He realises it's his paranoia being ramped up by seeing cameras and security measures everywhere, as well as the fear that his guilty intentions must be legible to his intended victim.

'I'm good, yeah. Thanks for your time, and for the tour.'

'My pleasure. I'll take you downstairs myself. I'm heading outside anyway.'

They stop off at Cruz's office on the way, so that he can pick up his coat and quickly reply to a couple of emails. Parlabane waits out in the lobby area, the clicking of Cruz's keyboard audible from where he stands next to the receptionist's desk. He notices a handwritten list of names in front of her, like she's been copying them from there into her computer.

Parlabane takes out his phone and surreptitiously snaps a photo of the list while pretending to type. There is a possibility, however remote, that one of these people is behind what he and Buzzkill have been sucked into, and any lead he can find into that investigation is likely to be more valuable than whatever else he takes away from this expedition. He's been here close to two hours now and the most he's learned about Synergis's potential vulnerabilities is that there don't appear to be any.

Cruz beckons him aboard the elevator and taps his ID to activate it: can't even exit without valid credentials, Parlabane notes.

'Was there anything else you wanted to ask before we wrap up?' Cruz enquires.

'Actually, now that you mention it, it occurs to me that you never told me what this epiphany actually was, because presumably it wasn't to do with Reg Holdsworth. I'm guessing this had to be something more recent.'

Cruz smiles rather wistfully, a hint of apology in there.

'For reasons that will only become apparent in the future, I'm afraid I can't be very specific about this. I realise it's frustrating for me to be so evasive, but . . .'

Something changes, like he's had a change of heart, or maybe run out of patience with all the restrictions he has to abide by.

'I've read up on you, Jack. Your past is almost as chequered as mine. Don't worry, I'm not about to get moralistic. It would hardly suit me. But the thing is, it occurs to me that you're probably a guy who understands what it is to be looking for a second chance, so what the hell, I'm going to take a risk. I can't be specific, and I won't confirm or deny, but I can give you an idea of where I'm coming from.'

'I'll take whatever you're offering.'

'Truth is, my epiphany was that I missed my old self. I had turned into someone I didn't like, and I hadn't even realised I didn't like that person until . . . Well, I had an encounter with someone else who had rediscovered his old self, and who remembered a different, better version of me. I realised that if he could recapture the spark he used to have, then together we might both be what we once were.'

'I take it you can't give me his name?' Parlabane asks, though he barely needs to.

Cruz merely smiles, saying nothing: telling him everything.

After twenty years in obscurity, Aldous Syne had emerged from the shadows with another game-changing invention.

# CHALLENGE ACCEPTED

I get off at Monument, swerving past a woman with a buggy so that I don't get stuck behind her on the escalators. I slow my stride as I reach for my phone to check the time, and while I'm not walking so fast I take in my reflection in the glass of an advertising video screen.

I look wired.

I want to seem brighter – less, I dunno, batshit mental – to Jack, so he doesn't regard me purely as a threat. I want him to see that this is a person he's dealing with, and not some faceless entity like Zodiac. He's always acted kind of standoffish, like he's afraid of me, even when I've been helping him. I suppose the measures I was taking to protect my identity were never likely to put him at ease, and what's happened recently isn't going to improve things.

It's about ten past eight. I said I'd be there on the hour, but I was unlucky with the District Line. Lilly is round at her friend Cassie's house this evening, so I've got until ten to get back there and pick her up. I realise I'm making it sound like it's Lilly that wanted to go out, but actually it was me who asked a favour of Cassie's mother. I've spoken to her a few times at the school gates. She knows about Mum and she lives pretty close. I told her I've got a late shift at Urban Picnic which I couldn't get out of because I'm new. I hate lying to her and I'm kacking it in case she finds out, but Jack and I need to do this out of office hours, and we need to do it in the dark.

I see him in the ticket hall, checking his phone. There's a paranoid part of me waiting for the cops to come swooping in now that I've shown up, bundling me away in a van, then thanking him for his cooperation.

He's about the same age as my mum, I reckon, though I'm not

always good at guessing. He's roughly my height, but wiry and taut whereas I'm Miss Spaghetti Legs. I look like one of those toys that you press the bottom of their stand and they collapse. By contrast Jack looks coiled, as though he could spring up and haul himself across the overhanging beams.

He's got the kind of hair that probably looks untidy no matter what: unruly and a dusty mix of grey and blond. It's the eyes you notice most, though. They go right through you. I reckon they'd sparkle when he smiles, but I haven't seen that yet. Mostly it's just been the x-ray treatment, and who could blame him.

He notices me coming and I offer him a smile, feeling stupid and pathetic for doing so. It's not like he's going to be pleased to see me, is it? He looks resentful, and I realise how the smile must have played: like I'm milking the power I've got. He seems wary too, which makes me uncomfortable. I'm so unused to this. I'm usually the one shrinking away from people. How can anyone be scared of me, right?

I want to say I'm sorry, but I don't want to open the door to him trying to persuade me again to go to the police. That isn't happening. Nuh-uh.

I'm about to ask how it went today but I can already hear myself sounding all wet. Besides, we already talked on the phone briefly. I decide instead to act all business. He hates me anyway: I might as well make that work for me.

'You said you lost the cameras. What happened there?'

He gives me a glare, real Superman heat-vision stuff.

'I didn't lose them. I ditched them, and I thought I'd made it clear why. If I was already burned I'd be no good to you. What would you do then?'

I decide not to respond, as I can see where this is going. It's the flipside of my mutually assured destruction strategy: if I make good on my threat, there's no reason for him not to give me up too.

'You're a reporter: you gotta have a good memory for detail. Why don't you tell me what you saw, break it down for me.'

'Sure thing. I can break it down for you very simply: it can't be done.'

I draw my eyes off him, giving him the response Mum always gives me when she thinks I'm acting like a huffy teen. It's an act though, so he doesn't see how scared this makes me feel. If I can't keep him onside, I can't deliver what I promised to Zodiac, and I have no doubt Zodiac will deliver on what he promised to do if I fail.

'Let's take a walk down Tricorn House,' I suggest. 'And on the way there you can tell me *why* it can't be done.'

I start walking. I honestly don't know what I'll do if he doesn't follow, but it doesn't come to that.

'Okay. I've got reason to believe that this prototype is a new invention from Aldous Syne, who has presumably been working on it in a cave somewhere for the past twenty years.'

'He's the geezer who invented the Synapse, right?'

'Yes. Cruz hinted that this is another game-changer. Cruz is a hype-merchant, that's his MO, but he's clearly excited, and we know he's not the only one. He seems aware of that too, so he's paranoid about industrial espionage. To that end, I'm sure he's keeping the prototype in a steel vault, to which I'm guessing only Syne, Cruz and maybe the head of R&D have access.'

Jack talks quietly, like he's afraid we'll be overheard. There's nobody else on the pavements, though.

Jack gives a humourless laugh.

'I mean, Christ, I enjoy a challenge,' he says, 'but the places I've broken into in the past, we're talking about shinning up a drainpipe or abseiling down from a roof and wedging open a window. This isn't just a different league. This is a different game. I don't even know where to begin.'

'I do. That's why we're here right now. You're a climber, aren't you?'

'Yeah, but I think the guy you're looking for is a cross between Peter Parker and Ethan Hunt.'

I have to convince him otherwise, speak to him in terms he'll understand.

'Don't be so down in the dumps. I'm not a climber but I'm guessing it can look pretty scary from the ground: maybe even impossible sometimes. You think: how will I ever get past that overhang, never mind reach the top. But then you find the tiniest bit of purchase somewhere, and it's enough to get you a little higher. And from there, now you can see the next tiny foothold that's going to get you up to the next ledge. It's the same with a hack.'

'So where is our first toe-hold?'

'Down in the dumps.'

We take a left down a narrow alley, wide enough for one vehicle. It traces an s-bend, ultimately curving to emerge around the back of Tricorn House, at a service bay for delivery vans and, more importantly, refuse disposal.

We stop at the corner. There is a control barrier and a manned security booth monitoring vehicular access to the bay. Beyond that I can see an enclosure housing the waste hoppers. It is walled off, locked up and has a steel mesh over the top to prevent anybody climbing in.

'Some toe-hold,' Jack says. 'Even the garbage here is locked up tight as a camel's arse in a sandstorm. Doesn't this tell you something?'

'Yeah. It tells me that we turned up in the wrong clothes.'

He splutters in exasperation. I have to remind myself that how I see the world and how a non-hacker sees it can be very different.

'You don't understand. This is good news.'

'How can the fact that even their midden is access-controlled be good news?'

'Because this suggests there's more chance of finding treasure in the trash. People are very careful about what they throw away these days, in case somebody like us is planning to sift through it. But when they know – or when they *think* – their garbage and data disposal are secure, then they worry that bit less about what they're chucking in there.'

'But how are we meant to get near it if it's secured and monitored?' he asks.

'Let me worry about that.'

# MAKE-BELIEVE

'Hello, Tricorn House, how may I direct your call?'

'Oh, hi there. I'm calling from DDS, that's Data Disposal Solutions. I wonder if you could put me through to whoever handles secure waste management for your building?'

'Certainly. That would be Nigel Holt, he's in charge of Maintenance and Buildings Operations. I'll just check if he's in yet.'

I can hear Lilly humming a song to herself in the bathroom while I'm on hold. She likes doing that when she's using the electric toothbrush. I don't know if it's the sound it makes or the way it feels inside her mouth, but she can be in there for ages, and the upside is her gnashers always get a decent scrub.

'Putting you through now,' says the receptionist.

The bloke picks up right away.

'Nigel Holt,' he says, sounding a bit grouchy. It *is* first thing in the morning. I decide to up the bubbly quotient, and even change my choice of false name to something more frothy.

'Good morning, Mr Holt. This is Pippa Sparks from Data Disposal Solutions. We're expanding into the City right now and I was wondering if we could offer you a free quote for secure disposal services?'

'We already have a contract for that, with ten months left to run.'

'If you don't mind, could you tell me who that is with?'

'SecuShred.'

'Of course. Know them well. We do like to plan ahead at DDS. Would you be interested in finding out if our quote might be cheaper?'

'Sure. We're always looking for a competitive tender.'

'That's great. And so we're quoting on like-for-like services, can you tell me a bit about your facilities?'

'If you give me an email address I can send you a breakdown.'

'That would be very helpful. And how often do they pick up? Is it weekly? Monthly?'

'Weekly.'

'And which day? I mean, we can change that to suit you, but so I know how it would work with our current schedule.'

'They're due tomorrow, as it happens.'

Lilly comes out from the bathroom and I check the time. Have to scoot soon.

'Just need a minute, Lill.'

I finish the call and nip to my bedroom, where I look up SecuShred's website, checking out promotional photos of their staff and paying close attention to what they get kitted in for work.

'Read-ee!' Lilly shouts.

I download some high-res images of the SecuShred logo and save them to a flash drive.

Lilly is waiting in the hall when I emerge, school blazer on and her bag already slung.

I walk her to the Loxford, figuring there's a place on Ilford Lane that will do the job rapid. All the way up there she talks about what she and Cassie are going to be playing at during interval, innocent games of make-believe.

I envy her so much right now. I've already lied at length to a stranger this morning and I'm planning to commit two crimes before lunch.

# DRESSED FOR SUCCESS

Parlabane is waiting in the ticket hall at Monument again, roughly eighteen hours since he was last here. He's the one running late this time, though with less emphasis on the running part. Ordinarily he considers lateness an arrogant discourtesy, but he's not so concerned about propriety when it comes to people who are effectively holding him hostage.

He's supposed to be working on a follow-up to one of the lines that emerged from his visit to the arms trade exhibition, though he has hinted to Lee that he has something else in the pipeline. He cleared up the issue of the "big story" tweets by admitting he was hacked by his Uninvited source as a prank, but if anything this merely seemed to boost his cred.

It may be desperation talking, but he has started to convince himself that he can maybe make this into a story. Everything would need to be anonymised, and his own part airbrushed out, but there is scope for a first-hand account of how one of Uninvited's self-styled digital insurgents practises the craft of infiltration.

It's no wonder she has evaded detection until recently. Every time he looks at her, his brain struggles to connect this skinny and awkward adolescent girl with the demonic cyber-Loki who has haunted and quietly terrified him since insinuating her way into his life, like she has slipped into computer networks across the globe. He learned the hard way not to underestimate her, but given some of the ruthless and connected bastards he's found himself on the wrong side of down the years, it seems incredible that this should be the one who has gripped him most tightly by the balls.

She acts like sustained eye contact is a struggle, let alone that she would be capable of hurting anybody, yet a little while ago she and her mates wiped several million off the stock market, and her finger remains over the nuclear button that could detonate Parlabane's career, life and liberty.

To put the buttercream on top of this dainty little cupcake, she's been hitting him for money too. It's not a shakedown in the classic sense, but he finds it pretty galling that as well as everything else, she's making him bankroll this thing.

First of all she got him to shell out for the spy cams and the SSD that he subsequently lost, and then last night she tapped him for sixty in cash before they parted ways, assuring him he'd find out why this morning.

She looks him up and down as he approaches. He thinks she's going to say something about him being late, for which he's warming up a tasty reply, but it seems she's appraising his appearance.

'Did you bring the tools I asked you to?'

'Yes. Are you going to tell me what they're for?'

She's playing a power game, drip-feeding him only as much information as she needs him to know at any given time. He senses there's a vulnerability there, but nothing he can use until he can somehow get a few steps ahead of her.

She reaches into her rucksack and pulls out a pale blue garment.

'You need to get changed into this.'

He unravels it, which is when he sees that it is identical to the one she is wearing under her jacket. It is a polo shirt, with a logo printed on the left side of the chest, saying SecuShred.

'Lovely,' he says, working it out. 'Start the day with an indictable felony, that's what I always say.'

She coaches him on what to say as they walk from the Tube station to the service bay where their journey ended the night before.

'Why don't *you* do the talking?' he asks.

'Good point. Because I'd totally look like your boss if I did that, and it wouldn't raise anyone's suspicions.'

'They say sarcasm is the lowest form of wit. That and Jim Davidson.'

'Who's he?'

'I envy your youthful ignorance more and more by the second.'

In contrast to last night's furtive peeking around the corner, they stride confidently up to the booth and speak to the uniformed guard manning the barrier.

Parlabane holds up his phone showing a fake email she has sent him, prominently displaying the Tricorn House masthead.

'Morning. John Saxton and Kath Hale. We're from SecuShred. We're responding to a report from Nigel Holt's office about a damaged hopper in your enclosure there.'

The guard gets them to fill out two temporary visitor passes, which he tears from a sheet and hands to them.

'And you'll have your own keys,' the guard says, at which point Parlabane stifles a groan.

He had assumed they only locked up the enclosure overnight. This is in keeping with everything else he has seen, and the only upside is that it might drive home to 'Barb' that this is a non-starter.

She doesn't appear to be seeing it that way, however.

'Sure,' she replies, without skipping a beat. 'Strict company policy that we sign out the keys for each premises before we leave the depot.'

'On you go, then,' the guard tells them, waving them through.

She sweeps off confidently towards the enclosure, Parlabane picking up his pace to pull alongside.

'Look, I know I told you I can pick locks, but I can't do it so quickly and inconspicuously that this guy isn't going to notice.'

'That's not how we're getting in. Come on. Role-play time.'

'I can do a really convincing pissed-off Scottish guy right now. Beyond that my parts are limited.'

'Good thing that's just what I need.'

Then he gets it.

He makes a decent show of bickering, then his 'subordinate' stomps off back towards the booth, where the guard is already on his way out to meet them.

'Everything okay?' he asks.

Parlabane nods to his colleague like she's a naughty child with some explaining to do.

'No,' she answers glumly. 'Like an idiot I've signed out the keys for the wrong place.' She holds up what Parlabane assumes to be her house keys. 'These are for SinTek over in Wapping. They're right next to each other on the board. Looking at a two-hour round trip to get back here, gonna knock our schedule right off.'

'Nah, don't be daft, love. Got our own set right here.'

'You're a life-saver, mate.'

# BURIED TREASURE

Upon Parlabane's suggestion, they take their haul back to Mairi's flat, so that they have somewhere private to sift through it. He had entertained some doubt as to the wisdom of letting Buzzkill know where he is staying, which lasted the fraction of a second it required for him to consider that she probably already knew and that if she didn't, it would hardly be a challenge for someone of her skills to find out. Besides, he reasoned, it would provide the perfect opportunity to make a start on levelling the playing field.

Most of the paper they discovered in the enclosure had been shredded, though there were a few complete sheaves; probably because they were innocuous, but you never know. They took as many of these as they could inconspicuously carry, but most of their hopes rested on the discarded USB sticks and a single hard drive that were lying in a hopper amid a bed of broken and burned-out circuitry.

'Barb' is hunched over the table in Mairi's micro-kitchen, performing some kind of surgery on her laptop in order to connect it to the hard drive. She boots up the machine then Parlabane hears a whine and a familiar purring from the HD.

'Result?' he asks hopefully.

She retains her look of concerned concentration, so he grasps that merely getting the drive to run doesn't mean she's home and dry.

'I'll know in a minute. I might need to take this elsewhere and put it through a few processes to retrieve what's on it.'

She rattles the keys, typing into a shell in an operating system that definitely didn't ship with a marketing campaign.

'Result,' she confirms.

That's when the real work begins.

'There's like a gazillion docs on this drive,' she says, as Parlabane hands her a mug of tea.

The simple civility of the act towards someone who is ruining his life seems at once natural and weird, like there are two versions of this reality and he is phasing between them. In one they are enemies, hijacker and hostage. In the other they are working together towards a common goal: friends even.

It is a fiction, however. As he leans over her to place the mug on the table, he slips his free hand inside her jacket with practised dexterity. He palms the Oyster card he saw her slip into her pocket earlier, carrying it back with him to the worktop where his own mug is waiting.

He glimpsed it before at the ticket barrier, enough to see that it was a student card with a photo and therefore a name. Now he has the chance to read it.

Sam Morpeth.

He glances back at her. She is totally immersed in what she is doing, enough for him to return the card as he passes behind her, as well as depositing a little secret something too.

'I think this came from a back-up server array,' she says. 'It's mostly accounts and admin stuff, going back years: got details of every last purchase of paper clips. Look at this shit: company policy on chewing gum. Who has a company policy on chewing gum?'

'I don't know, but I'll bet when they emailed it, they flagged it "highest priority".'

'It's going to take a while to sift through this for anything useful. That's the part they never show you when there's a hacker scene in a movie. Hard to do an exciting montage of someone pecking away at a keyboard for five hours straight, sipping Red Bull and brushing biscuit crumbs from their lap.'

'What about sorting by date?'

'Duh-uh. Obvious suggestion is obvious. I already did.'

'Okay. Then try searching for references to the abbreviation RBA,' he suggests.

'Why?'

'Because reasons. Just do it.'

She keys in the request, and the salvaged hard drive hums again.

'Two hundred and eighty results. What's RBA?'

'Exactly what you think.'

'Right Back Atcha?'

'I had a hunch it might be Cruz's codename for the project.'

'I'll ping these over to your machine for you to search through,' she says. 'I'm going to keep busy with this.'

'What should I be looking for?'

'Names of people working on the project. Job titles, departments, contact details, command structure. What jargon and terminology they're using.'

Parlabane settles down on the sofa, bracing himself for a long and tedious haul. He glances at her, patiently intent, not restive or frustrated the way he is likely to be pretty soon. He realises she was talking from personal experience when she mentioned pecking away for five hours. So much for the digital generation with their short attention spans and lack of application.

He flicks at the touchscreen, scrolling and scanning. He finds purchasing correspondence between Synergis and Optronix, the firm Cruz is considering acquiring according to the documents on his desk. It manufactures miniature laser equipment, and a quick look at its website shows that its lens technology is used in applications ranging from DVD players to holographic projection.

He notes names and details as she suggested. Large acquisitions for the R&D department mostly seem to come through Jane Dunwoodie, the shy but serious woman he met on his tour. Similar purchasing authority indicates the seniority of Will Ludemann in IT and Sanjay Singh in Security, as well as confirming Nigel Holt's position as head of Maintenance and Buildings Operations for the whole of Tricorn House.

He doesn't see anything to get excited about, which is why he is startled by Sam suddenly calling out with unguarded satisfaction.

'Yes. Wrecked.'

'What have you got?' he asks, getting up and looking over her shoulder.

'Gatekeeper Systems Europe. According to this, they're about to roll out a firmware upgrade.'

'Who are they?'

164

'Our foothold. A very big foothold.'

'How?'

'You'll find out.'

Parlabane slams her laptop closed, causing Sam to jump.

'No. Enough of the fucking teases and trails. You're like human clickbait. If you want my help, I need to know what we're doing and why we're doing it, at all times. You spell out to me very explicitly what you've got in mind, and you don't assume any knowledge just because of this "kindred spirit" bullshit, okay?'

She turns around and folds her arms. For a moment he fears she's about to go in the huff, but then she tells him to take a seat, whereupon she begins to explain her plan.

By the time she is finished, Parlabane has decided that she is quite possibly the most dangerous person he has ever met, which is saying something. Hearing her politely and plausibly lay out the means by which she intends to subvert multi-faceted state-of-the-art security systems makes him want to clear out his bank account and move to a desert island where there's no Wi-Fi.

She is inventively and resourcefully deceitful in a calmly logical way that he finds coldly unsettling, but the truly scary thing about her is that she has made him believe this job is possible.

# RESPONSIBLE BEHAVIOUR

Sam bundles up her kit in a hurry, evidently having lost track of the time.

'I've got to be somewhere,' she announces. The calm and calculating young woman has gone, and suddenly the nervous and awkward girl is back.

She leaves with such haste that Parlabane almost expects to find a golden slipper on the stairs. Not that he's anybody's Prince Charming, let alone hers. He's old enough to be her father.

He gives her a five-minute start, then heads out to follow her. She's probably halfway to the Tube station by the time he hits the street, particularly given the speed at which she walks, but he doesn't need line of sight. There is a tiny GPS tracking device in the lining of her jacket, which he secreted through a small tear he spotted while taking her Oyster card. He picked it up at the same time as he was buying those spy cameras he ended up sacrificing at Tricorn House.

He is able to track the location on another recent purchase: a second phone, one Sam doesn't know about, so that he has an uncompromised line of communications.

The signal disappears after only a few minutes. He feels a pang of concern that she has sussed his ruse already, but the more likely explanation is that she is underground. She didn't notice, but there was a receipt folded inside the SecuShred polo shirt when she handed it to him. She got them printed at a place in Ilford that morning. It's low odds she's on the District Line towards Barking.

Parlabane continues to Aldgate Tube station, where he buys a ticket and boards a train heading east. Sure enough, the signal pings back again as he reaches Bow Road. She is a couple of stops ahead.

He gets off at Barking, tracing her progress north towards Ilford.

He reckons she's still on foot but it's a tough call: between the speed she walks and the pace of the traffic, she could be on a bus.

Since she outlined her plan, and particularly since he realised it is feasible, it is all the more imperative that he gather as much information about her as he can.

He has a big decision ahead of him, one from which there is no going back. He hasn't done anything seriously illegal yet, allowing that stealing trash is a sufficiently grey area. All of his conversations with Sam can be considered hypothesis rather than conspiracy, especially if he frames it as part of an investigation to find out what she planned to do.

She is a loose cannon capable of inflicting great damage, but she is also young, she is naive and most importantly she is being manipulated by individuals far more dangerous. Parlabane still thinks the best solution is to ease her into police hands, but doing that without him ending up as collateral damage is going to be a delicate job. She is reckless, she is irresponsible and she has no grasp of the disproportionate real-world consequences of her online activities. Nor does she seem to appreciate how deep are the waters she is swimming, and what monsters lurk there. Maybe a night in the cells would be the wake-up call she needs.

He pinch-zooms on the touchscreen, noting that the signal has been stationary for a while. She is outside the Loxford School, and according to his phone, it is a couple of minutes to four: picking up time.

Parlabane keeps his distance as he approaches. It is easy to hang back and stay hidden. There are dozens of people waiting at the gates, cars double-parked all along the narrow streets nearby. He can see her talking to two people: an Asian couple.

Bang on four the bell rings and a few moments later he sees the pupils appear, the first of them emerging on wheelchairs, many heading towards waiting minibuses with hydraulic lifts attached. That's when he deduces that it is a special needs school.

He picks out Sam again, striding away from the Asian couple. There is a girl hurrying towards her, an eager smile on her face.

Parlabane gets a closer look at them both as they walk back

towards Ilford Lane, across the road from where he is standing between parked cars. He shrinks back and keeps his head down but there is little chance of being spotted. Sam is intent on listening to the girl, who is chatting away with gesticulative enthusiasm.

He recalls Sam's words in the coffee shop: *If I end up in jail, what happens to—*

She had cut herself off, and he hadn't speculated about what she left unsaid. He knows now. She means her sister. Begging the question: where are their parents?

Before she is even out of sight he has Googled 'Morpeth Loxford School Ilford'. He gets the name he is looking for – it's Lilly – but he gets a lot more besides. Beneath a few links to school and community webpages is a brief news story reporting on a Ruth Morpeth (47) of Ilford being sent down for drugs and firearms offences.

Parlabane follows the signal once more. Within half an hour he knows her address. He is filling in the blanks, but he already got the big picture outside the Loxford School. He saw the look on her face: both their faces. She loves her sister, and Sam is all Lilly has. Sam will do anything to stay out of jail, because she has to be there for the person she cares about most, and the person who is most reliant upon her.

Going to the police can't be his call. He doesn't want to be responsible for Sam ending up in custody. Even if it happened for reasons beyond his control, he knows he would feel culpable now. It's not just about her any more.

Everything has changed. The more he has found out, the more complicated it has become. Merely the fact of knowing Sam's real name has changed how he perceives her. The last vestiges of Buzzkill are gone, and now there is a real-world identity that fits this skinny, shy and vulnerable young woman.

Young girl.

She's just a kid, a kid with way too much weight on her shoulders, which is why she came to him. There is no decision to make any more. He's going to have to throw his lot in with Sam, for better or worse.

# COLLATERAL DAMAGE

'Hello, this is Samantha Morpeth. I'm trying to find out about getting some support for after-school care for my sister.'

'Financial assistance, do you mean?'

'Yes. To help pay for my sister to go to—'

'I'm sorry, that's not really my department. Let me transfer you to—'

'Please don't, please. I've been transferred about three times already and they put me through to you because they said you handled carer support.'

'Well, strictly speaking, I— Never mind. What's your name again?'

'Samantha Morpeth. My sister is Lilly Morpeth. Lillian, it would be.'

'Pulling up your records now. Ah. There's a note here about your case. Miss Morpeth, I'm afraid you're not eligible for Carer's Allowance because it says here you're in full-time education.'

'No, that's just it. I've left full-time education. I'm not at school any more. That's why I'm calling. I'm working now, but I can only do certain shifts because I need to be there to pick up my sister from school. I want to know if I can get some support to help pay for Lilly to go to an after-school club, so that I could do more hours.'

'How many hours are you working right now?'

'I've only just started, so it's not really—'

'Is it more than twenty?'

'No, not so far. In a week, do you mean?'

'Yes. I'm afraid you're not eligible for any assistance unless you are working more than twenty hours.'

'But that's why I'm calling. I can't work more than twenty hours unless I can get my sister into after-school care, and right now I can barely afford it. It would cost almost as much as I'd earn for doing the work.'

'Well, it doesn't sound like this is something I can help you with. If you like, I can transfer you to . . .'

I barely hear what she says after that. I mumble a response and hear the phone ringing but I hang up before the next person answers. It's hopeless. *I'm* hopeless.

Why am I like this when I am telling the truth? When I am forced to be me? I let them fob me off, like they're trained to do, and I fold up like wet cardboard in the face of any resistance.

It's only once Lilly's gone to bed and I've got out my laptop that I realise there's no internet. Or rather, there is, but it's only the piss-weak signal from two doors along that I've got access to. The flat below have changed their password, or more likely BT have been in and changed their router, as the old couple down there wouldn't touch the kit themselves. The good news is that this probably means they've got a fatter pipe for me to leech off, but I'm going to have to dream up a pretext for a visit tomorrow so that I can nab the password.

I'm trawling through the fruits of another dumpster dive, this time from Gatekeeper Systems. Had to tap Jack to spring for car hire because the UK headquarters is in Colchester, and it wouldn't look right if we were seen stepping off a bus. Gatekeeper's waste disposal was secure, so we did the polo shirt routine again to get access. Jack wasn't pleased to be doing more midge-raking, as he put it, and I can see how he might feel like we were actually moving further away from our goal by repeating what we had already done, and at a different outfit too. That's how it works with hacking, though: sometimes you have to take a couple of steps back so that you can move three steps forward.

I'm sipping black tea because we're almost out of milk and I want there to be enough for Lilly's cereal in the morning. My bed is covered in piles of paper, with the more manky sheets down on the carpet. This kind of stuff seemed more like fun when I was part of Uninvited. Maybe it was because it felt like I was working with friends, and we never knew what any of us might uncover or reveal the next time we all met up in IRC.

I'm lurking on there now, anonymous. I've got some channels open simply to see who's around, but not #Uninvited. I haven't been back there since Zodiac contacted me.

This time Jack brought a decent-sized shoulder bag, so we were able to heft more paperwork, though most of what I've read is useless bumf. There was a lot of shredded stuff in the dumpster, and it's often the case that if staff are switched on to security concerns, they'll only throw away complete sheets if they're sure there's nothing sensitive on there.

I'm sifting through it methodically, harvesting names, titles, departmental structures, and any on-the-job jargon that crops up. People always believe you have the right to more information if they think you're already in the know.

Then I get lucky. It's in a particularly grim pile on the carpet, which I have turned to last. I find a stack of crumpled pages all bearing wide coffee stains. Someone used the sheets to mop up a spill, then binned the lot without checking what was printed on them.

What's printed on them is just the break I need.

The sheets tell me that Gatekeeper are having contractors in to do some heavy-duty maintenance on their IT systems. They're going to be swapping out drive arrays, taking servers offline, updating operating systems, the whole shebang.

The memos warn of potential disruption, informing every department of the dates on which the work is likely to affect them. To me, the warped and coffee-stained print-outs are like an embossed invitation.

I'm starting to form a plan when I hear an alert and cast a glance at my laptop.

I tense up, my train of thought derailed with mass casualties.

Zodiac is online, inviting me to an IRC channel: #progressreport. And by inviting, obviously I mean demanding.

<Zodiac> Hello, Samantha. Long time no see. Hope the
    family are well.

171

&lt;Buzzkill&gt; What do you want?

&lt;Zodiac&gt; I trust you've been a busy girl. I hope things are progressing. I'd hate to think you were dragging your heels.

&lt;Buzzkill&gt; These things take time. You know that.

&lt;Zodiac&gt; I like to stay informed, though. So I'd appreciate it if you gave me a full breakdown of where you've got to and more importantly how you plan to proceed. I want full approval of your strategy before you execute.

&lt;Buzzkill&gt; And I want an MSI Titan laptop but I ain't getting that either. You don't get to dictate the fine terms and micro-manage this thing.

&lt;Zodiac&gt; Yes, that is exactly what I get to do. I think you're forgetting the alternative to you doing what I say, when I say it.

&lt;Buzzkill&gt; No, *you* are forgetting the alternative. You can only pull the trigger on your big threat once. If you give me up to the feds, I can't deliver on this thing you want so much.

&lt;Zodiac&gt; Don't kid yourself, love. You're not the only game in town. But you're right in that my first priority is getting what I want, so I am 'micro-managing' because I want to ensure the best chance of success. To that end I want to know how you are intending to go about this. I want a progress report, and I want to be kept up to date regularly.

I type the words 'fuck you' but my finger hovers over the Send button. I change my mind and delete it. Meanwhile my attention is drawn to an increase in activity elsewhere on the screen.

At the bottom there is a panel listing all the users active on the IRC channels right now. It's way busier than usual. You normally only see these kinds of numbers when there's an op going down. It shows how out of it I've been lately that I don't even know what's in the wind.

Zodiac is waiting for my obedient reply, and must be entertaining doubts as to whether it's coming.

172

&lt;Zodiac&gt; Remember that when this is over, you will want to
    remain on the right side of me. You will want to remain of
    value. If it would help for you to see what happens when
    someone proves they are no longer of use, then I
    suggest you turn on the news.

He sends me a link which takes me to a video feed on the BBC website. The banner at the foot of the frame states: 'Liverpool – Police make first arrest in RSGN hacking investigation.'

I see a scared-looking white guy around my age being led away in handcuffs, plain-clothes detectives either side as they march him down a gauntlet of officers wearing Kevlar and holding SMGs. Like us hax0rs are known for being tooled up with anything that doesn't run Linux. It's total overkill, purely for the cameras.

This is why everybody's on IRC. Bad news travels fast, especially online.

It's a running joke to post 'Feds at the door' when you are about to pop out of the room during a chat. I'm guessing nobody's laughing right now.

'Police have named the suspect as Paul Wiley, a twenty-two-year-old postgraduate student at Liverpool University,' says the reporter on the screen.

At once I'm sure this guy is Cicatrix. I picked up on hints that he lived up north.

He was the one who bailed out of our meeting. I wonder if he had already met with Stonefish when he got cold feet about a second rendezvous. Maybe he was intending to warn me but, like me right now, had no way of knowing who could be trusted. Guess I'll never know.

Zodiac decides I've had time enough to take it in.

&lt;Zodiac&gt; You're not the only member of Uninvited I've got
    the goods on. That one wouldn't play nice. Tried to hack
    me, the cheeky skrub. He forgot I was the one holding all
    the high cards. So, about this progress report . . .

I write out a text document describing how I intend to pull off the Synergis job, and the whole time there's a voice in my head saying, 'Lol. Yeah, right. As if.'

I keep Jack out of the story. Zodiac doesn't know about him, and that gives me some kind of edge; or at least some kind of comfort.

I consider how, given more time to play with, I could embed some malware in the next one of these docs I write: a Trojan that might help lead me to Zodiac's location or harvest some clue to his identity. Then I think of the fact that this poor bastard Paul Wiley must have pulled something similar and got caught.

It's as I'm blocking out my strategy for hitting Gatekeeper that two things hit me, neither of them good. The first is that by writing out this plan I'm basically giving Zodiac a signed confession up front. The second, and deffo the scarier one, is that what I've got in mind for Gatekeeper will require me personally to carry it out.

I had mentally assigned Jack the same field-ops role as I'll require of him when we hit Synergis, but looking at the Gatekeeper strategy written down, I realise he doesn't have the technical know-how. I could walk him through most of it in advance, but if anything happens that I don't expect, we're humped. And something *always* happens that you don't expect.

I lie awake, listening to drunks meander home, hearing sirens in the distance.

How am I supposed to do this?

I can't, I conclude.

I think of the call I made to the Social earlier on. If I can't even stand up for myself in a telephone conversation when I've every right to state my case, how am I going to handle myself face-to-face inside a building I've got no right to even enter?

Then I remember that I stand up for myself in telephone conversations all the time, in the very act of infiltrating places I'm not supposed to be. Throughout all those pre-hack calls, some of which can get really knife-edge as they threaten to go south, I always hold my nerve. I lie, improvise and manipulate instinctively, no matter who I'm talking to, so what's different about that? I ask myself.

That's when it hits me: it's not about phone calls versus face-to-face. It's about acting a part versus being myself. I'm never scared of what they might do or say as long as they think I'm someone else.

So when I hit Gatekeeper, I won't be Sam Morpeth. I'll be Buzzkill, unleashed IRL.

# HANDS-ON POLICY

It takes Parlabane minutes to search the people on the list he snapped on Cruz's secretary's desk, and to distinguish them from namesakes. In most instances this is achieved via personnel listings on tech-industry companies' websites, but in the case of the one he got the longest look at, Google Images does the trick. As soon as he keys in the name 'Danny Winter', that angry-gargoyle mug leaps out from the resultant grid of headshots like it's trying to bite him.

What proves more taxing is the job of nailing down what it is Winter actually does. His name pops up all over the industry and beyond, on the boards of several companies and in other elusively non-specific roles. Deeper digging establishes that he fronts a venture capitalist company with connections to an offshore hedge fund, though his specific relationship to the latter proves obstinately obscure.

Like Cruz, he has a reputation as an asset stripper, though his involvement with the hedge fund seems more oriented around invest-ment opportunities than fire sales. Unlike Cruz, it would appear he prefers the shadows to the limelight.

The closest he comes to high-profile involvement is his recent investment in a hi-fi company. Metal Box Audio was once a brand leader through its prestigious CD players, but with most people choosing to buy, store or stream their music online, the format has been rendered redundant. As a long-time print journalist, Parlabane can sympathise.

Metal Box opted belatedly to move with the times and manu-facture its own music streaming systems, but by that time it was heavily in debt, just when it needed to invest in new equipment, new expertise and new marketing strategies. This was when Winter stepped in.

'He was able to take a big slice of the company at that time, because we urgently needed investment or we were going to fold.'

Parlabane gets this from Agnieszka Savic, Metal Box's marketing director, who invites him to take a tour of their factory in Braintree. The cachet of the *Broadwave* brand seems to make people more eager to talk than Parlabane has been used to recently; though maybe it's also a sign that his own name is less toxic, largely through fading from notice.

Parlabane initially requested an interview with Winter. Savic sounded pessimistic regarding the chances of this, and Parlabane detected that she was reluctant to even ask. Thus she suggested the factory tour by way of compromise, adding that Winter would be on-site that day, so they might be able to improvise a quick chat.

'It will look like he got us for a song if we continue to grow the way we've been doing over the past three financial quarters,' Agnieszka tells him. 'But nobody else was offering to take the risk. We never lose sight of that.'

Parlabane acknowledges the gratitude but it's hard to miss the subtext. There must be times when 'never losing sight of that' seems particularly difficult.

'I've read some criticism of the firm's status as a British brand,' Parlabane suggests. 'Your critics say that you import all of your components from overseas and merely assemble the units here in the UK. Their beef seems to be that you still get certain grants and benefits as a British manufacturer.'

Agnieszka meets it with a shrug.

'It's the nature of the business these days. At this stage there's no economy of scale to manufacturing certain components ourselves. That said, Danny has intimated that this is something he might be able to remedy in the near future, though he hasn't given us any details.'

Parlabane thinks instantly of the Chinese facility owned by Synergis for manufacturing its generic handsets. Is that what Winter really has his eyes on?

The tour complete, she leads him to what looks like a small lecture theatre, its walls sound-proofed with thick foam in an endless tessellation of spikes and curves. There are speakers positioned all over the place: some floor-standing, some on plinths, some embedded in the walls and ceiling. This must be where they demonstrate the product, but today it's being used for a strategy seminar, which Winter is attending.

By the time he strides in, about ten minutes late, there are roughly thirty people seated around the auditorium, the company's forthcoming new model represented both in physical form at the front and in exploded view on a projector screen. Winter barely glances at the waiting assembly, and if he even notices Parlabane, he doesn't give any indication of recognising him, or of having any questions over his being here. Parlabane guesses he isn't sufficiently familiar with the personnel to have any expectations of who ought or ought not to be present.

Metal Box founder Craig Elder, something of a legend in British hi-fi design, kicks things off by delivering a presentation on the company's new music streaming system.

His talk is very techy, not a primer for a future marketing pitch, though the end user is clearly seldom far from his thoughts. Parlabane watches Winter to see what he is making of it all. He sits on the far right of the front row sporting a scowly and brow-furrowed expression, one that Parlabane initially interprets as intense concentration but which turns out to be growing disquiet.

He suddenly cuts Elder off, holding his hand out like a traffic cop while loudly saying: 'Woah. Woah. Woah. Woah. Woah.'

Elder stops and looks towards Winter. The room has descended into silence, one all the more profound from the effects of the sound insulation. There is a long, unnerving couple of seconds of this before Winter speaks again: one more word.

'Woah.'

Parlabane learns a great deal in that single moment. It's that superfluous sixth *woah* that says 'arsehole' louder than any sound that's ever been blasted from the speakers in this room.

'This is not what was agreed when I was here six weeks ago.'

'There have been a few refinements, certainly, but the overall—'

'Stop. Stop. Stop. Stop.'

Winter gets to his feet. It's a weird dynamic: he is addressing

Elder as though they are the only ones in the room, and yet Parlabane reckons Winter is only too aware this is in front of an audience.

'Why was the design altered from the one I signed off on?'

'It's hardly a fundamental alteration. When we built the prototype, we discovered that—'

'Look, I don't want to hear it, it's pointless. You'll say what you believe, I'll say what I believe and by sheer force of personality, I'll win, so why don't we save ourselves the bother and cut to that part?'

*King* arsehole.

When the show is over, Parlabane files out with the rest of the audience, Winter remaining behind for some one-on-one time with Elder, like Jack witnessed with him and Cruz.

Out in the foyer, Parlabane is expecting a little more awkwardness from Agnieszka due to having witnessed this. Instead she gives him a rather knowing smile, which is when he realises part of the reason she invited him today was that she wanted him to see something like this.

'He's got a very hands-on style,' Parlabane suggests.

'He's a complex individual,' is her diplomatic response.

'How will you handle it?'

'The usual. We'll tell him what he wants to hear and then carry on as we planned. He likes to come in and micro-manage, then you don't see him for weeks, but when he comes back he forgets everything he was so insistent about the last time and starts demanding other stuff.'

He spots Winter emerging from the lecture theatre and quickly ascertains that he has Agnieszka's consent to buttonhole him here.

Parlabane intercepts him close to the double doors from the foyer into a corridor leading to the main stairs.

'Mr Winter? I'm Jack Parlabane, from *Broadwave*. I was wondering if I could grab you for a quick chat.'

He can tell Winter is about to brush him off, but then something flickers in his face, and he needs a moment to process it.

'Do I know you from somewhere?'

His tone is accusatory rather than curious. He is making no attempt to be charming, and Parlabane isn't sure he would know how even if the notion occurred to him.

179

Parlabane takes advantage of briefly having the floor, effectively answering Winter's question with a couple of his own.

'Can you tell me about your involvement in Synergis? Are you looking to expand your interest?'

There's been an update behind his eyes. Back at Synergis, Winter couldn't have been pleased that someone had witnessed that little moment between him and Cruz. He is even less pleased that the witness has pitched up in front of him again.

'I can't talk about Synergis. I would be in violation of a non-disclosure agreement even if I were to confirm any involvement with the company.'

Parlabane suppresses a wry smile at the inevitable mention of an NDA. Any time he hears this excuse he is reminded of a kid saying 'Keys up!' while playing tig or hide-and-seek. To the speaker it's an invisible force-field nobody can penetrate, but to everyone else he just looks like a fanny who won't play the game.

'Off the record then, are you surprised that Leo Cruz is looking to grow the company when everyone assumed he was planning to break it up? Did you have designs on acquiring it yourself before he stepped in?'

Winter once more seems like he is about to blank him and walk away, but he appears to think better of it. Parlabane recognises the look: Winter is wondering if he might be the one who has something to learn from the encounter.

'I can talk to you off the record, but only as long as I know it really is off the record.'

'You have my word.'

'Which is worth considerably less than me knowing for sure that you don't have any hidden microphones, mobiles, body cameras, bugs or anything else stashed away. Ditch your jacket and your shoulder bag. You can leave them in the foyer. Then we're going to go some-where you can turn out your pockets and show me there's nothing under your shirt.'

'If that's what it takes.'

'That's what it takes. Follow me.'

Parlabane follows Winter out into the corridor, but instead of heading for the stairs, he is led around a corner into a narrow passage towards a fire exit.

'All right, pull up your shirt,' Winter says.

Parlabane complies, revealing that he has nothing concealed beneath.

With Parlabane's hands still gripping his shirt, Winter drives a fist into his midriff, winding him and lifting him off the floor. Less than a second later, Winter is behind him, slamming his face against the wall and bending an arm up his back.

He speaks right into Parlabane's ear, quiet but threatening.

'Who the fuck are you?'

'I'm Jack Parlabane,' he manages to splutter, his guts demanding he bend over for relief but Winter's hands pinning him upright. There is a proficiency about his violence. He is powerful and fast, with the speed and balance of a boxer.

'I'm with *Broadwave*.'

'I don't care who you're *with*. It's where you are and where you've been that bothers me. Leo Cruz might enjoy acting the showman, but I don't appreciate having cunts like you looking into my business.'

He sends a sharp, controlled blow into Parlabane's side, below the ribs. The pain is phenomenal.

'I see your fucking face again, I'll leave it so you can't look in the mirror without feeling sick. Do you hear me?'

Parlabane gasps enough breath to whisper a faint reply.

'Loud and clear.'

Winter strides away, leaving Parlabane doubled over. He needs a while before he can go back out where he'll be seen. He guesses he's looking pale and conspicuously shocked, not to mention shaking. He just wants to grab his stuff and get out of here, whereupon he will take great pains to comply with Winter's demand.

The fucker definitely isn't going to see Parlabane's face again. But that doesn't mean he won't be there.

# COVERT SURVEILLANCE

'I think I've met our prime suspect,' Parlabane says, filling Sam in on his encounter at Metal Box.

He's been trying to phone her for an hour. She apologises for all the missed calls, saying she had switched her mobile to silent at the cinema and forgot to reset it. He knows this isn't true. She had it on silent because she's at work, in a sandwich bar in Ilford. She still hasn't discovered the tracking device.

He wonders why she's lying. He knows she's struggling for money, but she clearly thinks there is some kind of shame attached to her work. He's still finding it tough to reconcile the cyber-menace whose felicitations have so terrified him in recent years with this shy and anxious young woman; the cocky and ostentatious hacktivist with someone knuckling under in a McJob in order to look after her vulnerable younger sister. He guesses there is only one side of her that she ever wants him to see.

'You reckon this guy could be Zodiac?'

'I'm not sure. But he's got claws in Synergis and he stands to gain if they suffer a loss. If their prototype plans get stolen, it would surely make the other investors less sure about seeing a long-term return.'

'We need to get up in his business,' she states.

It sounds less like a suggestion than a vow.

'Agreed. But we need to keep our distance. He already knows my face, and if he really is Zodiac, then he knows yours too. Any suggestions?'

'I'll need to give it some thought. First thing to come to mind is a Teensy HID, but I'm not sure that's an option.'

'Why not? What is it?'

'Teensy is a microcontroller system that you can use to program

182

a hidden internal device. The idea is you put one inside a peripheral that plugs into a computer: a keyboard or a mouse, for instance. Trojan horse principle, except you're using hardware to deliver the software.'

'So what's the problem?'

'It's not something you can pick up at Maplin's. I know one or two potential sources, but I can't trust them any more. So unless you happen to know a shit-hot electronics engineer who can be relied upon to keep his mouth shut, then like I said, it's not an option.'

Parlabane allows himself a smile, thinking of an electronics engineer in Paisley whose discretion can be guaranteed, not least because opening his mouth to talk to somebody would constitute unnecessary effort.

'Tell me what you need.'

# FILE TRANSFER PROTOCOL

I see from the clock that it's after half one. Urban Picnic has been going like a fair since before twelve, and I'm starting to worry that I'll miss my window. I had a break around half eleven, which was when I saw all the missed calls from Jack. I nipped outside to talk to him, partly so nobody could earwig, but also so Jack couldn't get a sense of where I was phoning from.

My problem is I need to make this next call during lunchtime, when there is a greater chance that the person I'm asking for will be out of the office.

Yeah, I know that sounds wrong, but bear with me.

There's enough of a lull around 1.40, and I indicate to the boss that I'm desperate for the toilet. She gives me the nod, gesturing with two fingers how many minutes I've got.

More than I'll need.

I close the door and take out my mobile.

'Good afternoon, Gatekeeper Systems, how can I help?'

I ask for David Frew, the bloke who issued the coffee-stained memo regarding the major systems upgrade that Gatekeeper have got scheduled for tomorrow.

'I'm afraid Mr Frew is on his lunch at the moment. Can I take a message?'

'No, that won't be necessary. I'm calling from Data Stream. I just wanted to confirm with David that everything is still set for our team coming in to work on your servers tomorrow.'

'Yes, totally. We're expecting you around ten, is that right?'

'Ten, absolutely. Looking forward to it.'

I have to drop Lilly at the school early so that Jack can pick me up and get us to Gatekeeper HQ in Colchester before the Data Stream

184

people get there. I get a bit short with her because she's dragging her heels. She doesn't understand why she's got to be ready half an hour earlier than usual, and she hates any disruption to her normal routine. She looks a bit huffy when I leave her at the gate, which makes me feel like shit.

I don't say much on the drive. I'm psyching myself up, as well as revising the info in my head: names and positions of people both at Gatekeeper and at Data Stream. I've been researching this for days, but you can never be sure it's enough.

As we pull into the car park, my guts are like jelly and I need to pee. All I can think about is Paul Wiley getting led away in handcuffs. I'm worried about what the cops might be finding out from him, what dots they could be joining. I picture them appearing outside our flat with their battering rams and their machine guns, imagine how scared Lilly would be. She'd have nightmares for ever.

We watch the Data Stream people arrive. I count seven of them. I'd have preferred more but the building is big enough that every face isn't going to be known to everybody else. My invisibility cloak here is that the Data Stream people are going to assume I'm with Gatekeeper, and the Gatekeeper people are going to assume I'm with Data Stream.

We give it half an hour after the visitors are inside, then it's time. I'm armed with two manila folders, a clipboard, a laptop and a lanyard displaying an ID I faked up last night, the Data Stream logo prominently displayed above my mug shot.

'You okay?' Jack asks as I open the car door. 'You want to test the blind speed dial one more time?'

'No, I got it. Just make sure you've got the right MP3 cued up in case of emergency.'

As I walk towards the building's front entrance I force myself to think about the *Teen Titans* episode I watched with Lilly last night. My instinct is to rehearse my lines in my head, but I suspect that's only going to make it more likely I'll trip over them. I picture Raven glowering at Robin; I can even see the scratch on the right-hand side of the reclaimed laptop's display.

There is a barrier system to the right of the reception desk, which staff can open with a swipe of their IDs. Visitors need to be buzzed through.

I walk towards the barrier briskly, hugging the clipboard and folders to my chest with my left arm, the laptop bag slung over my shoulder. At the last second I hold up the lanyard with my free right hand and turn to face the woman at the desk.

'Can you buzz me back in? I'm with Data Stream. I had to nip out to fetch something from my car.'

'Yeah, on you go.'

She barely looks at me, simply hits a button and the glass panels of the barrier slide apart. The irony of Gatekeeper's core business is not lost on me. They manufacture state-of-the-art controlled-entry barrier systems, so that unauthorised randoms can't simply walk in the front door.

I'm so read up on Gatekeeper at this point, they could be my specialist subject on *Mastermind*. The system they've installed at Tricorn House is top of the range, controlling not only the barriers at the main entrance, but the lifts and the doors to various restricted sectors of the building. It is operated using a program called GEM: Gatekeeper Entry Management.

Each client uses a tailor-made release of the software, identified by a code and an account number. Thanks to the hard disk we got from our first dumpster dive, I've got both for Tricorn House. I'm not here only to snag a copy of their unique version of GEM, however. I'm after the source code, and some nice person is going to give it to me, because I'm going to ask in precisely the right way.

I take off the Data Stream lanyard once I'm past the front desk. My heart is hammering but though I'm scared, I'm also recognising the upside of this sensation: it's like the buzz from a hack, except supercharged.

Hackers on steroids.

I explore the building, catching the occasional glance but rarely a second one. The other thing making me invisible is the clipboard. Whenever I pause to look at anything, be it an office, an individual computer screen or a group of people, I take notes. This was Jack's idea.

'Nobody will ask you anything because as soon as they see the clipboard they'll instantly be hoping you don't come over and ask *them* anything.'

So far it's working very well in terms of reducing eye contact. Nobody wants to be bothered while they're trying to get on with their work.

I watch several of the Data Stream people gathered around a server stack. I write down names, cross-referring with the lists I gleaned online. I identify Angela Pike and Ian Nelson, two of the senior IT staff at Gatekeeper. The former is working very closely with the Data Stream visitors, while the latter appears to be minding the store, keeping an eye on the everyday running of the network systems.

I locate the account manager named on the documentation we got from our dumpster dive. His name is Derek Travers and he is Gatekeeper's primary liaison with Tricorn House. He sits at a cluster of four desks in the Sales and Customer Care department.

I need to get Derek to trust me, and the best way to make that happen is to have him be the one who calls *me* for help.

I sweep the corridors looking for a discreet spot to base myself. I was hoping for an empty desk somewhere but I actually find an empty office. I'm not sure this is for the best, and I wonder if I should keep looking. My head tells me that hiding in plain sight would be better: sitting openly in view of other staff, all of them assuming I'm supposed to be there, rather than hiding myself away. My gut tells me that privacy is always preferable when you're up to no good, and I'm not sure my nerves can take the plain sight option.

I slip into the office and close the door, noting the name outside: Sophie Oswald, Head of Marketing. I get out my secondary mobile, an old crappy effort with a pay-as-you-go SIM. My proper phone remains in my hip pocket. I call the building's main number, which gets me through to the switchboard.

'Oh, hi, I've been calling Sophie Oswald and I keep getting bounced to voicemail. Do you know if she's definitely in today?'

'I'll just find out for you.'

I am put on hold for a couple of minutes. I hear a phone ring in a nearby room.

The receptionist comes back on.

'Hello? I'm sorry, Sophie's out of the office today. She'll be back in tomorrow. Can I take a message?'

'No, it's nothing urgent. I'll call back then.'

Result.

I lift the handset on Sophie's desk and make a quick call to Jack, then I dial Derek Travers's extension. He picks up on the second ring.

'Oh, hi, Derek, this is Jen from Data Stream. I'm working on the big server refit and I want to check that your computer's okay and you're still connected to the network.'

'As far as I can see, yes. No problems to report.'

I blow out an exaggerated sigh, sounding relieved but a little flustered.

'Thank God for that. We're having some major issues here and I thought your whole sector might have gone down. You're on port 3847, aren't you?' I ask, plucking the number out of the air.

'I wouldn't have a clue, to be honest.'

Good to know.

'Do you mind checking for me?'

'Sure, long as you can tell me where to find it.'

'If you have a look around the back of your PC, where the Ethernet cable plugs in, there should be . . .'

'There's a sticker, yeah. It says port 4751.'

I write down this vital piece of information on my clipboard.

'Well, that explains why you haven't been affected by any outages yet,' I reply with a chuckle.

'Am I likely to be?'

'I honestly couldn't say for sure. But tell you what, if your connectivity goes down, call me right away and I'll get straight on it.'

I give him the number of my burner mobile. I make him read it back to me, and he obliges.

'Fingers crossed you won't need it,' I tell him.

I take my laptop out of the bag and connect it to the local network using the cable I have just unplugged from the back of Sophie Oswald's computer.

Next I call Ian Nelson, the senior Gatekeeper IT guy who's *not* working with the Data Stream crew.

'Is that Ian?'

'Yes. How can I help?'

'It's Jenny from Data Stream. Sorry to bother you, but Angela's got her hands full and she said you would oblige. We're trying to isolate a glitch here. Could you shut off the connection to port 4751 for us please, for five minutes?'

'No problem. Do you want to call me when you want it back up? Or can I suspend it on a timer?'

'Timer's fine. Give it five minutes.'

'Okay. Shutting it off now.'

'Cheers.'

Then I wait for my burner to ring. It takes about thirty seconds.

'Hi, is that Jen? Derek again. My computer just went down. Well, not the whole thing, but I've lost network access.'

'Sorry, Derek. It's like pushing down bubbles in wallpaper today. No sooner have we fixed one outage than another problem springs up elsewhere.'

I keep him talking while I tap away at the keyboard in front of me, even though the PC it's connected to isn't switched on. I 'try' a few things then ask him to report the results, my series of failures intended to increase his concerns about how long he's going to be basically paralysed. This ramps up the corresponding relief and gratitude when my stopwatch approaches five minutes and I tell him: 'Wait, I think I've isolated the issue. Yep, here we go. Give it a try now.'

'You're a life-saver,' he reports. 'Thank you.'

And now comes the clever part.

'Don't thank me yet. I'm afraid we're not quite out of the woods. Looks like the outage was caused by a server crash at this end during a routine back-up. I'm running an integrity check on the files to make sure we haven't lost any data.'

'I'm sorry, what does that all mean in English?'

'Hopefully nothing, but I'm making sure no files have been lost. So far it's all okay, yep, good, good, good. Seventy per cent. Eighty per cent. Still all fine. Ninety . . . damn.'

'What?'

'We've got one file irreparably corrupted.'

'Irreparably? You mean it's gone? What was it?'

'No, not gone. This is the back-up server. The original should still be safe. But the problem is that right this second it's the only copy, so we need to back it up immediately in case anything else goes wrong.'

'Absolutely. How do I do that? Which file is it?'

'It's called GEM256SY66-SC, from a directory called GEM-SC. Is that important, or can we . . .'

'Christ, yes, that's important: that's really important. It's the source code version of the management system for a major account. How do I back it up?'

'Well, the automated back-up system is down because everything's haywire. The simplest way would be for you to send it to me and I can install it on to one of the new servers right away. Can you access the file okay at your end?'

'Yes, I'm looking at it right now. I'm attaching it to an email. What's your address? Oh, no, hang on, it's not letting me—'

'That's because you shouldn't be emailing source code to an offsite address, even though technically I'd be picking up the email from inside your building.'

It never hurts your trustworthiness when you're the one telling them not to do anything that might compromise their security protocols.

'So what do I do?'

I talk him through it, telling him how to call up a map of all the computers connected to his internal network. I've renamed my laptop to appear as 'DataStreamJen', and I tell him to look for that.

'Okay, found it. What now?'

'A simple matter of copy and paste.'

'Doing it right away.'

I see the transfer begin, and check that it's the right file. It's almost a gigabyte, so it's going to take a minute.

'Is it coming through okay?'

'Yes. But don't shut down anything at your end until it's complete.'

'I won't. I really can't thank you enough.'

'Please, don't mention it.'

To anybody. Ever.

The transfer completes and I disconnect the cable.

I have just plugged it back into Sophie Oswald's PC when the office door opens and a woman blocks the doorway, a suspicious look on her face. She knows this room is supposed to be empty. Knackers. Should have gone with the hide-in-plain-sight strategy.

'Who are you? What are you doing in this office?'

She looks like every school teacher I never liked: someone who lives for catching people out of line. I can tell she'd be disappointed to learn everything was in order.

'I'm just finishing up,' I say, closing the laptop, which is still showing the folder containing my stolen GEM source code file. 'I'm with Data Stream.'

'Can I see your visitor pass?'

I hold up the lanyard, but she barely looks at it.

'No, not your ID, your visitor pass, issued by the front desk.'

Uh-oh.

'I think I left it downstairs in the Accounts department. I've been moving around a lot, working on different systems.'

My hand reaches into my hip pocket, my fingers fumbling for the switch. Bugger. When I practised this I wasn't trembling.

'I'm calling Security.'

Fuck. She's lifting the handset, tying up the line.

'Hello, Security? Yes, this is Gillian Windham in Marketing. Can you come up to Sophie Oswald's office immediately.'

With her standing by the desk, away from the doorway, I think about doing a runner, but I know that would blow everything. Even if I was to get past the security guard who's already on his way up here, and make it out to the car park, it would alert them that there has been a breach. I have to stay calm, hold my nerve and wait.

I glance at the phone on the desk.

'Look, I'm done here,' I say, trying to keep the panic from my

191

voice. I'm pitching for pissed off, like this is an inconvenience I can do without. 'I can go and get the pass if you like, but I'm actually—'

'We'll go and get it together: all three of us.'

I glance again towards the phone. I'm aware she might notice, but I can't help it.

I can hear heavy footsteps in the corridor, growing nearer, moving swiftly.

I'm seconds from this whole thing crashing down upon me.

The security guard appears in the doorway, brows knitted together quizzically, game face on.

Before he can ask what this is all about, the phone rings.

I move to pick it up. I've no intention of doing so: I'm just prompting Scowlychops Bitchface to intervene rather than let it ring out on the assumption that it's for her absent colleague. If it goes to voicemail I'm fuxored.

She answers.

'Hello, Sophie Oswald's office?'

She fixes me with a look that says 'Don't you even think of going anywhere' as she listens to the caller. The security guard remains in the doorway, silently awaiting his instructions. I try not to look scared, but each passing second makes it harder.

Then her expression becomes a twisted mix of confusion and then disappointment.

I try to mask my relief as much as I masked my fear.

Jack is on the other end, giving her the script. In the quiet of the office I can just about hear his side of the conversation, and I'm guessing so can the guard. What I can't hear, but Gillian definitely must, is the hire car's stereo playing office background noise.

'Yeah, this is Mark Ferguson at Data Stream,' Jack tells her. 'Is Jen Webster still there? Only, she's left her visitor pass down here in Customer Accounts.'

'Yes, she's still here.'

Nicely improvised, I think. The line has been open on my mobile since I speed-dialled him and he's been listening carefully.

Gillian hands me the phone as the guard asks her why she summoned him.

'It's nothing,' she replies irritably. 'Never mind.'

'Sorry about the delay,' Jack says very quietly. 'Receptionist must have been busy. Took ages to answer and transfer me to the right extension.'

'No, thanks for letting me know, Mark. I was about to fetch something from my car too, so I'd have had to call you and get you to bring my pass out to the front desk.'

I keep talking well after the guard has departed, wittering on about technical stuff, dropping in names of individuals and departments. Gillian hangs around, wanting the satisfaction of at least seeing me vacate her colleague's office, but nobody escorts me anywhere.

A minute and a half later I am climbing into the hire car, its engine already running.

'We good?' Jack asks.

I nod and he reverses out of the space then proceeds at an easy pace towards the exit.

Once we are out of sight of the building, I ask him to pull over, which is when I open the passenger door and throw up.

# SINS OF THE PAST

I am walking through the gates of the prison again, wondering if the next time I do this I won't have the option to leave.

Last time I was here, I brought Lilly because it was a Saturday. She was delighted at first but distraught afterwards, as I knew she would be. It was almost a fortnight ago and I haven't been back since.

I tell myself I refuse to feel guilty about that, but I still do. I've been making excuses, saying I can't visit because of work. This hasn't always been true (at least in terms of Urban Picnic – though my other 'job' has been keeping me plenty busy too). There were times I could have squeezed in a visit, but I chose not to: partly because I want to drive the point home about the situation Mum has put me in, and partly because I'm still so angry with her. I'm angry about her landing herself in here and I'm angry about everything that happened before, all the things she did that ultimately led to this.

Despite all that, I feel a desperate need to see her, in case . . . I don't know what. I don't want to name what. I just need to see her, even though she can't help me.

I wish I could tell her all my problems, pour my heart out about what I'm afraid of, what I'm mixed up in. I wish she could protect me, put her arms around me and tell me everything's going to be all right.

I wish Dad was still here. I wish I was still living in that house we had in Newcastle.

Dad was an IT consultant, and his home town was the one time he had a contract that kept us in the same place for a few years. Mum had a permanent job then too, before having to become an agency nurse.

I was nine years old. I got a computer for Christmas. Dad installed a game called *Ultimate Spider-Man*. I played it while Lilly sat on

Mum's lap and watched, shouting out in delight as she urged me what to do next.

I'll never forget that look of wonder and excitement on her face. It was as though the comic strip world had come to life and I was some kind of god to her for being able to grant her wishes in making Spider-Man do what she asked.

We were all huddled around that monitor, the four of us sharing something joyful. We were a family.

Then a little later, while Mum was cooking the turkey, Dad showed me how to use a command shell.

Mum walks into the visiting room, dressed again in shapeless joggers and that horrible faded blue T-shirt. She looks tired, but her face brightens when she sees me. She opens her arms to offer a hug. The huffy part of me wants to keep my distance, but I need this too much. I hold her tight and just about manage not to cry.

'I've missed you,' I say, pressing my face into her shoulder.

'I've missed you too, girl.'

She draws back and looks at me.

'Is something wrong?'

I take a seat, wiping my nose with a piece of toilet roll from my pocket. Don't have the money for proper tissues these days.

'Everything's wrong, Mum.'

She has this startled rabbit look, the worst fears running through her mind.

'Is Lilly okay?'

'Lilly's fine,' I reassure her, and it's as I do so that I realise she didn't ask about Lilly first, or query again why I haven't brought her.

'I'll bring her to see you again soon,' I promise. It comes out before I can think about it.

'Has something happened, Sam? You all right for money?'

I can't hide the fact that I'm a mess about something, but neither can I confess what's really wrong. To give myself cover I tell her about Lush coming around to take the TV and DVD player, and about Ango and Griff strong-arming me at the cash machine.

Her mouth is hanging like someone switched off the power to her jaw.

195

'They took our TV? Was Lilly there?'

'No, she was at school, thank God.'

'What about her cartoons?'

'I've sorted something out, for now. A portable thing that someone threw out. I knew how to fix it up.'

She gives me a warning glare.

'A laptop?'

'No,' I lie.

She looks exasperated.

'And you just . . . Why didn't you do anything?'

'Like what?'

'You could have called the cops, for one thing. Or at least threatened to. There's more than one way to stand up for yourself.'

'Call the cops? And say what? Help, officer, I'm being ripped off by drug dealers claiming back the money my mum owes them. You may remember my mum: she's in jail for owning a firearm and possession with intent to supply.'

She has an expression like thunderclouds forming on the horizon. It's not the standard indignation though, which is usually about deflection. This is something else, something deeper.

She speaks slowly and quietly, like she's determined there should be no mistake about what she has to say.

'I don't fucking owe them money. I've had dealings with Lush, but we were square.'

The way she's staring at me, I know she's telling the truth. I realise I've been had. They knew she was inside. They knew I was vulnerable, and they knew there would be no come-backs.

'They're locusts,' she says, her voice trembling with anger. 'Christ, Sam, how could you just let them into our home?'

'What else was I gonna do? Fight them off? You're the one who brought them into our *lives*. You're the one who's left Lilly and me wide open to the likes of Lush because you're in here for being no better than him.'

I went in a bit harder than maybe I ought there, but I am furious. She looks wounded, angst-ridden now.

'That's not true, Sam. I told you, girl: I was set up. Those drugs were planted, and I would never touch a gun, let alone have one in the house with you and Lilly.'

I can't hear this.

'Oh, for God's sake, Mum. How long, eh? When are you gonna take responsibility for yourself?'

Her eyes are wide and red now, angry and sad at the same time. It would be affecting if I hadn't seen the show before.

'All I've known is responsibility. You don't know what it is to be bringing up two kids, and one of them . . . one of them with what Lilly's got. It was hard enough when Neville was around, but I lost him: my world revolved around that man and I lost him. You don't know what that's like.'

'We all lost him, Mum. You act like it only happened to you, but we all lost Dad. That's what you forgot when you let yourself disappear into drink and drugs and self-pity. You lost him, Lilly lost him, and I lost him too.'

'Yeah, then you should know that we can all do things that are selfish and irresponsible when we're feeling messed up. It wasn't what *I* did that meant we ended up banned from having an internet connection in our house.'

'Jesus, Mum, I was fifteen. You can't judge me like—'

'I'm not judging you, Sam. I never did. I'm asking you not to judge me.'

Her voice is soft now, her tone pleading.

I swallow back tears, reach a hand across to hold hers.

Yes, I was fifteen when I did what I did, but I'm not fifteen now. I think about all that I've hidden from her in the years since, and I don't just mean my hacking. I mean even owning a laptop. That's the main reason I keep it hidden. And for all I get on my high horse about the times she was out of it on drink or other things, the guilty part of me knows that I was often happy to see her like that, because I knew it meant I had time to get busy with no chance of her coming in and finding me at it. No need for me to be listening out, ready to slam my secret laptop closed and hide it under the covers.

I've always told myself I retreated into my online world because my mum was retreating into her own world of self-indulgence, but

197

these things are never that simple, are they? It was like how she blamed Dad for getting me interested in computers. That was true, but it took both of them to make me a hacker. Dad only taught me about programming machines. She was the one who taught me you can program people.

All girls, all kids, see their dads as the fun parent if it's their mum who's waiting at home for them when they come in from school, dealing with the everyday needs. Dad comes home from work later and scores all these unearned points just for showing up. It's not fair, but it's the truth.

Mum wanted to be fun too, and I think she wanted me to see her in other ways. She also wanted there to be something only between us that wasn't about Dad, or about Lilly. So she liked to show off to me. She knew clever ways of manipulating people: tricks to get them to tell her things they shouldn't. She knew dodges that let us skip the queue; strategies to get discounts she wasn't entitled to.

God, how close we felt when she did these things. Each one was a precious secret we shared: us and only us. I was less amazed by what she blagged than by the artfulness, the invention. It wasn't what she got, but how she got it. Sometimes it was subtle, sometimes a matter of bamboozling the target, and all of it relied on being tuned into emotions, reading the tiny signs that told you what people were thinking, how they were feeling.

The other side of this was that Mum was an expert in hiding those things when it came to herself.

Dad would talk all the time about his childhood, his college years, places he'd lived, crazy friends he had known. I always felt so close to him because of how much he shared. I felt like I was a product of that, of everything that had happened to him. Even after I found out he wasn't my biological father, I never felt like there was this asterisk over his status. I still felt shaped by him and by the life he led, unquestionably his daughter.

As for Mum, it was as though she didn't exist before she met Neville, as there was so much she wouldn't talk about. I was in my early teens before I realised I had never heard her say a word about her own childhood. I learned that she had been brought up in various care homes, but she wouldn't volunteer anything about her experiences. I know that's why she is so adamant that Lilly should never end up in state care, and why she went so mental when I had my own little problem back when I was fifteen.

She was in her late twenties when she had me, which leaves a glaringly large chunk of adult life missing from the picture: all the more so when a part of that is becoming a single mother.

I didn't even know Neville Morpeth wasn't my biological father until I was ten, when I saw a family passport application and asked why the date of their marriage was two years after I was born. They sat me down and told me, but it seemed like no more than an obscure technicality to me at that age. It was like how Auntie Janice wasn't a real aunt because she wasn't my mum's sister: it didn't change anything about how close we were. It didn't seem to matter.

It was only after Dad died that I really became curious. Obviously I was looking to fill a void; more than one void in fact, because not only did I not have Dad any more, but my mum was withdrawing too, and leaning on me more and more to look after Lilly. I couldn't honestly say whether it was my curiosity to find my biological father that drove my interest in my mum's past or the other way around, but either way, she wasn't encouraging it. She told me very little.

She said it wasn't about him – nothing to do with who he was and what he was like – but rather about who *she* was at that time, though she didn't offer any details.

'If it wasn't about him, did he even know?' I asked her.

She said no, he didn't, because she had already decided to cut off ties before she found out she was pregnant. She said he wasn't a bad person or anything, but neither were they in love. She needed to get away, to change a lot of things in her life right then, and he was far from reason enough to stay where she was.

I'm not sure whether all of this is true: whether she was lying for whatever reason or had just come up with a version of it that suits where she is now.

It made me curious about her connections, the ease with which she was able to slip into the places she did after Dad died. She was an agency nurse because we had moved around a lot with Dad's job. After he was gone, she began to fill the free days with chemical oblivion – she said she couldn't take the loneliness. Then she started to miss the shifts she did have, and became increasingly unreliable, until she ended up getting dropped.

I previously couldn't have imagined her going near some of the people she had dealings with. They terrified me, and yet she seemed so confident moving in their circles; moving in any circles. It made me rethink her ability to pull off those clever little tricks. I came to realise they were actually confidence scams.

She was never going to volunteer the truth about how she knew these things, but I knew that the one place she couldn't hide herself from me was online. I sussed the PIN for her mobile and the pass-word for her iPad, and in a reversal of the typical mother-daughter dynamic, it was me who started snooping on her browsing history.

There was nothing jaw-dropping or massively surprising, but one person did feature enough to grab my attention. Out of all the people she associated with on social media, his was the only name I wasn't familiar with. I guess that was my first hint, but the second, far bigger clue, was that she used anonymous accounts to follow him: accounts with fake names and profiles.

She didn't only monitor his activities on Facebook and Twitter: her search history was full of articles he had written, or that had been written about him, going back as far as records would allow. I wouldn't say she had an obsession with the guy, but she definitely had a fascination, and she didn't want him aware of it. Clearly, the guy knew her, or at least had once upon a time.

Of all the people she had associated with, why the interest in him above all? Why did she want to know what had been happening to him down the years, but was careful to prevent him returning the favour?

I won't pretend *that* thought didn't pop into my head, though I knew it was a reach on the basis of this evidence. But I knew he was a potential route into my mum's past. That's the real reason I sought him out. It wasn't so much about getting to know who my father really was, as about getting to know who my mother really was.

I tracked him down and drew him close in the only way I know how. I hacked my way into his life.

The more I got to know, the more I liked his style. We had a lot in common. He was a hacker too, in his own way. I felt we had a connection, even though I was always careful to keep my distance and protect my anonymity.

I'll admit it: I liked the idea of him being . . . you know. It became a comforting thought during difficult times, even though I knew that was all it was. One day I would find out more: that was the plan. I was playing a long game, but it was always my intention that when the opportunity presented itself, I would ask him about Mum.

Unfortunately, when I finally got to meet him, it was because of this shitstorm. I couldn't talk about the things I always wanted to, not least because he hates me now.

So here I am, having to ask Mum because time is running out, and knowing she'll tell me nothing. That said, I am my mother's daughter in that I can sometimes interpret a great deal from other people's nothing.

I wait until the conversation has become less charged, more mundane, then I throw it in there.

'Mum, have you ever heard of a reporter called Jack Parlabane?'
'Who?'

She's buying time. Why is she lying?

'Jack Parlabane.'

'No. I've never heard of him. Why? Has the press been sniffing around asking questions?'

I meet her lie with one of my own.

'Nothing like that. It's just I read an article by him and the name seemed familiar. I thought maybe I remembered you mentioning it once.'

'You remembered wrong, then.'

I don't know what I was expecting to see in her reaction: surprise, longing, curiosity? Something that spoke of warmth, nostalgia or regret, anyway. Instead she had looked instantly defensive. I'd even say she looked scared.

# HIDDEN POWERS

'Mr Parlabane. I'll take you upstairs.'

He is back at Tricorn House for an unexpected second visit to Synergis, after getting a call from Tanya Collier saying Cruz wanted to speak to him again.

Tanya is not exuding the same PR-mode friendliness this time. She's not outright frosty, but there's no small talk as she escorts him through the building, and he can't tell whether it's directed towards him specifically or evidence of a more general tension about something else. His paranoia neurones are starting to fire, wondering what Cruz might know, and what he's walking into when he reaches the man's office.

He gets a long, scrutinising stare from someone they pass in a corridor, and his discomfort is heightened further when the man does a u-turn and begins hurrying to catch up with them.

Fortunately, it turns out to be Tanya he's interested in.

'Do you think I could grab a quick word with Leo?' he asks.

'I'm afraid Leo is just about to have a meeting with this gentleman,' she replies.

Her tone is no warmer towards this guy than towards Parlabane, so maybe it isn't about him, he thinks. But it also occurs to him that her tone might be to warn the other guy that this is not a good time.

He doesn't seem dissuaded, however.

'I need literally two minutes.'

'I'm in no rush,' Parlabane says helpfully, looking to gauge Tanya's reaction.

'Well, if you don't mind waiting,' she replies neutrally.

'I'd rather not get in the way of the real work here.'

'Thanks, I appreciate it,' the new guy says. 'Hey, you're Jack Parlabane, aren't you?'

Parlabane is seldom comfortable with being recognised, but is trying not to read anything into this encounter, given that everybody at Synergis is likely to have read his article on them.

'Sorry, where are my manners,' says Tanya. 'Jack, this is Matthew Coleridge. He's our head of network security.'

Coleridge offers a hand and Parlabane grips it. He smiles, but that job title has got him wondering whether Coleridge recognised his name when Tanya mentioned it, or whether recognising his face was what prompted that u-turn in the corridor. Was the urgency of Coleridge's need to talk to Cruz genuine, or in fact a pretext for the computer security chief to shadow someone he knew to be wary of?

'You wrote the *Broadwave* piece,' Coleridge says.

'He did,' answers Tanya. 'And that, in fact, is what Leo wants to talk to him about.'

Her register doesn't suggest the meeting will be kicking off with grins and fist-bumps.

'Personally, I'd be more interested to talk about the one you wrote regarding Uninvited and the RSGN hack,' Coleridge says.

Parlabane is very rapidly trying to get a handle on this guy, unsure if he's merely curious or marking territory. He looks late thirties, still kind of boyish about the face, but widening at the middle. Parlabane reckons he's looking at a geek grown up, as opposed to a grown-up geek: someone who was making *Doom* mods twenty years ago but now plays *Minecraft* with his kids before rocking some *GTA* late at night to take his mind off the mortgage and responsibilities.

'That hacker you were in contact with, Buzzkill: I'm betting you know more than you could print. I mean, like, do you know his real name?'

Coleridge is looking at him intently, Parlabane's paranoia neurones firing with renewed vigour. He's telling himself there's no way this guy could know anything, but of late he's been moving in a world where he can never be sure of who knows what, or who anyone secretly might be.

'A journalist doesn't name his sources,' he replies. 'But as I'm sure you can imagine, these people go to elaborate and frustrating lengths to avoid being identified.'

'Everybody makes them out to be the bogeyman, which is precisely what they want. My guess is they're just kids showing off, same as LulzSec. For the most part they don't mean any real harm, but nor do they think much about the damage they can do. That's what keeps me awake at night and busy by day. It's why I need to talk to Leo, in fact.'

'You're beefing up security?' Parlabane suggests.

'Yeah. After RSGN it would be negligent not to heed the warning, so we're upgrading all our login systems. The whole of Tricorn House is implementing 2FA.'

'What's that?' asks Tanya.

'Two-factor authentication. Your username and password won't be enough anymore. Before you can even enter those, you'll need to key in a time-limited PIN that will be sent automatically to an app on your phone.'

It's all Parlabane can do not to physically wince as Coleridge says this, his heart plunging as he understands that his task has moved one notch closer to impossible.

Coleridge is as good as his word. He is in Cruz's office less than the promised two minutes, the brevity enough to further fuel Parlabane's concern that talking to the boss was not his primary motive.

'He says to go in,' Coleridge says, indicating the open door.

Parlabane glances to Cruz's secretary for confirmation and gets the nod.

Cruz appears at the door, appearing to hold it open by way of beckoning Parlabane inside, but the force with which he subsequently slams it shut indicates that this was the real reason.

'You've got some balls, I'll say that much. I wasn't sure you'd have the front to actually show up here after what you wrote.'

The *Broadwave* piece has been live for a few days now, and prior to encountering Tanya's coolness earlier, having heard nothing from Cruz, he assumed all was well. Maybe the CEO's been too busy to react, or maybe he's been nursing his wrath.

'What did I write?' Parlabane asks, keeping his tone neutral: neither defensive nor apologetic.

'You led with an angle that strongly hinted Aldous Syne has a new invention.'

'As I remember it, you're the one who strongly hinted Aldous Syne was back. I merely reported what I believed I was being invited to infer.'

'I didn't authorise you to reveal something so sensitive.'

Parlabane wonders, if this is the problem, why it has taken him so long to respond. He suspects something else has changed and Cruz is looking for a scapegoat.

'You don't get to authorise these things, Mr Cruz. Journalism doesn't work like that. I merely speculated on the basis of what I was told. And given the subsequent effect on your share price, I can't see what the problem might be.'

Cruz pauses, then lets out a chuckle.

'There is no problem. I'm just trolling you, Jack.'

Parlabane shakes his head, lets out a laugh despite himself.

'You really had me there,' he admits. 'Did you even get your PA to be frosty?'

'Tanya's very indulgent. It was a good piece. And I'm not just saying that because, as you say, it didn't hurt our stock. You gave me the benefit of the doubt. Nobody's done that for a long time. Thank you.'

'You're welcome,' Parlabane replies, uncomfortable as always when a subject sounds anything approaching gushy. Adversarial he can deal with. This kind of response makes him concerned that he hasn't been as analytical as he should, though he isn't lacking for mitigation. When you're plotting to rob somebody, it's understandable that you might disguise your intentions by being less critical than usual.

Cruz isn't merely responding to compliments, however. His sincerity indicates more that he is looking to be understood than looking to be praised.

'I know I probably don't deserve the benefit of the doubt, so I get why people have made assumptions, but when you're trying to turn things around, turn *yourself* around and do the right thing, you need a bit of encouragement, you know? We all need to know someone believes in us, even just a little. And when that someone is a cynical bastard like you, clearly it means all the more.'

Cruz's last remark is what they call in the theatre a treacle-cutter: a reaction to a preceding moment of unguarded and revealing sentimentality. Parlabane knows what it is to have everyone believe you're the worst of the worst, a bottom-feeding sleazebag low enough to rim a rattlesnake. You can be absurdly grateful to anyone who gives the impression they still see something better in you.

He gets it now: this is a man in search of redemption.

'It doesn't guarantee I'll be doing you any favours the next time,' Parlabane says. 'Just to be clear.'

Like when I'm breaking into this place and making off with your prototype.

'That's fair enough. But I'm going to do you a favour. I'm going to give you the scoop making it official.'

Parlabane's pulse surges.

'Aldous Syne?'

'Correct. I can confirm on the record that our product in development – still strictly under wraps – is something Aldous Syne has been working on for quite some years, and we are privileged to be the ones bringing it to market.'

'And I can interview him?'

Cruz pauses, breathes out a regretful sigh.

'That part, no. Aldous has always been a very shy, very reclusive individual. Maybe he'd have been cut a little more slack back in the day if we'd all been familiar with terms such as Asperger's syndrome and the autistic spectrum. But some of the ridicule he was subjected to, the things that were written . . . He's not as thick-skinned as you or me, Jack. It's no wonder he crawled back inside his shell.'

Parlabane recalls how Syne's reputation had so swiftly gone from genius to joke, visionary to one-hit wonder.

'He was extremely reluctant to put himself out there again, even when it came to presenting this new idea to people for development funding. I suppose there's only so much rejection and humiliation you can take. Consequently this has been very much another garden-shed-inventor type deal, though it's something considerably more technically sophisticated than the Synapse. We're talking about the fruits of a lot of labour, and a multi-disciplinary command

206

of electronic engineering. I think people will be forced to admit he is a true genius whose work requires a long gestation period.'

'And are you confident you'll be present for the birth? Last time we spoke you had concerns about a hostile takeover.'

Cruz gives an odd little grunt, like someone trying to make light of their frustrations.

'Certainly the upside of your article was that the resultant rise in our share price has warded off that particular predator – for now.'

'You mean Danny Winter?'

Cruz pauses, tripped by the question.

'That's confidential. How did you get that name?'

'If you recall, we've had a turn at the "naming my source" dance once. The steps are the same.'

'Equally, you'll understand that I'd be in violation of non-disclosure terms if I were to confirm that.'

'I don't hear you denying it.'

'What would be the point? I've nothing to say on the matter, though.'

'So what was the downside?'

'Huh?'

'Of my article. You said there was an upside, which implies . . .'

'Oh, yes, sure. Quite simply it's that bigger predators might start circling, especially now I've confirmed about Aldous.'

'So why confirm?'

'You always plan contingencies against what you anticipate going wrong. In this case I didn't plan for something going unexpectedly well. It alters your perspective. I was terrified of Win— of someone else taking over Synergis because I feared the very intentions people assumed of me: shutting down and asset stripping. But now that danger looks to have passed, the new danger isn't so scary. To be perfectly honest, if I have to dilute my holding, or someone else buys control of my company from other shareholders around me, I'm not as concerned as I used to be.'

'Why not?'

'If a bigger player is interested now, it's because they want what we can build, not what they can get from breaking us up. I feel I owe Aldous something, so if we can make this happen – and, let's not be coy, if I end up making a profit from it – then it doesn't matter so much about who is holding the pink slip at the end of the day.'

# HOSTAGE SITUATION

It isn't only Synergis's stock that is on the rise. Parlabane can do little wrong as far as his new employers are concerned. Since landing the gig by bringing them an exclusive interview with a member of Uninvited, he has followed it up with the interview in which Cruz hinted that Aldous Syne is back with a new idea. It is precisely the kind of tech-angled scoops *Broadwave*'s demographic-obsessed advertising department has been crying out for. Now he is delivering on the initial rumour with a follow-up of firm confirmation, on top of piquing Lee Williams's considerable intrigue with the suggestion that he is tracking another major development involving his hacker contact.

'I'm really looking forward to bringing Candace up to speed on all this when she flies in again,' Lee tells him. 'There's a big state-of-play meeting scheduled. Attendance mandatory.'

'She's coming to London?'

'Duh. She's throwing a huge party to mark the London office of *Broadwave* being open three years. She'll be wanting to show you off, so keep your diary clear.'

Three years. It told him the extent to which his head had been up his arse post-Leveson that his impression was that these arrivistes had only popped up in the last six months. He kept this to himself, naturally.

In everyone else's eyes, it seems he is solid gold right now, which is why he has to conceal the truth by acting like he's content and on top of his game. In reality he is on a runaway train that could explode at any moment, yet the only action open to him is to keep stoking the boiler.

He has in the past paid the price for breaking one of his profession's golden rules: don't make yourself the story. On this occasion that choice has been taken out of his hands. The only question is whether that story will be how he helped Buzzkill hack the *Clarion* or how he helped her hack Synergis.

He has seldom felt so lonely. He has nobody he can talk to about this, nobody who can help him. There's only him and Sam, to whom he harbours constantly alternating feelings of resentment and responsibility, like she's both his jailer and his ward. This duality is only enhanced by his own duplicity towards her. He has not revealed how much he knows about her, not even her real name.

She reminds him of someone and it's driving him crazy that he can't think who. What makes it harder is that she only reminds him of whoever it is in these tiny glimpses. Most of the time her head is down, withdrawn or intent upon a screen; but every so often – usually when she laughs, when there is a hint of devilment or scheming – that's when he gets this weird sense of déjà vu. It's like he's met her before, which is impossible.

Every stroke she pulls off is another crime, another fraud, one more line that can't be uncrossed; yet still she's keeping this train on the rails. It always goes the same way: she outlines the objective in what sounds like a *Mission: Impossible* briefing, and then patiently and methodically goes about making it happen. For instance:

'We have two primary targets: Synergis Network Security Director Matthew Coleridge and Synergis Head of Research and Development Jane Dunwoodie. We need their usernames and passwords, and to do this, we're going to reach deep into our bag of tricks.'

The first of these, which she calls 'baiting', delivers them nothing on their primaries, but it does bear some other fruit.

She uses her multiplicity of fake social media accounts to subtly infiltrate the online circles of Tricorn House workers, spreading a link to an appeal from the Facebook page of Trish Gomez, a (non-existent) fellow employee who has misplaced a red-coloured flash drive, which she is desperate to recover as it contains scans of childhood Polaroids she recently lost while moving flat. With a few carefully placed social media posts, Sam seeds the rumour that it isn't childhood snaps Trish is anxious to retrieve, but naked selfies intended for her boyfriend – ironically carried on the flash drive because she was worried about the security of storing them online.

At various points over the subsequent days, Parlabane and Sam make separate visits to the publicly accessible ground-floor concourse area of Tricorn House, where they plant red flash drives in places they might plausibly have fallen and settled: in toilet cubicles, behind bins, under coffee-shop tables and between cushions on waiting-area benches.

'The US government once did an experiment by planting a load of USB sticks in car parks outside their official buildings,' Sam tells him. 'Sixty per cent of people who found one plugged it into a workplace machine. Employees tend to be more educated about the danger these days, but that can change if they think they already know whose drive it is and what's on it. Or what they *hope* is on it.'

'What's really on it?'

'A reverse-shell RAT, hidden in the exe, backdoored with a Metasploit-based payload which will evade most AVs in common use.'

Her words make no sense.

'I did ask,' Parlabane concedes.

'Basically something that should get us the credentials of anybody curious enough to stick this in their USB slot. What's also on it is a folder containing a shitload of naked selfies of the same woman whose photo I used for the Trish Gomez profile. I figure they'll spend a while clicking through them, by which time my remote access Trojan will have had time to copy itself to their machine.'

They score a 70 per cent pick-up rate, though of those, more than half wait until they get home to check out the goodies. Unfortunately the scattergun method means that Sam has no way of targeting the departments she wants. This means she gets results from all over Tricorn House and beyond, but none of them is in Tricorn Security or Synergis R&D.

They do score one member of Synergis personnel: an electronics engineer named Oliver Greenberg. Due to the newly implemented two-factor authentication system, Sam can't log into his account on the Synergis network, but she can get into his personal emails.

'He and his buddies are doing a lot of bitching about Dunwoodie,' she tells Parlabane. 'She's been parachuted in as head of R&D: she came with Cruz as part of the package. People don't like it when someone is brought in over their head, and it appears you can double up on that when it's a woman in a techy industry telling guys what to do. They seem particularly tetchy about the implied lack of trust. Seems only the higher-ups know the nature of Project RBA. The rest are being asked to work on individual components but none of them have been told what they're for.'

The baiting tactic has come up dry on getting closer to Coleridge and Dunwoodie, but they are working other angles. Parlabane suggests that researching a follow-up story for *Broadwave* would provide the perfect cover to quiz the targets and glean some valuable personal details.

Sam looks at him with pitying disdain.

'No benefit in making yourself memorable to the targets. Imagine the inquiry after they're hacked. Who did you speak to, out of the ordinary? Oh, there was that journalist who was asking all kinds of questions I thought were kinda tangential at the time . . .'

'So how do you suggest we play it?'

'In this day and age, you don't need to go in person to ask things when people are telling the world freely if you know where to look.'

Within a matter of hours Parlabane knows more about the everyday lives of Jane Dunwoodie and Matthew Coleridge than he knows about most of his friends: marital status, number of kids, the names of their kids, what those kids look like, places of education, favourite pubs and restaurants, football affiliations, favourite music, TV shows, movies, video games, political and charity activism, who their friends are, what their friends look like, where they grew up, where they've been on holiday, what cars they drive.

'Have you used this on me?' he asks.

She doesn't answer.

'So what do we do with all this?'

'We go spear phishing.'

Spear phishing, she explains, is what you call it when you're aiming at a specific target, as opposed to spamming out emails and hoping some idiot bites. It is a matter of creating a bespoke trap, carefully tailored to the individual using the information you have gleaned.

They know Matthew Coleridge has an eleven-year-old daughter who is heavily into karate, and he spends many a Saturday driving her to competitions at various sports centres around south London and Kent. They have dates and locations for several of these, photos from the meets, lists of organisers, competitors, sponsors. They know he lives in Bromley, they know the name of the restaurants where he likes to go out for family meals and they know that he sometimes takes his wife and kids bowling beforehand. They know plenty more besides, but this was as much as they would need for now.

Using Coleridge's direct line – found by Sam on a group email in Oliver Greenberg's account – Parlabane calls the security chief mid-morning, when he'll have had time to deal with the most pressing matters in his in-tray and most likely be open to a moment's distraction. This gets Parlabane his first foot in the door.

'Is that Matthew?' he asks, putting on a generic English accent.

'Yes. Who is this?'

'My name is John White. I'm with the Sevenoaks Karate Association.'

'How did you get this number?'

He sounds irritated rather than accusatory, not welcoming an interruption this morning, but Parlabane can use that too.

'Oh, am I ringing you at work? I'm terribly sorry, it's just this is the number on the contact form I've got here from Bromley Junior Dragon Dojo.'

'No, it's no problem. Must have put down my work number on the form by mistake. Your voice sounds familiar, actually. Have we met?'

'Well, you may remember coming to a competition recently at the leisure centre here: your daughter Penny came first in the under-twelves open Kata.'

'How could I forget,' he all but purrs.

They chose the Sevenoaks Karate Association for this reason: people are always happy to reconnect with the scene of a triumph;

parents doubly so. In about ten seconds Coleridge has gone from mild impatience to oozing goodwill.

'The thing is, we're having a silent auction to help raise funds. I'm not on here asking for money, at least not today. Just want to know whether you'd be interested in taking a look at the auction website, and if there's anything you'd like to bid on, you can take it from there. All the businesses in the area have been very generous. We've got a pampering session at a local spa, a bowling session at Strike Lanes followed by dinner next door at Pollo, a corporate package at Selhurst Park, really a ton of great prizes to bid on.'

'No, that sounds great. I'd be delighted to take a look.'

'Thanks, that's brilliant. I didn't want to send out a mass email because everyone gets a million of them, don't they? And if you're fund-raising, it helps to be a bit more personal. Not to mention the danger of it ending up in the spam folder.'

'Well, I can assure you that won't happen with this if you want to email me the link now.'

'Sure. Well, actually I can't do it right this second. The Wi-Fi here has started playing up. Can I dictate you the URL?'

'Sure. I'm opening up a new tab now.'

Parlabane tells Coleridge the address.

'And can you make sure I spelled that right?' he asks. 'Is it loading okay?'

'It's taking a while, actually. Oh, no, here it comes.'

'Great. As I said, I'm not asking for credit card details. If there's anything you want to bid on, email the address at the bottom. Anyway, if you'll forgive me, I have to make about another twenty of these calls this morning, so . . .'

'No, no, not at all, and best of luck.'

The website does list the items for a fund-raising silent auction, all knocked up by Sam the night before with careful attention to detail. What it also contains is the reason the site appeared to be 'taking a while'. The first thing it did was deliver its payload of malware to Coleridge's computer: a remote access Trojan that connects back to Sam's laptop from inside the Tricorn House firewall.

They pull a similar trick with BMW driver and Arsenal fan Jane

Dunwoodie: in her case the hook is an invite to a VIP champagne opening event at a new dealership close to her home in Finchley, featuring a prize draw offering, among other enticements, a corporate hospitality package at the Emirates.

The runaway train stays on the rails, always accelerating. Parlabane thinks of all the cat-burgling break-ins he carried out, the simple deceptions that bagged him exclusives but ultimately earned him the opprobrium of the Leveson Inquiry. These were mere smash-and-grab jobs, opportunistic exploitation of unwariness and complacency. They were the work of an amateur.

Sam operates on a different plane: working multiple angles simultaneously, planning several moves ahead, improvising instantly when that next foothold shows her an unexpected rockface. At any given stage she is pursuing a variety of attack vectors.

It's only on the part left to him that they are making bugger-all progress.

# KEYBOARD PLAYER

Even the most ingeniously devised and perfectly executed strategy can yield nothing if your luck is out, especially when you're firing blind.

Sam bought what she needed from a place off Tottenham Court Road, then Parlabane shipped the components north to his friend Spammy, along with Sam's specifications. He got the finished product back three days later, which constituted a lightning turnaround for the big man. Spammy had done a grand job of the electronic engineering, then it was down to Sam to handle the social engineering.

She called Winter's investment firm, where she spoke to his PA, the man himself apparently unavailable. This was preferable, because Parlabane had been warned that he was suspicious of favours. Flattering him via a subordinate was therefore ideal.

Her voice was bubbly and enthusiastic, like she was calling her best friend.

'My name is Tess Jones, from Vizion Peripherals. That's Vizion with a zed. The reason I'm calling is we're launching our new top-of-the-range keyboard, the Vizion Maven, and as a marketing initiative, we're offering a limited number free to people who are considered electronics industry visionaries: mavens. Obviously what we're hoping is that they'll talk and tweet about the brand, but there's absolutely no obligation. We consider Mr Winter someone who has shown vision in his choice of investments, so I was wondering if he would be happy to try our new Vizion Maven?'

'As I said, he's not around right now, so I can't ask him personally, but he's always interested in new tech. I'm sure he'd be delighted.'

The keyboard was despatched the same day, addressed to the PA with a covering note reiterating what Sam had said on the phone. It was a backlit keyboard with the original logo removed and replaced by something Sam knocked up on her laptop. The result was an impressive-looking piece of kit, almost certainly preferable to whatever was already on Winter's desk, but the most remarkable properties were out of sight.

As soon as the USB cable was connected, a hidden internal device inside – known as a Teensy HID – would install a program that allowed Sam to access the target computer. However, that was only half the payload: the keyboard also contained a microphone equipped with a mini SIM card for a pay-as-you-go account. It was audio-activated, so that if someone in the office was talking, it would dial a dedicated mobile, which would then record the call.

It should have given them eyes on Winter's computer and ears on his conversations. Unfortunately, so far the bastard had never plugged the thing in.

Parlabane gets Sam to call again, ostensibly as a follow-up.

'Hello, is that Clare? This is Tess Jones following up, from Vizion. Just checking if Mr Winter's keyboard was delivered all right.'

'Yes, it was. Thank you very much.'

'And do you know is Mr Winter enjoying it?'

'I'm afraid he hasn't been in the office since it arrived. He is in China at the moment, but he's due back next week.'

Four days later, Sam rings Parlabane to say that the keyboard is finally live.

She gets Winter's login details for his office intranet, but annoyingly he is careful enough to use a different password for his email, so she can't access his account independently via the web. She is still able to read his messages, but only while his computer is active, and that is proving a limited window. He shuts it down when he isn't in the office, and he isn't in the office much.

'His security practices are sharp,' she tells Parlabane. 'He does everything I would do in terms of day-to-day protocols.'

'Like a person with something to hide?'

'Or a person who knows how to keep his stuff secret from people like us.'

'You mean a person who knows how hackers work?'

'It's looking that way. I haven't found any hacking tools but I

217

wouldn't expect him to keep them on an office machine, especially when the bastard is hardly in the office.'

Sam forwards as many emails as she has been able to copy, and Parlabane scans through them. In keeping with Winter's general discretion, there is little that is candid, and nothing that would be compromising were it to be read by persons unknown. On this evidence, Winter is either straight as an arrow or extremely disciplined about compartmentalising his communications. Parlabane thinks of how he was led to a quiet corner away from CCTV cameras and asked to demonstrate an absence of recording equipment before being physically assaulted by this man. Thus he's betting on the latter.

Adding insult to this particular injury is that he is now out of pocket nearly three hundred quid just to send the bastard a fancy keyboard that he never uses.

Eventually, however, the Teensy HID begins to deliver. The next day, Parlabane hears one side of a phone call in which it is clear from early on that the subject is Synergis.

'Yeah, well, the share price has gone up because of this fucking article. How was I supposed to see that coming? Regardless, I still believe it's going to be an extremely worthwhile asset to acquire.

'Yes, I realise that. I thought Cruz was grandstanding. We all did: it's how he operates. But it looks like he's got something of substance behind his posturing for a change. This only makes it even more worthwhile getting in at the ground floor, and my concern has always been that the window is limited. Once the other shareholders decide the long-term returns are worth it, we're locked out or priced out. But as you and I know, in this business, everything can change overnight.'

Parlabane takes another look through the emails, many of which now take on a markedly different resonance. Dozens of them are to a Mr Sunny Li of Sunstream Corp, and upon a second reading it is clear that the language in these is more neutral and its subjects cautiously concealed compared to Winter's exchanges with other correspondents. It's all 'the opportunity' and 'this potential acquisition'; whereas the emails to Metal Box about the unit costs of a particular model do at least name the model and the prices of individual components.

In the emails to Li, if Parlabane makes the assumption that they are talking about Synergis, the picture changes dramatically.

Not being particularly familiar with Sunstream, Parlabane calls Agnieszka Savic for a more informed industry perspective, though he doesn't disclose the reason for his interest.

'Well, they're legit these days,' is her sardonic and less than re-assuring overture.

'From which I can infer that this was not always the case?'

'Sunstream are a burgeoning force, a major player in the South-East Asian consumer electronics market: TVs, phones, laptops, tablets. But they've struggled to get a foothold in both the US and Europe, largely as a legacy of their origins. They were knock-off merchants, back when China was a Klondike for that kind of thing.'

'You mean before international intellectual property laws were enforced?'

'Yeah. Companies like Sunstream were the reason why those laws were being demanded. They just reverse-engineered from US and Japanese originals, and blithely sold their cheap rip-offs to the domestic market and beyond. They've cleaned up their act since those days, and discontinued all of the products that were cited in lawsuits, but it's fair to say that in the west, people are still wary of doing business with them.'

Then she drops the hammer.

'That's probably why Neurosphere wouldn't sell them Synergis.'

'Sunstream tried to buy Synergis?'

'That's the rumour, anyway. People assumed Sunstream were only interested in getting the Shanghai manufacturing plant at a knock-down price, and would have closed Synergis without shedding a tear. However, there's an alternative theory that they were principally interested in the brand, and that Neurosphere were even less happy about the implications of that than about them asset-stripping a division they long wanted rid of.'

Finally it starts to become clear. Winter is acting as a front for Sunstream to acquire Synergis at the second attempt, but has suffered a setback in that Cruz's investors may not be so easily tempted by a short-term return if the long term is looking peachy.

How much keener might they be to sell were some act of industrial espionage to befall Cruz's new project? As Winter told Li, in this business, everything can change overnight.

# RAILROADED

I am hunched on my bed, working on creating a clone of the Gatekeeper client support website on my laptop. Normally I would get off on this, but it's after midnight and I'm knackered after a full day at Urban Picnic.

My eyes are closing on me, and when they do I keep seeing sandwiches.

I decide I'll wrap it for the night, and am about to shut down when a message from Zodiac pops up in the corner of my screen.

That wakes me up sharpish, sending a jolt of adrenaline right through me.

> <Zodiac> I've looked over the latest progress report you sent me. I think you're stalling.
> <Buzzkill> That's bullshit. One does not simply walk into Synergis.
> <Zodiac> There's careful planning and there's taking the piss. I think you need a more pressing motivation, so I'm giving you a deadline. I want it done by this weekend.
> <Buzzkill> FFS. That's never enough. Most of the strategy is in place but I'm still working on how to acquire the code for the vault and I definitely need more time to circumvent the two-factor authentication.

He doesn't respond for a couple of minutes, then when he does, I shudder at the sight of the words.

> <Zodiac> There's more than one person working this.

I am terrified he is calling me out about Jack: letting me know he is aware I've got help, and that I have been keeping this from him. But then I remember about Cicatrix, and find myself wondering how many other hackers he has blackmailed, from Uninvited and beyond.

> <Zodiac> Another source has uncovered that the PIN for
>     the vault is changed on a daily basis, and the new code
>     is emailed to those with appropriate security clearance.
>     You just need to get into one of their email accounts and
>     you're go.
> <Buzzkill> I can hack their personal emails, but getting into
>     their Synergis email accounts still needs two-factor
>     authentication.
> <Zodiac> Not my problem. You have until midnight
>     Saturday. If you can't deliver by then, I will give the job
>     to someone who can. And I don't need to remind you
>     what happens to people who are no longer useful to me.

I go into the kitchen to make myself a cup of tea, because I know I'm not getting to sleep any time soon after what just happened. I look up at the clock on the wall, which reads 01.30. It is digital, but I can hear a ticking even so.

I am running out of time.

I should have seen this coming.

Jack told me how this Winter creep is in bed with some Chinese firm. Straight away I thought of Stonefish, the sly prick who lured me out into the open and pulled me into this nightmare. I'm not as clued-in as Juice when it comes to the stockmarket stuff, but this part seems simple enough: with the share price still rising, they must have decided they need to act before it gets too high.

So close but yet so far.

Most of what we need is in place. I stayed up late finishing my cloned website and this morning I tricked Nigel Holt, the buildings manager at Tricorn House, into downloading my hacked version of the Gatekeeper Entry Management software. I could make it sound like this part was really clever, but the real work was done when I stole the source code.

The big obstacle remains 2FA: the two-factor authentication system that sends a PIN to your mobile before you're allowed to log into the Synergis network. If I can't crack that, everything else I've acquired is worthless.

The clock keeps silently ticking, my time draining away.

I take a sip of my tea and glance down at the *Evening Standard* I retrieved from a bin on my walk home from picking up Lilly. The front-page headline is about a Tube strike. Desperate for a break from wrestling with the 2FA problem, my brain seizes upon a memory, but I find no respite there.

I recall my journey home on the day all of this started, when that girl Mia got on and I overheard her talking to her friend about Keisha.

I've been checking up on the news via my fake accounts on Facebook. She's conscious again, but they kept her in intensive care for more than a week. Every time I think about her, I feel sick. I hated her so much, but I can't forgive myself for what I did. I know what it is to be bullied by someone like her, but I also know what it is to have my life ripped apart by an anonymous figure on the internet, and there is no question which is worse.

Perhaps I deserve to go to jail: not for the RSGN hack, but for what I did to Keisha. Maybe that would be justice. But the problem is that Lilly is already being punished for Mum's mistakes. She doesn't deserve to suffer for my crimes too.

I scan the *Standard* front page, searching for details in case the strike is going to affect me. The tone is hysterical, acting like some Tube workers wanting better pay and conditions is going to turn London into the set for the next Mad Max movie.

That's when I realise I've been thinking about this the wrong way. I'm seeking hacks and exploits, exploring possible technical solutions to get around the problem of 2FA. I'm forgetting my hacking fundamentals. The best way to acquire login credentials − be they a username, a password or a PIN − is to get some sucker to straight-out tell you.

# ASPECT OF THE DEMON

Parlabane is standing opposite the reception desk at Tricorn House, taking a moment to run through the script in his head one last time. He is dressed in a suit in order to blend in. The only blokes turning up in this place wearing anything else during business hours are going to be carrying packages and requiring a signature.

He checks his watch. It is 1.40 p.m. He has timed it for when there is the highest traffic through the lobby, rendering him the most anonymous. He is nervous, though only slightly, but that's because this isn't show time. This is just a prelude, albeit still the first of several all-or-nothing moments.

He has done riskier things, but he has never done so much reconnaissance, so much research, so much technical preparation. He has never been in a position whereby the physical act of infiltration would be so simple. And yet he has never been so sure something feels wrong.

It's not about the risk, he realises: it's about the stakes. He has finally got his life back on track, and now he stands to lose everything. And what's making it worse is the fear that he is on some kind of collision course with fate.

The act of trespass has come to define him. It played an inextricable part in building his career, and an inevitable part in almost ending it. It's the aspect of himself he has most struggled to understand, probably because it is the aspect of himself that he most fears.

Despite his denials, he knows that Sam is right when she claims they are kindred spirits. They have the same addiction, the same demons. The buzz is in devising ways of sidestepping the most elaborate security measures, of coming at the target from a direction they didn't anticipate. In Parlabane's case this is often literal: that direction usually being the vertical. People thought that if

224

their office was three floors up, they didn't need locks on the windows.

But there are other ways in which he and Sam are alike. They each like to defend their dishonest practices as necessary guerrilla tactics against a mighty foe, but neither of them are conscientious freedom fighters, selflessly throwing themselves behind an altruistic cause. They are both outsiders who have often found it easier to unpick the locks and enter forbidden places than to walk into open rooms and feel like they belong.

The problem is that those forbidden places are always empty.

Parlabane is waved forward by a smiley but flustered young woman wearing roughly as much foundation as Joan of Arc would need for an open-casket funeral.

'Good morning, welcome to Tricorn House,' she says in a sing-song Cockney accent. 'How can I help?'

'It's afternoon,' Parlabane says with a smile, pitching for charming and reassuring. Instead she looks panicked, like this is something else she's got wrong. He's guessing first day. Shit.

'Sorry. Good afternoon. Welcome to . . . I mean, how can I help?'

'My name is John Finch. I'm doing some contracting work upstairs with Synergis. There should be a swipe card on the system for me.'

She looks blankly at him then glances at her computer screen, almost certainly consulting the list of pre-booked visitors.

'Who is it you're here to see?'

'No, I'm a contractor. I started working here yesterday but there was a mix-up with the swipe cards. They told me I would be on the system when I came back in today, so if you just print me a new—'

'I'm sorry, I don't see your name. It was John Finch, you said?'

'Yes, but I won't be on the visitors list. I should be on the system for a new swipe card.'

She stares back with a look of gormless confusion. She doesn't have a clue what he's on about.

'If you just tell me the name of who you're here to see, I can give them a ring upstairs and . . .'

He needs to extricate himself from this exchange right now.

'I'm sorry, I've got to take this call,' he says, pulling his mobile from his pocket.

He retreats towards the seating area, as though seeking privacy. The last thing he wants is her calling Synergis, because no matter who she speaks to, they won't have heard of John Finch.

Fuck.

Sun Tzu said no battle plan survives first contact with the enemy, and it appears that nor does any degree of sophistication guarantee a contingency against contact with a numpty.

He could try again in a minute and hope for a different recep-tionist, but it's not like the barbers where you can say you'll wait for the one you prefer, and he can't do anything that will make him memorable or draw attention to himself. He'll have to come back later, when this numpty is hopefully not on duty.

He is about to head for the exit when his mobile does genuinely ring.

It is Lee Williams, calling from *Broadwave*.

'Jack. Where are you?'

'The City. Near Monument.'

'Doing what?'

There is something testy in her tone, beyond the merely curious.

'I'm working on something. I can't really talk now.'

'You're supposed to be here at the office,' she scolds. 'Candace is in the building and we've got a meeting with her in twenty minutes.'

He gets hit with a full bucket of that forgotten-my-homework feeling, blindsiding him amid all of his other anxieties. He has been so preoccupied with what else needs to happen today that he has completely forgotten about Candace flying into town. Christ. This might lose him his job before anything else has even had time to go wrong.

'I'm sorry, I should have called. I'm following a lead and something came up at short notice: an opportunity to pin down a very elusive source. I kind of got caught up in the chase and lost track of time.'

'You need to get here, Jack. You've got eighteen minutes.'

'Understood.'

Fuck again.

That meeting could take the rest of the day. He may not have the option to come back later. He needs to act now.

What would Sam do, he wonders.

She'd be someone else, and she'd do it on the phone.

A few moments later he is launching an app Sam gave him that replaces the number you are calling from with whatever you key in. ('Honestly, if you want to make out you're calling from 10 Downing Street, long as you know the number, this will spoof it.')

He programs it to appear that he is calling from inside Synergis, then rings the Tricorn House front desk. He is standing a few yards away, next to the couches in the waiting area, watching the reception counter out of the corner of his eye.

'Good morning, Tricorn House,' says the same sing-song Cockney voice.

And thrice fuck.

He hangs up, waits a few seconds then tries again.

Finally somebody else answers.

'Good afternoon, Tricorn House. How may I direct your call?'

He steals a glance. It is the middle-aged black woman on the far left of the desk.

Parlabane puts on an English accent.

'Hello, this is Oliver Greenberg from IT up in Synergis. We've got a contractor coming back in this afternoon, name of John Finch. He was issued a dud swipe card yesterday.'

'Oh, sorry about that.'

'No worries, these things happen. But can you run off a new one for him please? He'll be in shortly.'

'A new guest card? Certainly, sir.'

'No, he's on the system. It's so we don't have to keep opening doors for him, you know?'

'What was the name again?'

'John Finch.'

'Oh, yes. Here it is. Printing that off now.'

'Thank you. As I said, he's due in any minute. Actually, I think that's him calling on my mobile. Pardon me just a sec.'

Parlabane mutes his phone for a moment, then comes back on.

'Are you still there?'

'Yes, sir.'

'Okay. Mr Finch says he's down there in the lobby. Can you wave so he knows who to . . .'

Parlabane turns and pretends to have his notice suddenly taken by the sight of the woman waving at the desk, her sights on nobody in particular. He waves back.

'I see him,' she responds.

'Brilliant.'

He hangs up and walks towards reception once again, where she takes his name and hands him a swipe card.

'The barrier is on your left and the lifts are just behind us here.'

He has somewhere else to be however, and he knows that won't look right.

'Can you tell me where the nearest gents is? I need to go before . . .'

'Certainly. Over to your right through the cafeteria.'

This excuses a rapid exit. Ten seconds later he is back on the street, and a minute after that he is inside a cab heading for *Broadwave*.

# TWIXT CUP AND LIP

It's Thursday. Almost show time. I barely slept for worrying about it, and I have been feeling like there's a rock in my guts from the moment I woke up. We go tonight. I'm dreading it, but the waiting is worse. I want the evening to arrive, the darkness to come down, but I've got to get through the day first, and it's not going to be an easy one. I'm guessing they cut the scene in *Ocean's Eleven* showing one of the guys putting in a half shift at a sandwich shop then cooking his little sister's tea before going on to rob the casino.

I make it through my demi-slog at Urban Picnic despite Snotworm dogging me throughout, looking for any reason to criticise my work. He left his phone in the back room during the break. I thought about the details I could harvest in only a few seconds, the fun I might have at a later date, but as soon as I did, I could only picture Keisha.

I saw Snotworm differently from then on. He's only a stupid kid like me, a bundle of fears and insecurities. I've learned my lesson about the law of unintended consequences. When it comes to vengeance, my efforts now are focused on Zodiac.

My half shift doesn't finish until six, so I pick up Lilly from the after-school club, getting there about quarter past. I'm trying not to think of the numbers, but I can't help it. It is costing me most of what I just earned to pay for Lilly to be collected on the minibus and looked after for two hours, purely so that I could make this half shift. The alternative, however, was to say no again and move one step closer to losing the job altogether.

Lilly is a little confused by the change of routine.

'Why do I have to go to the club instead of coming home after school?' she asks.

'It's so that I can work longer at the sandwich shop.'

'But why can't you work there during the day?'

'That's when my boss needed me, Lilly.'

'But your boss didn't need you there yesterday after school. What about tomorrow? Will you pick me up from school then?'

*What about tomorrow?* There's a question I don't want to dwell on.

The woman running the club says it would be better if Lilly came here regularly, so that the new arrangement becomes consistent.

I look at all the other kids who go there every day, amazed at how their parents afford it. I guess they aren't all working at places like Urban Picnic, but I'm pretty sure they're not all working in the City either. My suspicion is that they're getting assistance I'm probably due too, except they didn't throw in the towel when they were on the phone to the Social.

I'm rubbish at this kind of thing. I know it's pathetic. I'm nineteen, not a child. But the truth is I feel like I need looking after. I need my mum.

I know that if I let myself cry even once about this, I'll fall apart. I can't let Lilly see me that way. I dig deep to pull myself together, putting on a smile and leading her homeward.

One more push, I tell myself, as the flats come into view.

I've been feeling like my life is on hold, trapped and unable to see beyond this looming task, so much that it has blocked the view of all possible futures. Jack says that if we give him what he wants this time, Zodiac will soon be back asking for more. I know he's right, but after this I will at least be able to breathe out and plan my next move.

Plus, I have an idea to give myself some leverage.

'Jingle bells, Batman smells, Robin flew away,' Lilly is singing as we climb the stairs to our landing. She's been repeating it for the past fifty yards, getting so giggly that it is proving infectious.

'Mr Silly lost his willy on the motorway.'

I am laughing now too, more at her giggles than the song itself, my eyes watering as I open the front door.

It is almost enough for me not to notice that it wasn't locked.

The realisation has an instantly sobering effect. I never forget to lock this door. Never. I think back to this morning, try to picture leaving the flat. Was I distracted, maybe trying to get Lilly out on time and she was being difficult?

No. I dropped her at school then came back for a bit before heading out to work.

With a cold feeling in my gut, I nudge open the living room door. The first thing I notice is that the blinds are closed. I usually leave them open, and I didn't forget to do that either.

Somebody has been in here. There is stuff all over the carpet: books, magazines, DVDs, CDs, toys and ornaments tossed to the floor. I go to the kitchen and it's the same. Drawers and cupboards have been rooted through, items spilled when they got in the way.

I'm guessing they were looking for money, or drugs. Of course. Since her conviction, word must have got around that Mum was a dealer. Some desperate chancers have latched on to that part but missed the crucial detail that she was done for possession, which generally involves the police coming round and confiscating your stash.

'Sam. Sam. Sam. Samantha,' Lilly wails from down the hall, her voice high and panicky, like that time she burned her hand on the kettle.

I see her come out of her bedroom, eyes streaming.

'My DVD player is gone. My room is all a mess and my DVD player is gone.'

She means the laptop I fixed up for her. I never called it a computer in case it got back to Mum.

I run to join her. They've torn through her wardrobe and her chest of drawers, looking for anything they can sell. There are clothes, toys and books everywhere, and the bed has been hauled away from the wall.

The sight of it jolts through me. My bed. My laptop. If it's gone, I'm screwed.

I run to my room, which is trashed too. Worse, in fact. They have taken the drawers right out, and they've smashed the wood at the foot of my wardrobe so they can check underneath.

My bed has been pulled away from the wall. I step between piles of clothes and climb on to the mattress, a cold dread gripping me as I lean over and look down.

The carpet is still in place. It doesn't look like it's been moved, but I pull it back to check. I lift up the hatch and reach inside, my pulse soaring as my fingers feel the touch of neoprene.

Okay. So this is a mess, not a disaster.

Lilly appears in my bedroom doorway. She's trying to stop crying, I can tell. Trying to be a big brave girl like Mum tells her to be when we visit her in jail. Merely the sight of her efforts is threatening to set me off.

'Are you going to phone the police?' Lilly asks.

Probably not the best night to be doing that, I think.

'It wouldn't help,' I tell her.

'But if they catch the robbers, they'll get me back my DVD player.'

'That's not how it works. Even if the police catch them, they'll have sold it by now.'

As I'm saying this, I think of how little they'll get for it, compared to how much it was worth to Lilly.

'I'll get you another one, though.'

'Tonight?'

'Tomorrow.'

Everything will be simpler tomorrow.

She looks crestfallen, as though for a moment she believed I could make everything all right, only for me to let her down.

'Tell you what, why don't we have pizza tonight?'

That makes her smile through the snotty tears. I know that take-away is going to nuke the budget but I need to do something to take her mind off what has happened here. Besides, eating pizza on our laps from cardboard boxes will save me having to throw something together from the chaos of the kitchen, where I'm not even sure there's two whole plates intact.

We tackle Lilly's bedroom while we wait for the pizzas to arrive, returning to the task as soon as they're done. She wasn't that hungry, probably because of the shock, but it did lighten her mood. I put the leftovers in the fridge, grateful the burglars never took the microwave.

Her room looks relatively normal by the time she would usually be getting ready for bed. I had been hoping to get her off to sleep early tonight but I know there's no chance of that now. I need her tucked up and out of the way though, so I suggest she gets her jammies on and rereads some of her favourite comics.

I know she takes comfort in the familiar when she's upset. When Mum got arrested she lost herself in an ancient run of Batgirl comics that she's had since the age when she could only look at the pictures.

I tuck her in and warn her not to come into the kitchen because she might cut her feet on the broken plates and glasses.

'Will you read to me, Sam?'

It hurts to say no, but I don't have the choice.

'I need to do more clearing up.'

'Please?'

'I'm sorry, Lilly. I'll read to you tomorrow night, I promise.'

Feeling about an inch tall, I go to the kitchen where I place my laptop down on the table, next to my phones. I close the door and take the tiny memory card from its hidey-hole in my bra, insert it into the empty slot and boot up.

I see that Mr and Mrs Cohen's Wi-Fi signal is at full strength here in the kitchen. I must be almost directly above the source. In the end, I didn't even need to come up with a pretext for getting into their flat. They had a problem with their new router, so they came upstairs and asked me if I'd have a look at it in the hope that they wouldn't have to phone the legendarily useless BT technical support. I reset it for them, taking a note of the WEP key and the admin password.

I log on and launch my virtual private network program. It hangs on loading, giving me another minor heart attack, but then the glitch clears and suddenly my IP address is reading as Glendale, California. I run some diagnostics, making sure the rest of my tools are ticking over without any problems.

I hear a sound from outside. It's just some kid kicking a can down the street but it makes me jump, partly because I am so consumed by what I am doing on the laptop, but mainly because I am wired from the shock of the break-in.

I don't feel as safe in here as I usually do.

I go to the window and look along the landing. There's nobody outside, but I don't feel reassured. I walk to the front door to double-check it's locked and the chain is secure, then I go around to make sure the windows are closed and the curtains drawn.

I return to my laptop, put a headset on my ear, and finally, once again Samantha Morpeth is banished.

Buzzkill is online and ready to crime. We are good to go, all systems in place, and I'm getting the tingle before the rush to come.

I call Jack. It rings eight or nine times with no answer. He's on the Tube, maybe.

I give it a few minutes then call again. Still no answer.

I try a third time. A fourth.

WTF?

Ten minutes pass. Fifteen.

I try a seventh time. An eighth. A ninth.

I start to get a nasty intuition about this. A Stonefish kind of intuition.

Something's wrong. He's screwing me over.

# PRESSING ENGAGEMENT

Parlabane is barely listening, unable to concentrate on what is being said. This kind of meeting is always an ordeal, but it feels particularly interminable under these circumstances. Even when the subject comes around to him and the positive reaction to what he has delivered since joining, he feels disconnected, feigning his responses.

He is impatient, that's the real source of his anxiety. There's nothing he can change now, so he just wants to get on with it. He wants it to be over; except that it won't be. The Synergis job is merely the first hurdle. Their real task remains that of catching Zodiac.

In the aftermath of tonight, it is bound to become more obvious what this is really about: what Winter and the Chinese are trying to achieve. However, he is aware that they must be thinking beyond this stage of their plan too, and that is when things are likely to get far more dangerous.

Bag men, like assassins, seldom fare well in the second phase of a conspiracy.

The meeting finally concludes, but he doesn't escape unharmed. He has a piece to file on Britain's enduring love of the eccentric inventor, a suggestion from Candace that emerged towards the end of the discussion due to the mention of Syne. Even without his more pressing agenda, Parlabane would have thought it was a shit suggestion, and he is sure Lee thinks it's a shit suggestion too. Nonetheless, they both understand that it's one of those occasions when you have to suck it up and keep a dilettante proprietor happy in the short term so that you can be free to do your job properly the rest of the time.

He finds a free desk and opens his laptop. He reckons if he gets his head down, he can get it written by half-seven, definitely eight at the latest. That would still leave him an hour or so to get home, pick up what he needs and head to Tricorn House for the time he has agreed with Sam.

Two hours later he is giving the piece a read-through and a tidy up when Lee appears at his side. He has been so immersed in his task that he seems to have missed everybody else leaving. What he can't miss is that she has brought a change of clothes with her to the office. She has transformed from her usual working garb into, of all things, a dress. It is a red number with white spots, and she looks magnificent, with extra wow points for the matching red Doc boots she's wearing to complement it.

'Are you almost done?' she asks. 'Got a taxi waiting.'

'Yeah, ready to file. And can I just say, you really scrub up well. What's the occasion?'

'Are you kidding me? The party. Where's your head, Jack? Candace has invited half of London.'

Where is his head, indeed. This soiree is the principal reason Candace is in town, but it would be fair to say his mind has been on other things.

'Come on. You can share my cab, and you've no idea what it took to get one tonight with this Tube strike going on.'

'Lee, I think I'll have to give it a miss. You remember that jumpy source I had to bail on earlier? I really need to go and meet this person, and it's been a delicate business setting it up.'

Lee is wearing the same implacable expression as she had during the meeting when she was agreeing with Candace's shit idea for this article.

'You'll have to postpone.'

He notes that she isn't asking.

'If I don't show, this might not be so much a postponement as the one that got away.'

'The same might be said of your job, Jack. Candace has spent a small fortune on this affair tonight. It's all about face, and about faces. Questions were asked when she took the decision to hire you, and among her other agendas tonight, she wants to bask in the vindication. Yours would therefore be a most conspicuous absence.'

'Can I get there a little later? A couple of hours, maybe?'

'I already texted her we're on our way the minute the cab showed up.'

'I'd need to go home and change.'

'No, you don't, you look far smarter than usual. You scrub up pretty well yourself. Never seen you in a suit, I don't think. What's that about, by the way?'

'Camouflage.'

The party is in a place named Shallot. It's near the Angel, on the first floor above an art gallery, and the entrance vestibule alone probably cost more to fit out than the start-up budget of every restaurant beyond the M25. It accommodates a reception desk and a cloakroom, where diners are greeted by a hostess before being escorted along polished granite tiles to a staircase and a lift leading to the restaurant proper.

Upstairs is a sprawling and labyrinthine affair combining several bar areas and dining rooms, though no matter where you are, you can't escape the same music throbbing from a DJ deck at the very back of the darkened warren. It's that ambient dance pish that Parlabane always hears at trendy gatherings but which no bastard would ever choose to listen to for their own entertainment.

The place is mobbed: people gathered in groups around every flat surface that can hold a drink. Their eyes are scanning each person who passes in case it's someone more interesting than whoever they're currently talking to, or in whose company it might be more profitable to be seen.

Waiters in dress uniform are offering champagne. As well as the open bars, there are pop-up stalls mixing gimmicky cocktails, served in equally gimmicky receptacles, such as treacle tins and jam jars. Salvers of taster plates are being offered around by smiling staff, trying to shout the names of these dainty creations over the sound of the music. Everything is so on-trend that the leftovers are likely to be binned in a few hours for being out of fashion rather than for any of the ingredients being past their use-by dates.

Everybody is dressed to maim, which makes Parlabane feel even more uncomfortable for having been vomited into the place in this fucking suit. He feels like he's turned up in his school uniform. And then it gets worse, because Candace appears and it's like his mum has shown up to collect him.

He feels his mobile buzz moments after she has greeted him, and gets a literal slap on the wrist before he has even pulled it from his pocket.

'I don't even want to *see* a phone tonight, Jack. It's a party.'

Lee was right: Candace is all about parading him like a star signing this evening. She's got him on her arm and is making a show of introducing him to all these media types: people who are eagerly shaking his hand, congratulating him on his recent scoops. Bastards who wouldn't have given him a subbing shift not so long ago are now doing the full fake-and-shake. He's wondering whether Candace will be so pleased about marrying herself to his reputation twenty-four hours from now.

He keeps feeling the vibration in his top pocket. He can't answer but he knows who it is.

Buzz. Buzz. Buzz.

Kill. Kill. Kill.

He is supposed to be in position, ready to rob, but instead he's trapped here.

If Sam thinks he's bailed on her, there's no knowing what she might do. She won't take the zero option yet, surely, but she's bound to be getting twitchy, and having all these people glad-handing him is a timely reminder of just how far she could cause him to fall.

He recalls bitterly all the dark times when he might have fanta-sised about something like this: being led around an open-bar party in Islington on the proud arm of a new-media mogul keen to show investors and industry players what a real reporter looks like. Now that he's living it, all he can think about is how fast he can get away without offending Candace.

Then he realises he can use this.

He can't be in two places at once. A moment ago, this was his problem. Now it is his opportunity.

Half the media in London have seen him at this party, an affair where people will be drifting in and out of each other's company all night. The CCTV camera in the vestibule will have recorded his arrival. It will record him leaving several hours hence too. So if he can find another, unseen route out of here, and if nobody witnesses him sneaking back in later, he'll have one hell of an alibi.

# OUTSIDE INFLUENCE

I fish through the debris for a mug and make myself some tea, telling myself I'm not going to take any action until I've drunk it. With the roof falling in on everything I have been planning, it is a way of forcing me to calm down and attempt to be rational as I consider my options.

My first instinct is to think about how I can light a fire under Jack, though my whole problem right now is that I can't get in touch with him. I have already dug out the countdown blog post I blackmailed him with, but just the sight of it makes my heart sink. It strikes me that maybe the reason Jack isn't answering is that he's not scared of this anymore. Perhaps now that he has got to know the real me behind Buzzkill, he is calling my bluff, convinced I won't pull the trigger on my threat.

This leaves me to consider a harsh alternative: could I do it myself?

I have never been beyond the entry barrier at Tricorn House, so unlike Jack I have no prior knowledge of where I would need to go once I was inside Synergis. It would have been easier if he'd made it out of there with the video files he recorded, though if I have an all-access swipe card, it surely wouldn't take me too long to find the vault.

With a few keystrokes I confirm that I can still access the GEM system. What I can't confirm is if there is anyone on reception and if they would issue a new swipe card at this time of night. Plus, duh, conspicuous. Once they know they've been robbed, they are going to investigate, and someone going up to the front desk and asking to pick up a swipe card at nine o'clock at night is going to be very memorable. That was why Jack went to pick one up at lunchtime when the place was teeming.

Another issue is that I can't hack into the security systems and wander around the building at the same time. Well, strictly speaking I could execute the hack, but I would have to kill all the CCTV feeds at once before entering Synergis, which would alert security that something is wrong. There are good reasons why this was always going to be a two-person job. Which is not to say that it can't be done by one person – just as long as that person doesn't mind getting arrested for it a few hours later.

I am actually asking myself which might carry the bigger sentence – getting busted for hacking RSGN or getting busted for breaking into Synergis – that's how desperate this is getting.

How could he do this to me? Is this his revenge, for all the things I've done to him? Stringing me along and dumping me right at the moment when I thought we were about to carry this off?

Well, fuck you, I decide. I'm going to remind him that if he hangs me out to dry, I have nothing to lose by returning the favour.

I am getting ready to restart the countdown website I threatened him with previously, when suddenly my mobile rings.

'Jack, where the fuck have you been?'

'I'm sorry, I couldn't answer my phone.'

'Why not? I was panicking here.'

'It's complicated. I'm on my way now, though.'

He is panting, and there is a weird rhythm to the background noise of the call.

'Are you running?'

'Yeah. I got sidetracked. I still need to get home, get changed and pick up my gear.'

'Why don't you jump in a cab?'

'Are you kidding? Tube strike.'

'Sorry. Not thinking. You should be able to take a bus when you're heading for Monument. They'll be much quieter in that direction.'

'Appropriate too, for a heist. I always loved that bit in *Die Hard* when Hans Gruber got the Number 21 to Nakatomi Plaza.'

Jack calls again about half an hour later, to say he's a few minutes away from the target.

I have all my research documents open on the screen so that any information I am likely to need is to hand. Right now the file at the top concerns security personnel. I called a couple of nights ago to establish who would be working this shift, then went into social-media research mode.

I say a few things out loud to get into using this particular voice. I sound a little shaky, but it's not a bad thing if I come across as nervous. I take a couple of breaths and begin dialling, spoofing the home number of a genuine Synergis employee, in case they check the records later.

'Hello, Tricorn House.'

'Oh, thank God there's someone there. I wasn't sure there would be anybody still in Synergis at this time. Honestly, you're my saviour.'

He isn't, yet, but I've just given him a high status and he will be reluctant to strip himself of it.

'Oh, no, this is Tricorn House Security,' he corrects me. 'I thought there was still somebody up there in Synergis but I guess not, so that's why you've come through to here.'

'I see. Tricorn Security. Hang on, I know that voice. Is that . . . Aaron?'

'It is.'

He sounds pleased and surprised to be recognised. I chucked in the pause to give him that moment of hoping I get it right.

'Yeah, this is Cheryl from Synergis, Cheryl Hayes. You remember? We talked about Tenerife because you were going there on holiday.'

'Oh, yeah.'

It's my estimate that he must have a dozen small-talk chats every day. Chances are he's talked about his holiday destinations with enough people that he's not going to link the subject with anybody specific. The main thing is that it establishes me in his mind as somebody who passes through here all the time.

'May, you're going, isn't it?' (Thank you, Facebook.)

'That's right. So how can I assist?'

'Oh, God, Aaron, I'm like: help me, Obi Wan Kenobi, you're my only hope. What it is, it's taken me two hours to get home because of this Tube strike, and it turns out I've only gone and left my phone at the office.'

'Oh no.'

'Nightmare, right? But it gets worse. I've got this major project I need to get finished for the morning. It was supposed to be next week, but I just opened my laptop and there's an email saying the client has had to bring his trip forward, and he's flying in from China and blah-blah-blah. I could do it on my laptop here at home, but all the project files are on the internal network and I can't log in because I need my phone for the new login thingy.'

'The 2FA?' he asks.

'That thing, yeah.'

I take a breath. Here we go.

'Can I ask a massive favour? Could you run upstairs to Synergis and get my phone, then read the PIN to me? I'm pretty sure I've left it on my desk. It's dead easy to find. I sit right next to Oliver Greenberg.'

I have no idea where Cheryl sits, but I know from my research that both Aaron and Oliver are Spurs fans, so there's a greater chance Aaron remembers him, meaning the use of his name will further cement my credentials.

'Oh, yeah, I know Oliver. I'm really sorry, Cheryl. I'd love to help, but I don't have authorisation. My swipe card only lets me in certain areas. I'd only be able to override that and get into Synergis if there was a full-scale emergency.'

A fact I am counting on.

'Of course. I forgot. Thing is, I'd come back in and get it myself but it took me all this time to get home. So near and yet so far, eh? Could be looking at a three-hour round trip, all for the sake of a four-digit PIN number.'

I dangle this out there and let it hang. I'll ask explicitly if it comes to that, but it's better if I give him the chance to offer, so that he thinks the idea came from him.

'I know. There's nothing I can do, though. As I said, I can't get into Synergis. I mean, obviously I've got the 2FA app on my phone too, but I don't imagine that helps you.'

Oh, but you'd be wrong.

'No. 'Fraid not. Hang about, though, actually, it does,' I add, sounding like this has just occurred to me. 'Aaron, you're a genius.

The 2FA thing generates a PIN that lets you log into the system. Doesn't matter who uses it: that's what usernames and passwords are for.'

'So if I generate a PIN on my phone, you'd be sorted?'

'And owing you a massive, massive favour, yeah.'

'All right. Problem solved. Let me launch the app. Okay, here we go. You ready for this now?'

I've been ready for days, mate.

# CAMERA SHY

Parlabane calms his breathing as Tricorn House rises into view. This place has turned into a citadel in his mind, a prison he can only escape by breaking *into*. He can't remember being so nervous about an act of trespass; not even the first time he ever did this in search of evidence supporting a story he knew to be true.

He is still in the suit, a small rucksack slung over his shoulder. He worries a little that it might look an incongruous combo, but it's after hours. He is also wearing a hat and glasses to make his face that bit harder to recognise on CCTV footage, in the event that Sam isn't able to disable the cameras or erase the tapes. He has to look like he belongs, look like he does this two or three times a day.

Parlabane approaches the barriers, where he will confront the night's first big moment of truth. As he grips the card he is already rehearsing excuses that will allow him to retreat inconspicuously in the event of failure.

*Yeah, my card isn't working. Never mind, I'll get it sorted in the morning. I was only popping in to pick up a DVD I'd left in my drawer.*

He taps the card to the sensor and the glass gates slide apart.

It's on.

Somewhere inside the computer system, John Finch has been logged as entering the building at 21.02. Sam's hack of the Gatekeeper software has delivered on its first challenge. He feels a surge of relief, a pressure valve venting somewhere inside his subconscious, yet at the same time he can't help feeling that every door this card opens takes him one level deeper into the mire.

He follows the route he was taken on his previous visit, around the back of the reception area to the lifts, where he puts on his Bluetooth headset. He took time to devise call-names for both of them, as well as a series of coded references so that they would each know what the other was talking about without saying anything that might be incriminating were it to be played back in a courtroom. Sam just laughed and looked at him as though he had suggested using tin cans and hairy string.

She explained that such code words and aliases would be redundant as they would be using an encrypted voice-over IP connection and that – once she had jailbroken it – his mobile would be sending no audio telephony signals: only data.

In an attempt to regain some cred and establish that he knew what she was talking about, he had told her how he used one of the earliest VOIP iterations back in the late nineties, adding how its economic benefits for international communications were reduced by having to pay per-minute for a 28k dial-up modem connection.

From her expression he could tell that if she was at all impressed, it was by the fact that a man clearly over a hundred years old could still use a computer.

'Barb, do you read? I'm in.'

'I read. Where are you?'

'Approaching the lifts. Hoping my visit is not being recorded for posterity. How are you progressing on that front?'

There is an unsettlingly long pause.

'Working on it.'

Arse.

He enters one of the elevators and subjects the card to its next test. It passes, letting the lift raise him six storeys, while simultaneously plunging him one level deeper into the shit.

There is a friendly chime and the doors open on to a bright landing, the glass walls allowing him to look down into the vestibule. Pressing himself close and peering directly down, he can see the main reception area from behind. The angle reveals that there is a bank of screens running along the desk, embedded beneath the shelf where the receptionists' computer monitors sit. He is too high to make out any details, but it looks like CCTV feeds.

He glances around the landing, spots a camera high on one wall.

'Any word on Tricorn's Funniest Home Videos?'

'Still working on it.'

He taps the card against a sensor: another open door, another crime committed, another step further into damnation.

Synergis's expensively furnished interior reception area lies before him, partially lit by the glow from the landing behind him and the lights of the city through the windows dead ahead. Everything in between is in darkness, only the occasional blink of an LED visible among the desks and workstations.

He takes a moment to get his bearings, disentangling his memory of where Tanya first took him from his recall of where he actually needs to be. Then he walks forward, at which point the lights ahead of him begin flickering into life.

Exhibiting remarkable composure and lizard-brain reflexes, he freezes to the spot and just about manages not to shit himself before realising that this sudden illumination was merely the response of a motion-activated power-saving switch.

There is nobody here. More significantly, there are no alarms. Sam has deactivated the security systems.

As if reading his mind, her voice sounds in his ear.

'Did something happen? You made a weird noise.'

'Tripped the auto for the lights, gave myself a jolt.'

'Well, that's not all it tripped. I've tapped into the CCTV feed for the monitors that the security guard is watching. So far it's been running a sequence, toggling through locations in rotation, but when those lights came on, it switched straight to where you are.'

'Must be automated to do that, draw attention to anything unexpected. No alarms, though.'

'No, it didn't trigger anything,' she confirms.

'But the alarms *are* deactivated, right?'

'Yes,' she replies, sounding testy. 'I wouldn't have let you proceed unless—'

'Okay. Just clarifying.'

'Bear in mind you're going to be tripping the lights and camera feeds wherever you go. That shouldn't raise suspicion if you're only walking through some offices, but the thing to be aware of is that when you get to R&D, you'll need to wait for the camera feed to switch again before you start messing with the vault.'

'Roger. But I thought you were going to be in control of these cameras.'

'Working on it.'

'You've said that twice already. And I'm not going to be messing with the vault unless you can supply me with the daily code. How are you doing with that part?'

'Working on it.'

# UNWANTED GUEST

Shit toasters.

This isn't quite going according to plan. It's not falling apart on me either, otherwise I'd have given Jack the word to abort, but I can see problems ahead, and if I can't perform some top-of-my-game hack-fu on them, things might get very messy.

If I was being completely honest with Jack, if I was being completely honest with myself, I would give him the word to abort. I'm not sure I can handle this. That on its own ought to be reason to bail, but the bitch of it is, I'm not sure I *can't* handle this either, and I only have one shot. I'd say I'm gambling with both our fates, but the selfish part is that I'm actually only gambling with his. Whether I get caught in the act or I abandon the attempt, I am equally fucked. My only safe way out of this is via a result, so I have no option but to gamble with the stake I've got.

As soon as Aaron gave me a PIN, I logged into Matthew Coleridge's account, allowing me high-level access to Synergis's security systems. In case there were any session-time limits, the first thing I did was disable the 2FA on both his and Jane Dunwoodie's accounts. I could have disabled it for the whole show, but I don't want anybody logging in from home then reporting it up the line that the system didn't ask for a PIN.

Next I navigated my way through the building's alarm systems, which was where I first realised the waters were getting deeper than I might be ready for. When I tried to alter the settings, I got hit with a fresh password request, and Coleridge, like a good security chief, wasn't using the same one for everything.

I didn't lie to Jack. The good news is that all the Synergis alarms and sensors are currently deactivated: the vault, the server room, all restricted areas and, indeed, non-restricted areas too.

249

The bad news is that this had nothing to do with me.

They were like that when I got there, and I suspect it's not that they have been deactivated, but that they haven't been set yet. It could be that they don't get set until a certain time of night, which is worrying because it means we might be up against a clock we can't see. Or it could be that Aaron in Security hasn't set them yet because there are still people working elsewhere in the building.

Oh Jesus.

My mind flashes back to my conversation with Aaron.

*I thought there was still somebody left up there in Synergis but I guess not.*

At the time I didn't twig because I was so focused on getting him to give me his PIN.

Something cold starts trickling through me. I mute the audio feed to Jack and pick up one of my mobiles, the one set to spoof Cheryl Hayes's home number.

'Hello, Tricorn House.'

'Aaron, hello. It's Cheryl again.'

'Is everything okay with that PIN?'

'Yeah, yeah. I'm ploughing through this stuff now. With a fair wind I might get to my bed by about one.'

'Harsh.'

'Innit, though. The thing is, when I called, you said you thought there might be somebody still up there in Synergis. It would be really useful if there was someone on-site who could check a couple of things for me.'

'Yeah, but there wasn't, otherwise the call wouldn't have come through to me.'

'I know, but I thought: what if there *is* someone in there but they were away at the loo or something when I rang? Could you check the system to see if there's anybody who hasn't swiped out yet tonight?'

'Of course, sure.'

I hear the gentle tapping of the keyboard. Sounds like he's a one-finger typist, and the speed of his technique isn't doing my heart any favours.

'Hello, Cheryl?'

'Yeah, still here.'

'Looks like you're in luck. According to the computer, Mr Cruz is still in the building.'

# MIXED MESSAGES

Parlabane fears he's taken a wrong turn. He knows where he is relative to the street outside, but the corridor layout isn't an easily navigable grid, and sections of it are close to identical: desks, cubicles, computers, whiteboards.

He approaches the next set of doors and waves his card at the sensor, an electronic talisman charming an invisible sentinel. It's so quiet that he can hear the mechanism of the lock release, the silence making him all the more conscious of the sound of his own movements.

He pushes the door open and steps into the darkness beyond, listening for the faint click and buzz that heralds the motion-activated lighting. In the fraction of a second before it engages, he is sure he sees light spilling from interior windows on the left of the passageway. He stops dead again, looking for somewhere to hide. There is an open area to the right, a cubicle farm currently in darkness, but that would change should he head there, like an automated spotlight permanently trained on the intruder.

He listens out for any sound of movement, but hears nothing. The sight of the corridor lights coming on would have attracted the attention of anyone in that office on the left, surely: unless they didn't notice it from inside somewhere already illuminated.

He proceeds with the softest tread, crouching as he nears the interior windows before rising himself up on creaking knees to glimpse from the bottom edge of the glass. He sees a meeting room similar to the one he was left to wait in; though rather than one big table, there are six double desks all facing the smart board dominating the wall at one end. There is nobody inside. Maybe the power-saver lighting switch failed, or perhaps the electrics in here are on a different circuit.

He stands up straight and allows himself to breathe out.

That's when he hears footsteps above: sudden, swift and brief, then gone again.

He is about to speak but Sam beats him to it.

'Jack, we've got a complication.'

'No kidding. I just heard somebody moving upstairs.'

'Leo Cruz didn't swipe out tonight. He's still inside.'

'Arse. Do you know where? Because if he's in R&D, then I'm going to have to lay low and wait.'

'I'm trying to get a fix on him, but nothing so far. I don't think he can be in R&D, though. I haven't seen a feed from there yet, so I'm assuming it's in darkness.'

'You're assuming? Why can't you take a look, switch to that camera?'

'It doesn't work like that.'

'Fuck's sake. Tell me when something does work, *Barb*.'

And that's the other thing that isn't quite bending to my will like I hoped. Coleridge's login should have given me complete control of the CCTV system, allowing me to display whichever cameras I needed to see on my laptop, and to select which views I wanted Aaron to be looking at. Instead it's almost the other way around. I have no say over which feeds are live, so I am only able to see what I presume to be the same views as are cycling on Aaron's four security monitors.

What's truly worrying me about this is that it suggests there's somebody else logged in whose access privileges trump mine.

I am left waiting and hoping to catch a glimpse of Cruz in order to suss his location. I have to be patient, but I can't sit staring at the CCTV windows either, as I have other tasks to be getting on with.

I am simultaneously logged into the system as Jane Dunwoodie, glancing at the CCTV feeds every time the camera switches. I'm starting to recognise most of the views, though I don't know for sure which ones are inside Synergis and which ones are elsewhere in Tricorn House.

I wish I had a bigger screen. I have the CCTV feeds lined up in a row along the top, as small as my eyesight allows, and now have two separate windows open via the Dunwoodie account: one to trawl her email and the other to search her files for references to Project RBA.

I am focusing so intently upon this that I don't hear the door open. I almost hit the ceiling when I hear Lilly's voice.

'Sam? What are you doing?'

She's standing in the kitchen doorway in her pyjamas, looking distressed. I can tell she hasn't been to sleep.

'Lilly, you can't come in here.'

'I've got slippers on.'

I'm thinking, What the hell has that got to do with anything? Then I remember what I told her about the debris on the floor.

'Yes, but it's still dangerous.'

She's staring at the laptop screen. She's looking hurt, maybe even betrayed.

'You're watching TV,' she says, accusingly.

'No, it's not TV. It's my computer.'

'Why can't I watch it?'

'It doesn't have a DVD player. It's not as good as yours was.'

'You're watching TV on it, though.'

I realise she's looking at the CCTV feeds.

I can hear Jack in my headset, asking who I'm talking to. I mute the mic.

'It's not a show, Lilly. It's something I have to do. For school,' I add.

'You said you stopped school. Can I watch what you're watching?'

'Lilly, you need to go to bed.'

'But I can't sleep.'

'Well, you won't sleep if you're not in bed.'

'I'm scared in my room. What if the burglars come back?'

In my earpiece, Jack is asking again about the PIN.

I can't handle this. I lose it.

'Lilly, just get to your fucking bed.'

Her face crumples up into tears and she runs off, howling like I haven't heard her do in years.

Jesus. I hate myself. I hate my mum. I hate Jack. I hate Zodiac.

I get up from my chair, intending to go to her room, but then one of the CCTV feeds refreshes, and I find myself staring at it. I've seen it a couple of times before and assumed it was somewhere downstairs, but now that it has cycled back around I am seeing a different possibility in light of recent developments.

'Jack, I'm looking at a lobby area outside an office: there's a secretary's desk, a sofa and a coffee table.'

'Big modernist painting on the wall that looks like vomit?'

'Yes.'

'That's Cruz's office.'

'I can't see inside the office itself, but the door is ajar and it looks like there's a light on.'

'Okay. I know where that is. He must have come back downstairs. I can get to R&D without going too close to Cruz's office, but give me a shout if you see him on the move.'

'You got it.'

I get back to the Dunwoodie login, still keeping tabs on the CCTV feeds as they change. A new one flashes up each time Jack triggers the lights in a different area. Sometimes he's right there in the shot, others no more than a shadow moving in the background. Unfortunately I have no sense of where he is in relation to anything else: it's like something out of one of Lilly's Loony Tunes DVDs, with him disappearing from one window then popping up in another.

Happily I am getting more of a feel for the layout of the network. It's not been my most elegant of hacks, but I am finally homing in on my goal. After running into a dozen dead-ends, I have uncovered a sub-directory on one of the Research and Development servers, tagged 'R_B_A', the underscores having foxed my automated search.

Jackpot. I encounter a huge cache of documents and open a few samples to make sure I've definitely found what Zodiac is after. There are blueprints, circuit diagrams, exploded-view drawings of micro-architecture and a bunch of other stuff I could go over for hours without making head nor tail of. I open a video file, hoping to cut to the chase as to what this prototype is, but it just shows

Cruz standing in a dark room talking straight to camera, and I don't have time to watch it through.

I'm sending the lot to a trusted file storage server based in Finland. This will allow me to access it later without the stolen material ever being stored on my own machine. I always boot my laptop from a memory card that I can swallow or destroy if the feds ever kick down the door, but the Project RBA trove is too big to store on the card, and I can't afford to be connected to it.

Except, apparently I'm not sending anything anywhere. The files are restricted by copy protection. I'll need Jack to do this on-site.

'Jack, are you near a computer?'

He answers in a quiet tone, a little above a whisper, though there is an echo on his voice, as well as a slight break-up in the signal.

'This is literally the only time since I walked in here when I could answer no to that question. I'm in a stairwell. Why?'

'I need you to find a machine with a USB port. I'll talk you through it from there.'

'Any news on that PIN?'

'Shit, sorry. I've been concentrating on locating the Project RBA files. I'll get right on it.'

'Only if you're not too busy. Maybe during the ad break in *Come Dine With Me*.'

'Yeah, sure, Jack. You really nailed me. I'm loafing about here, watching my big blank space on the wall because the fucking TV got taken by drug dealers, and I'm enjoying the modern-art vibe of having what little stuff my sister and I still own smashed and emptied on the floor by the junkie bastards who ransacked my flat tonight.'

Jesus, where did that come from? I ask myself. And I told him I had a sister. That was stupid. I've been so careful to hide my home life and my family from him.

There is radio silence for a few seconds, though I can just about hear Jack's footsteps reverberating in the stairwell.

'I'm sorry. I had no idea.'

'No, I'm sorry. Pressure's getting to me, you know?'

'I know.'

A few seconds later one of the CCTV windows changes to a new view as Jack trips the lights. I don't see him at first, then he enters the edge of the frame and sits down at a PC.

'Go to the one on the other side of that cubicle,' I tell him. 'That way you won't be in shot – in case Aaron the security guard is taking an interest.'

'Got you.'

He takes a seat at a different PC shortly before the view automatically toggles to somewhere else. He's got latex gloves on now, so he doesn't leave prints on the keyboard. They're skin coloured and hard to notice on the screen unless you're looking at the fine rings around his wrists. I hope Aaron isn't paying as close attention as I am.

I go back to trawling Dunwoodie's emails while he waits for it to boot up. She gets a shit-ton of messages each day, and it's not apparent from the subject line which one contains the daily vault code. I really hope I'm not going to have to read the text of each one individually, as that could take hours.

'Okay, the machine is up and running and I can navigate the menus, but I don't have internet access.'

'You need to log in before you can connect to anything.'

I log out of Coleridge's account so that Jack can use it to get into the system, then I begin sending him a piece of software I need him to put on a USB memory stick. This will allow him to copy the RBA files direct once he gets inside the server room.

Jack confirms that the download has started and I go back to the emails. I change the sort filter so that it lists by sender, reckoning that will let me narrow my search.

At the top of my screen, the feeds refresh again, and I catch a flash of movement in the corner of one window, someone exiting the frame at speed.

'You on your way, then?' I ask.

'Just about. Blue line shows the transfer still has about half a centimetre to . . . nope, done.'

Shit toasters. Jack hasn't budged, so it wasn't him.

I stare avidly at the CCTV feeds, willing them to refresh. The window where I saw movement remains empty. I'm not sure where it is, but I think Jack passed through it a while ago.

257

Finally one of the windows shows me the lobby outside Cruz's office.

'Jack, you need to be aware, Cruz might be on the go. The door is still ajar but I can't say for certain whether it's in exactly the same position.'

I tell him this much because I don't want to admit the other possibility, which is that Cruz is still in his office and there's someone *else* at large inside Synergis. I recall Zodiac's warnings that I wasn't the only person tasked with this, and think of the weird lock-out on the CCTV system. I scan the feeds, but see no further movement other than Jack appearing in a new area.

If there is one consolation, it's that I still haven't seen the R&D lab, which would indicate that the lights haven't been triggered up there. But even as I think of this, I am hit by the disturbing possibility that someone else is executing my original plan: manipulating the cameras to conceal the movements of their own partner on-site.

I give myself a shake. Focus, girl. We need this PIN.

No matter whether it is Cruz or someone else moving through the building, one thing is certain: I don't have the time to comb through these emails. It would simply take too long, so I need to think this through logically and narrow the field.

I decide I can dismiss those from external domains or even people outside Dunwoodie's department, which is when I remember that in fact there is only one other person who would be party to emails containing this information.

I look for messages directly from Cruz or forwarded by him. Again, there's a lot of reading here. I scan a few via the preview window, seeing nothing obvious; certainly no numerical sequences leaping out from all the screeds of text.

'Okay, I am in sight of the R&D labs,' Jack states. 'First stop is the server room, but once I'm done there I'm going to need a result on that code for the vault.'

I look again at all the correspondence: high-level suit stuff. That's when it hits me that this would need to be automated. Both of these people are too high up and busy for the lowly task of resetting the vault PIN on a daily basis, and they're not going to trust anyone else with it.

I scan the list for any emails that look like they might be automatically generated, maybe carrying 'admin' or 'auto' as a prefix on the sender's name.

Nothing.

I search for 'do not reply'.

Nothing.

A new view pops up in one of the CCTV windows. I see Jack striding through Research and Development, moments away from the server room.

'You remember what you need to do?' I ask, as he taps his keycard and disappears inside.

'Insert the memory stick into the USB port on server Syn_Indigo. Doing that now.'

I hold my breath through a long, silent wait, then the connection lights up at my end. I run a sequence of commands to tunnel back via Dunwoodie's account, and a few seconds later, I have started copying the Project RBA files to my secure server in Finland.

'We good?' asks Jack.

'Yes, but don't touch the USB. There's a lot of data to transfer. Could take a couple of minutes.'

'If only there was something constructive I could do in the meantime.'

'Yeah, I'm still working on it.'

I try a search for messages to which both Cruz and Dunwoodie were recipients. Unfortunately this gives me another shit-ton of results, all sorts of cascaded spam that went out to everybody. But among this flood my trained eye homes in on a message that only went out to the two of them. Its sender is listed as Linda Collins and its subject line reads: 'What's the word?'

I open it, but the short paragraph of text makes no sense. It says:

Sister flower hope takes diary pouting for gable sentry
cardigan throw closes on pepper.

The feeds refresh again. I see a flash of movement, but once more it's on the edge of the frame. This isn't just bad luck, I'm thinking. This is someone who knows where the cameras are pointing – or has somebody telling him where the cameras are pointing. I ask myself the likelihood that Cruz would be trying to avoid appearing on CCTV inside his own building.

His office lobby appears again on the next refresh. I don't think the door has moved since last time. I'm not sure it ever moved at all.

At the bottom of my screen, I see the file transfer has about seventy seconds remaining.

I open the metadata on the nonsensical Linda Collins email and check the headers. The display address is linda.collins@synergis.com but the original header states that it came from aux.gms.Gatekeeper@ synergis.com. I run a search for the subject line, and there it is, repeated every day: 'What's the word?'

I open two more.

Sudden hold breaking for gloves to produce the wonder
   providing . . .

Curled certainly with convincing unafraid for other
   genuine . . .

Every time, it's utter bollocks. But my hacker's eyes, always looking for patterns, notice that in every message, the first word has six letters.

My eyes fall upon the shitty burner mobile on the kitchen table next to my laptop, with its ancient push-button dial pad. No touch-screen for texting.

'Sister' is the PIN.

'Jack, the code for the vault is seven four seven eight three seven. Confirm.'

'Seven four seven eight three seven.'

It's as he calls it back to me that the feed from R&D goes black.

# PRIZE POSSESSION

Parlabane hears a ping and a fading hum as the lab is plunged into darkness. It sounds like a surge-protector was tripped, or some automated system killed the juice to the lights, which would explain why he can still hear the fans in the server room. It makes sense that they would be running on a different circuit.

He holds his position, giving it a few seconds to see whether emergency lighting kicks in or the system automatically restarts. Neither of these things happens.

His next thought is that it might be closing time: perhaps the reason Cruz was on the move is that he has left the building, and maybe the last one out does truly turn off the lights, especially if he's a cost-conscious boss.

However, the stunned silence in his earpiece is arguing against this hypothesis.

'Jack, you still there?'

'Yeah. I've lost the lights, though.'

He waits for his eyes to adjust to the dark, for the glow through the windows to become enough for him to navigate without danger of tripping over a desk. He proceeds past the sub-zero room, the constant hum from within indicating that it is on a different circuit too. Its door is closed and he knows that the facility must boast near-impermeable insulation, so it must be only his own anxiety that is causing a chill to run through him.

Steady the buffs, he tells himself. He's almost there.

He holds up his phone as he approaches the vault door, using its flashlight to illuminate the keypad.

He punches in the PIN.

Nothing happens.

Shit. Did the electrics get killed? No. There is a red light on the keypad, so there is still power to the lock. There is a small orange light about a foot away on the wall too. Of course. A sensor plate for the GEM system. He taps his card against it and tries the PIN again. He hears the click and whir of an internal mechanism and the light on the keypad turns green.

'We're in.'

Parlabane plays the flashlight around the darkened chamber. There are tiers of metal shelving running almost floor to ceiling around the steel-walled cube, most of it empty. He counts four boxes of files, all stashed low on the right-hand side. He figures the excess capacity indicates Neurosphere kept a lot more stuff in here once upon a time, but it would have been shipped out and possibly shredded before they handed the door keys to Cruz.

'Can you see the prototype?'

There is no question but that what he is after is the item directly ahead: a compact brushed-aluminium flight case roughly the size of a hardback book. The object is sitting on the middle shelf opposite the door; it has probably been positioned there for convenience, but he can't help inferring an element of it being afforded pride of place, like it's the god inside a tiny shrine.

'I think so.'

Parlabane flips it open, revealing a metallic device nestling on a tight bed of insulating foam, like an oversized engagement ring inside its presentation box. On the inside of the flip-lid is a printed label stating: Synergis Dimension PHP> Prototype version 3.1.

'What is it?' Sam asks.

'I'm looking at it and I still have no idea.'

He holds it in his hand. It is the size of a slim matchbox, uniformly metal but for a tiny glass dot at the centre of one face. Its purpose remains baffling, and he resents how such a trifling thing could have tyrannised his world for the past few weeks. The power is in his hands now, though: literally.

He thinks about simply pocketing the device, but decides that taking the flight case would be a better option.

They're never worth as much if you don't have the original box, he muses, closing the lid gently and placing the flight case carefully inside his rucksack.

Parlabane clicks off the flashlight, plunging the chamber into darkness. He waits again as his pupils respond, watching the shapes of desks and monitors gradually resolve themselves against the rising glow.

He's on the home straight now. He admits to himself he never thought he'd make it this far, so he has to beware euphoria: stay frosty for the egress. It would be all the more painful were he to fuck it up now, especially if it was due to an oversight, an act of carelessness resultant of being too eager to GTFO.

With that thought, he suddenly remembers about the memory stick, still jammed into a port in the server room. He is wearing latex gloves right now but knows he must have handled the memory stick when he wasn't. He can't be sure, but it is possible Sam might have handled it at some point too.

He experiences a tiny surge of fright, like a trailer for the panic that *would* have hit him had this detail only occurred to him later.

Okay. Server room and then exeunt Parlabane.

He steps through the vault door and something hits him in the chest.

He is racked by a surge of the most enormous, convulsing pain, amid a riot of light. It is not a flash but a storm: a matrix of brilliant but agonising energy enveloping his whole body.

As he falls backwards, his first thought is that he has been shot, but when he hits the floor and he tries to reach for his chest, he finds he is unable to control his limbs. Not only are they powerless, but it is as though they are restrained, held in an invisible mesh. He feels them spasm.

He is aware of motion close by: the movement of air and the sound of soft footfalls. He senses a figure crouching over him, initially only an outline of black against the greys. In time he makes out a visage, though in his confused and disoriented state, he struggles to decode his own senses. He sees a face he recognises, yet it is a face that is not a face. What he sees, or thinks he sees, refuses to add up. It is blank and yet distinct; unmistakable and yet . . .

Anonymous.

A Guy Fawkes mask.

Parlabane tries again to raise himself, feeling sensation and control begin to return to his arms.

This proves a mistake.

The figure extends a hand and he is convulsed in a second storm of light and pain.

Then there is nothing.

# PART THREE

# WINDOWS UPDATE

I think I'm going to be sick. I stand up and head for the sink as quickly as I can, allowing for the scattered bottles of bleach, oven cleaner and a dozen other trip hazards. This is not like my previous hacks, which churned up my insides in a good way. The tension surrounding this has been growing for weeks, becoming close to unbearable since Jack entered the building, and that was before I lost visual contact. Now I've lost audio too. There was a weird crackling sound, then a thump, then more crackling, then the connection was dropped altogether.

I can't talk to Jack. I can't hear him, I can't see him, and I know this can't be good.

I grip the sink, staring out of the kitchen window at the street below, quietly getting on with itself. I wonder how many other silent crises are taking place behind the walls of all these other homes, while their neighbours obliviously assume the world outside their own door is calm.

In the past I would sometimes look up from my computer and realise I was starving or that my bladder was full; so much time had passed, so much drama had unfolded before my eyes and yet there I still was, still sitting in my bedroom. Whether hacking or playing video games, there was always that air gap between the places on my computer and the reality everyone had to live in. But the air gap has been completely breached, and everything that happens on this laptop tonight changes the world I will have to live in afterwards.

The sick feeling passes and I splash water on my face. The only way to get through this is to get busy. I need to hack into the works, take control of Tricorn House's internal electrics.

I remember about Nigel Holt, the buildings manager, and I scroll

267

to his username and password in the list among my research documents. I open another shell and navigate to a fresh login screen, but the fields are greyed out, looking for a 2FA PIN.

Shit. Coleridge's login allowed me to deactivate 2FA for Synergis, but not the whole building.

I'll have to do it analogue.

I call Aaron once again. It rings and rings with no response. Ten rings. Twenty. He could be on another call. He could be in the toilet.

Keep it together.

I hang up, force myself to wait a full minute, watching the second hand tick all the way around the kitchen clock face, then try again.

'Hello, Tricorn House.'

'Aaron, yeah, me again. Gotta stop meeting like this.'

I manage a chuckle and try to keep my voice light and breezy, though my hand is shaking as it holds the phone.

'People will talk. Least I know I'm not the only one working late. What can I do for you this time?'

'It's Mr Cruz. He's trying to get hold of Nigel Holt because he says the lights have gone out in the Research and Development lab. I said I'd call and ask you to look into it as well. Can you have a check on your system, see if everything is okay?'

'Yeah, I can call that up. Happens all the time. Usually them power-saver switches being a bit over-keen, though sometimes it's a blown fuse at a main junction box, and I can't do nothing about that. Need to wait until the maintenance guys get in tomorrow morning.'

I hear him type slowly as ever into his keyboard. It's excruciating.

'Let's see. Nah, according to the computer, all the electrics are running normal. No outages, no problems.'

*According to the computer.*

Sure, because that's how I would play it if I was messing with this place: bypass the fault detection so it reports all systems go. The good news is that if this is the case, then it should respond to a reset. The very bad news is that this would all but confirm there is somebody else messing with this place, and after a reset there would be nothing to stop them simply killing the lights again.

'Can you reset the lights in that area anyway? Just in case it saves Mr Holt having to come out?'

'I think so. Let me see. Research and Development, you said?'

'That's right.'

While Aaron is plodding his way through this, I run a program to list everyone currently logged into the system. It may not tell me who I'm up against, but it will at least identify whose account they're logged in from.

The results scroll down beneath the command line, showing only three. As well as the two I am responsible for – jdunwoodie and mcoleridge – there is one more user active: lcruz.

'Okay, I think I've reset the lights, but as it was showing okay before and it's showing okay now, I don't know if it's worked.'

'Thanks, Aaron. I'll give Mr Cruz a call and find out.'

I look at the CCTV views along the top of my screen. None of them has auto-switched to the R&D labs, which I take to be a bad sign, though it might need a few moments for the reset to take effect.

I watch and wait. Nothing changes. I watch some more, then glance at the clock again. It's been at least a minute and the windows are still showing the same feeds. The reset hasn't worked.

Then it hits me. The windows haven't changed. None of them has automatically cycled to the next view. Something is different.

I try the CCTV command system again and find I've got full control. I can select any camera and hold the view as required.

Whoever hacked into the Tricorn House systems must have logged out, having finished whatever they were doing. Something tells me this is not a good thing.

I refresh the list of active users. It now only shows jdunwoodie and mcoleridge.

I start toggling through CCTV views, looking for Jack. I've got access to a branching menu telling me where all the cameras are. I bring up the Synergis ones, opening a sub-menu listing cameras inside Research and Development.

I see one marked 'Vault', and click on that.

One of my windows now shows the view inside a dark chamber, light spilling in through the open door. Jack isn't there.

I click on 'Server Farm'. That's empty too.

I toggle through three more, each showing desks, cubicles, corridors, locked doors. Still no sign.

Finally I click on one tagged 'Sub-Zero Room', and my mouth falls open in horror.

# MURDER IN THE DARK

Pain wracks him. It is all he knows, all he can sense, as though these receptors are the only systems to have fully come back online as he struggles to reboot his consciousness. At first it feels like it is everywhere, too many parts of his body reporting damage for him to pick out discrete sources, but gradually his head, his face, his ribs and his chest make their cries distinct. There is an unmistakable metallic taste in his mouth, and he can feel its stickiness on his top lip and around his gums. He can hear absolutely no sound, other than the rush of his own blood in his ears, and when he opens his eyes it makes no difference: he can see nothing. He recalls several blows to the head, and fears he may have been blinded.

Memories of the violence are the freshest, but they make way for a swirling, woozy recall of what immediately preceded it. He remembers who did this: the V mask, the hoodie. He had a hand-held electroshock device and a telescopic baton.

The former was to render him helpless. It was the latter that did the lasting damage. He was dragged somewhere, still twitching from the second shock.

He remembers a voice, someone speaking.

Sam.

It takes him a moment to realise that he's cold: really cold. He is lying on his back and every point of contact with the floor beneath him is freezing.

He is in the sub-zero room. That's why he can't see.

Instinctively he puts out his right hand to push himself upright and winces in pain. He fears his arm is broken, possibly from a defensive wound. He reaches out his left hand and it touches soft material, something beside him on the floor. That's when it hits him that his latex gloves are gone. There is something solid beneath the cloth, and that's cold too.

There is someone next to him. Someone dead.

He manages to sit upright, his head spinning from the sudden upwards movement. Something wet runs into his eye. He wipes it away, following the path it traced. He is bleeding from his scalp.

He reaches for his phone so that he can use the flashlight, but his pocket is empty. It takes a second for the true import of this to sink in. Never mind the flashlight app: without the phone he has no way of letting anybody know he is in here.

He crawls forward in search of a wall, bashing his head on a shelf maybe, or a table. Using his good arm, he manoeuvres around the obstacle, which is when his eye is drawn to the only thing in the room that can be seen: a tiny orange light.

It's a card sensor. Thank fuck.

He begins scrambling slowly towards it, mindful of further invisible obstacles, when suddenly there is a click and the room is bathed in light.

He gets to his feet and turns around to look at the body on the floor, dead from multiple stab wounds. His face has taken a battering too, probably from the same telescopic baton, but there is no mistaking his identity.

It is Leo Cruz.

Equipment lies scattered about the floor, circuit boards and anti-static gloves from an upended table. It looks like evidence of a struggle, but it wasn't one he was a part of, and if the same assailant killed Cruz, he doubts that was much of a contest either: not with an electronic cosh in the attacker's armoury.

Parlabane fumbles for the swipe card. It is doubly awkward because he is having to reach with his left hand into an inside left-hand pocket, and because he is shivering.

He waves the card in front of the sensor. It doesn't respond. He taps it. Still nothing. Finally he rubs the card against it, as he once saw Tanya do when a pad wasn't proving sensitive.

The light remains red.

He looks frantically for options, and his eyes are drawn to a thermostat. It states minus ten, and he is wearing only a light suit. He has no way of opening the door and no means of contacting the outside world. He will be unconscious within an hour and long dead by the time they open this thing tomorrow morning.

# REVELATIONS

I expand the CCTV window to fill the whole screen. I see Jack standing in the centre of the room, clutching his arms to his chest, shivering. There is blood on his face and his hair is matted with it, but he is doing better than the other guy, who I'm pretty sure is Leo Cruz.

I don't get why Jack is simply standing there, why he doesn't leave; then it hits me that he can't. Something has gone wrong with the swipe card.

No. None of this is down to malfunction.

I open up a new shell and connect to the GEM system, logging in via the secret backdoor I created when I hacked the source code. It responds by telling me the account does not exist. It's been deleted and I've been locked out.

I pick up the mobile and call Aaron, no fake cheeriness in my voice this time.

'Aaron. You have to get upstairs to Synergis, right now. There's somebody trapped inside the sub-zero room.'

'Hang on, slow down. You say there's . . . Oh Jesus.'

I'm guessing the new feed from the sub-zero room has shown up on one of his monitors.

'You need to open the door. There's somebody trapped in there.'

His voice is shaky in response.

'There's somebody *dead* in there. That's . . . Shit, I think that's Leo Cruz.'

'Yeah, and he won't be the only one if you don't do something. It's an industrial chilling facility. You need to get up there and let him out.'

'Let him out? That bloke's just killed somebody. I'm not opening the door to him on my own.'

'It's not what it looks like, believe me.'

'Hang about, how do you know what it looks like?'

Uh-oh. His tone is accusing now. I've blown it.

'You said you were talking to Leo Cruz a few minutes ago, about the lights,' he goes on. 'How are you seeing this? You said you were at home. You sound different. Who are you?'

I make one last desperate appeal.

'Never mind that. This is an emergency.'

'Damn right it is.'

# COLD LOGIC

Someone has hit the alarms. The ringing is muffled, but Parlabane can definitely hear it from beyond the walls of his frozen cell. It is a faint sound of hope.

There is a CCTV camera high on one wall. Maybe Sam has seen him and raised the alert, or perhaps it was Aaron the security guard. If that was the case though, why wouldn't he simply come and open the door using the override outside? Why hit the all-out emergency button?

The bloodied mess on the floor answers his question. That's when he grasps that the best-case scenario right now is that he should survive only to be taken into custody and charged with Cruz's murder. That's what this has been about all along: setting somebody up to take the fall.

Setting Sam up to take the fall.

It was supposed to be she who was coming here tonight, as far as Zodiac knew. He had demanded that she keep him up to date with her progress and her strategy, right down to the specifics of when she was planning to hit Synergis. When the scene was discovered in the morning, it was supposed to appear to the police that Cruz had tried to fight her off, apparently after he had interrupted her mid-robbery.

The post-mortems would show that he died of stab wounds, while she died of hypothermia, either after being rendered unconscious or from finding herself locked inside the sub-zero room. Crucially, the temperature would disguise when Cruz had actually died. By the time morning came around, there would be no sure way of knowing the time of death for either of the corpsicles.

With the alarm having been raised, he is estimating – hoping – the police will make their discovery a lot sooner than Zodiac planned,

276

but he'll get his scapegoat nonetheless. They're going to find Parlabane in here covered in blood, not all of which, he is sure, will turn out to be his own. Somewhere else in this building, a knife will be discovered too, with his fingerprints on the handle, grasped while he was unconscious.

He has to get out of here before the cops arrive. He looks back and forth, scanning the walls, as though there was a second door he might have missed. There is only one door, however, to which his key no longer works.

Might as well be locked in the vault, he muses bleakly, a thought that causes him to reflect on the crucial ways that this is not true.

The sub-zero room is only a trap if he sees it as one. It wasn't designed to keep people in: it was designed to keep heat out. So it's not like the steel-walled vault at all.

His first instinct, as always, is to look towards the ceiling for a climbing route out of here. He reckons he could unscrew one of the panels and access the crawlspace between the sunken ceiling and the true ceiling above. Unfortunately the pain in his right arm is telling him he can't take the high road this time.

He looks down instead, paying closer attention to the floor material. He had been hoping for sectional tiles but beneath his feet is a rubberised surface, extending wall-to-wall. He crouches down and sifts through an upended tray of equipment, tossed there as evidence of the fatal struggle. There is a pair of shear cutters lying half buried under an avalanche of precision screwdrivers and a tangle of alligator clips.

As he lifts them he notices a darkened smear upon a length of metal, a corona of frosting distinguishing it from the other tools. It is a knife, deliberately discarded, blood freezing on the blade and his fingerprints doubtless on the plastic hilt. He wipes it down but in the frozen air can't be sure how effective this is. He considers taking it with him and cleaning it properly but he knows the cops are on their way and he can't risk being caught with it.

He uses a clamp stand as a hammer, driving the point of a screwdriver into the floor until he has made a rip large enough to introduce the tip of the shear cutters. Then he begins nibbling along in a line, tugging the matting upwards as he goes. It is stiff but just about pliable, and after a few minutes he has created a flap, beneath which he can see the original flooring. Throughout the rest of the R&D lab he has seen cables disappear into ducts beneath the carpet tiles, so he is confident there will be a crawlspace beneath, though how adept he will be at crawling in his injured condition remains to be seen.

He has to cut a bit further and tug back a larger flap until he reveals a seam between floor panels, either side of which are pairs of screws holding the sections in place. It takes a while doing it left-handed, but eventually he removes one end of a section and is able to lever it up like a hinge. There is a tiny passage underneath, extending beyond the walls of the sub-zero room. He is only a couple of yards from freedom, but every inch of it is going to be agony.

He crawls in head first, encumbered by having to cradle his right arm against his chest. His ribs are afforded no such protection, so the pain is constant as he squeezes himself along, hauling with his good arm and pushing with his feet.

As he struggles his way through the channel his mind is pulled back to the deduction that it was meant to be Sam who was framed and left for dead here tonight. For some reason this feels like another blow. He can't say why, but somehow this seems more wounding than that it should be him. After all, he's put himself in a lot of stupid positions, walked willingly into dangerous places. Who has she hurt to deserve this? She's only a kid: yet someone was planning to frame and murder a nineteen-year-old girl to cover up their own crimes.

Rage acts as an analgesic, either through distracting him from the here and now or filling him with a more overwhelming emotion.

He wants to hurt whoever is responsible for this, and he wonders why he didn't feel this way only a few minutes ago. He ended up being the one on the receiving end, and for this he is confused to feel grateful.

Sam.

He thinks of the sacrifices she is making in order to look after her sister, the danger she is putting herself in to stay out of jail. He thinks of the break-in she suffered tonight, pictures not one but two vulnerable young girls at the mercy of an enemy as ruthless as it is faceless. The depth of his anger surprises him.

She is a person he had come to detest, someone who had ripped his world apart when he thought his life was back on track. Now he feels personally outraged at the idea of a threat to her. Now he would go to any length to protect her.

# CONTAINMENT

It is dark beneath the floor, the light from the sub-zero room barely penetrating the gloom. He can see only shapes but he knows he is beyond the wall because the alarms are instantly louder. He twists his body through ninety degrees, wincing against a fresh wave of hurt, then pushes upwards against the panel directly above his face.

It doesn't move. He spends a brief moment wondering about the viability of remaining here throughout the police search, before remembering the rather obvious point of entry he has left in the sub-zero room. He pushes again, reaching a few inches to the left of his last attempt. It still doesn't lift, which makes him think of the screws he had to remove at the other end, driven downwards into a joist.

He comes close to panic, but thinks of all those cables he saw. The sub-zero room wasn't designed to allow under-floor access, but the rest of the lab would have to. His hands search for another join and he gives it a shove. He feels the panel move, though it is restrained by something on top of it. He gives it another couple of thumps and dislodges it laterally, enough for his fingers to feel the underside of a carpet tile.

It takes a further effort of contortion to get the shear cutters from his pocket into his left hand, after which he is able to rip a hole in the carpet. Then, with his left arm forced into the gap, he is able to wrench and worry his trunk through the resulting slit.

He gets to his feet and stands steady for a few seconds, getting his breath back and recovering from the dizziness of being suddenly upright once more. His inner ear is normally a better friend than this. He must have taken a very nasty whack to the head.

The alarm isn't helping. It's one of those deafening sounds intended to drive people from the building in case of emergency, though his principal worry right now concerns who might be coming *into* the building, and how soon.

He's not quite ready to break into a full run or even a jog, so he walks swiftly towards the lab's main entrance, where he waves his swipecard at the sensor, which gives it a damn good ignoring.

The card must have been deactivated. It is now going to open nothing, leaving him trapped in the R&D labs. He has squeezed himself painfully through a steel-framed intestine and shat himself out of the other end, but the only thing that has improved about his situation is that he's a bit warmer and no longer sharing accommodation with a corpse.

He has to get back in touch with Sam. She has high-level access to the GEM system, so she should be able to reactivate the swipe card.

He reaches instinctively for his mobile, only to remember that it's gone.

Arse.

It takes an embarrassingly long few seconds for it to occur to him that there are about a dozen telephones within feet of where he is standing, only for his embarrassment to be disastrously compounded by the realisation that he doesn't know any of her numbers. They're all on his handset.

He suppresses a scream of rage then remembers they weren't using mobile networks to communicate.

Parlabane hurries back to the PC he logged into earlier and opens a browser to download a copy of the VOIP software they were using. The program takes a few seconds to install, and as he watches the progress bar he notices he has left bloody fingerprints all over the keyboard and mouse.

He glances towards the electronic workbenches, where he recalls seeing a box of disposable latex gloves earlier. He rushes across while the software continues to install, grabbing a fistful of paper towels while he is over there. He is unable to clean the keyboard or mouse completely, but has hopefully smeared the plastic enough to obliterate the prints.

This sparks a recollection of his final thought before being hit with the electroshock: that he still needs to retrieve that memory stick from the server array.

Bollocks.

There is nothing he can do about that now, as his card will no longer open the door to the server farm.

The installation completes and a few seconds later he is keying in his login details. That is when he notices that the PC has neither a webcam nor an attached microphone.

He breathes, keys in an instant message.

<Jack> You there? I have no audio.

He waits for a response, which doesn't come.

<Jack> Hello? You there?

Still he waits.

<Jack> FFS, where are you?

# MULTITASKING

I am scanning the CCTV cameras in an attempt to see where Jack might emerge, as well as keeping one window on the lobby to check if the cops have arrived yet. I watched him cut a hole in the floor and somehow squeeze himself into it, but it's been ages since he disappeared and I'm starting to worry that he's stuck under there. It doesn't help that I don't have a camera that is labelled as being outside the sub-zero room, so I don't know which view he's likely to show up on.

I hear a sniff. For an instant I think it's Jack back online or some other audio feed I'm picking up. Then it's followed by a whimper.

'Sam, can I have a glass of water?'

Lilly is in the doorway again. She looks dead on her feet, red-eyed from crying and from fatigue. I recognise the exhaustion that comes when she should have been asleep hours ago but was too upset, and then actually too tired to slip over.

Asking for a glass of water as a pretext for reappearing well after lights out: she hasn't pulled this shit in years. That tells me how desperate she is. I can't turn her away.

I find an unbroken glass, fill it with water and walk her back to her bedroom. As I tuck her in again, I hear a chime in my earpiece: some kind of alert from the computer, though I don't recognise specifically what.

'Sam, tell me the story about Poogie.'

I used to do this some nights when she was younger. We shared a bedroom because she didn't like being alone in the dark. It was this silly story I made up about her favourite doll, Poogie, and her adventures when she got lost in the land through the bedroom mirror.

I turn out the light, leaving the door ajar and begin talking. It's been years, but I remember the basics, and she seems calmer as soon as I hit my stride.

I hear the chime again, and this time I realise it's the instant-message alert from the VOIP program, which it plays if you have the window minimised or something else open on top.

Jack is back online, but I've not finished the story.

By the half-light from the hall she looks wiped. I wonder if I should keep going until she's asleep, so that she doesn't reappear again, but I know I don't have time.

'I'll have to finish this later,' I say. 'I'm just going to the toilet.'

I pull the door over so that there is still a sliver of light spilling through, then I run to the kitchen where I begin to type frantically.

# ESCAPE KEY

Finally the screen shows Parlabane a response.

<Buzzkill> I'm here. What's with the instant messaging?
<Jack> He took my phone. Don't know your number.

She pings back her mobile number instantly. He writes it down on a Post-it note and sticks it in his pocket, then he dials.

'Is this number registered?' he asks, aware that the call records will be logged.

'No, it's a burner. Are you okay, Jack? I saw you all bloody on CCTV, and there was a body. Looked like Cruz. What happened?'

'I was attacked. He took my bag.'

'He got the prototype?' she asks, appalled.

There is no time to get into this.

'I need you to fix my swipe card. It's not working. I'm trapped in R&D. The alarms are ringing and I'm fairly certain the cops are on their way.'

There is a pause that he really doesn't like.

'I'm really sorry. I've been kicked from the system. Someone else has hacked this place tonight.'

'Tell me about it,' he spits, only stopping himself from kicking a chair in frustration due to the thought of his feet being among the few parts of his body not already damaged.

He hangs up and looks across the labs, walking briefly back and forth to widen his perspective. Other than the vault and the sub-zero room, there are three more doors, two of them controlled by the GEM system. The exception is the door to Secure Disposal, which allows him a moment of hope until he remembers that it is operated by a numeric keypad. Unlike the vault PIN, he sincerely doubts a

285

fresh code for that gets emailed out to everyone on a daily basis: not simply for getting rid of rubbish.

He recalls their dumpster dive inside the enclosure at the foot of the staircase this door must lead to, where they found just enough information to proceed with this insanity. If only that had been properly secured, rather than helpfully opened for them by an easily duped security guard. He pictures the hard drive they found, which causes him to also picture the lab worker he watched open this door for her colleague, carrying a tray of damaged components.

He'd filmed it. He had been standing only feet away: maybe close enough to see which numbers she pressed; definitely close enough to hear the key chimes. The information he needs should still be here, hidden where he stashed it when he saw the guard searching those visiting investors with a detection paddle.

He is about to head for the gents when a message pings on to the monitor in front of him.

<Buzzkill> Looking at CCTV. Two cops walking into the
    main lobby.

Parlabane runs for the toilets, hope and purpose helping him block out the pain. There is no deliberation over which stall: he remembers it as though he was in there that morning.

He uses the precision screwdriver he took from the sub-zero room, which makes short work of unsecuring the access panel behind the cistern.

It is less stiff this time, coming away smoothly. He reaches down behind the kickplate, the fingers on his left hand scrambling like the biggest spider back there until they locate the solid state drive. He hauls it out, one of the cameras still attached, the other lost behind the plumbing.

As he emerges from the stall, he catches sight of himself in the mirror. He looks a fright. There is blood caked around his nose and mouth, more of it matting his hair. It stains his jacket and his shirt, particularly conspicuous against the pale blue of the latter. If he does make it out of here, he isn't going to get far on the street without attracting attention.

He brought a cagoule and waterproof trousers in case he ended up being pursued and needed a quick change: man in a grey suit to man in baggy dark blue wet-weather kit. They were lightweight and compressible, ideal for this purpose, but they were in the rucksack.

Along with the flight case.

He washes the blood from his face at a sink, then hurries back to the computer. There is a message waiting for him on the screen. It is timed from twenty seconds ago.

<Buzzkill> They're in the lifts.

He tries to calculate how long this means he has until they make their way to the lab. Gives up. There's no way of knowing and it won't help.

He crouches down to connect the SSD to a port on the front of the computer, relieved to see a light blink into life on the slim black drive. Then he looks up at the monitor for a corresponding sign.

A message dominating the centre of the screen tells him there is a Java update available and asks if he would like to install it. Parlabane comes very close to putting his head through the monitor, then dismisses the prompt and proceeds with locating the video files on the newly connected drive.

There are two: one from each of the hidden cameras. He launches them both, quickly maximising the one affording a view at what he estimates to be the right height. He uses the slide bar to scroll along, squinting intently at the preview thumbnail in a frantic search for the very brief moment he needs to see and hear.

He is running through his visit in his head, trying to remember in what order he saw these things.

A new message appears.

<Buzzkill> They are in Synergis reception.

He finds the moment, notes the time on the progress bar for replays. The woman reaches for the keypad and he hears four chimes, but the position of her hand obscures all but the first press. He plays it again, jacking up the volume, trying to memorise the rise and fall in the pitch.

He rushes to the Secure Disposal door and tries a code: one five nine six.

No response.

He tries one two nine six, which produces almost the same chime sequence, but still the lock is unimpressed.

It occurs to him that they might have changed the code. He can't afford to think about that, however. It's the bins, for Christ's sake, and it is less than three weeks since he made that video.

He returns to the computer and plays it again. He definitely has the chime sequence right, but that first press could actually have been a four.

    &lt;Buzzkill&gt; They are passing through lobby outside Cruz's
       office.

That's got to be a minute at most; forty seconds maybe.

He runs back to the door, singing the chime sequence to himself, then punches in a new code. Four two nine six. It sounds right, but still nothing.

Four five nine six.

This time there is a buzzing and the door responds to his urgent push.

He hurries through, finding himself in a small room accommodating three plastic bins and a tall aluminium tray caddy on castors. There is also, merciful Zeus, a lift. As he pushes the button he glances at the trays slotted into the caddy, similar to the one he saw carried through the same door on the video. They are filled with damaged components, circuit boards, empty compressed air canisters, USB sticks and hard drives.

Oh no.

He remembers the SSD, still plugged into that computer out there in the lab. The videos on it identify exactly who he is and what he was doing there.

He has to go back.

He hits the green release button and sprints to the computer, tugging the SSD free from the cable. On the screen, the videos instantly vanish.

<Buzzkill> They are almost at R&D, walking down corridor.

Parlabane races for the door yet again, and is keying in the PIN when he remembers he has left the VOIP program running. It has all of their recent messages on screen, including Sam's mobile number.

Holy mother of fuck.

He can hear voices approaching, someone saying, 'The sub-zero room is inside the research and development labs.'

He lunges back across to the computer a second time and closes the program. He can hear the voices closer now. The screen shines out like a beacon and there isn't time to shut down the computer. In about three seconds they will be coming through the double doors, just around the corner.

If he runs now, they'll see him.

He hauls the power cable from the monitor, rendering the screen black, and ducks beneath the desk.

Their footsteps only yards away, Parlabane holds his breath as he huddles out of sight. He knows they will be making for the sub-zero room first, which gives him the chance he needs.

He skips across on feet as light as his pain and desperation will allow, then keys in the code once more. He closes the door very softly behind him and allows himself a breath.

Before him there is a length of white material sticking out from beneath the lid of a bin. He's hoping for a lab coat. What he finds is an old sheet, spattered with a dozen colours of paint.

It is better than a lab coat, he decides, tugging it free. If he wraps himself in this, he will be able to invoke the nutter-invisibility charm. People encounter someone walking down the street wrapped in a manky old sheet, they look away; and if they don't avert their gaze, the sheet is all they will see or remember.

Parlabane takes the lift to the basement level, his memory of the building telling him the rear is lower than the front.

He steps onto a dimly lit landing with a corridor to the left and a door directly ahead, leading out to the secure enclosure where he and Sam did their first dumpster dive. There is a lock and a security guard to negotiate that way, so it's not an option.

He follows the corridor around a corner, where it leads to a locked door, though a green release button indicates that like upstairs, access is only secured from the other side.

He emerges at the foot of a concrete stairwell, which he reckons could be the same one Cruz took him up during his visit. There is a door opposite the foot of the stairs, marked Emergency Exit. A sign warns that the door is alarmed, which isn't really an issue at the moment.

He pushes through and steps into the narrow alley that skirts the side and rear, leading to the loading bays and the security guard's booth. He is on the right side of it, only about fifty yards from the street.

He sweeps the invisibility cloak around his shoulders, draping himself from neck to ankles, then proceeds towards the main road with a shuffling gait, head down. As he approaches the corner he hears sirens.

Parlabane presses himself against the wall as two police cars whizz past the mouth of the alley.

He allows himself a quick glance towards the main entrance as he rounds the corner. He sees three cop cars and an ambulance, the two recent arrivals discharging their personnel in a hurry. Looks like the boys upstairs have been into the sub-zero room and called in some help in finding the perp.

Parlabane makes it on to King William Street where he is surprised and delighted to see a cab heading towards him with its yellow sign lit up. Must have just dropped someone off. He waves to hail it but the taxi continues past like he's not there, because he's wrapped in an old sheet and looks like a nutter.

# FILE NOT FOUND

I see cops and paramedics hurry around the building, popping up on camera after camera, but they are not who I am looking for.

I am searching, hoping not to find.

Every new feed that doesn't show Jack is a relief, every feed showing a policeman charge through a door brings a renewed anxiety.

Though he stopped responding, I kept sending him updates on what I could see, right up until he killed the VOIP link. I don't know whether he found somewhere to hide or he somehow made it out of the building, but I do know they're still searching for him.

When they broaden that search, they're going to want to know what he looks like, and they will have more than Aaron's description. The CCTV recordings will have picked him up several times before the lights went out in R&D, then there will be all that ultra-damning footage from the sub-zero room. Footage I was supposed to delete.

Jack walked in wearing a hat and glasses so that any eyewitness description would be flawed, the plan being that this would be the only clue as to what the intruder looked like. Once they get a hold of those videos however, it will take no time for him to be identified, and after that there will be no hiding place.

Wait, though. As I now have proper control over the CCTV system, maybe I can access the recording files too.

I log back into Coleridge's account, grateful that Jack remembered to log out of it, and within a few minutes I have located the videos. It looks like they are broken into six-hour blocks to limit the file sizes, the names indicating location, date and time. The recordings still in progress started at nine, and are ongoing. Everything that happened since Jack entered the building is on here, apart from what took place in the dark. It hits me that this means there ought to be footage of what happened in the sub-zero room before nine o'clock, and I look for that file.

It's missing.

I scroll through the lists, comparing the tags for recordings before and after nine. Several have been deleted.

It figures. But two can play at that game.

I select all of the files and click to delete.

A message appears stating: 'Cannot delete while recording is in progress.'

I navigate through the controls until I find the option to 'Stop recording and commence new' on the first camera. I hold my breath as I click. If it turns out I don't have the privileges, I won't be able to erase these videos until three in the morning, which will give the police plenty of time to watch them on chasing playback.

The recording stops and a new file is automatically created. Breathing out, I click to delete the old one.

'File is protected. You need permission to delete this file.'

Shit toasters.

Somebody sure had permission earlier.

There's no way of erasing the footage, as I don't even know which user account would have that authority, let alone the means to hack it. But just because a file can't be deleted doesn't mean it can't be amended.

I look out a piece of malware I once used to hold Jack's files and folders to ransom, back when I first wanted to grab his attention. The Synergis network identifies it as malware and tries to block my upload, but logged in as Coleridge I can disable the protection and allow the program through.

I try it out on the recording I recently stopped, and get the result I'm hoping for. Then I repeat the process, stopping all cameras and encrypting the video files.

I still haven't deleted a single file, but if anyone wants to look at this footage, they're going to need the password to do it.

# STOLEN GOODS

Everything is so quiet now. It's plooting down outside, as Dad used to say, so there are no late-night stragglers on the street, talking at pub-level voices or singing or arguing. Lilly must have finally nodded off, and there is no sound in my earpiece. I feel very much alone, disconnected from the outside world, and yet if I look at the laptop screen or at the mess around the floor, it is clear I am still in the eye of a storm.

I am compelled to keep looking at the CCTV feeds, but I know I have to log out. My standard hacking protocol dictates that I take certain steps not only to clear my own footprints, but to conceal that there was a hack at all. To this end I restore the 2FA settings and undo any changes I have made to the accounts I was using. Looking at the cops and paramedics swarming the screens, it seems all the more urgent and yet all the more trivial. A hack might appear to be the least of anyone's priorities tonight, but covering it up is among the most important of mine.

I'm exhausted but I know I won't be able to sleep. I don't know where Jack is and I don't know what is around the corner: what might be coming for us.

There is a thought that has been banging on the door of my mind like a team of feds: I have been refusing to let it inside, but it is smashing its way in and demanding to be heard.

That was meant to be me.

As far as Zodiac knew, it was me who was going in there tonight, a one-girl operation. It makes me feel all the more guilty about what I've done to Jack, but that's nothing compared to the impact of my fear. Until now the biggest thing I believed I needed to be afraid of was going to jail and leaving Lilly.

Zodiac intended to kill me; and not out of anger or revenge, but

293

simply to cover up his own crime. That's how ruthless he is, and now I am a threat to him, because I have information.

My mobile rings, shaking me from thoughts that were drawing the walls in upon me. I don't recognise the number, but it's from central London: a landline.

Jack's voice sounds out in my right ear, and my heart thumps in response.

'It's me.'

'Where are you?' I ask. 'Are you all right?'

'My evening has been sub-optimal so far, but I'm not in custody and I'm not locked in a freezer. Those are the positives, and I'm not sure how long the first one will remain true. I take it you can still access my mobile?'

'Yes,' I admit.

'Good. I need you to perform a remote wipe. Of everything. He took it so that I couldn't phone for help, and I'm betting it will conveniently turn up during the police search.'

'I'm on it.'

'Did you get anywhere with the CCTV?'

'I couldn't delete the files, but I have encrypted them. It's their own stuff, so they're going to find a way to decrypt it soon enough, but I've bought us some time at least. What happened back there?'

'Lights went out and I got sandbagged. After that I decided to chill for a bit. Woke up next to the late Leo Cruz, minus my rucksack and my phone.'

'Who did this? Was it Winter?'

'I don't think so. He used a hand-held electroshock device to put me down. Winter wouldn't need something like that. He's a street-fighter in every sense of the word.'

'Yeah, but he could have outsourced the hit. Zodiac certainly outsourced the scapegoat role.'

'Has he been in touch?'

'Why would he? I was to await instructions regarding handing over the prototype, remember? Can't see that happening, seeing as he already has it.'

'Ah, but he doesn't.'

I can barely dare believe it.

'He doesn't?'

'It was in a flight case, which I put in my rucksack. The prototype itself I stuck in my trouser pocket. I wasn't sure how soon this handover might take place and I had a paranoid notion it might involve a theft or mugging shortly after I left the building. Clearly I wasn't paranoid enough. Either way, I knew that once we delivered what he wanted, our only leverage would be gone, so I saw a way we might have two bites at this.'

'What is it? The prototype, I mean.'

'I still don't know. It's just a tiny metal box. That's what pisses me off most — after everything I've been through tonight, I'm none the wiser as to what this was all about or who Zodiac is.'

# MISSING PARTY

Parlabane feels the rain running down the back of his neck as he hangs up the payphone. He can't remember the last time he used one of these things, and is trying not to dwell on the irony that the primary reason for his call was to ask Sam to erase his mobile. He's still got the non-hacked one stashed at Mairi's flat, but he didn't want to wait until he got back there to make the call.

He touches his arm tenderly, probing to feel the response. It isn't as painful as it was, so he's starting to think it might not be broken.

The rain is getting heavier and the cabs are still giving him a wide berth. He doesn't want to risk the bus looking like this, as the invisibility effect isn't quite the same in a confined space. People won't want to make eye contact, but he will nonetheless be massively conspicuous and thus memorable.

It occurs to him that he could turn his jacket inside out. It would conceal the bloodstains, and although that might seem conspicuous too, he's seen pissed City boy cock-sprockets do it on a night out.

A night out. Oh shit.

He remembers his genius alibi. He is supposed to be at a party. He checks his watch. It is ten past eleven. It's not too late if he heads straight there. He ought to go home and clean up, but he doesn't have time, not doing it by bus. Besides, he can't get changed, as he has to reappear wearing the same clothes.

He ditches the sheet in a bin and reverses his jacket, pulling it tight around the collar to hide the blood on his shirt. It takes him twenty minutes and two buses but he is back in Islington a little after half past.

Parlabane presses himself into a doorway as he sees people spilling out of Shallot's main entrance into waiting minicabs. He doesn't recognise them but he doesn't know who might walk out next, and he can't afford to be seen outside.

He slips down a narrow alley leading behind the building and commences his climb. It is an ascent that he would normally manage in a matter of seconds, but doing it one-handed in the driving rain means he has to take his time and be ultra-cautious.

He stalls on the branch of a drainpipe next to the gents toilets window, listening for sounds from inside. He has to wait a couple of minutes through toilet flushes and running taps before deciding it's safe to proceed. He levers the window up using the pen he had left wedged at the base to prevent it falling fully shut, then tumbles awkwardly inside.

He catches sight of himself in the mirror. His hair and face are soaking, and the reversed jacket looks inexplicable in this context. The bloodstains on his shirt collar are obvious too.

He should never have come back here. He looks conspicuously like someone who has been outside in the rain, possibly to have a fight. He should leave immediately, he decides. The only question is whether it would be better to go back out the window unseen, or hasten directly out of the main entrance where he will be caught on camera as per his original intention.

His mind is made up for him when the door opens and two guys stumble in, clearly well refreshed. One of them is holding a glass of red wine that he rests on the edge of a wash-hand basin as he heads for the urinals.

'Shit, mate, what happened to you?' he asks.

Parlabane finds inspiration.

'Said the wrong thing, as usual. Someone threw a glass of wine over me. Got my face and hair.'

Parlabane spies a hopper full of used hand towels and looks for the fresh ones. They're all gone as it has clearly been a busy night. He settles for fishing one out of the hopper and gives his hair a rub with it.

'What was it you said that was worth that?' the other bloke asks.

'Oh, this woman was telling me how much she liked Dickens and I think I could maybe have phrased my reply a little more carefully.'

The bloke laughs a pissed laugh and Parlabane exits, still holding on to the hand towel as a prop for his cover story. He rubs at his head with it as he makes his way through the building, deliberately catching people's eyes and exchanging brief remarks. Once his hair looks dry he can make for the exit. It's all about what gets caught on camera: when he entered and when he left.

Then he sees Lee dead ahead, just inside one of the dining areas. She breaks away from the group she is standing with and heads straight for him. She doesn't look pleased.

'Jack, where the fuck did you get to?'

'Oh, sorry. Someone spilled some wine on me so I had to go to the bathroom and clean up. Got it out of my hair but my jacket and my shirt are—'

'And was the bathroom at home in Edinburgh? I haven't seen you in two hours.'

'Sorry. It's a big place.'

'Candace was giving a speech and she wanted you to say a few words. We had everybody searching for you. You're soaking and this looks more like bloodstains than wine to me. I ask you again: where the fuck have you been?'

He attempts an exasperated smile, as if to insist he is confused by her failure to find him, but he knows he isn't selling it. Lee wouldn't be where she is if she couldn't smell a story, far less a lie.

His alibi isn't merely collapsing, it has turned into the complete opposite. His absence has been made conspicuous before the entire gathering, meaning there is now a whole restaurant full of witnesses who can testify that he was missing during the very time the murder took place.

# BREAKFAST TELEVISION

I wake up to the sound of the alarm on my phone. It's set on repeat to get me up at seven each day so that I can get Lilly to school on time. There is a bleary moment in which the familiar sound is comforting, until I realise I am not even in my bed. I am slumped at the kitchen table, where I have nodded off in front of the laptop, a puddle of drool soaking into the crook of my arm beneath where my head has been resting.

I don't know how long I have been out: I feel knackered, so obviously not long enough, but like my laptop, there is no reboot required: we both come out of sleep mode lightning fast and ready to resume.

I look at the screen and remember the last thing I did. Makes sense. I could never have nodded off until I knew that task was finished. I remember seeing the clock read four-thirty, and according to the data, the upload was completed at 4.55.

Lilly is normally an early riser, up and dressed and fixing herself some cereal before I stagger my way into the kitchen in response to my alarm. Luckily she has not appeared yet, which gives me time to hunt through the mess for an undamaged bowl. I find an ancient plastic one with the Powerpuff Girls on the rim, which she's had since she was about five. I pour her some cornflakes and milk and leave it out for her in the living room, then stick my head around the bedroom door.

The soft sound of my voice isn't enough. She is still well out of it, as is sometimes the case if she has been up late the night before. I gently shake her into life, then give her a cuddle as I remind her about the state of the place and warn her to stay out of the kitchen.

'Can I watch TV on your computer?' is the first thing she says, priority one from before she went to sleep.

'Sure.'

I move the laptop to the living room and open a browser, figuring I can find some cartoons for her while I grab a desperately needed shower. I go to the BBC website and am about to run a search on the iPlayer when I see the headline: 'Controversial entrepreneur Leo Cruz murdered'. It's among the top stories.

Swallowing, I click on the link. A video package launches at the top of the story. There's a male reporter speaking straight to camera from behind police cordons outside Tricorn House. It is dark and raining behind him – this must have been earlier this morning.

'Police are releasing few details at this stage but have confirmed that Leo Cruz was found dead last night after the alarm was raised by a security guard. It is believed that Mr Cruz may have interrupted a burglar, and there are unconfirmed reports that Synergis was also the target of a simultaneous cyber-attack, in what may have been an extreme act of industrial espionage.'

I feel Lilly's hand nudging my shoulder.

'Sam, you said I could watch cartoons.'

'Just a sec, Lilly.'

I notice a LIVE link beneath the playback window and click on that. It takes me to a more recent page where the emerging details are laid out in hyperlinked bullet points beneath a new video, still buffering.

- **Police confirm theft of prototype device at Synergis offices.**
- **Cowboy or visionary: Leo Cruz's controversial rise and fall.**
- **Police on hunt for white male in his 40s.**

The new video begins to stream, a banner declaring it as being live.

'But you said . . .'

'Lilly, *in a minute*,' I scold.

I am watching a gaunt and dazed woman appear amid camera flashes and the clicks of a dozen shutters. She looks as tired and wrung-out as I feel: her eyes dark-rimmed and red from tears, her face a picture of shock and disbelief. She is holding a piece of paper in both hands, like if she lets go she will fly apart.

A caption says: 'Jane Dunwoodie, Head of Research and Development at Synergis'.

'You said a sec then you said a minute. Sam, it's not fair.'

'LILLY, A MINUTE,' I shout, turning up the volume on the laptop.

Her lip trembles then she goes off crying. I feel shitty again but I can't take my attention from the screen. I know she'll be back in a minute, as she hasn't touched her cornflakes. Her hurt will be gone soon. The hurt I'm staring at will last a lot longer.

Until a few seconds ago, to me Jane Dunwoodie meant only a name, a user account to be hacked and exploited. Too late, I'm seeing that this is a person, and it feels the same as when I found out what I had done to Keisha.

Her voice is faint and shaky at times as she reads her statement, but she just about keeps it together.

'I have only known Leo Cruz for a couple of years, but I very quickly learned that he was a remarkable man. Nothing like the caricature the media often drew, but rather someone inspired by innovation more than by money. I have seldom met anyone with so much enthusiasm or who was so determined that an idea should succeed. I have lost a colleague and a friend, but what I have not lost is his inspiration.'

I think she's finished and it feels like a relief, as I hate watching these things at the best of times: people suffering in front of my eyes, their feelings pouring out raw. Then she swallows, prompting another wave of flashes and shutter clicks, and a moment later she continues.

Her voice is flat, but this only heightens the impact, as though she is trying to hold back what she is feeling to get through this.

'I have spoken to Aldous Syne and broken the news. Having known Leo for more than two decades, Aldous was distraught and I am making this statement right now at this most difficult time on the understanding that his grief and his privacy will not be disturbed. Leo and I have worked tirelessly at realising Aldous's revolutionary new design, and we are in agreement that we should honour Leo by seeing it through. Clearly, there are people who feel threatened and envious regarding what we have been developing here, but we will not allow them to win by destroying Leo's dream. Whatever it takes, and whatever help we might need in completing it, his vision will live on. Thank you.'

There is another burst of shutters as she withdraws, and the camera turns to the reporter again.

'As you can see, Jane Dunwoodie is representative of the state of shock reverberating all around Synergis as people wake up to this news. You may have already heard that police believe Mr Cruz was murdered when he interrupted a burglar in the process of stealing a prototype device. Now, it is not known what that device does, but clearly those at Synergis are concerned that this design might be reverse-engineered, particularly as it has been confirmed that design documents were simultaneously stolen last night via a cyber-attack. Jeremy Aldergrave, the Attorney General's new cybercrime czar, has stated that all of his department's resources will be deployed in tracing the person or persons responsible and bringing them to justice.'

Lilly comes back in, looking sheepish and apologetic. I hate it when she acts like she's afraid of me. I never want her to be afraid of anyone, let alone her sister.

I decide to stop probing the hurting tooth, and click off the report, finding her some cartoons instead.

The full resources of the cybercrime task force are being deployed to find me. They won't even need to suit up if Zodiac decides simply to toss me to them like he did Cicatrix. I have to hope Jack is right about that bargaining chip he's holding.

I shower and change, welcoming the feel of the towel and of fresh clothes almost as much as the hot water. I caught a sniff of myself earlier and it was pretty ripe. The kitchen is never warm after dark unless the oven is on but I haven't sweated so much as I did last night.

It feels insane to be pursuing the usual routine this morning, when there could be feds at the door any second, but I don't have much choice. I can hardly take Lilly on the run, and I'd rather she was safely at school if they opt for a ludicrously overpowered show of force like they did for poor Cic.

'Let's go,' I call out, picking up her schoolbag from the hall floor. She ignores me, giggling at what is on the screen.

'Now, Lilly,' I warn.

Still she blanks me. I should have seen this coming. It's her way of hitting back at me for shouting at her.

'Do you want me to get you a new DVD player?'

'Yes,' she nods.

I don't need to fill in the rest. She grabs her blazer and steps out on to the landing as I lock the door. I wonder what the point of that is after yesterday, as there's nothing left to steal. Then I remember that my laptop is sitting in the living room, rather than tucked away in its hidey-hole. I was wrong-footed by Lilly watching her cartoons on that instead of her own machine.

I decide I don't have time. We're already running it close this morning, and I'll be back in forty minutes.

I am halfway towards the stairs when I hear the sirens. They're not an exotic sound around here but something tells me they're heading this way, and in a matter of seconds I see four cars slewing crazily towards the flats from either side.

I tell Lilly to stop where she is as I look over the balcony. I see cops charging from the vehicles, running towards the stairways at either side. They're dressed in body armour, carrying SMGs, two pulling up the rear with a battering ram.

I'm guessing they'll be coming in the back also, cutting off all exits.

I notice Lilly is peering over the side too.

'Are they here about the burglars?' she asks.

I can hear the clatter of boots coming from the stairwell. They'll be here in a few more seconds.

I hug Lilly to me and tell her I'm sorry.

# CANCELLED FLIGHT

Parlabane is woken by the sound of an insistent hammering and comes round with a horrible jolt of dual realisations. The first is that it is morning and he must have been asleep for hours: something that was not supposed to happen due to fear of the second, which is that the cops are at his door.

He's blown it, and for something so daft, so weak: telling himself he needed to put his head down for ten minutes as it was thumping and he was starting to feel a bit woozy. Ten minutes, twenty at most.

He was meant to be gone by now, though he'd have to confess he hadn't decided where. He only knew he couldn't wait around to be caught. He left the restaurant as soon as he could extricate himself from what appeared to be a job-threateningly awkward conversation with Lee (though it was moot if he wasn't going to be able to show up for said job any more), then rushed to find a cash machine before the clock struck midnight.

He made two maximum permitted withdrawals either side of twelve. He could already hear the prosecutor present this in court as the actions of a guilty man, but his hope in the meantime was that it might buy him a few days if his location couldn't be traced by any card transactions.

He headed back to Mairi's place and sat glued to the news sites for a few hours. Then he packed a bag with the intention of disappearing, of lying low somewhere he could make some calls and follow whatever leads Sam's hacking skills came up with. He didn't know where: he would work that out once his head was clearer. All he needed was to lie down for a little while.

The hammering resumes, hard and angry. A demand, not a request, to open the door.

He sits up and instinctively looks to the window. He could get out that way, but they're bound to have people watching all possible exits. Plus his arm still hurts like a bastard too, as do several of his ribs. He decides he'd best spare Mairi the damage and come quietly.

# THROWN TO THE WOLVES

I hear the hurried scuffing of boots on concrete rising from beneath us and I can't work out why I'm not seeing them yet. It's like that bit in *Aliens* when the sensors show the monsters as being in the same room but Ripley and Hicks can't see anything: then it dawns on them that the monsters are directly above.

In my case it takes the scuffing of boots on concrete to become the crash and splintering of metal on wood for me to realise that the intruders are directly below.

'Sorry for what?' Lilly asks.

'For shouting at you,' I say.

For some reason they've made a mistake and gone to the wrong address. I reckon I can get her down the stairs and past them, out of harm's way before they realise they've screwed up.

I lean over the barrier and have a look down, which is when I get it: they haven't made a mistake. They're piling into the Cohens' place. I carried out the entire hack using their Wi-Fi, and it's been traced to their address.

What I don't get is how. My location should have been anonymised throughout. The virtual private network was set to make it appear to anyone tracing it as though the hack originated in California.

I flash back to last night, and the moment of anxiety when my VPN stuttered on start-up, briefly threatening not to load.

Christ. I've been hacked. My VPN software has been sabotaged, though I can't see how that was possible. I always boot from the memory card I keep in my bra.

I think about how the place was torn apart, drawers opened, every potential hidey-hole uncovered. Now I know what they were really looking for. They got hold of my laptop and installed something

306

that would disable my VPN, then they put it back, apparently the only thing in the place left untouched.

Fuck. I walked into this with my eyes shut. Zodiac demanded to be kept up to date with my plans so that he could approve them, but I didn't see the real reason. It was also why he set me a deadline. He needed notice. He needed to be ready.

He knew I was going in last night. I told him how I planned to get around the 2FA obstacle using the Tube strike as my cover, then go directly to Tricorn House once I had remote access to the network.

Everything I did is going to be traceable. Somebody came here and did this to make sure the cops would turn up plenty of evidence of my hack after I was found dead in the freezer. They didn't bargain on Jack being there instead, but this gives them something even more damning: a conspiracy.

'Lilly, I need to pop back to the flat for something.'

'Won't we be late?'

'We'll have to walk a little faster, that's all. Wait there, I'll be two seconds.'

I leave her on the landing while I hurry back inside, as I don't want Lilly seeing what I'm up to and asking awkward questions. I grab my laptop from the living room and the neoprene cover from where I left it in the kitchen, stuffing one inside the other then both inside a shoulder bag. I take my extra phones and all the cash I've got hidden, then go to my bedroom where I lift a change of under-wear, an act that forces me to admit what I'm truly facing here.

I am going to take Lilly to school, but I won't be there later to pick her up.

Once the cops have got the Cohens down to the nick, it's going to take them no time to suss that this sweet old couple hardly even know how to plug in their router, never mind hack an electronics corporation. Then at some point the Cohens are bound to mention how, whenever they have trouble with this kind of thing, they tend to ask that helpful Samantha girl upstairs, as she knows all about computers.

I have to bail. I feel physically sick at the idea of abandoning Lilly, at the thought of her distress when she comes out of school and can't find me, but I know that this outcome is unavoidable now. Either I'm not there because I'm under arrest or I'm not there because I've made myself disappear. This way at least I give myself an outside chance of being around for her again in less than five years minus good behaviour, but only if me and Jack can find out the truth and expose it before we both end up in handcuffs.

# BOUND

Parlabane climbs to his feet, various aches announcing themselves now that he is upright. He walks delicately towards the door, which is still being urgently pummelled.

He hears a voice.

'Jack, open up. It's me.'

Then the hammering starts again.

It's Sam. She's standing outside in a heavy jacket with a bag slung over her shoulder. As soon as he opens the door she barges past him into the flat.

As she disappears inside, he hears the squeak of a hinge down the hall and sees Han's head sticking out. He looks sleepy but concerned.

'Everything okay, man?'

'Peachy. Sorry for the noise.'

'No problem.'

Parlabane turns to face Sam, who already has her laptop out and is reading the Wi-Fi password off the side of Mairi's router.

'What are you doing here? How did you find me?'

She answers with a sneery look that tells him precisely how stupid his question was.

'I thought you were the cops at my door,' he adds.

'I'm here because they've already been to mine.'

'What?'

'Well, to my downstairs neighbours, poor bastards. Saw them getting taken away in a police van. I was leeching their Wi-Fi so the hack got traced to there.'

'How could they do that? And so soon? I thought you used a VPN.'

'I did. Somebody burgled my flat yesterday. Trashed the place to

309

make it look like junkies, but they planted some malware in my laptop. I weeded it out on the bus over here. This whole thing was a set-up to put me in the frame for Cruz. If it wasn't that I was piggybacking on to their connection, I'd be in custody right now. It's only a matter of time before the feds work it out, so I needed to get gone.'

'And you thought the safest place to lie low would be with the guy the cops are after for the murder of the person you hacked? I was about to go on the lam myself. Would be gone already if I hadn't fallen asleep.'

The sneery face is gone. She looks frightened.

'I don't have anybody else, Jack.'

He nods, letting her know he understands she has nowhere else to turn. But the time has come to let her know he understands other things too.

'What about Lilly?'

Sam shoots him a look of surprise and vulnerability. He's not supposed to know this stuff.

'You're not the only one who can find things out, *Sam*. I know about your mum too.'

She stands silent for a second, and in that moment, something passes between them. Something unspoken, something important.

Sam swallows.

'Lilly's in school. I dropped her off before I came here.'

'And what happens at four o'clock?'

She lowers her head like it's suddenly heavy.

'We need to find who did this, Jack. Whatever it takes.'

'It's going to take us disappearing, you know that, right?'

She nods then swallows again, searching for her voice. It is quiet but determined.

'The only way I can be there for Lilly again is if we can find this bastard.'

'Have we anything to go on yet?'

'Not so far, but it's early. The worm is on the hook.'

'You mean your wee surprise package. What do you mean it's early? Shouldn't someone have bitten by now?'

310

'Not necessarily. My instructions from Zodiac were to upload the project materials to a particular file storage site.'

'And you did that last night, right? From Synergis.'

'Yes and no. Last night I uploaded them direct from Synergis to *my* file storage site. I didn't upload them to the one Zodiac specified until about four o'clock this morning, after I had installed my malware payload.'

'Which is what?'

'Something called Stoolpigeon. Once you download and execute the file, it tries to discover its physical location via every means available and sends the results to me.'

'But won't Zodiac's anti-virus software pick that up?'

'That's why I was up so late. I embedded it among the Project RBA materials and compressed the whole thing into a zip file. As soon as you click to open the compressed file, you execute the Stoolpigeon package.'

'Sounds very technical.'

'Actually the embedding is the easy bit: the real trick most of the time is convincing some sucker to download the zip file your malware is hidden in. In this case that part was a given, so now I'm just waiting for Zodiac to download the RBA stuff and for Stoolpigeon to tell us where he is.'

'Unless he's already got it by other means,' Parlabane reminds her.

Sam's look of determination fades instantly into doubt.

'You're right. He had other people working this.'

'Either way, we can't hang around here waiting for something to happen. We need to get gone.'

'Where, though?'

'At this stage that matters less than how. We can't use public transport because it's too exposed and we need to stay off the grid.'

'What does that leave?'

'We have to acquire a car.'

'Hire a car? We'd get caught twice as fast that way. There are registration-scanning cameras everywhere, and your driver's licence and credit card details would be logged.'

'You misheard me. I said *acquire*.'

# AIRPORT PARKING AND OTHER MODERN ROBBERIES

An hour later they are in a minicab heading to Stansted Airport. Parlabane is wearing a thick scarf around his neck and a winter hat with earflaps. He does not take off either article throughout the duration of the journey, despite the driver observing the statutory protocol by which it is required that the interior of a private-hire vehicle should at all times maintain a temperature adequate to safely cook a Christmas turkey.

Sam is wearing an improvised niqab that she has fashioned from a black dress she found in Mairi's wardrobe, an act of vandalism that he fears may cost him their relationship.

She has also performed varying degrees of surgery on his laptop and his back-up mobile. His instinct was to be wary but frankly he's past worrying. He is better simply accepting an abject loss of control and letting her handle it. If he gets out of this mess he's going to go live someplace where there are no computers, no internet and no mobile reception.

Only Sam's eyes are showing as she sits alongside him in the back of the cab, doing things on her phone that he cannot begin to comprehend. They don't look a well-matched pair: the devout Muslim woman and the weirdo bell-end. In fact, they look very conspicuously like two passengers who have a suspicious reason not to be identified.

However, this is not actually a problem, as he explained before they left.

'Shouldn't we have the cab pick us up somewhere else?' Sam had asked. 'Around the corner maybe? I suppose there's lots of addresses inside this building but they're bound to know you're living here.'

'That's what I'm counting on,' he replied.

'Why?'

'If the cops look, I want the cab company's records to show that two people got picked up from here and taken to the airport. It's to sow a bit of uncertainty. UK Border's systems will show that we haven't left the country, but they'll be aware that high-tech criminal types like us might have acquired new passports.'

Parlabane's phone vibrates while the cab idles at a set of lights. He feels his pulse quicken in apprehension about who the message might be from. There is literally nobody in his life that it would be good news to hear from right now. He pulls the device from his pocket and sees that he has an email alerting him that a new recording has been made by the device hidden inside the keyboard they sent to Winter.

What an auspicious day for the bastard to finally show up again at his office.

He clicks on the link and listens back to this latest one-way phone conversation, in which Winter is discussing the morning's tragic news. He doesn't exactly sound distraught.

'We're only a couple of hours into trading but the share price is already beginning to tank. No, I wouldn't make any offers yet: it would seem inappropriate, but more importantly, it's only going to fall further. Yeah, I saw it too. That Dunwoodie woman is all defiance at the moment, but it's emotion talking. In the cold light of day, once the tears have dried, trying to haul the carcass of someone's half-finished project up a steep slope won't look like such an attractive prospect.

'Absolutely. She and the other shareholders will be very amenable to a purchase offer so that they can all move on. Yeah, wasn't I just saying how things can change overnight? Not the way I'd have preferred it, but you don't look a gift horse in the mouth.'

*Not the way I'd have preferred it.* Sure. But then he would say that, wouldn't he?

The cab drifts on to a slip road off the motorway, the sound of a plane booming somewhere overhead.

'That Stoolpigeon squawking yet?' Parlabane asks quietly.

'Still nothing. My counter says the file has been downloaded, though: just hasn't been launched yet.'

313

'Bugger.'

'It'll come.'

'Do you still have the RBA files on that thing?' he enquires, indicating her laptop.

'No way. I deleted them from my hard drive as soon as I uploaded the malware version. The originals are still on my storage server, though. Why?'

'I want you to email a download link to my mate Spammy. The bastard probably won't be up for another four hours, but if he can take a look at the blueprints he might be able to tell us what this prototype actually is.'

Parlabane pays the driver then retrieves his suitcase from the boot. There's very little in it, but he wants it to look as though he and Sam have packed for a long trip. They watch the taxi disappear from view then hop on the shuttle to one of the long-stay car parks.

The rain is off, but there is a strong breeze blowing litter along the walkway. They choose a vantage point from where they can see the cars coming in, scrutinising each new arrival. They are on the hunt for someone travelling alone, with luggage large enough to indicate they will be gone more than a couple of nights. When such a candidate appears, they watch very closely what is done with their keys: zip pockets are a no-no, inside pockets too. Ideally what they are looking for is a strappy shoulder tote or a handbag with magnetic fasteners.

'Her?' Sam suggests, indicating a peroxide-blonde middle-aged woman who has exited a black Nissan Qashqai.

Parlabane gives her the nod, notes the registration, and they move in as rehearsed.

Sam adjusts her makeshift niqab, which has threatened to come down over her eyes, then strides ahead, a leather bag they found in Mairi's wardrobe slung over her shoulder. She intercepts and over-takes the target so that both of them are now heading for the shelter where the shuttle bus picks up. Once she is a few paces in front, Sam subtly pings free a clip from the shoulder strap, causing the bag to tumble to the ground. It spills coins, tampons, make-up, mints, gloves, wet wipes and a compact brolly on to the tarmac.

The woman comes to a halt behind Sam and crouches down to

314

help her retrieve the articles that are now scattered across an impressive radius. She places her own bag carefully down on the ground, conscious of the danger of items falling out as she bends over to pick up Sam's fugitive belongings.

Parlabane arrives at the rear, stopping his pull-along suitcase so that it screens the woman from her bag. He swiftly crouches down to remove her car keys from a flip pocket on the front, apparently on route to offering his own assistance.

'Thank you. Thank you so much,' Sam says, gathering the last of her things and standing up again.

They retrieve their various articles of luggage and continue to the bus shelter, where they and a few other waiting passengers board the shuttle. Sam takes a seat at the front, close to the door, Parlabane continuing further inside.

A few minutes later the bus comes to a stop in front of the main terminal and Sam gets off first. Parlabane encounters the peroxide woman again as they both retrieve their luggage from the shelves. She gestures towards the figure in the niqab now passing the bus window outside.

'At least we know that one doesn't have a bomb in her bag,' she says with a chuckle.

Parlabane allows himself a smile, which he knows she will misinterpret. He is always taken aback by how people simply assume complete strangers are going to share their casual racism, but on this occasion he is genuinely amused, because he is about to steal this woman's car.

Parlabane watches her wheel her suitcase towards the terminal. He caught a glance at her booking print-out when he was dipping her bag: she's off to Tenerife for a week, and she isn't going to be noticing the loss of her vehicle from a beach in the Canaries.

He doubts they'll be able to evade the authorities that long, but at least this gives them some freedom to manoeuvre.

He heads for the main parking office, near the passenger entrance to the short-stay car park.

'I'm really hoping you can help me out here,' he says to one of the attendants on duty.

His colleague is apparently on his break, eating a pot noodle in front of his computer monitor, which is showing the BBC website.

'My ticket just blew away in the wind as I was getting off the shuttle bus. I thought I'd better report it at this end of the holiday, you know? Can you issue me a new one?'

'I'm afraid that for the long-stay parking there's a minimum charge for lost tickets at a full week's rate.'

'I know, but my licence plate was scanned at the barrier, so you should have proof I only came in ten minutes ago. That's why I came here right away.'

'Let me have a look. What's your registration?'

Parlabane rhymes it off, though as he does so his attention is drawn to the screen in front of the bloke eating noodles. One of the images above a story link is a photo-fit that he is sure is intended to be him. The photo-fit is far from a close likeness, though it's a sight better than it would have been had he not found himself the focus of the security guard's attention by being trapped inside that freezer.

There is an immediate instinct to walk away, but that would only draw more attention. He has to hold his nerve, follow this through, analyse the situation rationally: the guy looking at the screen is not looking at him, and the guy who has been looking at him has not been looking at the screen.

He keeps his eyes down, resisting the strong temptation to steal another glance at the monitor, but he knows that might cause the attendant to check what has caught his attention.

The attendant hands him a ticket.

'Here you go, sir.'

'Thank you.'

He takes the ticket and turns around, feeling his heart thump. He just got lucky, but he knows that won't last. Like most such images, the danger is not going to be from a close encounter with a parking attendant or some other stranger who's never seen him before. Somebody at Synergis, somebody at *Broadwave*, or maybe even somebody who was at the party last night, is going to see that picture then put two and two together.

Parlabane rolls his case along to catch the shuttle bus, which Sam is already aboard. She is sitting near the front, tapping away at her phone as always.

'Don't you kids ever look out the window and watch the world go by?' he asks rhetorically, sitting down in the row behind her. 'What are you checking up on now?'

'Synergis share activity. After your Winter update, I thought I'd take a look.'

'So what's happening?'

'A lot of people are ditching Synergis shares, which is no surprise given this morning's news. But the weird thing is that after an initial dive, the price has been holding steady.'

'I'm sorry, this shit baffles me. What's weird about that?'

'With everyone trying to sell, you'd expect it to keep falling. The fact that it's not means someone is buying: somebody is picking up Synergis stock.'

'Winter.'

'Despite what he said this morning, he's already making his move: increasing his own holding so he has more sway and a bigger slice when the Chinese start carving things up.'

'Impressive intel. How do you know about all this stuff?'

'Juice, one of my Uninvited buddies, showed me some cool sites for tracking stock trades. He used to make a bit of money short-selling when he knew we were about to do a hack. There's always a drop in the price due to security concerns and corporate embarrassment.'

'You weren't tempted?'

'I never had the money to make it worthwhile, but even if I did, it's too close to blackhat territory for my taste. I know people think I'm a criminal, but I do have a code of ethics. There's lines I won't cross. Plus I was paranoid that someone might spot a pattern and trace the trades. Juice obviously wasn't so worried. He's been doing it for ages.'

'Why do you say "he"? Couldn't Juice be a she like you?'

'Rule thirty, Jack. There are no girls on the internet.'

The bus drops them at the long-stay car park once again, and soon they are climbing into the black Qashqai. Sam pulls off her improvised niqab and Parlabane decides he can finally remove the hat and scarf, both of which were concealing the fact that he has shaved his head; or more accurately, Sam has shaved it.

It was as they searched through the flat for any possible means of disguise that she happened upon Mairi's bikini line trimmer, whereupon inspiration struck. Parlabane would have to confess it wasn't the most enticing idea he had ever heard, but nor did he have a strong argument against it. Sam started with scissors then moved on to the trimmer, before finishing things off with his own disposable razor.

He catches a glimpse as he adjusts the rear-view mirror. The effect isn't as anonymising as the niqab, but he has never looked so unlike himself, which is both reassuring and unsettling at the same time.

Parlabane pulls on his seatbelt and starts the engine. Sam is already busy on her phone in the passenger seat.

'So, I guess the tricky question is where now?' he asks. 'I mean, there's an urge that says I should keep driving until we're in Ullapool or somewhere, but this isn't about running: this is about fighting back. We need an operations base, a staging post.'

Sam voices a suggestion with surprising conviction.

'I think we should head for Milton Keynes.'

'Why there?'

She holds up her mobile.

'Because my Stoolpigeon just started singing.'

# THE PENITENT

For a wanted fugitive with a criminal past, I realise this is the first time I have ever actually stolen anything. I tell myself we're only borrowing the car, and have every intention of bringing it back (with a full tank), but I don't know why I'm trying to sugar-coat this. I'm tangled up in cybercrime, industrial espionage and now murder, so it's not like twocking is going to tip some moral balance against me, but for some reason it's important that I don't see what we're doing as theft.

Maybe it's because I don't want to add another crime to the list of things I've forced Jack into. Everything that is happening to him is my fault. I've even cost him his hair. He looks like an angry egg, and I know that at some point he's going to direct that anger at me.

Right now all of his attention is divided between the sat-nav and the road, with maybe a little left over for the radio. He turned it on 'to hear if there's any news', but we both know that what we're listening out for is our own names, which would take us to the next Defcon level.

'I know it doesn't mean much, Jack, but I want to say I'm sorry about all this. I know you never did anything to deserve getting dragged into my mess.'

He doesn't say anything. I don't know what I was expecting, and I can't even say what I was hoping for either. My apology is meaningless, though: words are easy. I owe him an explanation, at least. It's not going to excuse anything, but it's all I've got to offer. I've come to realise there's never going to be a right time to do this, so I might as well choose a wrong time and get it out there.

'The reason I contacted you, in the beginning, when I hijacked your laptop . . .'

He glances across for a microsecond, like a dog that's spied a rabbit from the corner of his eye. It's pure reflex.

'I did it because I thought you might have known my mum, way back when. She never talks about her life before I was born, but I found out she had this interest in you. She was all over you on social media, but she kept it anonymous. I thought maybe you knew her in those days, and you'd be able to tell me what she wouldn't.'

'Her name is Ruth Morpeth, right?' he asks. I keep forgetting he knows everything, probably always did.

'Right.'

'It doesn't ring a bell. Has she been married? Remarried? What was her maiden name?'

'Roberts.'

He squints, like he's trying to see into the past, but he isn't finding anything.

'I still don't recall . . . Though we're talking more than twenty years ago, so it's hazy.'

'Last time I spoke to her I asked if she had heard of you, to see what she'd say. She denied it.'

'You didn't challenge her?'

'I didn't want to get into why *I* had heard of you.'

He searches the memory banks again. Now that I've given him her maiden name, surely this should make the difference.

'Nope. Still nothing. I'm usually good with names, but as a reporter, I've met so many people down the years, so I need more than that. Do you know what her job was at the time? Where she was living?'

'No. That's the problem: she's wrapped up tight when it comes to this whole subject.'

I feel hollow. All the time I've waited for this moment. I've been too anxious to ask before now, and when I finally open the box, it's empty.

From the passenger seat I am able to watch his reactions very carefully, no need to avert my own gaze while his is locked on the road in front. It is my blessing and my curse to be able to pick up on the slightest glimmer of people's reactions. Even when they're

320

covering up, the fact that I can *detect* that they're covering up gives me a glimpse. With Jack right now, there is nothing.

I contrast this with my mum: lying to my face while her own betrayed her fear at the mention of Jack's name.

I just don't get it.

On the outskirts of Milton Keynes I spot a Goodnight Inn and tell Jack to pull into the car park, close to the building.

'What for?'

'So I can leech off the hotel Wi-Fi. I need to work with my laptop and using my phone as a hotspot isn't stable enough for what I want to do.'

'Don't you need a pass— Forget that, look who I'm talking to.'

I am already connected by the time Jack has parked. There's a delivery van taking up three spaces closest to the building, but the signal is passable.

Stoolpigeon has been busy mining data, and I am able to set my laptop to the task of triangulating it. With the exception of one outlier so distant as to be clearly the result of a VPN (San Francisco, FFS), I've got the target pinned down to a specific point on the map.

'The download was made at 27 Bletchley Rise,' I tell Jack. 'And if that turns out to be Danny Winter's home address, then we've got the bastard.'

'It isn't.'

'How do you know?'

'Somebody beats the shite out of me and threatens worse, I find out where they stay. Winter lives in Hornchurch in Essex.'

'Shit. There must be a connection, though. Are any of the companies he's invested in based in MK?'

Jack opens his laptop to check his files, and while he's busy with that I run searches and tests based on what Stoolpigeon is telling me.

'Result. Winter does have a company in . . . Ah, bollocks. It's no longer a going concern: one of the firms he bought over cheap then broke up and sold off.'

'Look at this,' I tell him, angling my laptop so he can see. 'Google Street View of our target address.'

'It's all blurred out.'

'I've been using everything I can think of to probe the IP addresses Stoolpigeon is giving me for that property. Nothing doing. The place has digital Keep Out signs posted everywhere. Whoever he is, this is definitely our guy.'

# TARGET IN SIGHT

Props to the angry egg: for all my apps and expertise, it's Jack who gets us a name. While I was acting on instinct and testing whether I could hack my way in, he went straight to the electoral roll and searched for 27 Bletchley Rise. Hacker pitfall: sometimes you're looking so hard to sneak in around the back that you don't notice the front door is open.

'The residents registered to this address are Gareth David Lansing and Elizabeth Mary Lansing. I trust that you can—'

'I'm all over it.'

I'm wary as this sounds like a married couple. I think about my downstairs neighbours, marched off by the feds earlier today in a state of fear and confusion. A hacker could have done to the Lansings what I did to the Cohens. There's the fact that their house is blurred out on Street View, but that's a privacy option open to anyone who knows they have the right to request it.

A few seconds later though, my doubts are wiped. I don't even need to pull off any hack-fu to find a visible web presence for a Gary Lansing of Milton Keynes: he runs his own computer security consultancy. The firm is called Lance Guard, and according to its website, specialises in penetration testing for corporate networks.

'He's a hacker,' I explain. 'All pen testers are hackers at heart or they're no good to anybody. Their job is to think up how a hacker might get through your defences, then show you the holes. It's like hiring a burglar to find out if your home security cuts it.'

As I expected, his online discipline is pretty tight, so I'm awarding major points to whoever coded Stoolpigeon. That said, it just proves that no matter what anti-malware protection you're rocking, your best defence is never to run anything unless you're sure of what it is and where it came from. Lansing has made damaging assumptions about both.

There's an official email address for him on his company website but beyond that he hasn't given me much to work with. He has been careful about keeping his business email address separate from his private interests, and his social media presence is very limited. However, his missus is a different story. She is the assistant head teacher at a local secondary school, and with an active and visible role in the community, she leaves a big, messy online footprint, which unavoidably overlaps with her husband's private sphere. I get the organisations she's involved with, the health club they're both members of, every kind of details about their kids; even a home phone number.

What I don't get is a connection to Winter, but I haven't even started on this guy yet.

Jack drives us to Bletchley Rise, which is outside Milton Keynes, in a village named Little Aspley. Even before we have reached the street itself, it's obvious that computer security has been good to Gary Lansing. Little Aspley is a posh neighbourhood, the houses large and far apart from one another, in gardens the size of my local park. I'm glad we've stolen (or rather, borrowed) a Qashqai, because anything smaller and more downmarket is going to make us conspicuous.

We drive slowly past the address and park further along the street, getting the lay of the land, as Jack puts it. It's a corner plot. There's a Range Rover Overfinch parked in the double driveway, swings and a trampoline in the garden.

I'm finding it hard to picture a suburban family man with a successful business, a schoolteacher wife and two primary-age kids turning out to be the scheming crook behind Zodiac's mask, but I realise I'm falling for my own trick. I of all people should know that the face someone presents to the world and the hacker underneath can be two completely different personalities.

From the side, the property is hemmed in by metal railings, a row of planting alongside for added privacy. The garden slopes gently upward at the rear, towards a large outbuilding visible above the top of the shrubs. It looks like converted stables. Probably more square footage than our flat back in Barking.

'I think we're looking at someone with a lot of clout,' I suggest.

'And I think we're looking at someone with a lot to lose,' Jack replies.

We make sure that nobody is watching from Lansing's neighbour's house then get out of the Qashqai. We take a walk around the side, getting a closer look. Beyond a gap in the greenery we can see the glow of monitor screens through the stable building's double-glazed windows. This is where he works.

I don't see anyone in there, but suddenly the light through the glass changes as one of the patio doors opens. I catch a glimpse of him emerging before instinct forces me to step back out of his line of sight.

He is shorter than I imagined from his company profile headshot: maybe five foot six and slightly built. I can easily imagine him needing a hand-held electroshock device to overpower somebody. I know he's thirty-seven but he looks much younger: mostly it's the boyish face but the jogging pants and the Green Arrow T-shirt are shaving some years off too.

The crunch of his footsteps carries clearly as he walks across the gravel path bisecting his back lawn. He's left the patio doors slightly ajar, suggesting he's nipping over to the house briefly: a trip to the loo or a mug of tea, maybe.

'I suspect everything we need to know is right through those doors,' Jack says quietly. 'We need to get him out of the way.'

I'm reckoning he must have heavy-duty locks and an alarm system protecting that lot, so we don't only need him gone, but gone in a desperate hurry.

I've been there myself, so I know just the thing.

I get back into the car and open my laptop, pulling up some of the details I have cached. I call the Lansings' landline from my mobile, spoofing the number of his kids' primary school. He picks up after two rings. I figure he's in the kitchen, from the echo on the call.

I put on a posh voice, trying to make myself sound more mature.

'Mr Lansing? Hello, it's Justine here from the school office at Saint Anne's. It's nothing to worry about, but I have to let you know that Alice has been a bit sick. We've got this winter vomiting bug going around, and I think she's the latest to catch it.'

'How is she?'

'As I said, it's nothing to worry about, but she's kind of upset and she's been asking for you. We're quite keen that it doesn't spread to the other children, so if you could possibly . . .'

'I understand. You need me to come and pick her up?'

'If you could. I realise that when you work at home you always get these things thrown at you, but . . .'

'No, not at all. It's *why* I work from home. I'll be right there. Justine, did you say?'

'That's right. Or Alice may have called me Miss Collins.'

'I don't think we've met. Are you filling in for Mrs Orton? Is she still on maternity leave?'

'That's right, she is, yes. So if you could just . . .'

'Absolutely. I'll be there in five minutes.'

We hear an engine start a few moments later, then see the Range Rover pulling out of the drive through its hydraulic gates. We didn't see him return to lock up the stables before he left.

I recognise the haste. Any time Mum or I got a call to say Lilly was ill, we dropped everything.

As soon as the Range Rover is out of sight, we slip through the gates, which are already beginning to reclose automatically.

'How far is the school?' Jack asks.

'According to Google Maps, it should take him seven minutes in current traffic, but he'll be hammering it because he thinks his kid's sick. Add to that about ninety seconds at the school office to establish that the call's bullshit, after which I reckon he'll be heading back here even faster than he drove out.'

Jack checks his watch.

'Call it twelve minutes, tops. Let's make it count.'

We run around the house and out to the stables, where I am alarmed to see that the patio door is no longer ajar. There is a strong breeze gusting through the garden, and it looks to have nudged the

326

door closed. When we reach the decking, I see that it has only blown to, without the latch clicking home.

I step inside and my eyes jealously gobble up all the beautiful kit. He's got two curved-screen 4K monitors side by side, linked to two server array columns and a Vibox Proteus water-cooled PC.

However, my eyes are soon drawn to something considerably less state-of-the-art, but strangely all the more compelling. Against the wall to the left of his immaculate workstation is what appears to be a miniature museum, or maybe more like a shrine.

Inside a locked glass cabinet are several vintage computers: a Vic 20, a Commodore 64 and an Amiga taking pride of place on the top shelf, above an Apple II, a BBC Micro and examples of the full Sinclair ZX range, from 80 to Spectrum Plus. There are also ancient comms devices: an acoustic coupler, a Hayes Smartmodem and a Commodore modem cartridge.

Above these on the wall hang two framed newspaper articles. One is from the late 1980s, a shock-horror tabloid splash about a hacker causing an emergency shutdown of the Wintergreen nuclear power plant. Next to it is a cutting from the *Financial Times* dated May 2008, a full-page illustrated feature about how 'one-time teenage hacker Gary Lansing is the ultimate poacher-turned-gamekeeper, with a roster of corporate clients engaging his expertise to protect their networks'.

I look again at the ancient machines on the top shelf, staring more closely this time. The plastic is worn and stained, the logos scratched and sun-bleached in places. These are not acquired collectors' pieces: this is his own kit.

I step around the cabinet so that I can view the Vic 20 from the side, which is when I notice the thin ribbon of a punch-tape label: black text out of a red plastic adhesive strip spelling a single word. Compared to today's printing possibilities it is unbelievably low-fi, but the sense of pride with which it must have been stuck on there is unmistakable to me.

'OMG,' I say.

'What?'

'He's got his old hacker name printed on his machines.'

'And is it Zodiac?'

'No. It's Ferox.'

I pull myself away from the cabinet, knowing I am wasting precious seconds. On the monitors, the screen savers have kicked in but the hum of the water pump and the glow of blue light from the cooling tubes tells me the system has not gone into sleep mode. I shake a Razer mouse that's probably worth more than my computer and am relieved to see a split-screen desktop rather than a login prompt.

My eye is briefly drawn to a framed photo on the wall behind the monitor. It shows Lansing when he was about my age, pale and skinny, looking like his mother still bought his clothes.

There's a reason the geek stereotype gained traction.

He's standing with his arm around the shoulder of another teenager who looks smarter in comparison, or maybe just a bit more posh. There's something vaguely familiar about him but I can't place it. Maybe he ended up making *Warcraft* or something. I notice the handwritten scrawl: 'Ferox and Thanatos – hackers in arms.'

Thanatos. Another name from hacker lore. It figures he'd be buds with Ferox. God, I wish I had hours to root through this guy's drives, but as it is I've got ten minutes.

I run a search for the most recently accessed files and quickly find the Synergis documents, extracted from the doctored zip file I created last night. I check my watch again and glance out of the windows at the gravel path. If I hear footsteps on that, I'll know it's already too late.

We've got nine minutes left. The question is whether I should search further while I'm here, or just install some remote-access programs that will allow me to poke around from a safe distance. I decide I'll try for the latter. As a hacker, you seldom get unrestricted physical access to a target's computer. This means I can disable his defences while I install my full repertoire of dirty tricks, though there is still a risk that my malware will be detected when I try to run it remotely later.

I slip a memory stick from my pocket and slot it into a port in the front of the Proteus. Lansing's security scanner has a fit, warning me against what I'm trying to install, but I give it the green light.

'Who is Ferox?' Jack asks.

He is crouching in front of a steel cabinet at the end of the building, probing delicately at a lock with two slivers of metal. I'm not exactly sure what he's hoping to find in there, but I'm guessing a V mask, an electroshock device and a silver flight case would be a decent result.

'He was a hacker legend in the early days of the internet. Before that, even: all the way back in the time of ARPANET and the first bulletin boards. He hacked a radar array and caused RAF jets to be grounded. He even hacked NASA, looking for proof of whether Roswell was true.'

'Spoiler alert: it isn't.'

'And as that press clipping on the wall would tell you, he once caused a major incident when he hacked into a nuclear power station.'

While my spyware is installing, I open up Lansing's email and search for messages from Winter. His name gives us nothing. This is why I need remote access, so I can sift through it more carefully later and identify an alias Winter might be using, or a coded exchange.

I check the time again. We've still got seven minutes.

'Why the hell did he hack into a nuclear power station?' Jack asks.

'The usual reason. To find out if he could. He was fifteen.'

'He's put his talents to more lucrative use since then, it would appear.'

'Yeah, but he must have kept a hand in the game, made sure he's up to speed with the latest scams. No wonder he was able to infiltrate Uninvited. It's his business to be one step ahead of us, and he's been doing this shit since before most of us were even born.'

Jack lets out a sigh of frustration and changes his grip on the picks. It doesn't look like he's getting anywhere.

'We've found a hell of an opponent to be up against,' he says. 'Even his locks are state-of-the-art and super-secure. All of which begs the question . . . oh fuck.'

'What?'

I swivel in my chair and it rolls backwards, my feet kicking out in reflex. Gary Lansing is standing in the doorway. He is pointing a compound bow at Jack, an arrow nocked and the string fully drawn.

There were no footsteps on the gravel. He hasn't come from the house – maybe a side door to the garden.

Jack doesn't finish his question. He doesn't have to. I realise a guy like Lansing would not leave his computers on and his door unlocked any more than he would unthinkingly download and extract my Stoolpigeon malware.

He did this to draw us into the open, and now he's got us right where he wants us.

# DEADLY TENSION

'I spoke to Mrs Orton, the school secretary, when I dropped off the kids this morning. She's pushing sixty, by the way, so she's had all the maternity leave she's ever going to need.'

Parlabane watches Lansing step through the doorway, keeping the arrow pointed at him. He is aware that at full draw, a compound bow can fire an arrow more than three hundred feet per second, and with the right tip could penetrate bullet-proof Plexiglas. At this range it would go through his skull and out the back again.

As Lansing speaks he glances briefly at Sam, who has turned around and is rolling back in her chair. Parlabane spots the briefest flinch in his reaction, like he is surprised, which doesn't tally with the fact that he has lured them into a trap.

Parlabane has his hands in the air and is standing perfectly still. The situation is more precarious than the threat of someone pulling a trigger. The slightest slip or startlement could cause Lansing to let go.

'Here's what's going to happen. You're going to step slowly over to the desk, pick up that handset and dial the police. You're going to tell them to come to this address, where two burglars wish to surrender themselves, then you're going to hang up and we're all going to wait.'

This is not what Parlabane was expecting. If this truly is Zodiac, his first enquiry would surely be regarding the prototype; or maybe he'd shoot both of them so that they couldn't talk. If the people apparently responsible for Cruz's murder broke into his house, it wouldn't be a tough sell to plead self-defence.

Parlabane takes a breath.

'I'm not making any moves with that thing pointed at me,' he says, as calmly as he can manage. 'I don't want anything happening through panic.'

Lansing points the arrow towards the floor, but keeps it drawn.

'Thank you,' Parlabane says. 'And I'm happy to cooperate. But I'm not sure you really want me to call the police.'

Lansing's eyes narrow in anger, a twitch of his shoulder suggesting he might be about to raise the bow again.

'I went to bed last night after hearing on the news that the electronics entrepreneur Leo Cruz had been murdered during a robbery at his premises. This morning I received a link to download what turned out to be confidential files pertaining to the secret project Cruz was developing at Synergis: files evidently acquired and subsequently uploaded by you. Why the hell wouldn't I want to call the police?'

'Because, Mr Lansing, if we've been able to tie you and your computers to what happened to Leo Cruz last night, how hard do you think it's going to be for the police to tie you to it? Or to put it more bluntly, if we're going down, you're going down. So I reckon we should talk.'

'You didn't tie me to it. You sent me a link.'

'No, that's the point. We didn't send anyone the link. So how did you get it?'

He raises the bow again. He looks scared and confused, neither of which augurs for this ending well.

'Of course you're the ones who sent me the link. How else would I get it?'

He looks across to Sam, whatever troubled him before seemingly compounding his confusion now. There are certainties crumbling on both sides.

'Mr Lansing, I don't believe either of us is who the other thinks he is. I suspect we have a common problem and I really, really reckon we should talk.'

Lansing stares back and forth at the pair of them, then lowers the bow, easing the tension on the string but keeping the arrow nocked.

'You both stay where you are, though,' he warns.

'Believe me, mate, we've got nowhere else to go,' Sam tells him.

'Okay, so talk. Who are you?'

Lansing's eyes are fixed on Parlabane as he asks this. He gets the impression he means 'you' singular, which is when Parlabane works out why Lansing seems uneasy about the sight of Sam. Lansing already knows who she is.

'My name is Jack Parlabane. I'm a journalist. This young lady enlisted my assistance when she was blackmailed by someone calling himself Zodiac. He wanted her to break and hack into Synergis, in order to acquire a new prototype and the blueprint documents for it. We executed this last night, but then the lights went out and I was Tased and battered unconscious. When I came to, I found myself locked in a freezer with the body of Leo Cruz.

'My associate here had instructions to upload the blueprints to a specific storage site. She complied, albeit after installing the malware that brought us here, but the address of that storage site was known only to her and to Zodiac. That's unless you can tell us different.'

'How were you contacted?' Lansing asks Sam.

'It was all done through IRC channels. Zodiac also demanded to know how I was planning the job and when I intended to go in. It was a frame-up from the start.'

'And have you found any clues as to who this Zodiac might be?'

Parlabane intervenes before Sam can answer.

'Mr Lansing, I appreciate you must have lots of questions, but I am particularly intrigued by the one you're *not* asking.'

'Which question would that be?'

'Who I am,' answers Sam, who has sussed it too.

'I'm sorry. As you say I've got lots of questions,' he dissembles. 'So what is your name?'

'The point is that you already know,' says Parlabane. 'And we'd like you to tell us how come.'

'I truly don't. This is the first time I've seen either of you in my life.'

'Mr Lansing, my associate and I are what I would call ultra-fucked at the moment. In a matter of time, maybe already, the police are going to connect both of us to what happened last night, and we will end up in custody, charged with murder. We have nothing to lose from telling them that you were balls-deep in this conspiracy, and the electronic trail will back that up, so I would strongly recommend you cut the shite and start telling us your end of the story.'

Lansing's body language changes, the tension going out of his stance like it went out of the bow-string.

'You know what I do, right?'

'You're a pen tester,' Sam replies. 'A whitehat.'

'I was contracted to infiltrate Uninvited and other hacker collectives, in order to uncover hackers' real-world identities.'

'Contracted by whom?'

'Same as you, I never got a real name. He called himself Zardoz. I think we can assume it was the same person. He wanted the details on hackers who could then be tied to specific attacks. From what you've told me, I now realise that this was for leverage.'

'I think the word is blackmail,' says Sam. 'And once you had found out their real-world identities, what then? Were you the one who reached out to me? Are you Zodiac and Zardoz is the guy pulling your strings?'

'I'm not Zodiac, I swear. Exposing the hackers was my end done.'

'So how come you got sent the link?'

'I don't know.'

Parlabane looks at his watch.

'The school run is approaching, Gary.'

As he says it he can't help but steal a glance towards Sam. She glances back, biting her lip.

'So unless you're planning on introducing us to the family and explaining what we're doing here, I'd say the time we've got left to help each other is running out. Give.'

'Okay. He told me that I would receive a download link, and my instructions were to download the files, check them for spyware and then pass them on.'

'To where?'

'To an address he hasn't given me yet. To be honest, I'd forgotten all about this. My work on exposing the hackers ended weeks ago; some of it goes back months. Then I got the link this morning. Even then I had no idea it was related to the Cruz thing until I checked the files. I can prove this. I kept chat logs and screenshots of everything.'

Sam sits forward in her chair, no longer quite so frozen since Lansing removed the arrow from the string.

'You hired that Chinese guy to say he was Stonefish, but *you* were Stonefish. That's how you drew me out.'

'No,' Lansing counters. 'Stonefish *is* a Chinese guy: how do you know that?'

'Don't bullshit me. You set up that meeting. You drew out me and you drew out Cicatrix, who's now in jail because he wouldn't play ball for Zodiac.'

'I didn't. I did identify Paul Wiley, the Scouse kid, but he wasn't Cicatrix. *I* was Cicatrix. You remember I arranged to meet you in a café at Euston Station?'

Sam gapes.

'That's right. But you never showed up.'

'Oh, but I did, in a manner of speaking. I had people waiting in that café. I sent you a message that I wasn't coming, then they watched to see who got up and left. They tailed you, followed you home, and from there I found out everything I needed.'

'That's why you bailed out of the RSGN hack at the last minute. You knew it was going to be used against everyone who took part.'

Lansing nods solemnly.

Sam looks annoyed with herself, but also a little confused.

'How did they know they were following the right person? Someone else could have left at the same time. I could have stayed for a coffee and five different people might have left before I finished it.'

'Because you've got it the wrong way round. With the others, my job was to find out their real-life identities, but in your case I was tasked with finding out Samantha Morpeth's current online hacker alias.'

Parlabane watches her physically shrink back in the chair, her eyes widening with a shock she can't hide. She steals an anxious look back, anxious about what he might have seen.

'Why?' Parlabane asks. 'I mean, how would you or anyone else know she *had* an online hacker alias?'

'Because she and I have more in common than she has seen fit to reveal. Haven't we, Sam?'

# RECKLESS YOUTH (I)

Jack's looking at me like WTF, searching for a signal that the guy is bullshitting. The shock on my face must give me away – that and the fact that I instantly feel guilty. Jack's going to think I was holding out on him, but it's not like that. I'm not allowed to talk about this stuff, and what's really got me floored is that nobody is supposed to know about it.

'What am I missing here?' Jack asks. 'What have you got in common?'

I want to be the one who answers, but I feel like I'm crawling up inside myself again. Scared and pathetic Sam is back, banishing Buzzkill just when she's most needed.

'We both pulled off some audacious hacks in the dizzy naivety of our mid-teens,' Lansing says. 'Doing it to see if it was possible, driven by anger and ego and not thinking for a minute about the consequences. Difference is: I never got caught.'

Jack is looking at me like he's afraid the rug is about to get pulled.

'What did you do, Sam?'

I want to speak, but I feel my throat swell up and my eyes fill. I feel bad that I couldn't tell him, but I hate the idea that he thinks this is shame. It isn't. It's the memories of my fear flooding back in. It mixes with my fear right now and my shock that Lansing – and by the sound of it Zodiac – knows about this.

'She hacked the official website of the Royal Embassy of Saudi Arabia when she was fifteen. She caused an international diplomatic incident.'

Lansing says this with a hint of triumph, but it's not like he's playing a card that smacks me down. He doesn't sound sneery or judgemental. He sounds admiring.

'Oh, Christ, you didn't redirect their address to tentacle porn and bestiality videos, did you?' Jack asks.

I still can't find my voice, but to be honest, Lansing is doing a better job than I could of selling it.

'No, I think they could have more comfortably written that off as mindless vandalism. She replaced every picture on the site with photos of women in action: politicians and leaders giving speeches, scientists working in labs, athletes on the track, singers, footballers, astronauts.'

'Could have been worse,' Jack suggests. 'You could have shown a woman driving.'

'Oh, she did. Formula One.'

'You hacked a foreign government website when you were fifteen?' Jack asks. I can't decide whether he sounds impressed or appalled.

I offer him a nod and a glum smile. Somehow I find my voice, through the need to clarify something.

'Strictly speaking, I didn't hack the Saudi government. I hacked the third-party developers they had contracted to build the English-language part of the website.'

'So why didn't I hear about this?'

'Precisely,' Lansing replies.

'It was covered up,' I mumble.

I swallow and clear my throat.

'They took the site down within minutes. I've since learned ways to prevent that, but it was up long enough. The hack was traced to an address in the UK and the Saudi embassy demanded an investigation.

'It didn't take them long to find out whodunit: I learned the hard way about covering your tracks. But then somebody else in the Saudi government, who better understood the Streisand effect, leaned on the British authorities to keep the whole thing quiet so the world never found out their website had been hacked by a fifteen-year-old girl.'

'So there was no court case? No charges?'

'No.'

I swallow again, feeling the memory well up inside, threatening to drown me from within. I can't talk about this part. I don't know why, but I feel as though telling someone else lets it in and makes it real again.

I spent the worst three days of my life on remand in Graythorne Young Offenders Institution. I was easy meat, fragile and defenceless. It's what made me such a quivering and pathetic specimen. To this day I can sense that menace, that predatory violence in people who are instinctively drawn to weakness.

'Although, my mum did ban me from using computers or the internet,' I add. 'To this day she doesn't know I've got my own laptop, as I was only allowed to use her iPad with her watching. But officially the whole incident was airbrushed out. Nobody is supposed to know it happened and I signed documents preventing me from talking about it.'

'Presumably you weren't calling yourself Buzzkill.'

'No, I didn't have an alias and I didn't leave a signature. Apart from the trail that led to my IP address, obviously.'

'So how come you knew about this?' Jack asks Lansing.

'Computer security, police cyber investigations and hacking are all small worlds with large overlaps. The incident was covered up, but Sam's name ended up on a lot of lists.'

'But this Zardoz or Zodiac – who I think we can assume to be the same guy – how did he know Sam would still be active as a hacker?'

'He didn't, for sure, but it had a high probability. Someone who pulled that off at fifteen wasn't going to give it up. He was looking for someone highly capable and must have figured that with a few more years' experience, Sam Morpeth was bound to fit the bill.'

'So he tasked you with confirming she was still active and tying her to her new alias.'

Lansing nods.

'How were you paid? I mean, couldn't you follow the money to find out who your mystery client was? Weren't you curious?'

'Of course I was curious. But he paid me in cryptocurrency, meaning there was no way of tracing the payments.'

'Bollocks he did,' Jack states.

Lansing tenses up again, his fingers tapping the bow string. The briefly chummy atmosphere of a few moments back has evaporated. I've noticed that happens a lot around Jack.

'Look at this place, Gary. Business is good. Million-pound house and articles in the *FT*. Lance Guard is doing very well. You didn't need money from some shady anon: that's not why you did this. He's got something on you, hasn't he?'

'He paid me in Bitcoin, and he paid well. Business is seldom so good that you can't turn down clients, Mr Parlabane. Especially when the work is intriguing.'

'Pish. He blackmailed you, same as he blackmailed Sam. That's how he works. He's got something on you, and he's making sure he'll have even more on you by the time this is done. Why else would you be instructed to download files then forward them? That's a redundant step. It's so these files can be traced to you, tying you into this, so you'll keep quiet when the shit starts flying.'

I can see the truth of this hit him. Lansing thought he was clever, expecting the files to have a hidden payload and making that work to his advantage, but now he knows he was kidding himself.

'Jack's right. You willingly downloaded unknown files from an untrusted source. Why would someone like you do that, unless you felt you had no choice? You were under orders, same as me.'

He knows I've got him, and I think he finally knows we're all on the same side too.

# RECKLESS YOUTH (II)

'This goes all the way back to the earliest days of the internet, really,' Lansing says. 'When we all felt like we were true pioneers in a new land, with eldritch skills and arcane knowledge.'

'You mean like Commodore bulletin boards and FidoNet?' asks Sam. 'The pre-dial-up days?'

Parlabane notes a change in Lansing's demeanour. He's warming to his subject and, in Sam's case, warming to his guest. He's recognised a fellow hacker, albeit from a different generation.

Sam, for her part, is demonstrating that she isn't merely a hacker, but in fact a keen student of all things hackish.

'It started then, yes. I was first online in the late eighties, and it really did feel like I could do what I wanted. You weren't paranoid about who might be eavesdropping, least of all the authorities. The police were years away from plugging in their first modem, so there was no way they were going to find their way on to these bulletin boards.'

'These were essentially message and file exchange systems, right?' Parlabane asks, reminding both of them that there is a non-native present.

'Yeah. I mean, we get dozens of texts every day and don't even think about it, but I can remember what a thrill it was to see a message, a few bytes of text, appear on my monitor and know it had been typed on another computer somewhere else.'

'You had a monitor?' Sam asks.

'Not back then, actually: figure of speech. In those days my computer was connected to a portable TV. I traded messages with other users; files too. I can't believe how trusting we all were. I think the mere fact of having made our way on to these boards assured us all that we had enough in common, but we soon wised up. There were boards where people only used nicknames, aliases, and the reason became rapidly clear.'

'That's when you became Ferox?' asks Sam.

'Like all hackers, I had several aliases, but when kudos starts being accredited to one name, ego inevitably comes into play. I was a nerdy teen who had discovered a place where I was one of the in-crowd.'

'Can we cut to the part where our villain makes his entrance?' Parlabane asks, conscious that they don't have time for this mutual geeking-out session in which Sam and Lansing are threatening to become mired.

'This *is* when he makes his entrance,' Lansing replies. 'I got to know this character on there, a fellow hacker. He called himself Zebedee, like from the Magic Roundabout. When I say hacker, I should clarify. Back then it meant someone who was into programming, into tinkering with code. People who broke into networks and went where they weren't supposed to go were called crackers. So Zebedee wasn't one of those. In fact, he wasn't a major coder either. He was an electronics geek, as we all were, really.

'I was getting off on what I could do, and I posted things as proof of the places I had hacked into. Often it was really banal official stuff, but the value was in where it came from rather than what it was. I hacked into Motorola in 1993. To this day, only a handful of people know about it: the dozen or so hackers on that bulletin board and now you two.'

'What did you hit?' asks Sam.

'I accessed a server storing design blueprints for a new processor. It was such a high clearance level that to this day I get giddy thinking about it. I copied a few files as trophies and as proof. After that, Zebedee gave me a suggestion, or more like a lead, for what I could hit next. He had done some of the groundwork, but he didn't have the skills to pull it off himself. It was another electronics firm, far smaller though. I didn't think it was much of a prize, or a challenge, but he offered me cash.'

Lansing gives a wistful shake of the head.

'It was never about money in those days. It was about testing what we could do. Mostly, anyway. There was one hacker, come to

341

think of it, who got inside a few companies and then made stock investments on the basis of confidential information he had discovered. A form of insider trading, I suppose, but it wasn't exactly blackhat. Grey hat maybe.'

Lansing glances in the direction of the computer monitor then back at Parlabane.

'That was never me, though. Prior to that, I saw hacking as its own reward. But I was at uni by this point, money was tight and my phone bills alone were crippling. I knew I could pull it off and I knew I wouldn't get caught.'

'And those words never signal disaster, do they?' asks Sam.

'Except in my case I never did get caught. The sting in this tail was a long time in striking.'

'How did he pay you?'

Lansing grimaces.

'When I think about the ways I could follow the money nowadays . . . Back then it was cash in an envelope, handed over by a third party. We both had codenames. The courier never knew I was Ferox, or what I did for the money. I was Zeppo, the contact was Zuul. His aliases and codenames were always zeds. Zebedee said that using this third party was a way of ensuring we each protected our identities, but it was actually his strategy for discovering mine.'

'The same one you used on me,' deduces Sam. 'Lure you out into the open and then have someone follow you home.'

'That's how I learned it, yes, though it took me a long time to realise my mistake. Back then I was too busy enjoying myself. A little money makes a big difference when you're a student.'

'I can relate,' Sam mutters.

'I had never been one of the cool kids, and suddenly I felt like I had money and power. I was able to buy better kit, and I was getting off on this James Bond trip. Hacking into systems, getting files, meeting my codenamed contact in London and walking away with another wad of tenners. But then I was harshly apprised of how deep I was in over my head.'

'You were blackmailed?' Sam suggests.

'No. Not then, at least. Zuul, my contact, got in touch to ask for a meet, and this time it wasn't to hand over payment. We didn't know each other's names but we had built up a degree of mutual trust.'

'Apart from him conspiring to discover your identity,' Parlabane says.

Lansing gives him an odd look, like he's giving this careful consideration.

'It's possible, but I don't think so. Certainly the way I work it, the target never sees the person who follows them home. But either way, it was Zuul who warned me that our mutual benefactor might be far more dangerous than either of us had previously assumed. I learned that the boss of one of the firms I hacked had been murdered shortly afterwards.'

'I can relate,' Sam mutters again.

'As wake-up calls go, it was a bucket of ice-water to the face. I realised I had been utterly in denial about what I was really involved with. I had told myself it was just hacking, and indulged my adolescent cloak-and-dagger fantasies, but the truth is it was industrial espionage, and I had finally been made to understand the stakes.'

'Who was murdered?' Parlabane asks.

'I don't know. Zuul said it was best if I knew as little about it as possible, but thought I deserved to know what I was caught up in.'

'Which also meant you couldn't verify whether this Zuul character was telling the truth.'

'Why lie about something like this?'

'It's an established tactic of con artists and other crooks in order to make sure people stay quiet. If you believed your hacking activities were connected to a murder, you weren't going to tell anybody about it, were you?'

'Wait,' says Sam. 'Are you saying that's what's going on here too?'

'No. I can verify first-hand that it was Leo Cruz who was lying beside me last night, and he has definitely stripped his last asset. But my point stands: Gary backed off and never talked to anybody about what he had been up to. He wasn't told who was murdered, which company they worked for, or anything that would have let him verify the story, were you?'

'No,' Lansing admits. 'I mean, I tried to find out. I scoured the news, but back then it wasn't like you could simply key the names of a few firms into a search engine and see which one linked to a murder story. My contact was very spooked though, I remember that much. But I realise from what you're saying that this might have been an act. I don't know what to believe.'

Lansing sighs and looks out the window, back across his expansive garden towards his beautiful house. This must all seem very long ago, Parlabane reckons, but he also knows something has recently resurrected the past and threatened everything in Lansing's present and future.

'When did he get back in touch?' Parlabane asks

'About a year ago. I got a text message from a burner, untraceable. It said: "Hi Zeppo, long time no see. Let's have a chat about your Ferox days. Zardoz."'

Fear and distaste are etched sourly across Lansing's expression. This was the moment his new life threatened to come apart, so it was not a treasured memory.

'I knew straight away. Zardoz was Zebedee: another zed. Always zeds. His next text was a link to an IRC channel. We talked there. When I gave those publicity interviews to the *Financial Times* and the other papers, I only disclosed what I wanted them to know: a few high-profile but strictly prank-style hacks, incidents that I had checked to make sure were not still the subjects of legal investigation.'

'Whitehat stuff only,' says Sam.

'Yes. But Zardoz had kept evidence of my blackhat activity from back in the nineties. He had proof of the things Ferox had done – serious industrial espionage – and proof that Ferox was Gary Lansing. He threatened to ruin me if I didn't give him what he wanted. And as before, what he wanted was simply for me to do something I was already good at.'

# LOYALTIES

As we stand outside the automatic gates again, I feel a weird sense of deflation. When we arrived here I really thought we were going to find our man. I was scared, especially about sneaking into his office when we knew how soon he would be back, but I thought that whatever happened, we would be closer to the answers we need. Instead we've only found that the rabbit hole goes deeper than we feared: more than twenty years deeper, in fact. We don't even have a next destination.

Jack puts a hand on my arm, telling me to stay put as we watch Lansing's Overfinch drive away.

'We don't go back to the car until he's out of sight. I don't want him knowing our make, model and registration, because for all we know he could be on to the police on his hands-free right now, giving them our descriptions.'

'But you said he's tied into this.'

'Yeah, but his story would sound better than ours if he decided to go to the authorities. I'm not taking any chances.'

'I think we can trust him,' I say.

'Why? Hacker solidarity? That didn't count for much in Uninvited. Turned out he was screwing you over back then, remember?'

'Yeah, but that's the point. When we discussed that stuff, didn't you notice? He didn't name Stonefish and he didn't connect an online alias to Paul Wiley. He continued protecting their identities when he didn't have to.'

'He didn't protect them from Zardoz though, did he?'

'That's different,' I protest.

It's not exactly a killer come-back, but it's true. It meant something to me that Lansing didn't give those guys up to us, even if Jack doesn't understand that.

345

I felt something when I saw his museum. His bow scared me, but I realised he was the truly scared one. Then I saw someone I recognised: a hacker. He had posed as Cicatrix, and I realised some of the things he said in IRC must have been true, though they were only fragments in a kaleidoscope of lies.

I was sad watching him leave. Under other circumstances, I could have talked to him all night, but I'm less sure how long he would have wanted to talk to me. Besides, he had to go and collect his kids.

This thought makes me check the time, and that is when I accept that I definitely won't be at the Loxford to pick up Lilly when school comes out. I feel it in my gut, this combination of fear and guilt, knowing that only a helicopter might get me to Ilford from here in time to collect her, and I understand how much I was kidding myself this morning. Part of me must have still hoped I could pull off a solution to this inside seven hours, even though I haven't come close in the preceding weeks.

'You okay?' Jack asks as we climb into the Qashqai.

That's when I realise I am filling up.

'Yeah. Just need to make a call.'

I ring Cassie's mother on her mobile as the car pulls away.

'Hello, is that Mel? It's Samantha, Lilly's sister.'

'Oh, hi. Is everything okay?'

I realise my voice must have wavered. I'm usually better at keeping my emotions under control, especially when I'm lying. I was about to tell her that I had been roped into doing an extended shift, but the fact she's picked up on me being upset reminds me I can do better.

'Not really. We were broken into last night, and I'm still trying to make the place safe after the damage. I was wondering if you could pick up Lilly for me.'

There's a pause, which instantly puts me on edge.

'Cassie's off school today with a temperature,' she explains. 'She's actually at her gran's in Acton because I'm supposed to be working a late one tonight. I think I've got someone who can swap shifts with me, but I'm waiting for her to ring back and confirm. Can I give you a bell when I know for sure?'

'Course, yeah,' I say. 'But I'll try someone else just in case.'

'All right, love. Speak to you in a bit.'

I try Jaffer, from the recycling place, but there is no response: it goes to voicemail after a few rings. I try again, then a third time, and as it clicks to voicemail once more, I feel this horrible numb emptiness as it sinks in that I am out of options if Mel doesn't come through.

I have to hold it together. We are on the main street now, approaching traffic lights. I will be conspicuous and therefore memorable if I am sitting in the passenger seat in tears.

I decide I have to go back to Ilford. Come what may, I have to be there and pick her up. While it is still within my power, my decision, I need to know that I chose her. I know I'll be late, but I can call the school and tell them I'm on my way.

I am about to tell Jack, bracing myself for his objection, when I hear a siren from behind us. I look back and see a police car through the rear windscreen, blues and twos, its headlights flashing as it speeds ever closer.

The lights are turning red up ahead, cars slowing to a stop between us and the junction.

'Lansing went to the cops,' Jack says. 'I fucking called it.'

He grips the wheel tighter and he sounds so angry that for an instant I think he's about to put his foot down and do something crazy. There are oncoming cars in the way, though: nowhere to go.

Jack signals and slows, pulling in towards the kerb. Something inside me turns cold and toxic.

Then I notice that the oncoming cars are pulling in too, mounting the pavement to make a passage. The police car overtakes us, easing along the narrow channel between vehicles until it reaches the junction, where it pulls back into the left and accelerates with a growl of the engine.

I breathe out.

In that moment I glimpsed what would happen if I was arrested. Memories of my time at Graythorne engulfed me, like battery acid coursing through my veins. It wouldn't be three days this time though, and it wouldn't be a young offenders institution either. It would be years, in adult prison.

347

I know now that I'd do anything to stay out of their hands. I can tell myself that it's the best way for me to safeguard Lilly in the long term too, but deep down I know that this is only an added justification, and I can't hide behind her any more.

I don't want to go to prison. I'm just a girl. I'm nineteen years old, and I don't want to go to prison.

'We have to get off the road,' Jack says, and I don't argue.

Jack drives us back to the Goodnight Inn on the outskirts of Milton Keynes. I already checked they have vacancies and, almost as important, room service, as we want to limit our exposure. On the way there I also look up the BBC website and make sure they aren't running our photographs to illustrate the Cruz story.

It's still only the artist's impression of Jack, though the report now also mentions the arrest and release of 'an unnamed couple in Barking in connection with a concurrent cyber-attack on the computer network at Synergis'.

There's no suggestion that they think the attack originated from the same building, but they probably wouldn't tell the press that anyway. Do I dare to let myself believe the Cohens never thought to mention me after all? Or that I got extra lucky with an inadvertent double bluff? Maybe the cops reckoned the hacker was spoofing the Cohens' IP address, and it hasn't occurred to them that something so grand-scale and sophisticated would be carried out from the flat above by someone who *didn't* disguise their location.

Hmm. It's a comforting possibility, but I'm not sure I feel that lucky. Not on current form.

I don the makeshift niqab again and go to reception, where I rent us a room, paying cash. The girl offers me a twin or a double and I go for the former. I give the name Samira Rasook, which is one of my many fake Facebook profiles.

As she fills in the fields on her computer, I glance at the clock behind her.

It's just gone four. Mel hasn't called back.

Lilly will be walking out of the school doors any minute. She'll be looking for me, searching the usual crowd of faces, but this time she won't find me. She'll be confused, then she'll be worried, and then she'll cry. Someone will ask what's wrong. A few minutes later I'll get a call on my mobile asking where I am.

I feel sick. I'm glad nobody can see my face.

I put down a cash deposit for extras and she hands me a keycard inside a white cardboard wallet. The drill is that I will send Jack the number and he will follow separately in a few minutes. The room is on the second floor towards the end of a long corridor, close to the emergency exit. I wonder if we'll be needing it.

As I open the door, I hear a chime alerting me to a new email. I take out my mobile and my stomach knots to see that it is from Lilly's school. I finger the screen impatiently, already wondering if and how I should reply, but one glance is enough to tell me it won't be necessary.

Hi Sam,

Just to let you know Lilly has been picked up okay, so no need to worry.

Sorry to hear about the break-in.

Best,

Dorothy Miller

Relief envelopes me like a warm quilt. Mel got her shift changed, and I go from fretting to calculating in a shamefully short space of time.

With Lilly somewhere familiar, I can stretch it to an overnight. I'll have to blank Mel's calls, then phone and apologise when it's getting too late for Lilly to be heading home, at which point I will grovellingly request (or Mel might offer) that she simply sleeps there. Lilly doesn't have any pyjamas with her but she and Cassie are close enough in size. The main thing is that Lilly will feel safe. I know it might only buy me a night, but I'm living this hour to hour.

I breathe out, the release of tension lasting only until I remember all the things that haven't changed.

# FACIAL RECOGNITION

Sam has the BBC website displayed when Parlabane enters the room. Her laptop is sitting on the dresser at the foot of the nearer of two single beds, the Cruz story dominating the frame. It hasn't been updated since the last time he looked, about ninety seconds ago, and nor has there been any fresh news on the other feeds he is monitoring.

He takes a moment to more closely scrutinise the artist's impression on a decent-sized screen. A glance in the mirror reassures him that his still startling lack of hair makes the resemblance even less striking. The receptionist downstairs, for instance, could look up from this same web page and see Parlabane walking through the lobby without making a connection. However, it's not his present appearance that's a threat: the real danger remains the sketch ringing a bell with someone who already knows him.

At least this appears to be all the cops have to go on, for now.

'Looks like you were right about Lansing,' he says. 'He didn't sell us out after all. Not this time anyway.'

'What do you mean, this time?'

'As opposed to before, when he sold out you and Christ knows who else.'

Sam pouts. She seemed quite taken with Lansing, but then it wasn't her that he was pointing an arrow at.

'He didn't have much choice,' she states. 'We all do things we'd rather not when we're being blackmailed.'

'No kidding.'

Parlabane places his bag on the bed nearer the window and is pulling his own laptop from it when Sam's words dislodge something that was bothering him back at Lansing's place.

He turns to face her and she looks up, anticipating that he has something to say.

'What is it?'

'Lansing sold you out specifically. What I mean is, in the other instances he was commissioned to identify hackers from their aliases. It didn't matter who they turned out to be. In your case it was the other way round. Why did Zodiac want you in particular?'

'I don't know,' she responds with a shrug. 'I guess it was because I had pulled off something so big at fifteen. He must have reckoned that with a few years' more experience I'd be among the few hackers capable of what he was asking.'

He doesn't believe she's holding something back – not this time anyway – but her answer doesn't stack up.

'So would you say you're the best in the business these days?'

'Are you kidding? Far from it.'

'See, that's just it. Zodiac was already playing the field to ensure he had the right personnel for the Synergis job. Lansing admitted he delivered details on lots of other hackers, who Zodiac then blackmailed into doing what he wanted. You said yourself he had other people working different angles.'

'True, but so what?'

'So there has to be another reason he wanted Sam Morpeth in particular, and for the role of fall girl, no less. This was personal.'

She looks stunned. This hasn't occurred to her even in her most paranoid moments.

'You mean like revenge?'

'Perhaps. Or maybe there was something else that made you the perfect candidate to take the fall.'

'The Saudi thing,' she suggests. 'If that got dredged up as part of the investigation, it would make me seem a plausible perp for other crimes.'

This doesn't sound right.

'If having form was the issue, then anyone in Uninvited would fit the bill. Zodiac's got proof you hacked RSGN, remember, so it can't be that.'

'Well, the Saudis are the only people I can remember pissing off – that know my real name, I mean.'

There's the spark, the connection. She's right. It's not about something *she* did.

351

'Your mother,' Parlabane says. 'What did you say her maiden name was?'

'Ruth Roberts.'

It doesn't mean any more to him than it did before, but neither Ruth nor Roberts is particularly distinct.

'Have you got a picture of her?'

'Sure.'

Sam opens a folder on her laptop and toggles through a selection, from the very recent all the way back to a shot of Sam as a toddler, sitting on her mum's knee inside a soft play area. It's got to be sixteen, seventeen years old, taken on an early smartphone.

Parlabane swallows.

He feels shock and a jolt of disbelief, though the latter is not born of any instinct to doubt what he is looking at. It is the expression of his incredulity that only now is he seeing something that has been in front of him all the time.

He's aware Sam is reading him for the merest micro-response, so there's no point in trying to conceal his reaction. The woman he's looking at could read people too, like she was bloody telepathic.

'You did know her.'

Sam looks expectantly at him, tense with anticipation.

He's starting to see a lot of things. Something about Sam always seemed familiar but he couldn't quite place who it was she reminded him of. He can now.

'That wasn't her name. She called herself Aurore.'

'Aurore what?'

'Just Aurore. There are few people in this world who can get away with going by a single name, but believe me, she was one of them.'

'You never asked her surname?'

'Oh, I asked, and I tried to find out, but she was careful. I get it now. R. R. Aurore.'

'Careful why? How did you know her?'

Parlabane hasn't thought about this stuff for so long, probably because it was padlocked in the memory vault marked 'Regrets'. He thinks back to how he knew her: who she was, who *he* was, all that could have been.

'She was a source. At least, I was cultivating her as a source: a potential whistleblower.'

'On what?'

What indeed.

'Industrial espionage.'

Parlabane invests this with sufficient gravitas as to convey unmistakably that he believes she is tied to this somehow, but Sam is suddenly less interested in the matter at hand as about what happened back then. After all, she's been waiting a long time to find out.

'When was this?'

'It would have been twenty, twenty-one years ago. I was working in London, part of an investigations team on one of the broadsheets. That's why she only gave me an alias.'

'How did you meet?'

'Essentially we were in the same field, the same game. Funnily enough, she was the one who sought me out, like you did, and gave much the same justification, that she reckoned we had a lot in common.'

'Like what?'

'Even then there were rumours about how I worked. I found ways to cover my methods, claiming things had been leaked to me when I had actually, ahem, "acquired" them, but there were people who sussed that there was no way I could have got certain information by legitimate means. These fell into two camps: one was the people I acquired it from, and other was fellow players.'

'You're saying my mum did the same as you? Broke into places and stole information?'

'It would be a disservice to say she did the same thing as me. Aurore operated with far more guile and panache. Why would she break into a building when she could talk or trick her way in? I was risking life and limb scaling walls and picking locks, while she tended to breeze right in through the front door. She showed me a little of how she operated: a potent combination of charm, glamour, confidence and an unerring ability to read people.'

Sam seems rapt, eager to hear more, but she doesn't seem particularly surprised. She didn't get her talents from the wind, he guesses.

353

'Why did she show you? Was it for a story? Surely she'd be giving away her techniques.'

'I was never entirely sure. Magicians love to tell you how something *can't* be done, so that you're looking out for the wrong thing. She liked to play games with people, and I began to suspect she was playing me.'

'What for?'

'I was working on several stories at that time, and I thought maybe she was trying to get close so she could ascertain how much I knew about a particular investigation. After a while I came to realise there was an alternative explanation: that she was sounding me out to determine whether she could trust me.'

'And did she?'

'I think so, yes.'

'So why would she lie to me about knowing you?'

He left a lot of threads hanging when he made his hurried exit from London back then, and he now realises she was the largest of them. She's been following him on social media, he remembers, but taking pains to make sure he can't reciprocate.

'I guess it's a door she doesn't want you looking behind,' he offers.

There is a moment of silence.

Sam looks over at him.

He knows what's coming.

'Jack? Were you and she, you know . . .'

Parlabane sees it all now: why Sam got in touch with him; why she did so tentatively, by removes; why she kept saying 'friends don't keep score' as the favours kept totting up. He even sees why she snared him into the *Clarion* job, thus tying his fate to hers.

He knows the question she can't quite bring herself to ask, and the greater one beyond it too. But he can't give her the answers that she wants to hear.

# FIDELITY AND BETRAYAL

I surprise myself by not crying.

I think if Jack had answered otherwise, the tears would have flowed, but there is no release to start the waterworks, only an angsty choked sensation, like there's nowhere for all this churned-up emotion to go.

He doesn't speak at first, just shakes his head. There's a gentleness in his expression that tells me he guessed where this was going; what I was really asking him.

I know he's telling the truth.

In that moment, I realise not only how much I wanted this to be true, but how long I have already believed it. I've been in denial, pretending it was just a possibility, on the edge of my bigger quest to discover more about my mum.

I had not rehearsed an alternative scenario.

'I won't deny there was a spark of something between us, and I was flattered by the attention, but I wasn't sure what she was up to. I didn't trust her. And then when I realised that she might actually be looking for my help, that made it complicated in a different way. I couldn't take advantage of her. And more problematically, in the end I wasn't able to give that help.'

'Help with what?'

'She had been riding a tiger for a long time. She was involved with dangerous people and I think she wanted out but she wasn't sure how. Maybe she thought I could help because I worked for a big paper: if we exposed the people she was afraid of then she'd be protected as a source. She was never explicit about anything though, always elliptical, like she was afraid of the consequences of asking. It can be like that when you're trying to coax a whistleblower to come forward and go on the record.'

'So why couldn't you help her?'

'I was getting into deep trouble of my own, making too many enemies through my investigations.'

'Is that why you thought she might be trying to scam you for information?'

'Precisely. Sometimes it pays to be paranoid.'

'So what happened? Did you break off contact with her, or what?'

'I broke off contact with everybody, though not quite voluntarily. I came home one night to find my flat had been burgled, and not by some junkie looking to tan my video. The place had been gone through methodically: they took every computer disk, every file, every folder, every notepad. They even removed the hard drive, which not many people knew how to do back then.

'I called the cops, then about two seconds later it hit me that whoever had stolen all my research might also take steps to get me out of the picture while they were at it. A popular tactic back then was planting class-A drugs then tipping off the police. In this instance, like an idiot I had called the police for them, so I had to find the stuff before they got there. I tore the place apart, making far more of a mess than the break-in, and I found enough Charlie to send me down for a decade. It was a lucky escape but I took the hint. I left the country, moved to LA.'

I hear the end of this and at some level I take it in, but it's as though he has faded into the background. I feel the walls of the room racing away and Jack becoming distant too, leaving me alone and exposed as the realisation hits home.

He notices. I don't know if my mouth is hanging open or I look spaced out, but it's clear something is wrong.

'Sam? You okay?'

'My mum was telling the truth. All along she was telling the truth.'

'About what?'

'She's in jail for having a gun, and for possession with intent to supply. She told me the gun and the drugs were planted and I didn't believe her. Shit, I should have seen this last night. They turned the place over looking for my laptop, to sabotage my VPN. That wasn't the first time these bastards were in our flat. This was Zodiac.'

356

'The MO isn't unique, but it's a hell of a coincidence.'

'Why would they be planting drugs on my mum nine months ago over something she was linked to twenty years back?'

'Same reason as they were planted on me back then. To get her out the way, keep her from making connections, keep her from talking about what she knows. And if she were to talk, a convicted drug dealer doesn't have a lot of credibility. Jesus. We need to speak to her.'

'That's going to be tricky. It's too late to email a visit request for tomorrow. I could put one in for Sunday, but if I get named in the meantime, the cops would be waiting for me. That's if we're still on the loose by then.'

'What about phone calls? I know she has to call out, but can you get her a message to ring you? Through a lawyer maybe?'

'I'm not sure. I'll give him a call, though.'

As I dial Mum's lawyer, Anthony Bledsoe, I notice a notification from my Stoolpigeon program. Six more people have downloaded the zip file and it is busy homing in on their locations. Seven. Eight. It keeps going up.

I get lucky, catching Bledsoe at the office before he has left for the weekend. I tell him it's a family emergency but he's not happy to comply. He explains that if it's not pertaining to my mum's case, he's on dodgy ground making this kind of request, and the fact that I can't give him any specifics isn't helping sell it either.

'Can't you just tell them it's to do with the case and it's confidential? That way they'll never know.'

'Yes, but if they were to find out later that I was lying, the consequences would be severe. I can't put myself in a position whereby my client could effectively blackmail me in future by revealing my previous deceit.'

Bledsoe says he'll look into the possibilities, but it's last thing on a Friday so it sounds like a big no to me.

By the time the call is over, I am tracking seventeen new downloads of the Synergis package.

I feel another kick to the gut.

'Shit toasters.'

'What?' asks Jack.

'Lansing said he'd let us know when and where Zodiac told him to forward the files. He was lying. He's sent me nothing but the package is popping up all over the place.'

'Why so many?'

'Zodiac must have given Lansing about twenty addresses to send it on to. Probably has each of those recipients primed to forward it to multiple addresses too, so that it puts him at several removes. But the headline news is it looks like we might not be on the same side after all.'

'Tell me about it.'

Jack turns his laptop screen to face me.

Both our pictures are now heading the BBC story; probably on the homepage too. No artist's impressions any more: in Jack's case it's his photo byline pic, and in mine this goggle-eyed horror from my school website.

Jack's voice is a hollow whisper.

'The bastard's named us.'

# BREAKING STORY

Parlabane scans the text a second time, looking beyond the initial shock value to parse how much the police must know, and more importantly how they know it. There is no reference to the CCTV footage from inside Synergis, so at least they haven't decrypted that yet.

It doesn't say how he was identified, or how they got Sam's name either. Both of them coming in at the same time could only have been due to one source: Lansing is trying to stay onside with Zodiac while simultaneously scoring points with the authorities before they come after him. It's a tricky hand to play, but Parlabane reckons the devious bastard might have the right cards to pull it off.

There is no description of him having a shaven head, which is a mercy. Lansing must have decided it was wise not to share the minor detail that these two wanted fugitives had been to his house. There's nothing about the niqab either. Lansing never saw that, but this indicates he is probably the police's only source at this stage.

That won't last long now that their names and photos are public.

Sam takes out her phone and starts dialling.

'What are you doing?' he asks.

'I want to give Mel a quick ring and speak to Lilly, make sure she knows I haven't abandoned her.'

'You can't. In fact, you need to kill your phone, right now. Take out the SIM and the battery.'

'I just need to speak to her for a few seconds,' she pleads. 'It's not a contract phone. They don't have my details.'

'The police don't need your details. All they need is one person to tell them your number and then they can track that device.'

She looks hurt but she knows he's right. She snaps the back off the handset.

'What about yours?' she asks, with a hint of petulance.

'Literally nobody has this number. This is a back-up I got after you hacked my main phone.'

She looks sheepishly apologetic about this, but there's not time to dwell on sins of the past.

'I hope the Wi-Fi in this place is stable,' he says.

'Why?'

'Because we're going to have to find a way of extricating ourselves from this hyper-gravity vortex of shit without leaving our hotel room.'

Sam doesn't look particularly fazed by this prospect.

'You'd be amazed at the places I've been without leaving my flat,' she responds.

'Yes, but the problem is that they've all ultimately led you to where we're sitting now.'

He gets her to call room service. They haven't eaten all day and he doesn't know what the night will bring.

Sam dons the niqab again when they hear the knock at the door, while Parlabane hides out in the bathroom until the waiter has left. On his suggestion she ordered a starter, a main and a dessert to conceal that the order is for two people.

They eat on their knees in front of their laptops, both scanning news sites for any fresh updates. Sam reports that there are now more than twenty activations of her modified zip file, pinging in from locations all across the globe.

'Still no word from your mate Spammy?' she asks.

'I've learned not to hold my breath when it comes to the big man.'

'Sure. But it would be helpful to know what it is we've stolen.'

Parlabane is finishing off the last of the chips when he notices a new banner at the top of the BBC story.

'LIVE: Synergis to make "significant announcement" at press conference.'

He clicks on the link and is about to direct Sam's attention to it when he observes that her sharper reflexes have ensured she already has it open on her screen.

The live stream shows what he recognises as the reception lobby inside the Synergis offices, the camera pointed at an improvised podium created by erecting two pop-up banners displaying the company logo. Journalists and photographers can be seen still getting into position in the foreground, but nobody from Synergis is yet centre-stage.

A scrolling marquee across the bottom states: 'Synergis press conference imminent, live from Tricorn House', to explain why the stream is currently broadcasting the visual equivalent of dead air. Then, as a veteran of a thousand such events, Parlabane recognises the ripple that passes through a room when the principal has made an appearance.

It is Tanya Collier, Cruz's PA, who is preparing to take her place in front of the microphones, shutter clicks and flashes playing herald. Matthew Coleridge is standing behind her, grim-faced, placing a hand on her shoulder in a gesture of support.

Parlabane stiffens. These are the two Synergis staffers he most feared might recognise him from the artist's impression, but that's no longer relevant. Everybody knows who they're looking for now.

She is not here to talk about the murder, however.

She clears her throat, asks for everyone's attention and begins reading from a prepared statement. She seems nervous and uncomfortable, her bloodshot eyes indicating she is only able to get through this because she's already all cried out.

Her delivery is stiff and halting, not helped by the content. Parlabane recognises a statement worked out by committee and thoroughly lawyered.

'These are not the circumstances under which one would ever wish to announce a new product, particularly one that has taken years of quiet development by an inspired individual, and the concerted efforts of everyone at our company. In fact, it seems almost crass and barely even relevant to be talking about business and about electronics right now, but there are reasons why it is highly relevant. There are reasons why it is imperative.'

She takes a moment, swallowing and glancing down at the sheet of paper in her hands. In keeping with the rhythm of these things, her pause is accompanied by a renewed burst of camera activity.

'The work that has gone into what was stolen last night means that this announcement deserves a greater fanfare; the sum of our collective endeavours ought to be unveiled at a glamorous and polished event, with a marketing and publicity campaign primed and set to roll out. However, what happened to our boss, our colleague and our friend Leo Cruz means that we feel duty-bound to act in defence of his legacy.

'We have been made aware that blueprints and design documents are already being offered for sale on the dark web, and we are certain that our prototype was stolen for the purpose of retro-engineering. We are therefore taking the reluctant and otherwise premature step of releasing details of a project that we did not intend to reveal for at least eighteen months. These details consist of early marketing materials, proof-of-concept documents and development reports demonstrating how close we are to realising our vision. They are live on the Synergis website, as of now.'

Sam navigates there in a blur of fingers.

Tanya pauses again. Parlabane can already see reporters' arms shooting upright but a hand gesture indicates that she is not finished.

'As of yesterday, we felt we were at least two years away from bringing this product to market. We still intend to see this through. However, we are aware that a larger competitor, with access to our prototype and our blueprints, might be able to develop a similar device sooner, especially as so much of the development has been done for them. That is why we want the world to know what has been taken from us. Someone in this industry has blood on their hands, and we will not allow them to simply wash it away.'

There is an eruption of questions. She dips her head as though recoiling, turns to the side and retreats from view.

He looks across to Sam, who is already scrolling through what she has downloaded.

'So what are we looking at?' he asks. 'Is it something worth killing Leo Cruz for?'

Sam angles her screen towards him, her face a portrait of concern.

'Worth killing Leo Cruz, the two of us and anybody else who gets in the way.'

# GAME-CHANGER

Parlabane catches a glimpse of a logo and a name, the same as he saw on the flight case. The document on screen is entitled 'The Synergis Dimension', but before he can get a proper look at the text, Sam has clicked on a different file and launched a video.

The footage is not slick and professional. The definition is high enough, but it has been done for testing and documentation purposes, not for presentation. The framing is functional and the zoom static, suggesting the camera is on a tripod and being operated by someone who knows little more than how to point it in the right direction and set it recording.

It shows Cruz. He is filmed from a few feet away inside a blank-walled room Parlabane never saw on either of his visits. Given that there is an MRI scanner dominating the space, it seems safe to assume this was filmed somewhere else.

Cruz is holding the prototype device in the upturned palm of his left hand, then plugs a cable into one end, connecting it to the scanner.

Someone off-camera is talking to him, but Parlabane doesn't recognise the voice. Whoever he is, he sounds quietly spoken, a distracted air about his delivery. With a start, Parlabane realises he might be listening to Aldous Syne.

'You ready?' he asks.

Cruz climbs on to the scanner's bed, glancing beyond the camera to whoever is back there.

There is a low hum as the MRI scan commences, at which point the camera tracks right, focusing on the table where the prototype sits. After a few seconds, an image appears, floating in the air above the table. Parlabane is reminded of the briefing scenes in Star Wars movies, except that instead of a Death Star, he is looking at a human brain. Leo Cruz's brain, to be precise.

The device is rendering the MRI scan as a three-dimensional holographic model, in real time.

The implications are colossal.

'Okay, need to give my brain something to work with,' Cruz says. 'Like we discussed. Countdown. Give me a word.'

'Camouflage,' replies the other man.

'Right, let's see. Flame. Mole. Clam. Golf.'

Flashes appear like tiny fireworks on the hologram, displaying the live activity as Cruz searches for anagrams.

Parlabane feels a chill, listening to the boyish pleasure in Cruz's voice and witnessing the excitement in his face. This is the man whose corpse he woke up alongside less than twenty-four hours ago, here looking forward to a bright future that was literally in his possession.

The video ends. Sam turns to Parlabane.

'This is incredible,' she says, her voice almost reduced to a whisper. 'Real-time 3D modelling of scanner data. Do you have any idea what that means? It could be the start of a new understanding of things like Lilly's condition.'

Parlabane goes to his bag and takes out the prototype. Sam all but pounces to snatch it from him, turning it over in her hands. Lacking a scanner to connect to, the device remains a lifeless lump of metal, but Sam is nonetheless regarding it with rapt reverence.

'How does it work?' she asks.

'You're asking the wrong guy. When I was in Cruz's office, I saw documents pertaining to the purchase of a firm called Optronix, which makes laser projectors. And among the stuff we got from the dumpster dive was a bulk purchase order for e-cigarettes.'

He points to one edge of the device, where there are two tiny circular apertures side by side.

'One of these is the laser and the other must be a vapour outlet, for projecting holographic images without a surface. However, the real magic must be in whatever interprets the data. A new chipset devised by Syne.'

'This could change lives, *save* lives,' Sam says, still reeling from the implications. Then she's reeling from a new one.

'Unless we've just helped someone put a spoke in it. Jesus, I couldn't live with that.'

'Nobody's going to be able to put a spoke in this,' Parlabane assures her. 'Not now that the world knows about it. The entire medical profession is going to be coveting this device, not to mention the entire electronics industry. This will put Synergis right back in the vanguard.'

'I guess that's why they were calling it RBA.'

As she says this, Parlabane remembers that there is someone who has already been coveting it for a while.

'Winter has the inside track on this. He's an investor.'

'Lansing told us Zodiac was an electronics geek.'

'And the industry people I spoke to said Winter was a sociopath with a keen eye for innovation.'

'He wants the Dimension for himself.'

'Yes,' Parlabane agrees. 'Though this announcement is going to throw his strategy a curve. His slice of the company will be worth a lot more, but if his main game was to buy out his fellow investors after Cruz's death caused the share price to tank, then I suspect he's out of luck.'

'But surely Winter couldn't profit from cashing out his Synergis stock then develop his own rival product from a stolen idea? Someone would join the dots back to a guy who had prior inside knowledge of the Dimension's development.'

'There were all kinds of non-disclosure agreements covering the project, so it might not be that easy to prove who knew what when. But right now that's moot, because whether it's Winter or anybody else, Zodiac doesn't actually *have* the prototype. We do.'

Sam glances down at the Dimension like it's an alien artefact.

'So why hasn't he been in touch asking for it? Is it possible he hasn't actually opened the flight case? Or was the person who attacked you another middle man who hasn't made his drop yet?'

It's a question that has been troubling Parlabane too, but it's only as Sam asks it that he sees the answer.

'It's because he has a problem: he doesn't have any leverage. He blackmailed you into this using the threat of prison, but with the cops after you for robbery and murder, the RSGN hack is barely an issue any more. In fact, right now he has a vested interest in you *not* being caught until you've handed over the merchandise. He knows he's got nothing to offer, nothing to scare you with, so he won't be back in touch until one of those things changes.'

'So like you said, we do have a bargaining chip.'

Parlabane lifts it from Sam's hand and places it carefully back inside his jacket.

Her eyes trace the movement, reluctant to have given it up. The Precious.

His mobile vibrates against his chest. Must be another email, as nobody has this number to be sending him any texts. He swipes the screen and sees that the message is from Lee, its entirety displayed in the preview window:

Where the fuck are you? Answer your phone or you're fucking fired.

She's been calling the other number, the phone that got taken last night.

He goes into the bathroom for at least a token degree of privacy and calls her, wondering as he dials how quickly the cops can trace a signal.

'Lee. It's me.'

'Jack, for fuck's sake. Where have you been? Where are you?'

Her tone is testy, to say the least.

'I'd rather not disclose that. It's complicated.'

'You don't say. The cops have been here looking for you, asking questions, taking statements.'

'What did you tell them?'

'I told them the truth: I don't know. I tried calling you right in front of them. I've left about six messages. We're not at the stage where I'm prepared to lie to the police for you.'

'We're not at the stage where I'd ask you to.'

'Anyway, it's not just me they spoke to. They asked if anyone knew where you were last night, so they've got several statements to the effect that you conspicuously fucked off from a party for several

366

hours then came back spattered in what you claimed was red wine. What the fuck is going on?'

'Is there any point in saying it's not what it looks like?'

'Well, to the police it looks like you murdered Leo Cruz. They've been to your flat, must have been talking to your neighbours. Somebody saw you leave with a woman in a niqab, so they were asking us who that might be, whether you had a girlfriend.'

He knows it's the least of his concerns, and that what happened between them wasn't supposed to mean anything, but he can still hear an edge of hurt to her voice.

It's the lying. The mistrust. She deserves better.

'I'm sorry,' he tells her, meaning it on so many levels.

He hangs up.

Parlabane allows himself a sigh, a moment to gather his breath. He wouldn't have thought it possible two minutes ago, but everything just got a lot more complicated.

# EXTREME METHODS

Jack goes into the bathroom, phone in hand. I don't know who he is talking to, but it makes me edgy that he would want to be keeping secrets right now. I decide I will stand at the door and earwig, but as I get to my feet I hear a ping from the laptop that sends a bolt of ice right to my chest. It is the direct message alert I have assigned specifically to Zodiac.

I look back at the screen and see the text, automatically opened in a small window on top of the browser I'd been looking at.

<Zodiac> You delivered me an empty box.

My heart is thumping, the sound of blood pulsing in my ears as it always does whenever his words are on the screen. Then I remember that he can't threaten me anymore. The only ammo he ever had was that he could turn my name over to the feds. Well, they're already looking for me, so he's shooting blanks now.

<Buzzkill> You planned to frame me and leave me to die in
    a freezer. So I guess we both have trust issues now.
<Zodiac> You will bring the prototype to the Lawn at
    Paddington Station tomorrow at 10.30.

I allow myself a smile. Does he think I'm fucking stupid?

<Buzzkill> I'm busy tomorrow. Can we reschedule? Never's
    good for me. How about never?
<Zodiac> It's up to you, but I thought you would wish to
    make the exchange as soon as possible.

There is a link underneath the text. It's a live webcam address.

I am about to ask what we would be exchanging but the darkest part of my instinct already knows. I think back to the message from the Loxford School, the question I avoided because I was too busy feeling relieved: why would they be emailing me?

I click on the link, my mind whirring like an old hard drive as it searches desperately for alternatives as to what Zodiac's exchange might be.

Lilly is sitting on a chair, staring blankly towards me. There is no sound and she seems oblivious of the camera. I guess she is looking at a laptop. I can tell she has been crying. I can tell she is scared.

<Zodiac> The Lawn. Paddington Station. 10.30. Or are you still busy?

I thought I knew helplessness. I thought I knew emptiness. I thought I knew fear.

Now I know differently.

I believed my concerns for Lilly's safety were a result of my burden of responsibility, but now I understand that they are totally about how much she means to me. It's not because I'm all she has now: it's because she's all *I* have now, and I only grasp this as I see her frightened face on the screen. I love her so much that I can't imagine surviving in a world without her, especially if I knew it was my fault.

Jack steps out of the bathroom and I look up at him. He reads it in my face even before he looks at the screen.

I turn the laptop away. I can't bear to look at it. Jack stares at it intently. I know he's analysing it, searching the image for clues. Zodiac's too smart for that, though. It looked like a blank room to me. Could be anywhere.

'How?' he asks.

'I don't know. I got this message from the school saying she'd been picked up. Zodiac knew I wasn't going to be there. He must have spoofed my email address and sent them a message faking my consent for someone else to collect Lilly.'

'Can you call them? Ask who it was?'

'There won't be anybody there until tomorrow morning.'

Jack casts around the room like he's assessing options.

'We have to go,' he says.

I'm relieved he isn't suggesting anything other than complying with Zodiac's demands.

'Damn right we have to go. I'm gonna be at Paddington at ten-thirty tomorrow with that prototype no matter what it takes.'

'No, I mean we have to go now. I just spoke to my boss. The police know I was seen leaving my building with a woman in a niqab. That's going to be public knowledge at any moment, if it's not been added to the reports already.'

'So I'll need to disguise myself some other way in the morning,' I argue. 'It's still best if we lay low here overnight where nobody can spot us.'

'Somebody has *already* spotted us: the woman on reception.'

'She didn't see us together, though,' I remind him. 'We came in separately. She won't call the cops purely because a woman checked in wearing a niqab. She and the hotel would be wide open to racism charges.'

'And what about if the woman in the niqab offered no ID and insisted on paying in cash? Do you fancy those odds?'

'Not much, no.'

I shut my laptop and stuff it into my bag. We both use the toilet again, aware that the next time we need to go, it may be at the risk of exposure. Then we make our exit.

We leave via the fire escape so as not to go through the lobby again. I almost lose my footing on the aluminium stairs because I am feeling so shaky, afraid that someone is going to see, that at any second I'll hear them shout 'Stop!' I know that if I get caught now, if I'm not free to hand over the prototype, then I have no idea what will happen to Lilly. Given that Zodiac was prepared to murder me simply to cover up another killing, I am under no naive illusions about his attitude to loose ends and liabilities.

We climb into the Qashqai and drive quietly out of the car park. Jack's given me his hat so that, at a glance, neither of us looks like the media images, but I feel sick every time we stop at lights.

I see a sign for the motorway but the car heads in the other direction.

'Aren't we heading for London?' I ask.

'Eventually, but not yet. There's another potential danger now that they know about your fancy dress costume. Witnesses are bound to come forward saying they saw a white male and a woman in a niqab at Stansted Airport. If they check the CCTV cameras they're going to see us getting on a shuttle bus to the long-stay car park, and if we're really unlucky, they might even clock the Qashqai.'

'Number-plate recognition,' I say, feeling the walls of the car close in tighter.

We head out into the sticks, keeping off main roads as much as possible until we have left the glow of streetlights behind. The rain makes the darkness seem impenetrable, the Qashqai's headlights barely picking out the bends in the road. Usually I would find it scary but tonight it feels oddly comforting. When we pass oncoming cars I feel reassured when I fail to make out any faces behind their windscreens.

Jack pulls off the main road into a country lane between a line of trees on one side and a hedgerow on the other. But for the sat-nav I would have no sense of where we are. He kills the lights but keeps the engine running for the heat.

'It's desperate,' he says.

'Anything that keeps us hidden until morning is okay by me,' I say.

I think how my priorities have changed. Less than an hour ago, I could think of nothing other than how to stay out of the hands of the police. Now I know I will be delivering myself into their custody by returning to central London, but as long as Lilly is safe, I will feel better than I do now.

'No, I mean it's risky of Zodiac to be taking Lilly. He needs that prototype and he knows that his window closes the second we get caught by the cops. He had to act quickly, get himself some leverage in a hurry, but he's walking a thin line to do it. If the authorities find out Lilly's been abducted, then it would be catastrophic for Zodiac to be caught with her.'

I think where he might be going with this and know I have to put the brakes on it quick-style.

'We can't tell the cops he's got her. If they went public or if it leaked out, she would become a . . .' My throat dries and I can hardly bring myself to say it. 'A liability.'

'I'm not suggesting we tell them. Not yet anyway. I'm saying he's had a lot of time to plan all the rest of this, but now he's winging it and he might have made a mistake.'

'I'm not doing anything that puts Lilly at risk.'

'Lilly's already at risk. And when the best-case scenario is a successful broad-daylight handover in a London railway station with half the Met already looking for us, then that sounds pretty risky too.'

'Have you got any better ideas?'

He stares through the windscreen, into the night beyond.

'There has to be something we're missing. Some edge we can use to get her back.'

I gaze out into the rainy blackness also, the pitter-patter of it on the roof hypnotic as I allow my mind to drift. So much information, so much data came pitter-pattering down upon me today that seeing the connections might be like linking two random raindrops. But then I recall a jolt and I see where both our thought processes got sidetracked.

I was focused on the possible link between Jack and me, the possible link between Jack and my mother. That wasn't the link that mattered.

'You said my mum was trying to blow the whistle on someone or something when you knew her. It has to be linked to whatever connected Zodiac and Lansing back then too. What if this murder Lansing mentioned wasn't just a scare story to keep him quiet?'

Jack takes out his phone.

'What indeed,' he says.

He's waving the handset and frowning at the screen. He's got no service. We need to get back on the road.

Jack drives while I monitor the signal, which improves as soon as we crest the first slope. There's no let-up in the rain, which a blustery wind is rattling against the car in angry handfuls as Jack pulls into a passing place and turns on the hazard warning lights.

He switches his handset to be used as a mobile hotspot and opens his laptop, upon which he starts searching paid-for subscription news archives. Hackish instinct and my innate desire to be obliging combine to make me wonder how I might crack the login to score Jack permanent free access.

I realise I'm an addict: I can't see a security measure without feeling compelled to circumvent it.

I see him open a link in a fresh tab and strain to read the tiny text from the passenger seat.

'Found anything significant?' I enquire hopefully.

He grimaces.

'I don't think so. Drowning of a senior executive on the UK board of IBM. Ruled suicide. Guy's wife had just left him. It's too early anyway: 1991. Wait, though.'

'What?'

'Here's one that overlaps with the time I knew your mum. Liam Skelton, proprietor of Skeltronix Limited. Listen to this: murdered after disturbing a burglar during a break-in at his offices.'

'Woah. Where have we heard that before?'

'There's a whole stack of results on this one. Yeah, listen to this: "Daniel Stroud, 49, was convicted at Cambridge Crown Court of murdering Liam Skelton, 35, at the offices of Skeltronix Ltd in Saffron Walden. Stroud, who has a string of convictions for burglary, was sentenced to life for bludgeoning the electronics entrepreneur to death."'

'What was Skeltronix?' I ask, never having heard of it.

'Hang on, there's a lot more.'

Jack opens several tabs and toggles back and forth between them faster than I can keep focus.

'This one didn't go away. Stroud maintained his innocence and his conviction was the subject of a TV documentary claiming it had been a miscarriage of justice. How does this sound? "Stroud always claimed that he had been hired to break into the offices but was never able to come up with a name for the third party. He said he had been contacted only by phone and been paid a small advance on the job left in a dead drop.'"

'Anonymous third-party outsourcing, intended to put a patsy in the frame,' I say. 'I think this is where I came in.'

Jack opens still another link and scrolls down the page at speed.

'It appears Stroud was released seven years into his sentence following a media campaign and an appeal. Officially the case remains open, but as always with these deals, the police didn't go busting a gut to find a new perp and thus prove that they'd got it wrong the first time.'

'So who was this Skelton?'

'He's described as a workaholic obsessive who was divorced before he was thirty. Survived by his ex-wife, Frieda, and a daughter, Sarah. Says here he designed micro-circuitry for Marconi and Texas Instruments before setting up his own firm.'

'And what did he make?'

'Looks like Skeltronix was a real Mom-and-Pop outfit. Or just Pop, significantly: the firm folded after Skelton's death. It was a small-scale operation making diagnostic circuit testers.'

I can't help but feel disappointed.

'Doesn't sound like anything worth killing for,' I say.

'No. I got the impression your mum practised fairly high-level industrial espionage, and Lansing was subcontracted to steal documents and blueprints pertaining to state-of-the-art innovations. In Skelton's case, I don't see what was worth stealing.'

'What are diagnostic circuit testers?'

'Two electrodes connected to a box, according to this picture. Beyond that I can't say.'

But I can. The grainy photo sparks an image in my mind, electrodes and wires running to an electronic panel. I see my mum in hospital, with that thing attached to her hip. I feel a buzz run through me, like I get when I've just cracked someone's password.

'I've worked out what was worth stealing. The Synapse. It was Skelton's invention.'

'Jesus,' Jack responds. 'You're right. That's it.'

'Skelton was killed so that he couldn't kick up a fuss when Cruz's ripped-off version hit the shops.'

374

'Except it wasn't Leo Cruz who stole it.'

I am about to ask who else it could be, but I don't have to. I'm only moments behind Jack in getting there, and it comes like a rush, as though the wind outside is suddenly whipping through the interior of the car.

The answer has been there all along, hiding in plain sight: an electronics geek, highly protective of his privacy; a reclusive 'genius' who had one great idea and then disappeared back into the shadows when he failed to follow it up.

The name without a face. The invisible power behind the throne.

I mouth a single word.

'Syne.'

# PHANTOMS

Parlabane is staring at the only photograph of Aldous Syne that he can ever recall seeing. This is the highest-resolution image of it he has been able to find, but it's a scan of an already grainy original. It is familiar to him from seeing news stories and features back in the nineties, though it usually ran small alongside far larger, usually commissioned shots of the publicity-hungry Cruz.

'It's so obvious now,' he says. 'All those years ago, he stole Skelton's revolutionary design for an ambulatory cardiac monitor. He had the vision to recognise that it would transform an entire industry, and the ruthlessness to ensure its true creator wasn't around to take the credit.'

'Using much the same MO he is still employing today,' Sam observes bitterly.

'Syne sought out Cruz and together they marketed the Synapse, but when technology moved on, Syne was unable to come up with anything new.'

'Or more accurately he was unable to *steal* anything new.'

'Cruz told me he got back in the innovation game because Syne emerged from the shadows with a new idea. Syne must have stolen the Dimension too. But from who?'

'Speaking from experience, it's possible the victim doesn't even know they've been robbed. Uninvited hacked lots of places that to this day don't know they were hit.'

'You're right. And what better way to cover up the fact that you've stolen an idea than to stage a break-in and say it's been stolen from you?'

'But that wasn't the only reason he staged the break-in,' Sam reminds him. 'Why did he kill his partner?'

Parlabane thinks back to the conversations he had with Cruz: charming, personable, maybe even needy.

'Could be Cruz belatedly found out the truth about the Synapse and had a fit of conscience,' he suggests.

'Or maybe he found a way of using Syne's big secret to try and cut himself a bigger slice,' says Sam. 'Either way, he messed with the wrong psycho.'

The photograph shows Syne at an electronics workbench in what looks like a garage or a shed. The colour is washed out, which is probably why in Parlabane's memory the shot was black and white. Syne looks a lot like an Open University professor tinkering around on his day off. He estimates it must have been taken in the early eighties or even late seventies, but this is an assumption based on very little evidence, as there is nothing in the shot to date the image: no magazine covers, cassette boxes or even technology that would impose a cut-off date.

There are book spines visible on a shelf in the background, but even at this resolution the titles are only legible enough to convey that they are not in English. In fact, Parlabane remembers speculation as to Syne's background largely due to these pictured volumes appearing to be Hungarian, Polish and German.

The thought that Syne could be orchestrating all of this from far outside the UK is not one he chooses to share with Sam immediately. At the moment he knows it is crucial that they concentrate on the good news, which is that they finally know who they are dealing with. The bad news, which he also keeps to himself, is that as far as Parlabane knows, nobody has ever been able to locate this man.

'I feel sick to think that this shifty creep has Lilly,' Sam says. 'But like you said, he's made a desperate move. I get what you're saying now about bringing in the cops. If he turns up to Paddington with Lilly and the feds swoop in, we've got him nailed.'

Parlabane wishes he still held his previous belief in this strategy, but the picture has changed.

'We have to consider the possibility that it wouldn't be Syne who turned up with Lilly. He's outsourced just about everything else.'

'No,' she says, her expression adamant. 'He's acting alone on this. He has to be. He subcontracted some things, but others he had to have done himself. You can pay someone to break into a place. You can blackmail someone to break into a place. But what happened at

Tricorn House is more complicated. All the swipe-card IDs are tracked, for one thing.'

'Syne could have all kinds of access to the computer system,' Parlabane argues. 'He could have set up an ID for his paid assailant. He could have an invisible login.'

'No, that's just it. When I suddenly got control of the CCTV system, it was because whoever was controlling it had logged out. Why would they do that *then*, when the job wasn't finished? It's because there was only one person involved: Syne. He couldn't be in two places at once, monitoring the computers *and* mugging you for the prototype. He had to log out and clear his cyber tracks before he could go dump you in the big freezer then exit the building.'

'I suppose it would fit with the electroshock device,' Parlabane admits. 'I've no idea how old this photo is. Syne could be in his seventies for all we know.'

'He's on his own, Jack, I'm sure of it. Syne has got Lilly, he's going to bring her to Paddington – and feds or no feds, I'm going to be there.'

Parlabane meets her gaze poker-faced, masking the fact that he isn't convinced. He is getting a strong impression that she *needs* to believe this, which is a dangerous state of mind.

There are too many unanswered questions for him to feel comfortable making any assumptions, and the biggest hole in the picture is the exact dimensions of a certain metal object he could hold in the palm of his hand.

'Why would Syne abduct Lilly in order to trade her for his own prototype?' he asks.

'I don't know. Maybe because the prototype itself is stolen and he hasn't been able to copy the original yet. Or maybe because it's built from stolen blueprints and he's worried if it goes public the real developers will recognise the design. Does it matter? If he's prepared to trade Lilly for it, then that's how it's going to be.'

A light is blinking on Parlabane's phone. He's got new email but he doesn't need to read it. Like every other message he's received in the last hour, it will be from someone asking why he isn't answering his phone. That said, he can't think there's anybody left in his address book who wouldn't be aware of the very obvious answer to that by now.

Except maybe a guy who sleeps most of the day, practically lives in his recording studio and pays almost no attention to the news, on the grounds that it's 'mostly shite'.

Parlabane wakes the phone, verifies his deduction and hits dial.

'Spammy? It's Jack.'

'Awright, mate? What's the script? You fuckin' trollin' me or what?'

'No, my phone got stolen: that's why I didn't answer.'

'I'm not talking about that. I mean this Synergis Dimension pish you've asked me to take a look at.'

'What about it?'

'It's the fuckin' Underpants Gnomes, so it is.'

'I don't follow.'

This was a phrase Parlabane found himself using at some point in most conversations with Spammy.

'You know, from South Park. They had a three-stage plan on a blackboard. Step one was collect underpants. Step three was profit.'

'What was step two?'

'That's the point: they only had question marks. They didn't know. You see what I'm saying?'

'Eh, not quite.'

'These docs, man. I'm seeing blueprints for a few components and circuits, and I'm seeing artwork for the finished product, but how you get from stage one to stage three is anybody's guess.'

Parlabane looks to Sam.

'Is it possible any files were missing from the RBA stuff?' he asks her.

'Absolutely not. I triple-checked that I had everything, and I verified the integrity of all files. Nothing was missing and nothing was corrupted.'

'Sam says everything that should be there is there,' he relays.

'Well, in that case it's a useless load of shite.'

'The plans are incomplete?'

'That's one way of putting it, aye. Kind of in the same way that if you'd sent me blueprints for the chassis of a Nissan Micra and a photo of the Millennium Falcon, you could say those plans were incomplete as well.'

# MARKET FORCES

The rain still does not let up, but its sound is so constant that it never becomes white noise. I'm permanently conscious of it drumming the roof and lashing the windows. I'm grateful to be inside the car but at the same time I can't help feeling trapped in here too.

'It's a pump and dump,' Jack says. 'That's all it's ever been, from the start.'

He speaks excitedly, sometimes tripping over his words as he thinks aloud, his tongue struggling to keep up with his over-heated brain. Between us we've worked out what's going on, but the problem is that it hasn't changed anything, and there is only one implication I care about.

'I should have seen it. This is why Cruz wouldn't let me leave.'

'When wouldn't he let you leave? What's a pump and dump?'

'It's a stock market scam. You pump up the share price artificially, then dump your stock when it hits a high. Cruz played me. He played everybody.'

'Not quite everybody,' I remind him.

'Sure, but the point is he and Syne were in this together all along: I just don't know how far back the plan goes. Cruz bought back Synergis for a song, and everybody assumed he was going to break up the company and sell off its assets. Instead he confounded expectations by pumping money in and attracting fresh investment. It was all to give the impression he was building for the future.'

'Very much assisted by a profile piece on *Broadwave*,' I suggest, to let him know I'm keeping up.

'That's why he was so cooperative, so keen to give me the tour. And then at the end of my visit, he kept hanging around despite otherwise making out he was a hectically busy man. He talked about an epiphany and then left it hanging, inviting the question. He kept saying things like "Is there anything else you want to ask?" He wasn't going to let me leave until he had dropped the hint that Syne was back with a revolutionary new idea, but he wanted it to seem like I was the one who wheedled it out of him.'

'Why?'

'Because it's a bigger story if it appears they were trying to keep it under wraps. We all fell for it. The story of Syne's return went viral and Synergis's profile was as high as it's been since the beginning.'

The inside of the car is briefly illuminated by the headlights of a passing vehicle, the first I've seen in a while.

'Then comes the really big play,' Jack says. 'Staging a break-in so that everyone believes Synergis has a new product its rivals would go to extreme lengths to obtain. And the story is even bigger because there's a murder involved.'

'I'm guessing Cruz didn't sign up for that part.'

'It worked, though. Because of the murder, and Synergis's "reluctant" decision to release information about the Dimension, they've got worldwide advertising for their game-changing product. And those conveniently incomplete blueprints will be going viral too.'

It's as he says this that I am able to make sense of something else that was chafing in the back of my mind:

'That Tanya woman said that the stolen design documents were already being offered on the black market, but at that point, Lansing had forwarded them at most a few minutes earlier. That statement must have been written *before* anyone else had downloaded the files; plus the documents are worthless, as they don't really contain any design secrets. It was all to make people believe the Dimension is legit, sending the share price through the roof.'

'Which is when the dump part comes into play," Jack says. "Syne and whoever else is in on this will offload their stock and be counting the profit as the house of cards collapses.'

'Whoever else. Do you reckon Winter?'

'It fits. Winter's role might have been to dangle the bait in front of the Chinese: tempt them into acquiring stock in a hurry, rather than with the due diligence of a formal buy-out. They snap up as much Synergis stock as they can, thinking they're getting in on the ground floor, only to find their holding worthless when the truth emerges.'

'What happens to Synergis then?'

'Exactly what everyone thought would happen when Cruz bought it back. It will fold and be broken up. Everybody who's been working away in good faith, maybe even taking stock options in part lieu of salary, will be out of a job.'

'But won't the feds come after Syne for fraud?'

'They'll have the same problem as us: they'll have to find him first. But it's my bet that his official stock holding will be pretty small and he'll be able to demonstrate that he never sold it. The same will turn out to be true of Cruz, who made great play of being determined *not* to sell Synergis. It was all a front. If we look into who currently owns Synergis stock, I'm certain we'll find that the largest shareholder won't be an individual – it will be a company; maybe even a host of companies. The trail will be labyrinthine, shell companies within shell companies, but the stock will ultimately be owned by Syne and Cruz.'

Jack starts searching stock ownership databases, opening several in different tabs and keying Synergis into all the search fields. The reception is getting patchy, all of the sites showing blank pages and spinning wheels. I can't see that it matters.

'It still leaves us exactly where we were though, doesn't it?' I ask. 'Except that maybe the cops will be more prepared to hear us out if we can pull the plug on a multi-million-pound fraud. We meet Syne at Paddington like he said, except this time he's the one who gets a nasty surprise.'

'No,' Jack says, his expression grim in the glow from his laptop. 'We can't go to Paddington. That's absolutely the last thing we should do.'

'What are you talking about? We can't negotiate with this guy. He's got my sister.'

'You remember I asked you why Syne would want to trade Lilly for his *own* prototype? Ask yourself the question again now that you know the prototype is a sham.'

I ask, but I can't bring myself to admit the answer.

Jack is less reticent.

'He's using Lilly as bait, but he's got no intention of showing up with her.'

'He has to,' I insist. 'I'll message him on IRC, tell him if we don't see her at Paddington, we walk away.'

'We'll never get that far, that's the point. Syne will tip off the cops that we're coming: that's been his plan since he abducted Lilly. He doesn't need to go anywhere near the place, let alone bring his hostage. As soon as we show our faces, we get arrested, and to nail down the lid on our guilt, we'll be in possession of the stolen prototype. The cops then hand the Dimension back to its rightful owner and we go down for murder and robbery.'

My mouth dry with dread because I already know the answer, I manage to croak out my question.

Jack knows the answer too, but I need him to hear me ask this.

'And what happens to Lilly?'

Jack swallows.

'We have to find Syne. We have to get to him before the police get to us. It's our only course of action.'

'Find out where he lives, you mean?'

'Well, that would be a start, but no journalist was ever able to trace him back in the nineties.'

No journalist had my kind of resources back in the nineties, I think to myself. I will find this bastard even if I have to post naked selfies on 4Chan to get the info.

I wake my laptop but the first thing I notice is the power.

'Shit. I'm almost out of juice on this thing.'

'Why didn't you charge it at the hotel?' Jack asks, like that helps.

'I thought I was going to be there all night, didn't I?'

'You can use mine.'

'No. I can't do this using a mobile hotspot in the middle of a storm. I need a stable connection and I need my own kit.'

'For what?'

# PARKED OUTSIDE

Forty minutes later they are in the car park at Luton Airport. Sam suggested it was somewhere big and anonymous where she could plug in her laptop in a quiet corner and log into the Wi-Fi. Parlabane's first thought was that it is also a place where there is a permanent police presence, but he kept that reservation to himself.

Sam climbs out of the Qashqai and stands motionless in the pouring rain. Parlabane watches her, willing her to proceed, fearing that she's lost her nerve.

Before setting off from the lay-by, they had searched their belongings for anything that could be used as a disguise. The best they came up with was from a First Aid kit they found in the vehicle's boot. Parlabane placed a gauze patch over Sam's left eye and secured it in place with surgical tape. It obscured a large section of her face, and though the patch itself made her conspicuous, they were placing their trust in the effects of British politeness. Once anybody caught a glimpse of the eye patch, they would make a point of not staring.

She suggested she should go alone, and though Parlabane's protective instinct urged against it, he couldn't argue with her logic. They couldn't go together because it would massively increase the chances of being recognised. Still, he doesn't like the idea of being the one sitting here hidden in the relative safety of the car while she walks into a public place patrolled by armed cops.

He figures maybe she's starting to see it that way too, then finally she makes a move, striding towards the airport building with that brisk gait of hers, a young woman who always seems to be going places in a hurry. He hopes that's true for a long time to come.

The rain is coming down hard and cold as I step out of the car, big drops I can feel on my scalp. The sensation makes me think of a previous soaking: Lilly laughing as I came into the flat with my hair plastered flat to my head and my face.

'You don't look like you,' she said.

I stay where I am and let it soak in for a few seconds, flattening the wet hair down with my hand so that I look nothing like the photo the media are using.

I walk into the airport clutching my laptop in its neoprene bag, keeping my head down, trying to avoid eye contact. This fails when I see two cops stride across the concourse in front of me with machine guns slung from shoulder straps. I can't help it: some reflex makes me look at them to check if they're looking at me. My heart speeds up as one of them glances back, but he looks away again, the two continuing on their way like they're out for a leisurely evening stroll.

I make my way to a seating area and grab a spot by the wall. Jack was right about the eye patch. Nobody looks at me for longer than it takes to see the plaster and gauze. For the same reason, I'm betting nobody comes over to give me shit about plugging my laptop into their power supply.

One of the Wi-Fi hotspots is part of a national network I've got a hacked login for, so that saves me any registration bullshit. The signal is middling but stable. Better than a mobile network out in the wilds anyway. I launch my VPN then send up the bat signal and cross my fingers that the guy I'm looking for is online.

I wait, watching the tiny chat window while I scroll the BBC website in the background. The story has been updated but there's nothing new on us: it's all about the Dimension. It's crazy to see everybody getting so excited by what I know to be a lie. They're quoting tech and business experts from Wall Street to Silicon Valley, talking about the implications of the useless sliver of metal I've got tucked into the pocket of my jeans.

I stole it while Jack was out at the boot, rooting through the first aid kit. He'd left his jacket across the back seat, so I reached through and lifted the prototype from his pocket. I don't like deceiving him, but when it comes to Lilly's safety, I have only one priority.

I stare at the screen, willing text to appear on it.

* * *

Parlabane shifts restlessly in the driver's seat, checking the dashboard clock and glancing in each of the mirrors once again. He watches buses arrive and disgorge their travellers, dragging rain-lashed suitcases towards the terminal. He looks at his phone, speed-reading the latest updates, agonised that he is at the heart of the day's hottest story and unable to file a solitary word on it.

This is the hardest kind of waiting. There is nothing to do but fret, helpless, useless. He sits there asking himself what's keeping her, when he has no way of knowing the answer. He doesn't know precisely what Sam has in mind, what its execution requires, what difficulties she might be encountering and most pointedly whether she has been recognised and already arrested.

He should never have let her go in there alone, he tells himself for maybe the fourth time, before conceding to his internal advocate that there was no choice. It still feels wrong though, instinct telling him he should never have let her out of his sight. He knows he's her best hope, but that doesn't mean Sam sees it that way. She's scared, she's tired and, because of Lilly, she's desperate.

He sighs and slumps in his seat, reasoning he should try and get some rest while he can, even if it is only a matter of not moving, not driving, not reading, not typing. But even as the thought plays across his mind, he notices a coloured flickering and turns around to see flashing lights approach through the rear windscreen.

Something in me surges as I finally see activity in the chat window.

> <Stonefish> This is the last person I expected a message from right now. Is this really you?

I know this isn't just him being surprised. It's a verification test. I tell him the exact time and date we met at Paddington. I describe what he was wearing, as much as I can remember it, and I mention the Rubik cube.

> <Stonefish> I haven't heard from you in ages, since before Paul Wiley got busted.

&lt;Buzzkill&gt; Kind of had my hands full. Plus I thought you were the one who set me up. No offence. I know different now.

&lt;Stonefish&gt; None taken. Until today's news, I thought it was you who set me up. I thought you set all of us up.

&lt;Buzzkill&gt; Did you have dealings with someone whose handle started with a Z?

&lt;Stonefish&gt; Zero-Cool he called himself. Meta bastard.

&lt;Buzzkill&gt; What did he make you do?

&lt;Stonefish&gt; I'd rather not confess in case it turns out you're not who you say. Do you know which one of us was the rat?

&lt;Buzzkill&gt; It was Cicatrix.

&lt;Stonefish&gt; Damn. I thought Cicatrix was Wiley. Do you know who this bastard is?

I stay my hand as I am about to type. I recall how Lansing didn't give us Wiley's online name, didn't sell out anybody's identity, even when he had nothing to gain from holding this back. We assumed it was Lansing who named us to the cops, but in light of recent revelations I'm not so sure. The most obvious person would be Syne: the guy who most wants us caught. He knew my name already and he saw Jack in the flesh last night.

I cut to the chase.

&lt;Buzzkill&gt; I need your help.

&lt;Stonefish&gt; NYPA.

Not Your Personal Army. It's the first thing that's come close to making me smile in days.

&lt;Stonefish&gt; Sorry. Just a prank, bro. Fire away.

&lt;Buzzkill&gt; I need an address for somebody who doesn't want to be found. That's one of your specialties, iirc.

&lt;Stonefish&gt; Give me the name. I'll get right on it.

We are only typing text into computers, unable to see each other's faces or hear each other's voices, but it still feels awkward to ask for a favour and then tell the guy I'm asking that I don't trust him. Or more like I can't afford to trust him. I need to do this myself, see the results with my own eyes. There's too much at stake for me to take it at face value if I give him Syne's name and he hits me back with an address. I don't know for sure this is Stonefish any more than he knows I'm Buzzkill.

&lt;Buzzkill&gt; I need to do this first-hand. I know it's a big ask, but I want you to tell me how you do it.

I wait for a reply, suddenly conscious of the airport sounds all around me that my mind had previously muted. Then he replies.

&lt;Stonefish&gt; I've got a high-level login for the electoral register and another for HMRC.

I put a hand to my mouth to stifle a gasp, daring to hope.

&lt;Stonefish&gt; Between the two there's no UK address I can't get. Every year I send a picture of my dick to Jeremy Clarkson as a Christmas card.

Two links appear in the chat window and I click on both. Hardly breathing, I type my next line.

&lt;Buzzkill&gt; What are the logins?
&lt;Stonefish&gt; Not just like that. I want a quid pro quo.

I tell him he can ask for anything. I mean it.

I wait again. Once more it's like somebody turned up the volume on the hubbub, the music, the tannoys.

&lt;Stonefish&gt; Another meeting IRL. But this time it's a date.

I get a lump in my throat as I consider how I am making my promise in good faith, but may not be around to keep it.

<Buzzkill> You got it. Long as I'm not in jail.

He sends me the usernames and passwords, and in a few seconds I have access to two vast government databases at such a high level of clearance that I can picture snow on top of the browser windows.

I get to work, tapping in my searches.

As Stonefish explains, if someone is a resident of the UK, or if they have ever been a resident of the UK, I can see where they live and where they used to live. I can look up any name. I can see the before and after on names that were changed by deed poll. I can find details on anyone who has lived here and worked here, going back decades.

I can do all of these things, but I what I can't do is find a bloody listing in any of them for Aldous Syne.

I think about that photo Jack showed me. It looked like there were foreign-language books in the background. I worry that Syne is someone who doesn't live here, who has never actually lived here. It hits me to the gut that Jack could be right about him outsourcing everything, carrying out his plans at a distance. But then I remember how he was celebrated as a great British inventor. Quintessentially British in fact, the lone eccentric working in his shed. So even if he was of foreign stock, he must have been born here, he must have lived here.

For Lilly's sake, he has to *still* live here.

I hear a commotion and look up, startled as I always am at my own vulnerability when I've become so lost in what I am doing that I forget my physical circumstances.

I see flashing lights through the windows.

I feel myself go rigid before I spot the paramedics rushing through the concourse. They are heading for the security search area, where I can see airport staff beckon them frantically. I hear someone call out the words 'heart attack', and feel my own thumping through my ribcage.

These databases are necessarily very specific, so I try again in case I've got some minor detail wrong, like misspelled something or transposed a couple of letters. Even as I type I know this is as desperate as it sounds, but I do it anyway.

I still get nothing.

As I shift in my seat, I feel the phony prototype in my pocket pulled against my thigh. Suddenly I understand what the evidence on my screen is trying to tell me.

Aldous Syne does not exist.

They say that when people think they are about to die, the reason they recount their life flashing before their eyes is down to their brains rapidly searching all of their memories for information or for a previous experience that might show them how to survive. Something like that happens to me as I stare at the blank search results. In a moment that starts off in shock and panic, my mind goes into an accelerated state, calculating so many things in a rapid chain of logical deduction that it's like my brain has been swapped for a high-end processor.

I know who is behind this.

Jack was wrong when he said the prototype was worthless. Right now this piece of metal in my pocket is worth millions. Tens of millions. It's all the leverage I need to get Lilly back.

To make that happen, I will have to do what I do best, and I'll have to do it the *way* I do best: on my own.

I reach for my mobile and dial.


Parlabane watches the paramedics load a stricken figure into their ambulance on a trolley, one of them hand-pumping air through a mask clamped to the patient's face. Looks like it might be a cardiac arrest, and it may not be the only one before the evening is out.

He is growing more anxious with each minute that ticks away. There's no let-up in the rain drumming down upon the car, and he peers intently through the windscreen between beats of the wiper blades, alternating his scrutiny with glances at each of the mirrors.

The paramedics close their doors and the ambulance high-tails it away from the terminal, blue lights flashing. He saw it arrive and now he's seeing it leave again. He couldn't say how much time has elapsed in between, but he knows it felt like an eternity, and his waiting isn't over.

To distract himself, he opens his laptop and begins looking up stock databases, using his mobile as a hotspot again. He strikes out a couple of times, then finally happens upon a recent listing of who owns Synergis stock. As he predicted, there are a lot of shareholdings owned by companies, the most substantial of which is a firm called Ridge Break Associates.

RBA.

So near and yet so far. He looks again towards the terminal, a sick feeling taking hold. The longer this goes on, the less he's sure Sam's idea was a wise one. He has to hold his nerve, but the waiting is gut-wrenching.

'Why is this taking so long?' he says aloud.

He runs a search on Ridge Break Associates, discovering that it is in turn wholly owned by a company named Milton's Lake, which means nothing to him. This is the labyrinth he predicted.

His eyes are drawn from the screen by more flashing lights, this time accompanied by the sound of sirens. This time it's not an ambulance. Police are arriving at speed from different directions. He can only hope they aren't heading for the terminal to arrest Sam on a tip-off.

It doesn't look like it.

Police vehicles slew across all exits from the car park, while another two pull up only yards in front of where Parlabane is sitting. They rapidly disgorge men in Kevlar to surround the Qashqai, levelling sub-machine guns.

One of the officers stares at Parlabane through the windscreen and commands him to step out of the vehicle with his hands above his head.

Parlabane lets out a sigh, muttering to himself as he reaches for the handle.

'Here we fucking go.'

# BY APPOINTMENT ONLY

It only takes half an hour from Luton Parkway, but it feels longer as I am impatient to make the call. I daren't attempt it while I'm in transit: it's going to be one of the most important conversations of my life and I can't afford to have it cut off because I've gone into a flipping tunnel.

The train pulls into St Pancras and I step on to the platform.

I put the battery back in my phone and make sure the signal is strong. I check the time. It's 9.30 p.m. but I know the offices will still be manned given everything that's been going on today.

The receptionist picks up on the second ring and I make my request. A moment later I am being rebuffed, as I knew I would.

'I'm sorry, but I can't give out anybody's home or mobile numbers. If you give me your number, I can ask—'

'Her to give me a call, yes. Please do that urgently. It's very important.'

'And can I have your name please?'

'Just tell Miss Dunwoodie it's regarding her ten-thirty tomorrow morning. She'll know what it's about.'

I hang up and make my way along the platform, the eye patch still working its magic. I have Jack to thank for that, I reflect, and I hope he's okay. I look up at the arches and the brickwork. Any other time I've been here I've allowed myself a little Harry Potter daydream, but right now he's all I think about.

It was in a little café just around the corner from here that I first arranged to meet him: first laid eyes upon him in the flesh, though he didn't know I was looking. I went there armed with the threat of dobbing him in to the authorities. Now I'm back here after calling the cops on him for real.

# TRADING FUTURES

She was the first face I saw, the first voice I heard in my head as soon as I allowed myself to accept that Aldous Syne was a fiction. Syne had been dreamed up by Cruz to help market the Synapse, and to hide the fact that he had stolen the design and murdered its inventor.

I sussed that Cruz was Zardoz, the anonymous electronics geek who had paid Lansing to steal files for him during the nineties, in his Ferox days. Cruz must have been the person my mum was entangled with back then too, when she was involved in industrial espionage. (A horrible thought crept in at that point, but my internal defences backgrounded it, blocking out anything that might distract my brain from processing what was urgent.)

The murder of Skelton must have been what spooked her and made her realise she was in too deep. That was when she sought out Jack, but he ended up fleeing the country. Twenty years on, Cruz leaned on Lansing again, this time to find out the online identity of the hacker he knew to be Ruth Roberts's daughter. He knew Mum's real name, and he knew about the Saudi website thing. (Still I blocked it. Vital processes only. Interrupts locked out.)

He roped me in as a warning to Mum to keep quiet. That was it: he was planning the biggest con of his life and he must have feared she knew something that could threaten him.

His plan was to use the Syne myth one more time, buying back Synergis for buttons then selling its stock for millions. But he wasn't working alone. He had a silent partner, one who did exist, but not one he could trust, as it turned out.

It was that statement this morning that gave her away. Such a great performance too, so convincingly shocked, tired and grief-stricken. I've played it back since to double-check I wasn't misremembering, but even before that I could recall every word.

393

*'I have spoken to Aldous Syne and broken the news . . . Aldous was distraught and I am making this statement right now at this most difficult time on the understanding that his grief and his privacy will not be disturbed.'*

She could only have stood up and said that if she knew there was no danger of being contradicted. Only one other person knew Aldous Syne never existed, and she had murdered him the night before. At that point the question remaining was why, but I've answered it since.

My phone rings as I reach the shopping concourse. Most of the shops are closed, but there's a café open and still tables outside. I take a seat and answer.

'Jane. How good of you to call back.'

I keep my tone neutral. I think of Lilly as incentive not to lose my rag, but it's a double-edged sword, as the thought of what this woman might be prepared to do to her fills me with volcanic rage.

'I thought the terms of the deal were agreed. If there's a problem, can we discuss it tomorrow? I don't really have time to talk right now.'

She's forcing politeness too, hiding how shocked and angry she must be that I've sussed her identity. I'm partly focusing on the background, wondering where she is. It's quiet, no echo. I reckon she's probably at home or maybe a hotel room. I wonder where Lilly is, then instantly block the thought.

I find my focus. This is what I do. This is how I do it.

'I know Syne is a phantom. I know the Dimension is a fraud. And I know you've got my sister, so I suggest you make time and you pay close attention to what I am about to say.'

I leave it a moment, listening to her response; or more accurately the absence of one. Even in such silences, I can always hear what someone is telling me, and in Dunwoodie's case it's all panic and swearwords.

'Tomorrow's meeting needs to be rearranged. Not rescheduled – just a change of venue and an alteration to the agenda. The whole point of asking me to Paddington was for me to get arrested and for the cops to then give you back the prototype. Trust me, the last thing you want is for that to happen. I know what the Dimension is worth to you, but that value only holds as long as people believe it's real. If I get arrested, I will tell everybody that both your invention and its inventor are pure fantasy. After that, Synergis will be worth nothing.'

I hear her swallow. Her voice is quieter, her mouth dry.

'What do you want?'

'I'm going to text you a link to a location. I want you to hang up and call me back once you're looking at it on the map.'

The process takes about three minutes in total, including the necessary wait time I build in.

She calls back.

'What the hell? It's the Tate Modern. You could have just told me that, especially as your first link didn't even work.'

I look at my laptop, and the invaluable information that is now staring back from the screen. As I suspected, Cruz was the hacker of the two; or at least knew how to operate safely in that sphere. But now she's on her own.

'If I had simply told you that, then I wouldn't have been able to install the malware on your phone that's just told me your exact location.'

She's at home. I guess a hotel was too risky with an effective (and memorable) hostage in tow. I read her back the address.

'I could send the cops there right now, catch you with Lilly. I could have her back within the hour and I'd be able to pull this whole thing crashing down around you. But that's not what either of us wants.'

There's a pause, while it sinks in that I'm offering a way out of this for both of us.

'I know your story, Jane. I know who you are, what you've done and why you did it. We've both been through all kinds of shit and we both understand that you do whatever it takes to survive. I'm prepared to make a deal because we've got more in common than you'd believe.'

I hear her breathing at the other end of the line. If I strained harder I could probably hear her heartbeat.

'I'm listening.'

'We make the exchange tomorrow at the Tate Modern. I give you back the prototype and you give me back my sister. But before that, we make another exchange.'

'Of what?'

'Our fates. I give you mine to hold over me, and you give me yours.'

'I don't follow.'

'Yes, you do. We're kindred spirits. There's a way we can make our interests mutual, and our destructions mutually assured.'

She pauses.

She gets it.

'You want stock.'

'Yes. I've earned it for my part in this. I'm emailing you the details and the numbers right now. At the closing price today, this holding is worth just under seventy grand. In terms of what you stand to gain, I'm sure you'll agree it's a small price to pay.'

'A small price today,' she states irritably. 'But according to market projections, this slice of the pie could be worth a couple of million by next week.'

'And that's the point. Even after I've got Lilly back, it would only hurt my interests if I told anybody the truth. I become complicit in the whole fraud, and we both have a bright future as long as neither of us divulges what we know about the other.'

'You don't have that bright a future. The police are looking for you, so presumably this all falls apart if you're caught.'

'They won't be looking for me much longer. They're only after me because you fed them my name as a tip. You can tell them it was a mistake. They don't have any solid evidence against me. Besides, I'm not the one the cops are really interested in. They're after a killer, not a hacker. Give them that and they'll be satisfied.'

'Except that it leaves your partner twisting in the wind,' she observes. She almost sounds impressed.

'As I said, you and I are kindred spirits: I'm only interested in me and Lilly. Besides, it's better than what *you* did to your partner: I'm not murdering the poor bastard. I can send you the password to decrypt the video files from last night, and that will give you all the proof the cops need to pin everything on their prime suspect.'

'You're willing to sell out Jack Parlabane to the police?' she asks, like she wants to believe it but can't quite allow herself.

'You should refresh your news feeds. I already have.'

# DEAD TO RIGHTS

'*If you want to catch Jack Parlabane, the bloke you're after for killing Leo Cruz, you need to get to Luton Airport right now. He is in the short-stay car park, sitting inside a black Nissan Qashqai, registration number . . .*'

Parlabane hears Sam's voice booming through the speakers. The insulated walls of the interview room are absorbing all the reverb, making the sound so dry that she could be sitting only feet away, except he's never heard her speak so loud.

Detective Superintendent Feeney nods to DC Kalawo and she stops the playback.

Feeney looks across the table at Parlabane with a faux sympathetic expression, even a tinge of regret thrown in. Parlabane finds it almost reassuring to be patronised by an old-school middle-aged polisman several years his senior. It's a cliché because it's true that you feel your age when the cops start looking younger, though he's not sure what freaks him out more about junior CID detectives such as Kalawo: the fact that they seem so young or the fact that they're so polite.

'Horrible night out there,' Feeney says. 'Absolutely tipping it down. Hard to see a thing at any distance, and there you were, tucked away out of sight inside your stolen vehicle. Strikes me as very unlikely under those circumstances that somebody just happened to catch a glimpse and recognised you, especially with that nice new haircut of yours.'

Feeney sighs and gives his head a gentle shake, a combination gesture he's probably been doing for close to three decades.

'Your partner already rolled on you. That doesn't suggest she's going to show much loyalty when we get hold of her, which is only a matter of time, so I suggest you cooperate.'

Parlabane would have to admit that it doesn't look good.

'Aye. What were the odds a lassie who trades in deception would go behind my back?'

Feeney gives him a grim smile, a man who knows surrender when he sees it.

'I'll give you what you want,' Parlabane tells him. 'But I have a couple of requests. First one is a pen and paper.'

Feeney gives Kalawo another nod. She nudges a notepad across the table and rolls him a biro.

'Second is I want to speak to someone a wee bit higher up.'

Feeney lets out a dry laugh of bemusement.

'I'm a detective superintendent. As it stands I wouldn't normally be conducting this interview if it wasn't such a high-profile case. How high up did you have in mind?'

Parlabane writes two words on the pad, one above the other.

'I want to speak to Jeremy Aldergrave. He's the assistant to the Attorney General in charge of the government's new cybercrime task force.'

Feeney looks like he's enjoying this.

'I know who he is. But why stop there? Why not the AG himself? Why not the Prime Minister?'

'The Prime Minister can't help me. Aldergrave can.'

Parlabane tears off the top sheet from the pad and holds it out.

'I want you to get in touch with him right now and tell him exactly what is written on this piece of paper.'

Feeney folds his arms and sits back in the chair, leaving the offered note in Parlabane's outstretched grasp. Kalawo reads her boss's gesture and places her own hands on the table. No dice.

'I've been in this game too long to let you start playing silly buggers with me, Mr Parlabane. We've more pressing things to get on with here. If you've something to say, you say it to me. I'm a good listener.'

Parlabane places the note down flat and slides it across so that it is sitting in front of Feeney.

'It's your call, officer. But in less than forty-eight hours Jeremy Aldergrave is going to be mired in a media shitstorm that will probably cost him his career, and afterwards I'll be sure to let the Home Office know you could have helped them avoid the whole thing.'

# LIFE HACK

The museum is already very busy, humming with kids in the tow of damp-jacketed adults as I knew to expect. It's a wet Saturday morning after all.

I chose the Tate Modern because I've brought Lilly here a few times to fill part of a Saturday or Sunday. It's free and she likes it. She finds some of the installations funny, some of them fascinating. Mainly she likes the space itself, I think: the high-ceilinged and expansive galleries and the turbine hall in the basement. Sometimes there's nothing going on down there and so it's just full of kids running around.

I told Jane we would meet on Level Two, and that I would be waiting for her on a bench close to the north-west corner. I've been in position for a while, scanning the crowds as they approach from two directions. I'm shaking. Face to face is not my A-game, but I saw no other way to do this.

I know Lilly's safe: that helps, but I'm still nervous. She's been safe since I made the call last night; safe once Jane understood that Lilly's wellbeing is worth tens of millions to her. I can't trust Jane as a person but I can trust her to act in her own best interests, same as she can trust me to act in mine.

A couple of tall Scandinavian-looking hipsters change course to look at a sculpture, and suddenly I see my new best frenemy. She's on her own. My stomach somersaults. Then a few paces behind her I see Lilly. I let out a whimper as the second she spots me her anxious face is transformed into the smile I know so well. Neither the eye patch nor the baseball cap I'm wearing prevents her recognising me. It takes all my effort to stay where I am and not sprint towards her. That and the fact I don't have to: she's already running towards me.

She overtakes Jane, giving her a brief glance to ascertain permission. I wonder briefly if she told Lilly to stay a couple of paces behind at all times, so that it didn't necessarily appear to witnesses that they were together.

It doesn't matter now. We're all here, and the game has moved to a different phase.

Lilly hugs me and I hold her tighter than I ever have. I sniff back tears and dig deep for the final trade-off.

'What's wrong with your eye?' she asks, clocking the patch.

'It's nothing,' I assure her.

'Are we going home right away?'

That's Lilly all over. I've been through hell to bring us back together, and she's checking she isn't getting dragged from the museum too soon.

'Not quite yet. I need to talk to Jane here for a minute.'

'She said her name was Sharon,' Lilly replies, confused.

'My mistake.'

I hand Lilly a new Batgirl comic and tell her to take a seat at the end of the bench while we talk.

Jane sits down on the other side of me, far enough away that it's not clear we're together, but near enough for us to talk.

'You got an infection?' she asks.

It takes me a second to realise she means the eye patch.

'This is to make sure I don't get recognised. I spent the night in a hotel around the corner, to minimise my time on the street.'

She puts out a hand, palm up to receive.

'Okay, let's get on with it. I delivered my side. Now you deliver yours.'

'There's no rush. Once I hand this over we're never going to see each other again, so I'd like to talk for a moment.'

'What, do you think we're going to be pals just because you've hitched your fate to mine? More like you're leeching off it. Either way, I don't have anything to say to you, so give me what's mine so we can cut to the "never see each other again" part.'

Even though she trusts me not to screw my own future, she's still as anxious to get the prototype as I was to get Lilly. While it remains out of her hands, so potentially is her fortune. If anybody discovers that the Dimension does nothing before she dumps the stock, then the ball's on the slates, as Dad used to say.

'Given what you had planned for me the other night, under the circumstances I'm being shockingly nice. I figure the very least you owe me is to fill in a few blanks. Like why you did this to me?'

'It's nothing personal,' she replies, looking ahead.

She still hasn't met my gaze. Maybe she's thinking about the CCTV cameras and she's paranoid about us being seen talking.

'It was personal for you though, wasn't it?' I reply. 'Cruz murdered your father, and that's why you killed him.'

Oh, she's damn well looking at me now.

'Your name was originally Sarah Jane Skelton. Your father was Liam Skelton. You gave it away with the name of your ghost company: Milton's Lake. It's an anagram of your father's name.'

She's looking at me differently now, the surprise becoming mixed with pain; the stony-faced defiance for the first time becoming something hinting at vulnerability.

"When your mum remarried you became Sarah Jane Dunwoodie. Then just Jane Dunwoodie, so that Cruz didn't see the threat. He killed your dad and got rich on his invention. Meanwhile you're going off the rails, into drugs and street crime by the time you're fourteen.'

'How do you know this?'

'I'm a hacker.'

Stonefish's logins got me her previous names and addresses. After that I had other sources to draw upon.

I know all about her now: in and out of institutions, learning all the wrong lessons, mixing with more and more dangerous people as a result. Shoplifting, assault, car burglary, house-breaking: juvenile convictions soon graduating to the adult versions. It gave her an apprenticeship and a contact list that would serve her well in her quest to even the score.

'I was in one of those young offenders places,' I tell her. 'Only for a few days. I was lucky. I got saved because of politics, lap of the gods shit. I could have gone the same way as you, except I don't think I would have survived like you. I'd have been crushed by it. Doesn't excuse you trying to kill me, though.'

'I'm not apologising,' she says. 'You've no idea what I've been through, the life I've had.'

'I'm not expecting an apology. But I think I'm due an explanation.'

Something in her softens. She swallows. She looks at me fleetingly, but when she begins to speak, she's staring straight ahead again, like it's easier that way.

'It was a few years ago when my mum got sick. I had to look after her because she didn't have anybody else. I knew she wouldn't be getting better, but it's a funny thing: helping her helped me straighten out, or maybe it kept me too busy to get into anything I shouldn't. I was on Carer's Allowance, living off that.'

'I got bumped from Carer's Allowance because they found out I was in full-time education.'

I hate sharing this, hate sharing anything with this bitch, but it has an effect. She nods, so subtly you might not notice, but it's there: an acknowledgment that we do have things in common.

'After my mum died, I was clearing out all her stuff. Took me days. While I was up in the loft I found this old computer: turned out it belonged to my dad. She got it when the firm shut down. It still worked. I looked through it like it was an electronic treasure chest, trying to get a sense of him. That's when I found the designs.'

'For a miniature cardiac monitor.'

'It was the Synapse, from the exterior design right down to the chipset. That's when I knew what had been taken from me, and by whom.'

I can feel her anger driving her to speak: driving what she has to say, driving the need to say it. She's never been able to tell anybody this, and she might never get another chance.

'I had a purpose for the first time in my life, and I dedicated myself to it.'

'So the whole thing was your idea? The Dimension, the pump and dump?'

'I'm my father's daughter. I inherited his gift for intricate design. I worked out a way I could use Cruz and then destroy him.

'I got myself a meeting with Cruz ostensibly to pitch the concept of the Dimension. He knew his stuff, reckoned this kind of technology was still a decade away. That's when I told him I hadn't come to him because I thought we could build it: I came to him because he had a proven track record of selling something that doesn't exist.'

'Syne. I bet you really had his ear at that point.'

'Cruz thought I was there to blackmail him. When he found out what I really had in mind he was delighted. Like you, he thought we were kindred spirits.

'My plan was to buy up some failing electronics firm, any outfit we could get cheap, but it turned out Cruz was already in preliminary talks about buying back Synergis.'

'Was it you I was talking to on IRC? Were you Zodiac all along?'

'Sometimes it was him, sometimes it was me. We both needed to monitor your progress, make sure you were going to pull it off.'

'So you knew I was spear phishing for your login? Why did you give it to me? No, I know: you had another login. High clearance and secret.'

'We both did. You didn't think we'd invite hackers into our shit without taking precautions.'

'Was anyone else in on the scheme? Danny Winter, for instance?'

She gives a dismissive snort, amused and yet derisory.

'No. Winter's just a useful idiot. He had his eye on Synergis too, and Cruz suspected he was acting as a front for the Chinese. They'll all be in for a big disappointment after they've paid to see my hand.'

She gives a thin smile of cold satisfaction.

'So now that we've had our little chat, how about you hand me the prototype and we can both be on our way?'

I take the device from my pocket but I keep hold of it, gripped tight so she can't make a snatch for the thing.

'I only have one more question.'

She tuts, but she knows she's in the home straight: the prototype is almost in her clutches.

'And what's that?'

'The same one I asked back at the start: why me? That's all I want to know, then the Dimension is yours.'

'No particular reason. We needed a plausible scapegoat, a hacker.'

I put the prototype back in my pocket.

'Bullshit. There's more than that.'

She frowns, busted.

'Early on I asked Cruz if there was anybody else who knew about Syne, who could put a spoke in our plans. There were two people who might *potentially* have worked out the truth about the Synapse. They had both been involved in different aspects of acquiring the design, though only one of them had ever met Cruz. The one who hadn't was a hacker. He was never going to be a threat, especially as Cruz said he had blackmail material on him. But the other one was—'

'My mum.'

'What about our mum?' Lilly asks, suddenly looking up from her comic.

'I'll tell you later, Lilly. Two more minutes, okay?'

'Okay.'

Jane is eyeing me cautiously, wondering how much I already know and how I know it. She isn't going to lie any more: there's nothing to be gained from it.

'That's why the drugs and the gun were planted in our flat, wasn't it? To discredit her in case she came forward.'

I keep my tone even, hiding the anger. I don't want her thinking I'm about to do anything rash.

'It was Cruz's idea,' she insists.

'Who physically did it, though? Was it one of your house-breaking contacts from the bad old days? Should we be worried that they are a loose end or a loose tongue?'

She shakes her head.

'It was me. I wouldn't trust anyone else. I'd have had to pay them more than the drugs themselves were worth to be sure they didn't just bugger off with them. Plus, as you say, it would be another loose end that might unravel.'

'How did Cruz know who my mother was, though? She went by an alias back then.'

'Maybe she let him get closer to her than she intended.'

I struggle to keep a reaction from my face, but Jane isn't looking for one. She simply wants this over with.

405

'He kept tabs on her from a distance down the years, in case she ever turned up trying to shake him down. He had all kinds of channels of information, contacts from his old hacking days. That's how come he knew about the Saudi website business. So when I said we needed a hacker as the centrepiece of the plan, he insisted it be you.'

'Why?'

'Because when you got done for robbing Cruz's company, you would tell your mum you'd been blackmailed into doing it. Then she'd make the connection and get the message: whatever you know or think you know, keep your mouth shut, because we can get to your daughter.'

I nod, deciding that I've heard enough. I get to my feet and take the prototype from my pocket.

'Come on, Lilly. We're making a move.'

Jane holds out her hand and I pass her the device.

'There's one final thing we've got in common,' I tell her. 'We both inherited talents from our parents. Yours from your father, mine from my mother.'

'What talent is that?' she asks scornfully.

'I have this gift for being able to get some idiot to trust me – to tell me all kinds of precious secrets that she really ought to have kept to herself.'

The look on her face is delicious. This is the bit you don't get to see when you're doing this online, the moment they realise they've been hacked. I have to say, it's so much better IRL.

There is half a second during which she knows something's up but can't tell where the threat is coming from. Then she sees that the answer is every direction. All around her, art lovers reveal themselves to be undercover cops.

# PLAYING TO THE GALLERY

*It was personal for you though, wasn't it? Cruz murdered your father.*

Sam's voice is crisp and clear through the loudspeakers, one of the officers tweaking the settings to filter out the background noise. Parlabane is standing in the Operations Centre watching the action unfold on a vast bank of monitors, while cops in headsets sit before individual screens, quietly talking to their counterparts in the field. There are feeds from CCTV cameras inside the gallery, as well as several more from bodycams attached to the undercover police on-site. The principal audio is coming from a microphone pinned inside Sam's jacket, but there are auxiliary feeds from devices hidden on the underside of the bench and from directional mics being carried by officers in the vicinity.

They've been tracking Dunwoodie all the way here from her home, first by car to the railway station, then followed by officers on the train. The police have had eyes on her since around midnight; strictly speaking, they initially had thermal-imaging cameras on her. They picked up two heat signatures inside the house where she lived alone. Dunwoodie appeared to be downstairs on her laptop, while there was a second person asleep in an upstairs bedroom.

*The whole thing was your idea?*

*I'm my father's daughter.*

Minute by minute, Dunwoodie is confirming everything Parlabane told them, Sam teasing out an inadvertent confession from someone who believes she has bought off her confidante.

She called him from inside the airport, her voice shaking with her impatience to let him know. She had worked it out, and her reasoning was incontrovertible.

'We can't go straight to the cops, though,' she said. 'Even if they find her with Lilly, she could make up God knows what story;

407

probably got it planned out in her head as a contingency. I can get her to cough, though. It's what I do.'

Then she outlined her strategy, and he couldn't fault that either, though the part requiring him to be arrested wasn't particularly welcome.

'I can't simply rock up to the nearest nick and hand myself in,' he reasoned. 'I might end up sitting in a cell for who knows how long, waiting for them to get in touch with the right people. I need to be dealing with a detective on the Cruz investigation: someone sufficiently senior that they'll see the full picture. It would work out better if the cops came for me.'

It was after Sam's call that he remembered an object that had caught his eye in Lansing's office. It was a framed photograph that Parlabane hadn't deemed significant at the time and thus hadn't questioned Lansing about while there were far more immediate issues to discuss. However, it struck him as pretty bloody significant now that he was waiting for the police to respond to Sam's call and huckle him away.

That photo – and what was scribbled on it – was going to give him direct access to an individual far more influential than whoever was running the Cruz investigation.

Someone sufficiently senior indeed.

*You gave it away with the name of your ghost company: Milton's Lake. It's an anagram of your father's name.*

As Sam speaks these words on the monitors, Detective Superintendent Feeney sends a glance Parlabane's way. It is a subtle gesture of gratitude, though it is Sam who deserves credit for sussing that one.

They have all been working through the night, journeying through the corporate labyrinth Dunwoodie and Cruz constructed in order to pull this off. And they have discovered that it is a labyrinth with a deadly trap at its heart.

When Cruz bought Synergis, he performed an initial stock dilution: a *fake* stock dilution, it turns out. The shares all went to companies he and Dunwoodie set up, all of which were ultimately owned by Milton's Lake. Milton's Lake was registered in Dunwoodie's name so that it couldn't be traced back to Cruz later, after the buyers realised they had been sold a pup. That was why Cruz was giving interviews stressing his determination to realise the project and his refusal to sell his own stake. It was part of his alibi, at least as far as he understood the plan.

However, Cruz would surely never have agreed to Dunwoodie effectively owning the whole shebang unless he had guarantees. There had to be a document somewhere, secretly agreeing that she would sign over his share once the fix was in and the cheques had all cleared. Unfortunately for Cruz, the problem with secret agreements is that if one party murders the other, she gets to scoop the pot.

*I worked out a way I could use Cruz and then destroy him.*

Jeremy Aldergrave is standing nearby, nodding with quiet satisfaction, no doubt anticipating the headlines.

This is part of what Parlabane promised him: that Aldergrave would be able to stand before the media and report how he was personally involved in the operation to catch Leo Cruz's murderer, as well as revealing who had been behind the Synergis hack. As the recently appointed cybercrime czar, he is in need of an early win, and this isn't a scrappy one-nil against unfancied opposition.

'The timing should be perfect too,' Parlabane had pointed out. 'This thing will dominate the Sunday papers.'

But just as important in Parlabane's bargaining was the story that *wouldn't* be dominating the Sunday papers.

*We needed a plausible scapegoat. A hacker.*

He called up Lansing from the car at Luton Airport, told him what was really going on – about Cruz, about Dunwoodie, and most pressingly about Lilly.

'Cruz was Zardoz?' Lansing said. Parlabane could almost hear face meet palm. 'Of course. All those names with a zed.'

'How come you didn't call us when he told you where to send the files?'

'I didn't think it would help, given he sent me twenty addresses. Plus I figured if I was sending the same zip file package with Stool-pigeon embedded, Sam would know soon enough where it went.'

'No, you were playing both ends until you saw which way the cards were going to fall. I don't blame you, but seeing as we're the ones digging you out of this, I figure you owe us a favour.'

'We'll see. What do you have in mind?'

'There's a framed photo in your office of you with Jeremy Aldergrave back when you were both teenagers: "Hackers in arms." He was Thanatos. When they're bigging up Aldergrave they talk about how he made a million by his twenty-first birthday. I saw you glance up when you mentioned a hacker who was effectively insider-dealing back then. I thought you were looking at the monitor, but you were looking at the photo. That was him, wasn't it?'

Lansing said nothing.

'I need to rope in some senior influence on this thing fast. I want you to give me the name of just one company that he hacked for an insider trade.'

Parlabane heard him swallow.

'You can't ask me to do that. He was a friend. He still is. And I'm certainly not making an enemy of him now he's the bloody cybercrime czar. He's got as much dirt on me as I have on him. He could destroy me.'

Parlabane knew this was never going to be an easy ask, but he hadn't played his full hand yet.

'I get that, Gary. Sam noticed how you didn't reveal the identities of those Uninvited hackers. You're loyal, and if I could find another way, I wouldn't be asking this.'

'Then *find* another way. I'm sorry. I appreciate the situation you're both in, but I have to think of my family.'

'You know, it's funny you should put it like that . . .'

*I asked Cruz if there was anybody else who knew about Syne.*

One of the cops has the famous solitary picture of Syne up on her screen. They're trying to find a source for it. Parlabane reckons it will turn out to be from some Eastern European magazine predating the fall of the Iron Curtain. An image that Cruz reckoned nobody in the west would recognise. An image nobody in the east was likely to encounter and say: 'Hey, that's me!' In the event that they did, Cruz could always have claimed he fed it to the press as a prank, or in defence of Syne's privacy.

*I have this gift for being able to get some idiot to trust me – to tell me all kinds of precious secrets that she really ought to have kept to herself.*

He watches the undercover officers move in, swiftly and without fuss. Dunwoodie is in cuffs within seconds of Sam stepping clear. There is a palpable release of tension from all around the Operations Centre.

'Your girl did well,' Feeney tells him, putting a firm hand on his shoulder.

Parlabane smiles.

She isn't his girl, not in the way she once hoped, but nonetheless he feels the warmest glow of pride.

# CELL BINDING (II)

I am determined to keep it together but the sight of my mum already filling up as she walks towards me is threatening to set me off.

I still had to leave my phone and my keys in a locker then go through the whole airport-style security rigmarole, but I have been shepherded through on my own, out of normal visiting hours. We're meeting in a private room too, which means I don't have to sit in that horrible waiting area with its permanent stink of cigarettes, anger and despair.

We hug, and neither of us lets go or says anything for a long time.

I do, somehow, keep it together.

'I'm sorry I didn't believe you,' I tell her.

She squeezes me a little harder, then finally breaks off and wipes her face.

We both take a seat.

'You've more than made up for it. I'm sorry I wasn't so easy to believe. I'm going to make up for it too. Jesus, Sam. I'm just so glad you're okay. What the hell happened?'

I take a deep breath. It's time.

'I was always afraid that this story would end with me in prison. Turns out I was right . . .'

# DECODED

I've told her everything.

She's crying again, but not in an upset way. I've never seen her like this, in fact. She looks moved. She looks proud.

'Everything's gonna be different now, Sam,' she says, sniffing back more tears. 'I'm all cleaned up. They told me they still have to sort out some red-tape stuff, but once they formalise the charges against Dunwoodie, I'll be out of here. I'm gonna be a born-again mum, I promise.'

'Does that include being more upfront with me?'

She looks kind of edgy about this, like she hasn't quite anticipated all the implications of the promise she just made, and is wondering whether she ought to clarify terms. It's almost a relief. If she wasn't still looking for the angles in every potential loophole, I'd think they had replaced her with a doppelganger.

'What do you mean?'

'Why did you lie to me about knowing Jack?'

She sighs.

'Why do you think?. He was a link to things I didn't want you finding out about. I'm assuming I don't need to explain why. I've always been frightened of my past coming back to haunt you. I was paranoid bordering on superstitious about it, like it would be my punishment for the things I did and thought I'd got away with.'

'And how bad were those things, Mum? How much did you know about what happened to Liam Skelton?'

She looks down at her hands. I know her signs, and this usually means a difficult truth is coming.

'People always assumed Cruz was this idealistic entrepreneur who ended up as a cynical wheeler-dealer. The reality is, Cruz was always a cynical wheeler-dealer, who spent a brief period posing as an idealistic entrepreneur. He was a slippery bastard when I knew him – that's *how* I knew him – but I didn't realise what he was truly capable of.

'He was wily. He always gave the impression he was working for somebody else, like he was a middle man between the likes of me and whoever was really calling the shots. So when I learned Skelton had been murdered, not long after I was hired to steal his project designs, I didn't think Cruz did it, but I knew we were both connected to whoever had.'

'Did you know the Synapse was the invention you had stolen from Skelton?'

'Yes. But when the company launched, I reckoned Syne must have been the real power all along. I thought he had killed Skelton and passed off his invention as his own, and I was scared of what he might do to anyone who knew otherwise.'

'Is that why you reached out to Jack?'

She looks glum; I'd even say ashamed.

'Yes, but . . .'

Mum sighs, needing a moment. I hope it's not to compose a plausible lie.

'I thought maybe he could be my way out. If I decided I could trust him, I could tell him what I thought I knew about Cruz and Syne. Unfortunately, Cruz found out.'

'He knew you'd been in touch with Jack? How?'

'I don't know. He always had sources; except, as I said, I always believed they were Syne's sources. Anyway, acting the middle-man, he said his employer wasn't happy that I'd been liaising with an investigative reporter. I was ordered to plant drugs in Jack's flat. I knew it was a loyalty test, and I didn't fancy the consequences of failing it. I was a lot more confident that he could hurt me than I was that Jack could save me.'

'Is that why you were always searching him online? Guilt?'

She nods.

'When the drugs and the gun got found in our flat, I knew it was a message to stay quiet. I was scared they'd come after you and Lilly if I didn't keep it shut.'

There's a silence. Mum looks apprehensive, though I haven't asked her anything else yet. I'm feeling the same. I think we both know what's coming.

'Mum, I need to know. Was Leo Cruz my father?'

Mum looks down at her hands again.

She shakes her head.

'No,' she says calmly but firmly.

'Then who was? I deserve to know, and I've waited long enough to find out.'

'It's never been that simple, pet. You have to understand, when you were growing up, even if I'd wanted to tell you, I couldn't have. I never knew his name.'

My heart plummets and she misreads my expression as disgust.

'Don't look at me like that,' Mum bridles. 'I'm not talking about a one-night stand I met in a club. We worked together, in a manner of speaking. He was younger than me, a little naive, very sweet. I did care about him, you should know that.'

'So how come you don't know his name?'

'I didn't say I *don't* know it. I said I didn't know it then. But I do now, thanks to you.'

'You've lost me.'

She offers me an apologetic smile.

'I met him through Cruz. I was a go-between, a contact. We used codenames.'

Something inside me ignites.

# CONDITIONAL OFFERS

Parlabane takes a long pull from a bottle of Schiehallion, impatient for the alcohol to do its thing. He's trying to relax, though the principal impediment to this is finding himself in the unaccustomed role of chaperone to a young lady as she meets a gentleman for drinks. The beer is good, but it's not strong enough. One of Han's caipirinhas: that's what he could to with right now; rapidly followed by two more.

Never mind relaxed, he ought to be in celebration mode. He's published one hell of a story, though not exactly the whole truth. Large sections of his original account have been redacted due to horse-trading arrangements with Aldergrave and with Gatekeeper, but he can't complain too much, given that they are keeping all the right people out of jail. In the case of the latter, the firm was only too happy to waive any charges pertaining to trespass and theft if it prevented its clients finding out a teenage girl simply strolled in its front door and made a mockery of its entire secure-entry system.

Even in its censored form, the scoop has proven massive enough for everyone at *Broadwave* to overlook his disappearing act at their Islington party, as well as that always socially uncomfortable 'wanted for murder' business that followed. It has been only half-jokingly suggested Parlabane be given the title 'Editor at Large' so that in future they have an in-built excuse when nobody knows where he is or what he's up to.

Professionally speaking, everything is as okay as it's been in quite some time. That's not the problem. What's really bringing the awkward is that the bloke Sam is chatting to is the one traditionally ascribed the minder role, being as he is the young woman's father.

When Sam broke the big news to Parlabane, he had to confess not only that he had already worked it out, but worse, that Lansing

416

knew too. It was how he got him to give up the goods on Aldergrave. Parlabane told Lansing he believed his codenamed contact had been Sam's mum, then gave him Sam's date of birth. Simple arithmetic took care of the rest.

He feels like a gooseberry, an effect exacerbated by the anxious and delicate nature of the conversation. It's like being a fly on the wall at a first date, the two of them treading on eggshells, trying really hard to please each other, determined not to screw this up.

'How did your wife take it?' Sam asks.

Lansing has a sip of his pint. Either the taste is more bitter than he was anticipating or he's wincing at the memory.

'It wasn't the easiest conversation of our marriage, but she knows it's not like I did it deliberately. I didn't conceal anything from her – how could I? I guess she's okay about it though, because she told the kids.'

Sam's eyes widen in nervous surprise. She seems pleased, though.

'Thing is, my wife and I were both only children, so the kids don't have any aunts or uncles or cousins. The idea they have a half-sister who's old enough to take them places has got them very excited. My apologies if this is a bit premature.'

'Don't worry about it. I'd like to meet them.'

'You're back at your studies, I gather,' Lansing says.

'Busy catching up after some lost time, but yeah.'

'I know finances are always stretched when you're a student.'

Sam sits up straight, her face more serious and determined than Parlabane has seen since Lansing pitched up tonight.

'I'm not looking for money,' she says. 'You don't owe me anything.'

She takes a drink of her cider.

'Of course, Mum doesn't quite see it that way. Some things haven't changed in the twenty years since you both knew her. She's always playing an angle, but I've told her to butt out.'

Lansing listens, nodding sincerely. He looks like he's biding his time.

'I'd like to offer you a job, Sam,' he says. 'Part time, to help pay the bills when you go to uni.'

'I meant what I said. You don't need to feel obliged towards me.'

417

'I'm not offering this out of obligation. We do penetration testing, and with your CV, I'm sure you can understand how valuable you would be to the company. Plus, it would give us a chance to get to know each other.'

Sam beams. Parlabane knows Lansing doesn't need to sell this.

'That would be amazing,' she says, with the same fangirling enthusiasm he first heard when she was scoping out Lansing's mini-museum.

Yeah, these two are definitely family.

'I have one condition,' Lansing says.

Sam looks up expectantly. Parlabane reckons there's little she wouldn't agree to.

'No more hacking,' he tells her. 'No more illegal hacking anyway. If you work for me, you're a whitehat from now on.'

Sam takes a moment to reflect upon this, longer than Parlabane is comfortable with. He's just had so much peace of mind dangled tantalisingly in front of him, the prospect of a renewed trust in his information and communications devices.

'Okay,' she replies. 'It's a deal. But at the risk of sounding like an addict, I do need one last hit.'

# REKT

'Here you are, gentlemen,' the girl says with a smile, placing down their coffees. The order is one double espresso for him and cappuccinos for the other two amateurs. Unlike this pair, Lush has actually been to Italy. They'd scoff at them there. Cappuccino is a morning drink, and it's half past two in the afternoon. To be fair, none of them has been up for more than an hour, but still.

He takes a look at what Ango and Griff have been presented with. The new waitress still ain't got the hang of the frother, but in that spray-on T-shirt and skinny jeans, it's not like it matters. She'll keep the customers coming. The Japanese say, 'First dine with your eyes', and she's offering a great menu.

'That's lovely, sweetheart,' he tells her with a smile and a winning twinkle in his eye. 'You enjoying the gig?'

She takes a second to work out that he means working here. She's not so bright. Again, like it matters.

'Yeah, it's all right.'

'Well, I'm planning on opening up a bar real soon. You play it smart, I'll soon have you pouring cocktails instead.'

The bar is looking six months off, according to the architect, so this is merely to remind her that he owns the place, and an invitation for her to show a bit of ambition, if she knows the right way to go about it.

He's building an empire here. Got two coffee shops now, two barbers and a ladies salon too. It's all about the cash: unquantified transactions, putting more through the tills than comes over the counter.

Ango and Griff pull out their iPads, which is a relief. He's not in the mood for their attempts at banter right now. Usually takes something stronger than coffee to manage that.

419

Lush has a sip of his espresso as he waits for his laptop to reboot. It's taking its time, but that's a relief. It's been acting sluggish, which always makes him worry he's got a virus, but it usually turns out that it's been downloading a ton of updates which install themselves when he restarts.

He keeps track of everything from this machine: *from*, but crucially not *on* this machine. It's all on the cloud, held by a file-storage company based fuck knows where. He is schooled up on the law for this. It would take the cops literally months to get the court orders necessary to compel an overseas firm to hand over what he's got stored with them. By that time he'd have long since cleaned it out.

He has to laugh at these thick actresses and pop stars crying because their sex tapes got stolen from the cloud. What were they using as a password: qwerty? Nah, ain't nobody guessing his. Never leaves it on automatic login neither, in case it gets stolen. He logs in fresh every time, username too.

The cops ever seize this thing, all they're getting is some top tunes to listen to while they apply for that useless court order. They ain't even getting his videos. Those are on the cloud too, his mementoes of special nights: hidden-camera keepsakes that the girls who shared those nights don't know about.

The laptop finally finishes rebooting, and he goes to his music, planning to compile a new playlist.

He gapes.

It's almost empty. There should be thousands of files there, but there's only one, and it isn't even a track he recognises: Nerf Herder – 'The Backpack Song'.

WTF?

Griff splutters, dribbling coffee down his chin. He ain't laughing, though.

'The fuck is this?' Griff asks Ango, pointing to his iPad.

'What?'

'Your Facebook status, mate: "Last day here among the kuffar. Shipping out tomorrow to join my brothers in jihad. Every day we bring the worldwide caliphate closer."'

'I never wrote that,' Ango protests.

420

Ango checks his Facebook. Apparently he did.

'Fucking hell. The feds are gonna be all over me. How did this shit get up there?'

Ango scrolls the screen then his eyes bulge at something else he has read further up. His shock is turning to laughter.

'Looks like we all got secrets, bruv,' he tells Griff.

'What?'

'Your status from two hours ago: "In the struggle against the Islamification of Britain, I have joined the English Defence League and will be raising money for them every night on Hampstead Heath. Support our cause: stand up for white values while I give you some Anglo-Saxon head."'

Ango is pissing himself at the horror on Griff's face, but Lush isn't laughing. He's contemplating how long his laptop took to reboot, and thinking about how he received a package in the mail a few days ago. It was a single sheet bearing one line of text:

'I want ten grand or the world sees this.'

Also inside the envelope was a flash drive. When he plugged it in, there was a single mpeg file, which to his relief turned out to be a pop video. Some skinny eighties dude singing about how he was never gonna give you up.

He assumed it was a prank, and was expecting the sender to reveal themselves. Nobody had yet, so he'd forgotten about it.

He's getting a nasty feeling about it now, though.

Lush double-clicks on the single music file that's still on the laptop. He hears thrashy guitar and some American bloke singing, over and over, 'I'm gonna get revenge on you.'

Hurriedly he goes straight to iTunes to check on his music, all of which he'll have to download again. It'll take days.

He gets a login screen, maybe because of the updates and the restart, but he's thinking maybe not. He puts in his username and password.

It tells him his login details are wrong.

He clicks to retrieve a lost password, filling in his email address.

It tells him no account exists for that email address.

Online and off, it's all been deleted.

Starting to panic, he logs into his cloud storage to check on his docs. It's not just the money-laundering stuff that's on there. Every last drug deal is logged: who bought what, how much they paid, which dealer holds what, how much cash they all owe. His whole empire.

It's all gone.

There is a single document listed where there should be dozens. It is entitled: Readme.txt.

He opens it. It says only: '#lushwank'.

WTF, he thinks. Then it hits him: a hashtag.

His heart thumping, he fires up Twitter. He gets a login screen. He's locked out of his account.

Lush grabs Ango's iPad off him and stabs at it with sweaty fingers as he launches the app. He searches for his username and sees that a tweet has been posted from his account while he was asleep. It contains a link to a video, the preview image telling him someone has had complete control of his computer in a way that is far worse than he could have possibly imagined.

> Check this awesome webcam selfie vid of me jacking it to porn on my laptop. #lushwank

As sickness rises in his gut, his eye is drawn to the same word listed in the top left of the window.

#lushwank is trending.

# FINAL SHOWDOWN

It's my last ever shift in Urban Picnic, and I'm feeling an unexpected pang of regret. I've actually kind of enjoyed it here since all the pressure came off me.

I'm back at my sixth form college, but I decided to stay on at the sandwich place to bring in a bit more money until Mum gets regular shifts. She's working with a new nursing agency. It's on a trial basis right now but it's looking good.

Wherever possible she insists on being at the Loxford to pick up Lilly from school, which allows me to pull a few hours at Urban Picnic after college. At first I missed seeing Lilly's face when she first comes out of the building each afternoon, but I've learned she looks just as pleased to see me when I come in the door after work.

I'm finishing at Urban Picnic today because I'll be working part-time for Gary soon as Christmas is out the way. I was keen to start straight away but he's insisting I use the holidays to catch up on the school work I missed.

That's another reason I've come to think again about working here. Studying for maths and physics sure makes you appreciate the calm simplicity of slapping a few sandwiches together.

Somebody's asked for a Double Meat Picnic. I recall how stressy I used to get about those, whereas now I can rattle them out with my eyes shut. I expertly wrap the DMP into a tight package and hand it over the counter, which is when I look towards the door and see Keisha walking in.

I had forgotten how much I once dreaded this, but at least I don't feel scared of her any more. My heart sinks but I can't begrudge her it after what I did. She's due this.

I glance across and notice that Snotworm is free too. I could keep

423

my head down with some prep, let him deal, pretend I haven't seen her. But I decide no, I need to suck this up, take it on the chin.

She might not say anything with other people here, but she won't need to either. The triumphant look on her face will be enough for both of us.

She reaches the counter and I stand up straight, presenting myself for her to do her worst. It doesn't happen, though. Instead she seems kind of sheepish.

'Hi,' I say, or more like mumble.

'Hi,' she says back.

She doesn't look anything like as sure of herself as she used to, and as she stands there I wonder if she's forgotten who I am, as well as what she came in for.

I feel like I've got to say something.

'You feeling better? I heard you were ill, in hospital.'

She looks surprised, properly taken aback. Her usual scowling and suspicious expression is absent. I can tell she's asking herself how I could possibly not know all about this.

I see the relief on her face as it strikes her that maybe not everybody was party to her humiliation. After all, she thinks I'm a complete square, totally disconnected from her social networks.

'I'm much better, yeah. Thanks for asking.'

She actually says this. It sounds like it wasn't easy, but she did it all the same.

'I heard about you on the news,' she tells me. 'Ain't you off to uni or something? What you doing working here?'

'Have to get my exams first. And I need the money if I'm going off to be a student.'

'I heard that. I'm wanting to go off too. Not uni, obviously.'

She smiles as she says this, the first self-deprecatory thing I've ever seen her do.

'I want to be a nurse. When I was in hospital the nurses were brilliant.'

'Is that always what you've wanted to do?' I ask, realising I know almost nothing about her.

'Nah. Never knew I wanted to do anything, to be honest. But

424

that's changed. I really want to find out all about nursing, how to get a training place or whatever.'

This is the hardest thing I've ever had to say, and somehow also the easiest.

'My mum's a nurse. If you like you could come round some time, ask her a few questions. She knows lots of people who could probably help.'

It takes her a second to accept this.

'Could I? For real?'

'Sure. I'll give you my number.'

This is probably the most adult moment in both our lives. It's like we both understand we're drawing a line under who we were before – stupid kids who didn't know any better and didn't understand the harm we were doing.

A little while later I check my phone and see that Keisha has sent me a friend request on Facebook. I've got a proper account that's genuinely me, the only account I'm using right now.

I click to accept, and can't help but smile.

I'm totally owning at this Real Life game.

425

# ABOUT THE AUTHOR

Since his award-winning debut novel *Quite Ugly One Morning*, Chris Brookmyre has established himself as one of Britain's leading crime novelists. His Jack Parlabane novels have sold more than one million copies in the UK alone.